THE PRINCE OF STARLIGHT

LOU WILHAM

Midnight Tide
PUBLISHING

To my biggest fan, Mika.
Embrace your dreams.
Let your imagination run wild.
Tell your story, whatever form it takes.

THE HEIR TO MOONDUST: BOOK ONE
THE PRINCE OF STARLIGHT
LOU WILHAM

PROLOGUE

The tricky thing about stories is this, they all have to start somewhere. For some it is with "once upon a time", others with "it was the best of times".

This story begins thus…

In a kingdom along the shore of the ocean Selene (named so for the great goddess of the moon who cried the ocean into being when her beloved Endymion was lost) there lived a young king called Jaxith, who was very happy. For in not but a fortnight his darling wife would give birth to their first child, and his family would be complete. He would have his loving wife, and their bouncing baby who would fill the halls of his castle with laughter and light like it had not known when Jaxith was a child.

But as with many good things, this too had to come to an end. And as with all good stories, this one too, is fraught with sadness.

When the time came for the queen to give birth, there were many complications. And though Jaxith had called for the best midwife in the land, she could do nothing to save child or mother, leaving Jaxith alone once more.

For many years, the young king lived with his loneliness by filling his life with the care of his people, but it was not enough. There was an emptiness still inside of him, a deep, dark pit threatening to swallow him whole at all times. And so, one evening as he stared up at the moon, he sent up a quiet prayer to the goddess.

"I do not ask for much, Selene. I give my life in service to your kingdom, and its people. I give my days to see that they are well, and happy, and fed. And for these long years, I have asked for nothing in return." Jaxith's voice was low.

A soft breeze carried petals from the cherry blossoms past Jaxith's window, flickering pale and gentle in the moonlight, as if to say, *What is it you ask of me?*

"I want only this," Jaxith said, swallowing around a well of tears that threatened to choke off his request. "I would have a child of my own. An heir to your great kingdom. Who will care for and look after your people when I am gone. Surely, that cannot be too much to ask."

Jaxith waited for an answer, staring up at the moon. When no breeze, nor animal, nor any other sign came that the goddess had heard, he exhaled deeply. Shoulders slumping forward, the king pulled himself from the window and retreated to his bed.

Many moons passed, and spring turned to summer, then summer turned to autumn, before Jaxith received an answer. (It was quite a long wait for one's greatest wish to be granted, but if you ask anyone who knows anything about magic, they'll tell you this, "Magic, good magic, takes time.")

The king's hunting party had been prepared for the

annual Lunar Festival Midnight Hunt for a fortnight. So, when the time came, even the horses seemed to feel the excitement. Their hooves stomped the ground in a steady rhythm as the moon's bright face rose high into the sky. When she was at her zenith, the first sound of a flute rent the air, and they were off.

Jaxith and his brother Sunil, some years Jaxith's junior, led the way. They traveled deeper into the wood to the west of Lunette, moonlight dappling the forest floor in her grey-blue gaze. Making it difficult to see, and even more difficult to find prey. The two brothers parted ways as the hunt continued, and some minutes later Jaxith saw a flash of white from the corner of his eye.

The long-eared rabbit streaked across the lush undergrowth, fluttering in and out of view like a specter as it hopped from one pool of moonlight to another. Jaxith dismounted quietly, holding his finger to his lips to still his horse, and tied the beast to a tree. Then he pulled a glinting dagger from his boot and crept after the scuttling creature.

It led Jaxith deeper and deeper into the forest (which should have given him pause, but as things go in these stories, it did not) until there was hardly any light left to show him the way. Jaxith lost sight of the creature then, spinning in place to find it again, but instead of the soft white fur of a rabbit, his eyes caught on a single beam of moonlight filtering through the leaves to light the recesses of a tree hollow.

A branch snapped beneath Jaxith's boot as he walked closer, and then a cry broke the stillness. A child wailing at having been awakened from their slumber. Jaxith jerked and stumbled, nearly falling to his knees in the mossy undertow of the forest. When he regained his feet, the child was still weeping. He clenched his fists, took a steadying breath, and approached the tree.

Bathed in moonlight, the child's midnight blue hair glittered with stardust, and their blue eyes seemed almost silver as they met the king's dark gaze. In that breadth of a second, the wailing had stopped, and the child peered at the king curiously through thick lashes.

"Hello there, little one," Jaxith whispered, reaching out a hand toward the babe. To Jaxith's surprise, the child reached back. Their chubby fist closing around Jaxith's little finger and gripping it tightly. "And what's your name then?"

A blink of wide blue eyes was the child's only answer.

"Hmm, then what shall we call you?" Jaxith continued, his other hand moving to scoop the babe out of the tree and into his arms.

The king turned and a soft breeze rustled the trees above, dragging with it leaves, and the faint sound of crickets. It was as if it were a gentle message from Selene herself.

Take care. Teach him to be kind.

Although the words went unsaid, Jaxith heard them all the same, and he nodded in understanding.

"I think Cricket will be fitting, don't you?"

The child squealed, his eyes squeezing shut in joy and a gummy smile lighting his face.

"Yes, that will do quite nicely." Jaxith nodded to himself. Another flash of white fur caught his eye, and he smiled softly. "Will you lead me back, then?"

The rabbit didn't answer (they never did, even magic rabbits didn't answer silly questions), it merely hopped in a small circle and darted through the forest again, leading Jaxith back the way he'd come.

NEARLY EIGHTEEN YEARS later finds the young prince Cricket much grown, but no less jovial, and mischievous for it. His midnight hair is long, sweeping well past his back, trailing stardust in his wake. His smile...is just the same, though not quite as gummy anymore.

BOOK I
THE CAPITAL

CHAPTER 1

Scrambling over the wall used to be a lot easier, he remembered that much. Before they'd lost that twisting willow that sat right next to it. Why had they lost that again? Oh yes, it'd been struck by lightning last summer. Stupid lightning just had to go and spoil the best escape route along the whole perimeter.

"Great moon and stars, when did I get so out of shape?" Cricket asked, not expecting an answer as his fingers clung to the top of the wall and his boots scraped against the smooth stone.

"I think it was about the time Lieutenant Chiaki retired to be with her grandchildren," came a sarcastic drawl from behind him. Looking over his shoulder, Cricket could just make out the red clothed figure of Ignacia where she stood, no doubt looking cross, behind him.

"Iggy!" Cricket yelped, releasing the top of the wall and falling to his feet with a soft thud. "What brings—" A few loose pebbles from the wall fell, littering the prince's dark tunic in a fine layer of dust. Cricket brushed it away, laughing nervously. "What brings you out this way?"

"Fumiya is looking for you."

"Is he now?" Cricket dusted his hands off on his trousers, blowing a stray strand of hair out of his eyes.

Ignacia raised one auburn brow, her light brown face taking on a look of impatience. She was going to have a go at him, Cricket could just feel it. If he were anywhere else, he might have tried to step back from her and make a run for it. But there was a wall behind him, and if he tried to run past her, she'd just catch him.

"Whatever for?" He tried to sound innocent. He sounded innocent, right? Nothing to see here. Just a prince skipping out on his lessons to go play in the streets like a common—

"I believe you know whatever for."

Oh. Oh no. She was mad.

"Is this about the history lessons? Because I know all of it, Iggy. I swear I do. And besides, Fumiya is so boring. There is nothing at—"

"You know it all, do you?" Ignacia's lips had turned up in a teasing smile. And oh, great Selene, that was *worse*. That was so much worse.

"Y-yes?" He looked from the corner of his eye to see if there was a quick way out, but it was just wall and yard and more wall and yard. She'd catch him, no trouble, her foot work had always been superior.

"You don't sound terribly sure."

"I'm sure."

"Are you?"

"Yes. Positive. I know all the material—"

"Who was the king of Helio when your great-great-grand-mother Jeong was queen?" Ignacia's pink lips were tipped up at one corner, showing off a truly impressive dimple that Cricket might call cute. You know, if he didn't want to live to see his eighteenth name day.

"Trick question, it was twins." Cricket bounced on the toes of his boots, brushing a long dark blue strand of hair from his face. "A brother and sister. Queen Alrika, and King Ajax."

Ignacia narrowed her eyes, lips pursing. "And who was their heir?"

"Their great niece, the lady Kyong."

"What year was the Great War?"

"8902, the year of the Rabbit. And the participants of the war were Helio, Lunette, and to a smaller degree Hermes. Although their ruler, Queen Calixte refused to give her full forces," Cricket recited, his pale blue eyes twinkling.

Ignacia drew down her brows, annoyance painted across her features.

"Did I pass?"

"It was satisfactory." She uncrossed her arms to pull a little purse from her pocket. "Honestly, I don't know how you can memorize an entire textbook in a week, but you can't seem to recall what dignitaries visited for dinner."

Cricket shrugged. "Textbooks are easy. You just read the words, and recite them. People are harder."

"Oh?" She seemed to be counting something in the little purse. He wondered how much longer she'd keep him there before she called the guards. Surely, she didn't intend to drag him back to his lessons on her own. Or at least he hoped she wouldn't drag him back by herself. That always ended in pain.

"Yes. They're all...." He frowned trying to think of a word that could describe them. "Fiddly."

She stopped counting, looking up from the purse to send him an incredulous look. "Fiddly?"

"Fiddly." Cricket nodded. "That's why I need to go into the city. So I can understand them better."

"Is that what you were doing? Going out to *learn*?" The air quotes were implied, but Ignacia was too refined to use them physically.

"Yes."

She didn't say anything, just went back to counting whatever was in the purse.

"Textbooks aren't going to teach me to be king," he said when it looked like she wasn't going to let him off. "And honestly, I haven't been into the city since my seventeenth name day. That's nearly a year, Iggy. A year!"

"Here." She held out the purse when she'd finished her inspection of its contents. Still not acknowledging his obvious distress.

"What's this?" He took it, weighing it carefully in his palm. He supposed there was money inside, but he didn't really know how that all worked. He had never had to pay for anything before.

"If you're going out into the city, you ought to have some spending money. And we had better pick up some dumplings for Fumiya to make sure he doesn't tell your uncle." Ignacia moved to the wall, looking up at the top of it thoughtfully. Then she leaped up, her fingers holding onto the edge, and pulled herself to sit on the top in a motion that seemed to Cricket so smooth it had to have been practiced. Cricket looked up at her dumbfounded. "We need to be back before your meeting with your uncle and Marwa. If you skip another advisor meeting, I fear he might just send you off to the monastery like he's been threatening."

Her feet swung from where she was perched on the ledge. The heels of her boots scuffing against the stone as she looked down at him, unimpressed. You'd never know that of the two of them, Ignacia was the servant, and Cricket was the prince. And honestly... how in the name of Styx did she make it look so easy?

"You coming, or what?"

"Uh... yeah! Yeah, I'm coming. Give me a hand up?" He scrambled to get his fingers onto the ledge again.

"You're a big boy, you figure it out." Ignacia scoffed, and turned to leap off the other side.

THEY SPENT the next few hours winding their way through the market of the capital. Zigzagging from vendor to vendor as they sampled dumplings and the last of the season's strawberries. The day was warm, the company was good, and it was all too easy to lose track of time. Really, Cricket couldn't be blamed for it, wasn't it Ignacia's job to keep him on schedule? He was fairly certain it was.

By the time the bells chimed throughout the city, they were already late.

"Is that the three o'clock bell?" Cricket asked, dread gripping his insides into a vice.

"Hmm?" Ignacia mumbled around the mochi she was stuffing into her face. She stopped chewing for a moment to count the bells, and then her face paled. "Oh no."

"Thank you again." Cricket smiled, bowing to the owner of the little stall selling the mochi. "It was truly delicious. I especially loved the—"

But he didn't get to finish as Ignacia grabbed him by the wrist and started dragging him back toward the castle. Cricket yelped, feet pounding on the stone behind her. They dodged a vendor moving his cart to the other side of the street to get out of the late afternoon sun, and a small herd of ducklings.

"Excuse us! Excuse me! I'm so sorry! My apologies! Excuse us!" Cricket shouted over his shoulder as they nearly knocked over more than one old granny out shopping for her weekly vegetables. Stars, where had the time gone? Hadn't it just been eleven?

"Your uncle is going to kill us. He's really going to this time. He'll skin me alive, and then have me sent to a convent. And he'll ship you off to that monastery up in the mountains. The one where the monks beat you with those giant wooden ladles if you speak more than once a week." Ignacia was saying, only half paying attention to the nonsense coming out of her mouth as she dragged him along.

"I won't let him skin you alive." Cricket aimed for reassuring, but when Ignacia turned to cut him a look as if to say *this is all your fault,* he decided it probably wasn't helping. "Or send you to a convent."

Ignacia shook her head, and kept running. T'would appear she didn't have time for his nonsense, and honestly, neither did he. Because she was probably right, Uncle Sunil was definitely going to try to convince Father to send him to the monastery after this.

"This is the fourth meeting you've been late to this month," Ignacia hissed through her teeth.

"I'm sorry Iggy. I really am."

She turned to level him with another glare. Which was impressive when they were still running full speed ahead. And there it was. There was the castle wall. All they had to do was make it over and pretend they'd merely gotten caught up in some discussion or other in the library. Cricket had left the library window open. No one would be the wiser. Absolutely—

One moment Cricket was running, the next he and Ignacia were a tangle of limbs in a mud puddle on the side of the street with another person.

"Why don't you watch where you're going!" The person snarled as the three fought to get themselves extricated from one another. Ignacia was free first, then she helped the irritable man to his feet while Cricket sat in the mud. Because sure, why not, things couldn't get much worse.

"We're very sorry," Cricket said, leaping to his feet and pulling the long braid over his shoulder to assess the damage. Mud. Mud everywhere. There was no time to change, no time for a bath, and little chance Uncle Sunil wouldn't notice.

"Yes, well you shou—" The man stopped mid-sentence when he got a look at the long braid that Cricket was trying to pull the worst of the debris out of. Cricket looked up with a frown at the sudden pause. The man was wearing a truly gaudy velvet tunic (he'd never get the mud out of it, and that thought pleased Cricket greatly), and a rather ridiculous expression of only just now realizing he might have put his foot in his mouth.

"No time." Ignacia grabbed his wrist, and they were off again before the man could pull his foot from his mouth and say anything else.

They made it to the wall in record time, and then Ignacia was crouching down, weaving her fingers together into a basket. Cricket put his foot into her hands, and let her give him a lift to the top of the wall. He turned back to offer her a hand up, but she'd already made the jump and was scrambling up the side without his aide.

"Don't worry about me," she grunted as her boots scuffed for a foot hold. "Get your ass to the meeting hall!"

"Right." Cricket leaped off the other side into the soft grass, the force of it bringing him to his knees. "Grass stains."

"Add it to the list." Ignacia huffed, dropping down beside him. "Run!"

Pushing to his feet, Cricket took off at a run. There was

no point in scuttling through the library window now, he'd only get mud all over the books. The best he could do was head in through the kitchen entrance, and try to think of a good excuse on the way.

A good excuse. A good excuse. A good excuse.

CHAPTER 2

He'd thought of one, he really had. Cricket had thought of a wonderfully valid excuse (a lie, he'd thought of a lie) for why he was, what? Fifteen minutes late? No. That wasn't right, the clocks read thirty after three as he raced past them. Oh no. Oh great Selene! Uncle Sunil really was going to send him to the monastery. Thirty minutes late and covered in mud. But the moment he skidded through the doorway into the meeting room to see Uncle Sunil, Marwa, Anstice, and... oh wonderful... an emissary from the kingdom of Hermes, if the deep blue robes were anything to go by, he'd quite forgotten what the excuse (lie) was.

"Uncle," Cricket said, plastering on a charming smile (the one that showed off his dimples, and usually got him out of trouble or into more of it depending), and standing up straight just how Father had taught him kings were supposed to stand. "So sorry to keep everyone waiting."

Uncle Sunil's face had turned a new shade of red, somewhere in the vermillion family. Which would have been funny, and spectacular, and all things hilarious if it weren't for the way his dark glinting eyes were fixed on Cricket of all people. Cricket saw Marwa shake her head as she struggled to suppress a fond smile, and Anstice duck her head behind one of her beautifully hand painted fans. Well. They weren't going to be any help. Some advisors they were.

"I don't think we've been introduced." Cricket took two great steps around the table, careful to avoid Uncle, and held his hand out to the emissary. "You're from Hermes, yes?"

The man looked down at his outstretched hand, and Cricket saw his lip curl. Glancing down Cricket found the hand was caked in still drying mud. He laughed nervously, and tucked it back behind him, opting for a respectful bow instead.

"Cricket," Uncle Sunil said, his voice strained for politeness. There was a vein on his temple which Cricket and Anstice had taken to placing bets on. They'd watch Uncle Sunil get truly enraged, and then bet how many beats per minute it was pulsing at. Right that moment it looked like it was about to explode. "This is Lord Benoit. He was visiting to bring your father a message, and decided he'd like to stop in and see—"

"And see how the young prince was doing with his matters of state," Benoit interrupted, which only made Uncle Sunil's vein pulse harder. Anstice made a noise like a laugh, then covered it with a cough and her fan. Benoit took no notice. "We'd heard that your father had given you a few villages to manage?"

Honestly, Cricket had to give it to Benoit, the man knew how to put up a front. If he hadn't cringed away from sullying himself with Cricket's grubby hands not but a few minutes ago, Cricket would believe nothing was amiss in this room. This room where Uncle Sunil's face was hot enough to fry an egg, Anstice was nearly doubled over where she leaned against the table, and Cricket was trailing muddy footprints everywhere he went. Nothing at all to see here. Just a normal day in court. And really, it kind of was just a normal day in Lunette, but Cricket wasn't about to say as such.

"Ah yes." Cricket nodded, his smile softening around the edges from the charming thing that it had been into something more thoughtful. "I've been taking care of Candra and Natsuki since... How long has it been again, Uncle?"

"Since your seventeenth name day," Anstice supplied. She'd recovered from her bout of giggles, dropped her fan, and was pulling some reports from the piles of papers on the table. "About eight months, if I'm not mistaken."

"Nine," Marwa corrected softly. "Well... nearly nine."

"Thank you, Mother." Anstice pulled a sheet of paper from the stack to let Cricket and Benoit look over statistics on the crops from that year. "It was a very good season for both villages."

"And there you have it." Cricket tapped the paper as if it held all the answers. "You can return home to Hermes and tell everyone that Lunette is in safe hands with me."

"Of course. Of course." Benoit nodded agreeably. "There was never any doubt. Now, if you'll excuse me, I do have to deliver that message to his highness."

"It was a pleasure meeting with you, Lord Benoit." Cricket pulled the charming, dimpled smile back onto his lips, and offered the man another polite bow.

"You as well, Your Highness. Please, next time you are in Hermes, feel free to pay me a visit." Benoit bowed even lower, and when he rose there was a twinkling of mischief in his eyes, as if he thought this whole thing rather funny. And well, maybe it would be if Uncle Sunil didn't skin Ignacia alive, and send Cricket to a monastery. Benoit had just risen in Cricket's esteem though.

"I will," Cricket promised.

Benoit said his goodbyes to the others and left. Once he

was out of ear shot, Cricket hunched his shoulders waiting for the shout that was—

"You impudent, immature, impetuous, rude, moronic, little brat!"

Ah... there it was.

"Sunil," Marwa said. Her tone was soft, but there was a hint of warning there, as if advising Uncle Sunil not to take this dressing down too far. And oh, great Selene, what had Cricket ever done to deserve Marwa and her loyalty? Other than being adopted by the king, of course.

"No, Marwa. He's gone too far this time. Skipping lessons. Jumping the wall. Falling into mud puddles. Being late. *Embarrassing me.*" Uncle Sunil said that last bit as if it were Cricket's worst sin of all, and Cricket supposed maybe in his eyes, it was.

"I didn't mean to be late. I just lost track of time." It was a weak defense even to his own ears, but he had to try, didn't he?

"I'll have you shipped off on the first carriage out of here. You can go up the mountains and let the monks teach you some manners. Mark my words." Uncle Sunil was wagging his finger in a rather dangerous way, Cricket hoped he didn't hit himself or someone else with it. And then he turned and stormed off.

"Well," Cricket said when he was gone, deflating into a chair. "That could have gone better."

Anstice tutted, moving over to him to smack him lightly on the head with her fan. "Where were you?"

Cricket held up a hand, smiling a little, and then he pulled a small box of strawberry mochi from his bag. Anstice squealed in delight, scooping them up.

"I take it back. I don't care where you were!" She took a bite of one with a happy murmur.

Marwa was not so easily swayed, she stood behind

Anstice, shaking her head in disapproval. "You went over the wall."

"I'm very sorry I was late." Cricket ducked his head. "I didn't mean to be. We just got caught up in everything."

"Tell me you at least took Ignacia with you." Marwa sighed, defeated.

"I did."

"Thank you." She stepped over to pat his shoulder, a gesture that had always made him feel much better in spite of everything. Then she snatched a mochi from Anstice's hands, eliciting a squawk of protest, and headed for the door. "Go get cleaned up. Dinner is in a couple of hours, and if your uncle sees that mud still in your hair then he'll try to take scissors to it again."

"Yes ma'am." Cricket offered her a salute, a smile, and once she was gone, he rose from his chair, stretching. "Can you drop these off at my room? I've looked at last month's numbers, but I assume these are updated?"

Anstice nodded, her cheeks puffed up around what appeared to be a mochi in each. Cricket snorted, which turned into a full belly laugh. He rolled forward, holding his stomach as he chortled. When it finally wore off, and Anstice had somehow managed to chew, and swallow the two mochi without choking, Cricket leaned over the papers again to look at them.

His mouth pressed into a line, muddy fingers scrubbing over his face, leaving smudges in their wake. "Tell me they're happy, Anstice."

"They're happy. I know your father tries, but these smaller villages need updated agricultural tools so they can make enough off their crops to sustain not just themselves, but also their homes. You've done that for them."

The initiative had been simple. Cricket had ordered the latest in farming and magical technology be provided to the farmers of Candra and Natsuki. The people there hadn't seen an update in decades, probably longer. Like Anstice said, Father tried, but there were too many outliers, and not enough help. Then there was the issue of importance, and those who had a higher population were higher on the king's list. It was as simple as that. No one's fault. Cricket believed that the best thing he could do for those people was not to throw money at them, but to give them the tools they needed to succeed. It wasn't much, maybe Father would have done something else, but he'd entrusted them to Cricket. And Cricket had done what he thought was best.

"I'm sure Uncle would disagree."

"Yeah. Well." Anstice rolled her eyes. "Your uncle wouldn't know a good idea if it bit him in the ass."

Cricket nodded in agreement. Uncle Sunil was... He was... He was a bit backwards, as far as Cricket was concerned. And completely inflexible.

"Right. I better go have a bath. I'll see you later."

Anstice turned back to the papers, stuffing another mochi in her mouth, and began to gather them up as Cricket retreated to his rooms.

UNCLE SUNIL WAS STILL FUMING, and a little red, by the time their soup arrived.

"And then he waltzes in, happy as you please, with a backside covered in mud!" he spat, hand gripping his spoon to the point of near bending the metal.

"I'd thought with that tree gone that'd be the end of you sneaking out," Father commented dryly, but there was a twinkle in his eye like he found the whole thing very amusing.

Especially the way Uncle Sunil was turning a not-so-subtle shade of fuchsia. At least he wasn't vermillion again, Cricket counted that as a win.

Cricket shrugged. "I've gotten taller since the last time I tried to climb the wall without the tree."

"So you have."

"That is not the point!" Uncle Sunil hissed, brandishing a shaking finger at Cricket like a weapon. "And you damn well know it's not, Jaxith."

"No, I suppose it's not." Father sighed, sitting back in his chair. "Cricket, you're not supposed to skip lessons. You know better."

"I do," Cricket agreed. "But I had Iggy quiz me on the material before we went out, and I answered all of her questions spot on. I didn't see the harm."

"Didn't see the...he didn't see the harm, Jaxith." Uncle Sunil repeated, his voice quivering on the edge of a shout. Except he wouldn't do that. He wouldn't shout in front of Father. He wouldn't shout in front of the servants. He was too dignified for all that.

"We could have Fumiya set up a test for him, to prove he's learned this month's material," Marwa suggested, ever the voice of reason. Cricket was struck again that he was lucky to have her on his side. She wasn't a mother, no. He'd never had one of those. But she was as good as one.

"And if he fails?" Uncle Sunil's dark eyes had fixed on Cricket, and Cricket wanted nothing more than to melt into his chair and never be heard from again. He hated when Uncle looked at him like that. Like he was nothing but a trial. Had been since the day Father had brought him home. Maybe he was, to Uncle, but no one else seemed to think so. Sure, he got into trouble, but he never did any irreparable harm. He often wondered if Uncle would find his behavior excusable if he were officially of royal blood.

"I won't." Cricket lifted his chin, meeting Uncle's eyes as best he could. Which was rather hard when Uncle was doing his best to look down on him.

"We can decide what to do with him after the results are in." Marwa had turned her attention to Uncle Sunil. Her eyes were hard and sharp. Cricket knew they didn't get along, although he was never sure why. It seemed to him that both of them wanted what was best for Lunette, and for Father, but neither could agree on what that was. "Does that sound reasonable, your highness?"

"Exceedingly. Have Fumiya prepare an exam." Father nodded as if that were the end of the matter.

Cricket picked up his spoon, intent on ignoring the rest of supper's conversations. Or at least only half paying attention to them now that he wasn't being sent directly to a monastery.

"Don't look so smug, you insolent—"

"Sunil," Father cut him off, sending Uncle Sunil a warning glare. "Cricket is the crown prince, and you ought to treat him as such. I understand that you think his education is lacking, but his marks are good, and I have never once had a complaint from any of his tutors."

"The monks would teach him better manners. That's where Helio sends their heirs." Uncle Sunil still had yet to touch his soup, and it seemed he was intent on not going down without a fight tonight. Which was a pity, because Cricket wasn't in the mood for a fight. "And all of them are upright, well-behaved children."

"It has never been our practice to send our heirs off to be schooled," Marwa reminded placidly when Father refused to say anything.

"There is a first time for everything."

"There is, but this is not the time for that. And besides, Cricket isn't a child anymore."

Cricket looked over at Anstice, and watched her eyes volley from her mother to his uncle with rapt attention. Honestly, how she could live on this drama, Cricket didn't know. He'd rather they just eat their dinner in companionable —or even tense—silence as opposed to this. And that was saying something as he hated silence.

"And his manners are fine," Marwa continued, setting down her soup spoon so she could meet Uncle Sunil head on. "There has never been a complaint about him from any of the emissaries, or the staff."

"He's impertinent." Uncle Sunil was bracing himself on the table now as if at any moment he'd push to his feet.

"He's brave."

"They're laughing at him! And why shouldn't they be?! Look at him! He bandies about like a commoner! His hair is longer than any woman in any of the kingdoms! And he sloughs off all responsibility! He is a spoiled, arrogant, foolish child and you mark my words Jaxith—"

"That is enough!" Marwa rose to her feet, slamming her hands on the table. "They aren't laughing at *him*; they're laughing at *you*."

Cricket stopped dead, his spoon clattering down to the table as he drank in the scene. Marwa looked more angry than he'd ever seen her, and Uncle Sunil had skipped the rest of the red spectrum and gone straight to ghastly white in fury.

"They're laughing at *you*," Marwa continued, her voice a cold hiss. "With your backwards, and self-important attitude."

"Are you going to let her speak to me like this, Jaxith?!" Uncle Sunil asked, his head swiveling to look at Father.

Father was silent. Taking his time to sit down his spoon, wipe his fingers on his napkin, and take a deep inhale. When he was done, he looked up and met Uncle Sunil's eyes. "Yes. I am."

"She is your advisor. A servant!" Uncle Sunil spat the words, slinging spittle along with them. "She's a *servant* and she sits at our table and eats with us like she's one of us. Like she's of royal birth! I am your brother! Your blood! And you choose her side over mine!"

"No. I choose my son's side over yours. Marwa is correct in her assessment of Cricket, and not entirely wrong in her criticisms of you." Father's voice was quiet. It always was. He didn't have to yell, or get angry. He spoke calmly and told the world as he saw it. It was one of the things Cricket admired most about him. Where Cricket could be mercurial, and passionate, Father was steady. The difference between a bubbling brook and a rushing river-bend. "The world has changed. We must change with it. And it starts with getting to know our people better. We do not now, nor have we ever, sat on a mountain apart from our people. If Cricket thinks his best chance to be a good king is to learn from them, then it is our responsibility to give him that opportunity."

Uncle Sunil's face went from ghastly pale to red again, thoroughly chastised. Cricket blinked in surprise watching as he stood from his chair, and left the table without another word.

CHAPTER 3

Marwa Dresden was dead.

She was the king's closest friend. His most loyal advisor. An auntie to his son. A mediator. An intelligent, outspoken, just woman. A mother. And she was dead.

Marwa Dresden was dead, and it was all Cricket's fault.

She fell ill some days after her argument with Uncle Sunil. One evening her and Cricket had been caught out in the rain trying to round up the rabbits in the yard. By the next morning she'd developed a ghastly cough. Before a fortnight, Selene had called her home.

Marwa Dresden was dead, and it was all Cricket's fault.

"You can't just hide in your rooms for the rest of your life," Ignacia said, but Cricket hardly heard her. All he could think of was how he couldn't possibly face Anstice. Not after he'd killed her mother. She'd never forgive him, and she never should. If there was any kind of justice in the world, Cricket would be next to catch a cold, and he'd die before the week was out. "Are you listening to me?"

"No," Cricket mumbled, staring out across the lawns.

Rain pelted the glass of his window, distorting the world outside in a melting mess of color. The grass was still green, the flowers were still blooming, the world was still so full of life. But it would never be the same. Never again. Because Marwa Dresden was dead.

"No?" Ignacia asked, her tone annoyed and incredulous. And that was fine, because Cricket deserved her ire. He deserved that and so much more. "What do you mean 'no'?"

Cricket shrugged, unable to say anything else. He wasn't even really sure what they were talking about anymore. His sketchbook lay discarded in his lap, a half-finished drawing of Marwa on the page. Already he could feel the image of her fading. Going fuzzy and indistinct around the edges as memories do. He'd wanted to paint her, so that Anstice would have something to remember her by. A real painting, not one of those stuffy portraits that hung in the hall of ancestors. Something that showed her at her best. But there was something about the eyes... it wasn't right.

Ignacia said something else. He didn't hear her over the pounding of the rain on the glass. It didn't matter anyway. They couldn't hold the funeral until it stopped raining. And it had been raining for four days. Since Marwa had passed. That seemed fitting, didn't it? For Selene to wash the earth away in her grief over the loss of one so loyal and true as—

The sketchbook on his lap was tugged away, and he jerked around to narrow a glare at Ignacia. She wasn't paying him any mind, her eyes were fixed on the sketch, assessing it. "What's wrong with it?"

"The eyes aren't right. They're not as... something, as they should be." Cricket sighed, leaning over to bump his head against the glass with a thunk.

"You can't keep blaming yourself for this. What happened isn't your fault, and Anstice doesn't blame you." Ignacia sat the sketchbook down on a nearby table, and perched herself on the window seat next to him.

"She should."

"No. She shouldn't. People catch colds, it happens. It's no one's fault."

"She shouldn't have been out there with me rounding up the rabbits. It was my responsibility. Father told *me* to do it." Cricket's head lulled to the side so he could look at her, but even then, he couldn't meet her eyes. "Uncle said I should have taken care of it by myself. Like a man."

Ignacia huffed, rolling her eyes. "Your uncle needs to learn when to keep his mouth shut."

Cricket opened his mouth to argue, and she wrapped her hand around it to keep him from doing just that.

"Marwa would have said the same thing. She didn't like how he always bullied you. It's not right. You're his nephew, he should be kinder."

Cricket tried to reply, but was muffled by her hand.

"I won't hear any more of your nonsense. Get up. We're having lunch with Anstice in the bunny sanctuary, and she'll be expecting you." Ignacia pulled her hand away, and picked up the sketchpad again. "And I think you should put this on canvas. I know you've got some other sketches of her from your earlier work. Maybe those will help you get the eyes right. She'd want Anstice to have it."

"You think so?"

"Don't you?"

"Yeah... I suppose she would." He took the pad, looking down at the sketch. The eyes would be an easy enough fix once he started adding color. He could bring a life and light to them that just pencil couldn't. Or at least he hoped so, because he didn't think he could live with himself if he didn't pay homage to Marwa the only way he knew how, with paint. "Wait. Lunch?"

"Yes, lunch." Ignacia had moved away from him and was tidying his room. Scratch that, she was merely moving the mess from one place to another as there was really no way to tidy Cricket's room. The maids had long since given it up, and he honestly didn't want them to have to clean up after him when it got to be this bad.

"Whose idea was that?"

"Yours." She'd extricated a basket from somewhere amongst the mess and was piling his dirty laundry into it. "You really ought to have Callie come in here at least once a month and clean up."

"It's not Callie's job to make sure my room is tidy, it's mine. Father said so."

"Hm..." Ignacia grabbed a paint-stained pair of trousers from a chair.

"Not those! Those are my painting pants." Cricket leaped up to snatch them from her. "And when did I decide to schedule a lunch?"

Ignacia dropped his "painting pants" where she found them and continued on gathering up the rest of the laundry. "Last night. When you fell asleep at your desk, and I wrote the invitations."

"That's illegal," he accused, carefully folding the pants and hanging them over the stool in front of his easel.

"I'd like to see you prove it." Ignacia smirked, dropping the basket just outside the door for one of the maids to pick up. "Now come along then. It'd be rude to schedule a memorial lunch with a grieving daughter, and then not show up."

"I hate you," Cricket said with no real bite.

ANSTICE WAS WAITING for them with red rimmed eyes, and no fewer than five rabbits in her lap when they arrived. At the sight of Cricket, she let out a soft, but happy sob.

"Cricket! Oh, thank Selene, Cricky! I've missed you! Where have you been!" Anstice shooed the rabbits from her lap, picking her way across their pen, careful not to step on them. Then she was in front of Cricket, and her eyes were so wild, hopeful, and sad that Cricket wanted to cry. But instead of smacking him, as she rightly should, she threw her arms around his neck to hug him close.

Cricket's wide gaze jerked to Ignacia, who was wearing an expression so smug he wasn't quite sure what to do with it.

"Come sit. Come sit," Anstice said, pulling back to let them in through the gate of the little enclosure.

"Anstice, I'm—" Cricket started, but before he could go any further, Anstice smacked his arm with her fan. "What in the name of Styx was that for?!"

"Don't you dare apologize. I don't want to hear it." Her tone had gone hard, her eyes narrowing. Cricket felt his stomach drop.

"Right. Of course. I'll just... I won't..." Cricket swallowed roughly around the rawness of unshed tears in his throat. He'd known this would happen; he'd just hoped to avoid facing that reality at least until after the funeral. "I'll leave you alone."

"What? What are you talking about? What's he talking about?" Anstice's head jerked to Ignacia, her expression confused.

"He thinks it's his fault," Ignacia supplied helpfully.

"Well, where did he get a stupid idea like that from?"

Ignacia didn't answer, but the look she gave Anstice must have spoken volumes.

"Why that self-righteous, arrogant, old goat. You know Mother always said he shouldn't be allowed to scold Cricket like he does. That yes, he's Cricket's uncle, but he shouldn't be allowed to help raise him." Anstice's face had gone quite red. She tapped her fan angrily against her open palm. "And you," she said, smacking Cricket with the fan particularly hard in the neck.

"Ouch!" Cricket hissed, rubbing the already reddening skin.

"Don't you start listening to him now. As your advisor, I'll tell you exactly what Mother would have said, whatever Sunil says, you just ignore him and do the opposite. He's usually wrong anyway, so that's a safe bet." Anstice nodded to herself, looking quite pleased with her words.

"But if I hadn't—"

Anstice smacked him again with her fan. "Honestly, Ignacia, how do you spend all of your time with this stupid boy?"

"Hey wait a minute. I'm not stupid." Cricket huffed, pouting.

"He's only stupid when he opens his mouth," Ignacia said with a shrug.

"Which is all the time," Anstice argued.

"I suppose that's fair."

"I'm still right here!"

"Come, Annie, let's have some tea." Ignacia held out her arm for Anstice, and then guided her over to a table set up in the middle of the rabbit pen. Both of them completely ignoring Cricket's continued sulk.

The playful air and banter continued for the duration of their lunch. It was as if a bubble surrounded the trio, blocking out the rest of the world. As they sat together, they were not crown prince, not lady in waiting, not royal advisor. They were simply Cricky, Iggy, and Annie. Three very old friends, finding comfort in one another the way only old friends could. Cricket was not sure how long they could keep the sadness that lingered outside their bubble at bay, but he would make every effort to fend it off, to keep Anstice's eyes from clouding over with tears again.

THE RAIN CLEARED SHORTLY THEREAFTER. As if Selene herself had taken comfort in their reunion, and found peace in the loss of Marwa Dresden.

The funeral was held the very next day. A small ceremony, which was no less meaningful and heartfelt for its meager numbers. Those who had come to face the mud were people who truly loved Marwa Dresden. People who were truly saddened by her passing.

Cricket's mind flashed back to the last Dresden funeral he'd been to. Five-year-old Anstice straight backed, and decked in traditional mens' mourning silks as her father was lowered into the ground. They'd spent half the funeral trying to subtly scratch each other's backs without drawing Uncle's notice. Anstice looked more at home in the soft gown and shawl in white that she'd chosen for her mother's funeral. He was grateful for this small mercy as her body shook with sobs. She deserved whatever would make this day the littlest bit less horrible.

Uncle Sunil spent the entirety of the ceremony glaring at Cricket where he stood holding one of Anstice's hands, while Ignacia held the other. Cricket studiously ignored him, the day wasn't about Uncle Sunil and his strange penchant for propriety. It was about finding comfort in one another during the loss of one of their own. And if Uncle Sunil couldn't see that...well...

Father gave a moving speech that left not a single dry eye in the small gathering. And when it was all over, Anstice let out a whimper, and Cricket pulled her into a tight hug so she could press her running kohl-rimmed eyes against his itchy silk tunic. Ignacia waited with them, her hand making slow circles up and down Anstice's back to sooth her as the others left.

"She's gone, Cricky. She's really gone." Anstice's words were a muffled wail against his chest, but he didn't have to hear them well to understand. "She's gone and I'm all alone."

"You're not alone," Cricket murmured, squeezing her tighter to him. "You've still got me and Iggy and Father. We're going to take care of each other, just like we always have."

"We are," Ignacia said.

"I don't know if I can replace her." Anstice gripped the front of his tunic, wrinkling the silk. Cricket didn't complain, it was ruined anyway, and what was a tunic when it came to his best friend's comfort.

"You can't replace her," Cricket said, words soft. "No one can. And you won't."

Anstice pulled her head from his chest to look up at him. Her eyes were red rimmed again, puffy from crying, and she had streaks of kohl down her cheeks. He was sure he didn't look much better, and he knew Ignacia didn't either. In spite of everything, Marwa Dresden had been mother to them all in a way. She may have given birth to Anstice, but she'd raised the three of them. Made them siblings. Taught them how to rely on one another. Lunette would not be the same without her.

"I won't?"

"No. You won't." Cricket took a deep breath, forcing himself to hold Antice's gaze. He hated saying things like this. He hated making grand declarations. That was Father's job, Father's place. But he supposed now was as good a time as any to get a little practice. "You won't because like you said, no one can replace Marwa. And that's okay. You don't have to replace her; she wouldn't want you to. What she'd want is for you to do the job your way. Don't be Marwa Dresden, Royal Advisor to the king of Lunette."

Anstice blinked at him, her tears slowing as confusion replaced despair if just for the moment. "No?"

"No. Be Anstice Naveen Dresden, Royal Advisor to the king of Lunette, best friend to Prince Cricket, and hand-painted fan connoisseur." Cricket smiled a little. It was weak and wobbly around the edges, but it was a smile, nonetheless.

Ignacia was looking at him in awe, and then she winked, her lips tugging just a little at the corners into a grin of her own. "You think you can manage that, Annie?"

"Yeah." Anstice nodded. "Yeah. I think I can."

CHAPTER 4

Anstice chose the flashiest purple gown Cricket had ever seen in his life for her appointment ceremony. It had a long flowing train, and enough sparkly bits on it that he was sure they could see it in the mountains of Helio. But she was happy, and that was all that mattered to him. Between himself and Ignacia they had managed to twist her hair up into a crown braid befitting a queen, and Cricket couldn't have been prouder.

"Is it too much?" Anstice asked, giving them an elegant twirl, which Cricket found truly impressive for if he'd been in a dress that long and tried to spin around, he was sure he'd have tripped. But that was Anstice, elegance and grace. She'd have made a wonderful princess, a beautiful queen, if she'd just been born to a king and not to the royal advisor.

"Maybe a little," Ignacia said, but there was a light in her eyes that only shimmered there when she was teasing.

"Oh you!" Anstice swatted Ignacia with her fan, and then laughed. "Fine. Fine. Cricky will tell me what I want to hear. Won't you, Cricky? That is your duty, as prince."

"Is it?" he asked, lounging back on the foot of her bed,

ankles crossed casually. "I didn't realize that had been added to the list."

"It was added the day I was born, and you tried to drop me down the stairs." Anstice nodded primly.

"First of all," Cricket said, sitting up, and shaking a finger playfully at her. "I'm not even a whole season older than you, I wasn't much bigger than you were by the time you were born."

"That's because you were a runt." Ignacia snickered into the back of her hand, covering it with a cough, or trying to anyhow.

"Oi!" Cricket shouted, reaching over to shove Ignacia's shoulder, causing her to fall over onto the bed with another giggle. "No ganging up on me!"

"That's not in the rules."

"I've checked," Anstice added, turning to give herself another once over in the mirror. "And what's the second of all?"

"Well now I don't think I'll say, since apparently no one here has any respect for me." He crossed his arms over his chest, poking out his lower lip in a spectacular pout, if he did say so himself. "Annie doesn't deserve my compliments if she's just going to be mean to me."

Ignacia snorted, giving him a shove. "You heard his royal highness; we have to be nice to him now."

"Oh ew. No. Whatever shall we do, Iggy?"

"Clearly, all that's left for us is to run away together. Come with me my darling Annie and leave this all behind." Ignacia rose, taking Anstice's hands in her own. "I'll take you away from this horrible, horrible prince."

They stared at each other for a long moment, and then the spell was broken, and they dropped into obnoxious giggles. Both throwing their heads back and cackling like old crones.

"Stop. Stop. It is too much. You'll make my makeup run." Anstice took a steadying breath, running her fingers carefully beneath her eyes.

"You're both terrible to me!" Cricket whined, flopping back onto the bed to stare up at Anstice's painted ceiling.

"Oh, you love us." Ignacia dropped back down beside him. "Besides, even if you didn't, we're all you've got."

"Don't remind me." He huffed.

"Hey!" Anstice shouted, kicking him in the shin with her shoe.

"Oi!" He sat up quickly, clutching his leg to himself, and cradling what was surely already bruising skin. "What was that for?! That's going to bruise!"

"Come and tell me I'm pretty on my special day or I'm kicking your ass out and you can go sit with your uncle." Anstice pointed her fan at him. It was a beautiful piece, commissioned specifically to match her gown. All swirling purple night skies, and glistening stars.

"You really shouldn't threaten people like that. It's unbecoming of a young lady."

"Here. Now. Compliments." Anstice pointed to the space right in front of her and raised a brow expectantly.

"All right. All right. So demanding." Cricket rolled to his feet to stand before her. He took Anstice's hands in his, giving them a light squeeze. "You, my dear baby sister. My best friend. The most ridiculous woman I've ever known. Look positively stunning. But not a lick of it would make any difference at all if it weren't a farce to cover up that insanely cunning brain of yours, would it?"

"Great Selene! I asked you to tell me I'm pretty, not to make me cry, you big oaf!" Anstice laughed wetly, giving him a hard shove so he fell back onto the bed next to Ignacia.

"Careful what you wish for," he chided playfully, and earned a smack to the face with a pillow for his trouble.

NOBLES from all over Lunette were in attendance at the new royal advisor's appointment ceremony. Each had their own motivations, but Cricket couldn't help but think a number of them were there to see a spectacle. He knew that his uncle was. Anstice was the youngest advisor appointed in centuries, and she was a quarter of the king's age. But that made no difference, Cricket knew she could do the job well. She'd serve Lunette just as well as her mother had.

A hush settled over the hall as Anstice made her way across the dais. Her train dragging behind her, fan tucked behind her back, and a serene look of certainty on her face. It was the most grown-up Cricket had ever seen her, and he nearly cried at the sight.

"Please repeat after me. I, Anstice Naveen Dresden, do swear," the master of ceremonies was droning. Honestly, if they could get a new master of ceremonies that'd make things a little more interesting. Cricket leaned back in his chair, and then sat up again when Uncle Sunil cut him a look.

Anstice stood up straighter looking for all the world like a queen about to make a declaration to her people. Cricket couldn't fight the grin that took over his face. If it weren't for Uncle Sunil to the right of him, he may have leaned over to the lord on his left, nudged him and told the man that that was his best friend up there. But he was sure Uncle Sunil would have something to say about that.

"I, Anstice Naveen Dresd—"

A clattering of noise from the hall drew everyone's eyes, including Anstice. A messenger, hair disheveled, eyes wild, ran down the center of the room. His feet slapped against the stone, echoing in the now silent space. Cricket heard more than one nobleman gasp as he climbed the steps of the dais.

"Excuse me. Excuse me. I'm so sorry to intrude. Excuse me." The man panted, falling to his knees before Father. "I'm sorry, Your Highness, I didn't...I couldn't... This is too important."

Father reached for the man, pulling him to his feet. "What is it? What's happened?"

The man whispered something to Father that Cricket couldn't hear. Father glanced to Anstice, and she nodded quickly.

"Is there a way to hurry this along? It seems I have a duty to fill already?" Anstice asked the master of ceremonies.

His long white beard quivered, looking thoroughly put out by the whole affair, but he rushed through what was left of it. Cricket had never heard the man speak so fast in his life, and he was sure he never would again. But it didn't matter, because not ten minutes later they were all dismissed, the guests ushered to the dining hall for refreshments on Anstice's orders, and Cricket trailed behind Uncle Sunil into Father's private study.

The messenger had been provided with tea, and a comfortable chair. He looked less harried now than he had fifteen minutes ago, but no less worried. His fingers trembled around the porcelain teacup.

"Please. Tell the others what you have told me," Father said from where he stood looking out the large circular window that overlooked the city below. The only sign of his distress, the clenched hands behind his back. Cricket had known him long enough to recognize it, though he'd rarely seen it. That was the most worrying thing, Father didn't get distressed. He remained calm, and upright, always. But Cricket could see a curving about his shoulders, exhaustion maybe. It had been a long couple of weeks.

"There's been an outbreak!" The man's hands shook violently, splattering tea on his fingers.

"Let me," Anstice said softly. She took the cup from him and set it on one of the tables stacked with books. "Slow down, start from the beginning."

"An outbreak of what?" Uncle Sunil demanded. The messenger wilted in on himself a little more.

"Don't scare him, Sunil." Anstice frowned, taking one of the man's shoulders to give it a gentle squeeze. "Go on, Theo. Tell them exactly as you told the king."

Theo nodded, a loud gulp coming from his throat before he started over. "For the last few weeks, we've seen a rise in magical activity all over the kingdom. At first it was little stuff; it could be shrugged off as that time of year. You know how it swells when the seasons change, and with all the rain we've had...well...it only made sense that nature would be a little off kilter. And none of the magic seemed malevolent, so it seemed normal."

"Which villages were these?" Anstice asked, moving to the table in the middle of the room that Father had sprawled a great map across.

"It's all over," Theo breathed.

"Keep going," Father said, still not turning to face the room.

"Two days ago, the magic turned dark. Destructive." Theo reached for the tea again, seeming to need something to hold onto to steady himself. "There are reports from all over the kingdom of goblin attacks, whole villages disappearing, witches running amok, fairies stealing children. It's chaos."

"Do you have the reports?" Anstice was clenching the table, her knuckles turning white. Theo looked up at her confused. "I need exact locations."

"We should send out the army," Uncle Sunil said. "I'll send word to General Eytan. We can start planning the attack—"

"No." Anstice cut him off. She took the scroll of reports from Theo, reading over them quickly and waving a hand across the map. When Cricket moved to her side little lights glowed in the places that had been attacked. Cricket frowned down at the map. Anstice's eyes had gone sharp, as if she were seeing something he wasn't.

"No?" Uncle Sunil asked, sounding irritated. "I beg your pardon, Anstice, but you've been the royal advisor for a grand total of two minutes. You don't get to make that decision. Jaxith. We must send out the army at once. If this is some kind of magical warfare, we have to get ahead of it."

"Your Highness, you need to see this." Anstice rolled the scroll back up, setting it aside. Her hands clasped and unclasped around her fan. Cricket took a step toward her, tilting his head to see it from a different angle. But it didn't make sense. None of it made sense.

"What is it?" Father asked, leaving his place at the window to join them at the table.

"Jaxith!" Uncle Sunil argued, but Father waved him away.

"It just doesn't make sense," Anstice muttered, tapping her fan on the table. "None of it makes sense."

Father leaned over, a growing tightness between his brows as he looked over the dots. They glittered like jewels on the pale paper. Flickering with the magic Anstice had embedded in them.

"This doesn't look like a war strategy." Anstice shook her head. "They're too scattered. And look, they're not even hitting any of the cities close to the capital."

"Do we have dates for them?" Cricket asked, tilting his head the other way.

Anstice nodded. "Let's do them in order of brightness. The brightest the first, the dimmest the most recent."

Another tap of her fan on the table and some of the lights dimmed while others grew near blinding. Cricket huffed, crossing his arms over his chest. That made even less sense. "There's no order to it."

"No. It doesn't even look like they're moving in a straight line," Anstice agreed.

"If anything, they're moving away from the palace and toward the mountains that border Helio." Father's finger stroked a path from the brightest to dimmest of them, showing what he meant.

"Yes, but in a zigzag. How does that make any sense?" Anstice shook her head.

"Since when has terrorism made sense?!" Uncle Sunil barked from too close to Anstice's ear. She winced, rubbing at it with a frown.

"No need to shout." Anstice glared at him.

Cricket's brows drew together. He took a step back from the map, tilting his head one way and then the other. When that didn't help make sense of what he was seeing he walked around the table. Doing a full three laps while Anstice and Uncle Sunil bickered. Anstice was right, it didn't make sense. Not even for a terrorist attack. No. This was something else. It was strategic, but made to look random it was—

"A distraction," Cricket muttered.

Anstice and Uncle Sunil stopped growling at one another to look at him.

"What was that, Cricket?" Father asked.

"It's a distraction. It's not a terrorist attack, it's not any kind of attack. It's a distraction. To draw the army away from the palace, and leave us defenseless." He nodded to himself, surer of it now than before. "If you send the army out, we will be attacked, and we will be overtaken."

"Then what would you suggest we do?" Uncle Sunil crossed his arms over his chest, his expression every part smug and self-satisfied. As if he knew better than anyone else.

Than Father. Than Anstice. Than Cricket. But he didn't. Cricket had never been more sure of it.

"A small envoy, to break up the disturbances. Don't you think, Anstice?"

Anstice tapped her fan against her temple. "Yes, something that won't leave the palace defenseless, but will ensure our people know that they're being cared for. Most of these will probably resolve themselves in time when whatever spell was cast wears off, but someone should be sent. A representative."

"Me." Cricket smiled. "I'll go."

There was a shatter from where Theo had dropped his teacup, and every head in the room turned to look at Cricket. Each wearing a slightly different worried expression.

"Cricket. Son. No." Father shook his head.

"That's insanity." Ignacia glared at him. He wasn't sure when she had gotten there, but she'd heard enough of the conversation apparently to make the assessment that he'd lost his mind.

"No, it makes sense. We want our people to know that we care about their suffering. That we want to see this resolved. We want to make sure they feel heard. The best way to do that is to send one of our own." It was reasonable, he thought. And why shouldn't he go? Father couldn't, neither could Uncle or Anstice. He was the best qualified. "And if it is a distraction then they'll be counting on us sending the army out. They're likely planning to attack the palace. We need the soldiers here."

"We should send one of the higher-ranking soldiers," Ignacia said. "Someone with enough clout to make them feel safe, but who isn't the heir."

"The people don't know any of the soldiers," Cricket argued.

"So?"

"No. He has a point," Anstice said, tapping her fan to Cricket's shoulder. "They don't know any of the soldiers. Our army tends to work as a faceless unit with the king at the head. It's not that none of them could handle this, they all could. But the people don't know them. They don't know their names."

"This is a stupid idea." Ignacia frowned.

"I agree with Ignacia, we can't take this chance." Uncle Sunil moved to stand beside her, and Ignacia took a not-so-subtle step away from him.

"In the end, this is your choice, Son." Father sighed, his shoulders sagging. He looked tired. Defeated. Heartbroken. Cricket hated it. He hated that he was the one making Father look like that. But what other option was there? None.

"His choice?!" Uncle Sunil shouted, turning pink, but before he could move further into the red family Father shook his head.

"Yes, his choice. Whether we approve or not, Cricket is going to do what he thinks best, as any good king would. And we cannot stop him."

"This is...Jaxith... He could..." Uncle Sunil was floundering for words.

Cricket met Anstice's eyes, and saw her nod. There was a twinkle there in her eyes, a reminder of what they'd said not but a fortnight ago in the bunny pen. Whatever Uncle Sunil said, Cricket should do the opposite.

"I'll go."

"Then he should take one of the soldiers." Uncle Sunil sounded defeated, like he was being beaten at some game he didn't know he was playing. "I'll appoint you a—"

"Uncle," Cricket laughed, shaking his head. "I don't need a bodyguard. I'll take my sword, and I'll take Iggy. That will be enough. Have a little faith in your nephew, yeah?"

"Unless you don't think he's capable?" Anstice asked, but it didn't sound like a question. It sounded like a challenge.

"I never said that." Uncle Sunil huffed, deflating.

"Then you can leave in the morning." Father nodded. "Sunil, have a servant prepare a room for Theo. He deserves a rest after riding all this way. Ignacia, I trust you can handle the horses. Anstice, I'd like a map made up for Cricket. He ought to head to the places where the magic is at its most dangerous."

"Yes, Your Highness." Anstice and Ignacia nodded. Then they, Uncle Sunil, and Theo all left to complete their respective tasks.

It was quieter than Cricket would have liked once they were all gone. Father still had his hands folded behind his back; his eyes fixed on the map.

"Father—" Cricket started but then stopped, unsure of what he was going to say. Was he going to apologize? Was he going to say thank you? What? He didn't know.

Father sighed, leaning heavily against the table. "You must be careful, Cricket. And come back to me in one piece."

"I will." Cricket nodded. "I'll make you proud."

"Of that, I have no doubt." Father smiled, shaking his head. "Just try not to get into too much trouble along the way, yes?"

"I don't make promises I can't keep."

Father laughed, the worry leaving his features. "Go to bed. You have an early start ahead of you, and I know how you hate mornings."

"Yes, Father."

BOOK II
TOCHTLI

CHAPTER 5

Cricket might not hate mornings quite so much if they happened a little later in the day. An opinion of which he had been told on numerous occasions was ridiculous by Uncle Sunil, Ignacia, many of the royal guards, and even Father. Anstice, however, seemed to agree with him. And yet, there she was, looking well put together in a pair of trousers and a crisp waistcoat, her eyes lined in kohl, and her hair in a neat bun. Where she'd found the time to get dressed-up and do her makeup before the sun had even properly risen, Cricket would never know. Perhaps she simply hadn't gone to bed.

"You'll need this," she said, holding out a hand mirror.

"Why? So Uncle can keep tabs on me?" Cricket didn't care if he sounded whiny, not in the least. It wasn't even six in the morning yet, and already he'd been bossed around by Ignacia, the stable master, and now Anstice too. The one solace was that Uncle had not seen fit to see him off.

"No. You dolt." Anstice smacked him on the head with her fan for good measure. "It's so *I* can keep tabs on you."

"Oh." Cricket pulled the satchel around to his front, stuffing the mirror into a pocket. "Well, that's all right then."

Anstice snorted. "You're going to do just fine, Cricket."

"I know." And he did. Well...sort of. In the back of his mind, he could hear Uncle Sunil. Could hear all the times Uncle Sunil had berated him, told him that he was a failure as a prince, that he'd never be good enough to be king. That he was not born to it, as Uncle and Father had been. That king-hood did not sing in his blood. Maybe he was right. Maybe Cricket was just...

"Hey." Anstice took hold of his shoulders, giving them a firm squeeze. "Wherever your head is at, you don't have time for that right now. You can't disappear into that brain of yours like you do. Your people need you."

Cricket wanted to ask if they did really. If Anstice thought he could do this. But the truth was, she wouldn't have agreed to it if she didn't think he could. So instead of putting sound to those uncertainties, making them that much more concrete for it, he swallowed them down. "Right. Where are we headed first?"

"Tochtli," Anstice said, looping her arm through his and leading him toward the main entrance. The tall double doors stretched up to the ceiling, and a servant stood in front of each, holding it open to let a warm summer breeze glide through into the main hall. Cricket could see Ignacia standing outside with the horses, a brow raised in their direction.

"And what's going on there?"

"The town keeps disappearing and reappearing. No one has heard anything from those who live there in a fortnight." Anstice pulled out the map she had made up for him, tapping the blinking dot that was Tochtli.

"How do we know its disappearing and reappearing if no one has heard from them?" Ignacia asked, her fingers brushing down over her horse's muzzle.

"A band of traders was out that way. Tochtli is their stop in between Ilkay and the capital. The leader said that he saw the town disappear just as they approached it, and it didn't reappear again until morning. He's the one who reported it." Anstice's darkly painted nail scraped against the paper, her red lips tugged down into a frown. Something was bothering her, but she seemed to want to keep it to herself.

"What did the people in town say?" Cricket hooked his chin over Anstice's shoulder to look at the map, trying to better understand what could be upsetting her. But all that he saw on it was the glowing dots of affected areas, Tochtli blinking like a firefly amongst them.

"The traders didn't stop in there; they were too spooked." Anstice sighed, rolling up the map, and holding it out to Cricket.

"So, we have no idea what we're dealing with. It could be a curse. It could be a goblin having a laugh. It could be...anything." Ignacia's lips twitched into a frown, a wrinkle appearing between her eyebrows. She was worried. And she had every right to be. Cricket didn't like the idea of going in blind either, but they didn't have much choice.

"It could." Anstice nodded. "That's why you two need to be careful. Go in during the day, ask around, see if anyone can tell you anything. Then get out before it disappears."

Cricket tapped his chin thoughtfully.

"Right then. Let's saddle up and get out of here. We're wasting daylight, Cricket." Ignacia swung herself up onto her horse, blowing Anstice a kiss from her perch. "We'll let you know when we get to Tochtli."

"Please do," Anstice said. Then she turned to Cricket and pulled him into a too-tight hug, squeezing hard enough to trap the air in his lungs. "Take care. Be safe. Try not to make anyone angry with you."

Ignacia snorted, muttering something under her breath.

"I heard that!" Cricket glared at her over Anstice's shoulder.

"Then what did I say?"

"That's not the point!"

Anstice laughed, shaking her head. "Try not to strangle him in his sleep, Iggy. We need him back in one piece to run the kingdom."

"Aye, aye Advisor Dresden." Ignacia saluted, and winked.

Anstice stood at the gate, waving her fan to them until they were out of sight.

TOCHTLI WAS A QUIET LITTLE TOWN—QUAINT, Father had called it—set along the river of Usagi that flowed from the capital down through all of Lunette. Cricket had been there once, when he was about five or six, but he didn't remember very much of it. Only a faded and washed-out memory of a vendor painting his name on a rabbit lantern in intricate, swirling characters.

"You're going to stick out like a sore thumb," Ignacia complained. They had crested a hill that overlooked Tochtli and stopped for a brief supper. The horses grazing nearby.

"I'm sorry?" Cricket asked, shoveling another quarter of a sandwich into his mouth. Youta, the youngest of the kitchen's staff, had taken to cutting the crust off his sandwiches when he was a child, and she'd just never stopped. He loved her for it.

Ignacia reached over to grab his wrist, dragging it upwards so his already folded up sleeve fell further down his arm, and the two moon-jade bangles clacked against his forearm. "These."

"Marwa gave them to me for my name day." He yanked his wrist from her, holding the bangles to himself protectively. "They match the ring Father gave me."

Something flickered across Ignacia's face, guilt maybe, but then she shrugged it off. "Put them in your bag. You can keep the ring."

"Why?"

"You look like a royal brat." She grabbed one of the quarters from his unwrapped sandwich and took a challenging bite.

"I am a royal brat." He didn't like the term brat, but it was true enough. He'd never had to want for anything. He'd never known hunger, or a cold winter's night. Father had seen to all of his needs. And those things that weren't needs? Crustless sandwiches? The staff catered to those. He knew that well enough.

Ignacia frowned, shaking her head. She didn't argue with him on that fact, and he didn't expect her to. She'd been one of the ones to say it, after all. "Right now, you can't be a brat. You have to be their prince. The man they want to be king. Take this seriously."

"I am taking this seriously!" He didn't know why everyone seemed to think he didn't take anything seriously, but he was getting a little tired of it.

She gave him an unimpressed stare, and Cricket begrudgingly wriggled the bangles from his wrist to tuck into his bag. "Better?"

"We should wait until tomorrow to go in."

"Why?" Cricket stuffed the last bite of sandwich into his mouth, his cheeks puffing out from being too full. If it weren't for the too-large bite in his mouth he might have sounded whiny.

"So we know what time it disappears, and when it reappears. Anstice said we shouldn't get caught inside just in case."

"But Iiiiiiggy." This time he did whine, stretching out her name purposefully to annoy her. Ignacia's face remained impassive, but the twitch in her eyebrow gave her away. A little more prodding and—

"Fine, but just for an hour. We get out before the sun sets. Are we clear?"

"Yes ma'am!" Well, that was easy.

They left the horses on the hilltop to graze, and bask in the early evening sun, a neat circle of magic woven around them to keep them from wandering off and passersby from stealing the supplies left behind. Ignacia hadn't liked the idea, but Cricket didn't want to lug all of that into town. He'd won out in the end.

A market was set up in the middle of town around a glittering fountain with an intricate statue of the lady Selene at the center. She was kneeling in a field of moon flowers, her face set into a smile.

"'scuse me." A child giggled as he brushed past Cricket into the square.

"Jingyi! Get back here!" his mother shouted, trailing after him in a pace that wasn't quite a run, but couldn't be considered a walk either. "I'm so sorry." She bowed to them, a rueful smile on her lips. "He's just excited about the Sunday market, is all."

Then she was off again, only just managing to get a hold of the boy's shoulders before he toppled headfirst into a stand of melons.

"Sunday market," Ignacia repeated the words, her brows furrowing. "We left on a Monday, didn't we?"

Cricket wrinkled his nose in thought, looking up at the white clouds drifting through the sky as if they could provide him with an answer. "I thought so. And it's only been a couple of days. But I could be wrong?"

"I'll check my journal when we get back to camp." Ignacia decided, her fingers tapping a tattoo against the sword on her hip. Something was bothering her, niggling at her. Cricket could see it. But she hadn't figured it out yet, and she didn't want to put words to her unease lest she be wrong. Ignacia hated being wrong. "We'll talk to some of the vendors. See if they've noticed anything strange."

"We don't have much time. Let's split up."

Ignacia opened her mouth as if she might argue, but she snapped her jaw shut in spite of whatever was going through her head. "You go that way."

Cricket turned off to the right to begin with the melon vendor little Jingyi had almost toppled.

"Excuse me sir." Cricket offered the man a little wave, and a wide smile. "I was wondering if you could—"

"Only melons for sale here." The man's beard twitched in irritation. He took an appraising look up and down the length of Cricket, and turned his attention instead to a woman who was knocking on the melons as if trying to root out a gnome from inside them.

"I understand, but you see I'm—"

"Only. Melons."

"Yes but—"

"Just! Melons!"

Cricket frowned, but moved on to the next, undeterred. "Good afternoon ma'am, I was wondering if you could tell me if anything strange was going on around here?"

She blinked at him.

"Oh...all right then." Cricket frowned, and moved on to the next stall, and the next, he was almost to the end of the row some minutes later. Each of the vendors had refused to answer him, all looking perplexed, and a little annoyed at an obvious outsider. He thought he should have worn his bangles. Maybe if he looked wealthier, they'd have been more apt to talk. Or perhaps it was that he just wasn't approaching this right? He'd never done this sort of thing before. He glanced over and found Ignacia deep in conversation with an apple salesman. Hopefully, she was having better luck.

"Oi," someone whisper-shouted from the stall at the end. Cricket couldn't tell what the man was selling, it just looked like a table full of junk. "You're looking for something strange?"

"Yes," Cricket breathed. His shoulders relaxed a little. "Have you seen anything? There have been reports that perhaps the town is—" A flash of light-colored movement caught Cricket's attention from the corner of his eyes. But when he looked toward it, he caught just the end of a white cloak as whoever it was rounded the corner of the nearby alley out of sight.

"I've got lots of strange things here." The man gestured to the table.

Cricket turned to look down at the collection of junk. A broken wristwatch stuck on the time 6:30, a hand mirror missing the stones from its frame, a small painting with a tear at the edge, and even a fork with bent tines.

"Oh um...you have some very nice things, but I don't think any of this is quite what I'm looking for." Cricket tried to offer the man a polite smile, backing away from the stall. "Thank you for your time."

"Oi, no need to be rude!" The man shouted after him.

Cricket ignored him to turn down the alley, following the whisper of a white cloak that had rounded another corner some feet away. He cast one look back at Ignacia still chatting away with the apple vendor, and followed it. He'd be back before she noticed. And figures running through shadows to keep from being seen were far more exciting and suspicious than talking to vendors who didn't seem to know anything. As far as he could tell, they were going about their everyday lives as if nothing had changed. They likely didn't even know their town was disappearing. But that figure, it'd been moving much too fast, as if to keep from drawing too much attention. It was up to something.

He rounded the corner, coming out in a less trafficked part of town, some streets away from where the market had been. The homes here were quiet, everyone had probably gone to the market, leaving their windows dark and washing hung out to dry on balconies. With light steps, Cricket walked down the street, eyes looking for any sign of movement, any hint as to where the white-clad figure had gone. His hand clenched the hilt of his sword, ready for an attack. But there was nothing, no sign of life at all. The person had just disappeared, leaving nothing behind.

"I'll have to check again tomorrow," Cricket decided, turning to head back to the market.

Something else strange caught his eye.

A pale, jade luna moth fluttered in front of his face, landing on his nose for a moment, playful and light. Then it flitted in front of his eyes, before bouncing through the air tracing a path in the opposite direction.

"You shouldn't be out this early." Cricket tilted his head, eyeing the soft glow of the moth in confusion. It danced through the air, weaving in circles around his head, as if urging him to follow it. "What? Do you know what's going on here?"

There was no answer. There wouldn't be. Insects were small, easily affected by whatever magic lingered in the air, sensitive to it in a way the elven clans long descended from Selene and Helios no longer were. Moths like this one were more in touch with the natural magic in the earth. But they couldn't talk. Still this one was trying to tell Cricket something, something important if its frantic bouncing was anything to go by.

"All right then. Let's see it." He nodded, resolving to follow the little creature wherever it may lead.

The moth led him through the streets. He let it guide him past a smithy, and an inn. They reached the edge of Tochtli as the sun kissed the horizon. The moth did another quick twirl about Cricket's head, and he huffed, stepping over the boundary from town to open field. There was a soft pop, like the uncorking of a bottle of fizzy wine that had gone flat. He turned back, and found...

Nothing.

Just swaying grass where the town had once been. Everything, the streets, the inn, the smithy, the market, the laundry, Ignacia, was gone.

"Iggy?" The name drifted from his lips, more prayer than calling. "Ignacia?"

But she was gone, just as the town was. Cricket turned ready to glare at and interrogate the little creature, but it too had disappeared. Leaving Cricket alone, surrounded by tall grasses that waved in the wind, and the subtle rush of water from the river.

CHAPTER 6

Cricket stared at the space where the town had been. Panic swelled sharp and aching in his throat.

Gone.

Everything was gone.

He had supplies for the evening, he knew how to set up a tent, he could protect himself if need be. That didn't matter. None of it mattered. Because Ignacia was just... she was gone. Swallowed up with Tochtli as the sun sank below the horizon.

And he was alone, well and truly alone, for perhaps the first time since he was a child and he'd gotten lost while they were traveling. He remembered it vividly. Remembered getting distracted by something, he wasn't sure what anymore, and wandering off. Remembered realizing too late that he'd lost sight of Father and the others, and sobbing himself sick.

And then he remembered Ignacia finding him. Her tone soft but chiding as she scooped him onto her back, and carried him to the inn where Father was waiting. His friend, his sister, his protector. She was gone. And he was alone.

"Time. What time is it?" he asked, dragging himself from the memory. He turned to dig through the bag on his shoulder. Dropping the bangles, the spare scarf, his sketch pad. When he didn't find what he was looking for, he dropped to his knees and upturned the whole bag, so the rest of his personal items fell out. There! The little silver pocket watch Uncle Sunil had insisted he bring along. Cricket had never found a good way to carry it—it just didn't fit his look. It opened with a soft *tink*. "6:35."

Cricket fell back onto his backside, looking at the space where the town had been again. What was he supposed to do now? Without Ignacia there to tell him, he wasn't sure. She was in charge; she'd always been in charge. Shaking himself, he collected his things, and stuffed them unceremoniously into the satchel. It took him another few minutes to gather his wits enough to climb the hill to the horses, set up his tent, and build a small fire.

He'd just have to wait until the town reappeared. Hopefully, it wouldn't be too long. Possibly at first light. He *hoped* it'd be at first light. He needed Ignacia to help him figure this out. There had been nothing in all the books he'd ever read about magic like this. Whole towns didn't just *disappear*. The power that would take was astronomical. It had to be...it had to be something. A curse? Maybe? But what kind? And why would someone curse an entire town?

His musings were cut short by a gentle chiming sound coming from the vicinity of his satchel. After more rapid digging, he found the hand mirror Anstice had given him. The glass, instead of showing Cricket his own reflection of warm copper skin, a dusting of freckles, and starlight eyes, showed Anstice. Her lips pursed into a look of annoyance.

"You were meant to call when you reached Tochtli," she said without preamble. "Your father has been worried."

"Annie." Cricket breathed, relieved, pulling the mirror up

to get a better look at her in the fading light. He wasn't sure what he looked like, but Anstice seemed to see something in his visage that bothered her for she dropped the haughty look, and replaced it with one of genuine concern.

"What is it? What's happened?"

"Iggy is..." He whined weakly, and turned the mirror to the field where the town had been. Now lit by moonbeams and starlight, the grass was a pale ocean of...nothing. Just nothing.

"Iggy is what? You have to talk to me Cricky. Use your words." Her tone was patient, but it didn't erase the worry in her eyes.

"Iggy was still inside when it disappeared. As soon as the sun went down, it was just gone. And I was following this person in a cloak. And then there was this moth. And we split up to ask the townspeople. But no one knew anything. And there was the Sunday market. And suddenly, I just turned around and poof, everything was just... It was all gone. Iggy was gone."

Anstice had leaned forward at some point during his explanation, and now she was rubbing the bridge of her nose. That worried wrinkle at the corner of her right eye was there, the one she'd inherited from Marwa. Not quite twitching down into a frown, but almost.

"What time did it disappear?"

"I don't know exactly, but I looked at my watch after and it was 6:35. Why? Does it matter what time?"

"It doesn't. Not really. But that might be when it reappears?"

"Is that how this works?" Cricket looked back at the vacant plot of land where the town had stood. Squinting as if he could see it there, but there was just grass and the soft twinkling of fireflies as they drifted about where buildings used to be.

"I don't know. I don't know how any of this works." Anstice huffed, sitting back in her chair. She hated it when she didn't know something almost as much as Ignacia hated it when she was wrong. How did he surround himself with women who had to know *everything*? "But if that's the case..."

"Then I should be up with the sun." Cricket groaned scrubbing at his face. "So, I have a full day to poke around."

"Right." She smiled, though it didn't reach her eyes. "Then you need to be out before 6. In plenty of time for the town to disappear again. Bring Iggy with you this time. Don't get separated. All right?"

"Right." Cricket nodded, some of the panic melting away at this. There was a plan. There was something to do. He didn't have to stress over the what of the thing, not tonight, because tomorrow he'd get to the bottom of it. Tomorrow he'd be able to ask more questions, and get answers.

"Did you say Sunday market?" Anstice's nose wrinkled.

"Yes. Why?"

"Cricky, it's Wednesday."

"That's...that's weird, isn't it?"

"It is. I'll do some digging through the books here, and see if I can find anything on curses that could make entire towns disappear. In the meantime, you get some sleep." She pointed at him through the mirror. She waited for him to nod, to agree, and then she waved her hand over the surface and her image disappeared, replaced with his own harried reflection. Great Selene, he was a sight, wasn't he?

"Sleep." He reminded himself and curled up in his tent to do just that.

EARLY MORNINGS WERE a loathsome thing that should not exist. But what Cricket found far more loathsome was knowing that one of his dearest friends was trapped in a disappearing village. He rose with the sun, just as he'd told Anstice he would. He ate a quick breakfast from their stores of dried fruits, and then the village reappeared at precisely 6:30. He recorded it in Ignacia's journal right alongside her annoyingly neat handwriting.

She'd likely skin him alive for writing in her journal, but he had to have somewhere to keep his observations, and he was not about to use his sketchbook for that. That'd be preposterous. Plus, she wasn't there to stop him. That thought ached more than it ought. He couldn't seem to find the joy in doing something he knew would irritate her like he usually did.

"Ouch," he grumbled rubbing at the clenching in his chest. There was nothing for it, the only solution was to go and get Ignacia back. So, he refreshed the magic keeping their horses there, and headed off.

As the sun rose slowly in the sky, the town of Tochtli was teeming with life. Children playing. Mothers hanging out laundry. The smithy was in her barn banging away at some horseshoes. It was much different than it was the evening before. But, just like the evening before, when Cricket made his way to the center of town, the market stalls were set up.

The vendors were much more lively in the morning. Shouting their wares to everyone that passed. And there was Ignacia... Talking to the apple salesman?

"Iggy! Iggy!" He ran toward her, waving, and she looked up to frown at him a little. As if she'd just parted ways with him. As if he were interrupting something important.

She said something more to the merchant and then turned to give Cricket an unimpressed look. "And where have you been? I look over and you're just gone."

"Iggy!" Cricket breathed, trapping her in a hug so tight he was sure he'd leave bruises. But he didn't care. Because she was here. She was here and she was safe. And he didn't have to do this alone. "I was so worried when the town disappeared. I turned back around, and you were just gone. Everything was just gone!"

"What? Gone?" She snorted, shaking her head. "I've been here the whole time. You were going to go and talk to the vendors over there, and I was chatting with the apple vendor and then..." Her auburn brows wrinkled, lips pursing. "And then..."

"And then what?"

"Well...I don't remember. I turned to look, and you were gone. I was going to finish up talking and go and look for you. It was late, I thought we should be getting out of town."

"You mean nothing happened after that? You didn't go and find a place to stay? Or wake up this morning? Or... What about this, what did you have for breakfast?" Cricket pulled the journal from his bag and scribbled down some notes in his mangled, disjointed handwriting.

"Well, we had what was left of the eggs and—"

"No, that was yesterday. What did you have this morning?"

"That's not funny, Cricky. You were there. We had the eggs and—"

"No, Iggy, that was yesterday," he said softly, earnest. "What did you have this morning?"

"I don't know." The words left her on a breath, and she wobbled a little on her feet. She was going to cry; Cricket could see it. It'd been so long since he'd seen her cry.

"Hey..." He stuffed the journal back into his satchel, and scooped her up into a tight hug. "Hey... It's all right. We're going to figure this out. All right?"

"But I was just gone."

"And you won't be gone again. I promise. We'll investigate, and we'll get out before the town disappears. It was 6:30 yesterday, so if we leave at 6, we'll be okay. I promise." Cricket pulled back, meeting her eyes to show her that he was serious. He was so serious. He'd never been more serious about anything in his life. He wasn't going to let Ignacia disappear on him again. Never again. "So, what did you find out from the apple vendor?"

"Nothing. He didn't know anything. None of them did. They're just going about their day like it's normal." She shook her head, scrubbing at her eyes to dispel the last of what would have become tears. "You? What did you find out?"

"It was the same with everyone else. They don't seem to realize what's happening." He scrubbed at his nose, looking around them. "They're just..."

"Gone." Ignacia finished, choking on the word a little. Then she cleared her throat, and tilted her chin up. "All right then, we've done the market, let's check some of the other townspeople. Maybe the local inn?"

"There's a smithy near the boundary, maybe she's seen something. Let's go there first."

"We could split—"

"No! No splitting up. No more." Cricket took her hand, squeezing it tight. "We stick together this time, so neither of us gets stuck again."

Ignacia nodded, her fingers squeezing his back in gratitude. The walk to the smithy was a quiet one. Cricket's eyes flicked around, taking in the townspeople. Everyone was just going about their day as if nothing at all was different. He wondered if they were tired. If in that gone place, they'd gotten any sleep. None of them looked like they were exhausted from days without sleeping, so he supposed they did.

The smithy was sitting on a stool in the middle of her

shop, banging away against a miniature anvil. She didn't look up when they came in, just kept working. Her hammer singing against the hot metal of the horseshoe she was forging.

"Excuse us but—" Cricket started, but stopped when she held up a finger. When the horseshoe was dunked in water to cool, filling the small open space with the soft sizzling of steaming metal, she finally turned to them.

"What do you need made? Horseshoes? Daggers? I can do swords, but it'll take me a bit longer so if you're in a hurry we should stick to something small." She wiped her sweaty hands on the leather apron over her chest then held out her hand to Cricket. "Ava."

"I'm Cricket, and this is Ignacia." He shook her hand, a delighted smile spreading his lips.

Ava shook Ignacia's hand then narrowed her eyes on him, looking thoughtful for a moment. "You're the prince."

"Yes...I...I am." He laughed nervously.

"What are you doing in Tochtli? Don't you usually stick to the capital?" She moved to her work bench digging through the bits of metal in various stages of progress there. "I don't think I've got anything that would really be fit for you here. Unless you need your horse shooed."

"No, actually, we have some questions." Ignacia stepped forward, all smiles. "And we'd be happy to pay you for your time of course. You seem like a busy woman."

"Never too busy for the prince." Ava smiled back, her eyes flicking over the long braid that hung down past Cricket's waist. "Ask away."

"Ah, yes." Cricket cleared his throat, scrubbing at the back of his neck. "It seems Tochtli is experiencing some strange magical activity. You wouldn't happen to have noticed anything like that? You've got a pretty good view of the edge of town, and we thought maybe you'd seen something."

"Not really." Ava shrugged. "There was a traveling trader through here a few weeks ago, selling a bunch of junk, but nothing out of the ordinary. What're they saying has been going on here?"

"Well, it seems the—"

"Just some weird occurrences. Nothing at all to worry about. Thank you for your time." Ignacia grabbed his arm and dragged him away.

Cricket waited until they were a ways away, and he could hear the sound of Ava working again before he rounded on her. "What was that?! She's the first person I've gotten to answer any of my questions since we got here!"

Ignacia shook her head, looking around to be sure they were alone. "From what I got from the few vendors I spoke to, there seems to be some level of dissonance about this thing. If you say the town is disappearing, they get angry. The girl with the berry cart almost took my head off."

"And we don't want someone with a bunch of weapons trying to take our heads off." Cricket sighed. "So we need to be more careful."

"Yes. Now, let's head to the inn. Maybe there will be some travelers who have noticed something." Ignacia suggested, taking hold of his hand again and tugging him along. He pulled the pocket watch from his bag to check it. It wasn't even quite noon yet. They had plenty of time.

CHAPTER 7

The sweet old woman at the inn, Madam Shen, insisted on seating them at her best table to conduct their interviews. It was set back into a private room, large enough for a party of ten.

"This really isn't necessary," Cricket argued. "We can chat with people just fine out there."

"Nonsense. Nonsense. I won't have the prince of Lunette taking his guests out in the main dining room like some commoner. Please, please. Sit. I'll have some tea brought." She gave Cricket an insistent, but gentle, shove and then slid the paper doors closed behind her.

"How are we supposed to choose who to talk to if we're closed in here?" Cricket frowned.

"I told you not to tell her you were the prince." Ignacia huffed, dropping into a chair, and crossing her arms over her chest. "I could go out and pull people in."

"It's not like I meant to! The hair kind of..." He gestured to the long braid he'd thrown over his shoulder. "No, it'd be better if we were out there, mingling. Then we could see who looks suspicious." He shook his head, tugging the door open a little to look out into the main dining room. "Do you think we can convince her to let us back out there?"

"How much of the room can you see from here?"

"All of it. Every corner. But with the door pulled shut, they won't be able to see in here." Cricket's eyes flicked about the room. There weren't a lot of people, mainly wait staff. But lunch time was coming, and then those who were staying at the inn would return to have their midday meal.

"Then we'll use this as our base of operations. I'll retrieve anyone who looks suspicious, and you question them while I keep a lookout."

It seemed like a good enough plan. Maybe it wasn't ideal, or what he'd intended when he suggested they head for the dining room and skip questioning the staff. But it would do.

"Tea?" the innkeeper asked, bustling into the room with a tray which she deposited onto the table. "And I'll have lunch brought in shortly, then we'll be out of your way."

"Thank you, Madam Shen. You're such a dutiful host." Cricket smiled, returning to the table.

"Nonsense. Nonsense. I won't have the prince of Lunette thinking my inn is some shabby..." She stopped, clearing her throat. "Well. If there is anything else you need, please do not be afraid to ask."

"Yes ma'am." Ignacia bowed politely, and turned to pour a cup for herself and Cricket. "Thank you."

Madam Shen left, and a few minutes later two waitresses came in bearing trays laden in enough food to feed a small army. Ignacia rolled her eyes in exasperation, and Cricket did his best to look gracious.

"Tell Madam Shen thank you. We very much appreciate her hospitality," Cricket said bowing shallowly to both women. When they were gone, he dropped into his seat looking over the plates upon plates of what seemed to be every dish the inn had to offer.

"Well, Your Highness, eat up." Ignacia snickered, a smug smile twitching at her lips.

"Oh, no, ma'am. You are helping with this. I can't eat it all and if we leave too much behind, they'll be offended. You have to help me." He wagged a finger at her playfully, and it pulled a real laugh from Ignacia. "Maybe our guests will want some."

"We can only hope." Ignacia sighed. "Open the door a little so we can look out and see if anyone looks worth talking to."

With their plates piled high, and the door open to let in the gentle murmur of the inn's patrons, Ignacia and Cricket filled their bellies. The tables outside slowly began to fill as those staying at the inn filtered in for lunch.

"Those two merchants first," Cricket said, pointing to two men who had just ordered their second round of ale. "They'll have travelled through the most towns, and may be able to give us a hint as to who is behind all of this."

"I don't know, Cricky. They don't look like they pay attention to much outside of themselves. Merchants are like that. They stay out of everyone's business." Ignacia shook her head.

"Then who do you suggest?"

"Her." Ignacia pointed.

Cricket followed where Ignacia's finger led to a straight-backed young woman. She had a pair of glasses perched on her slightly upturned nose that she'd buried deep in a book.

"Her?" Cricket frowned. "She doesn't look like she sees anything outside of whatever she's reading."

"She's a traveling scholar," Ignacia insisted. "Ergo, keen observational skills. A more than rudimentary understanding of magic. The ability to string a coherent sentence together. Less likely to be impressed and distracted by the prince."

"And she's pretty." Cricket added, the frown twitching into something else. Mischief lighting his eyes.

"That doesn't hurt." Ignacia shrugged, leaning back in her chair.

"Fine. We'll start with her. But no flirting. This is serious, Iggy." He grabbed a bit of cheese off her plate and popped it into his mouth, looking smug.

"You're not the boss of me." She huffed, standing from her chair, and sauntering out into the dining room. Cricket chuckled, shaking his head. He looked around the room for who they should speak to next, deciding on a young messenger in the corner. When his eyes returned to Ignacia and the woman, they were headed his way. Ignacia had her arm slung over the other's shoulders, a wide smile splitting her face, and Cricket had to suppress the urge to roll his eyes. "Your Highness, this is Genevieve. She's a scholar from Hermes, passing through Tochtli on her way to the capital."

"Y-Y-Y-Your...Your Highness." Genevieve curtsied awkwardly, her knees shaking a little either with the weight of Ignacia's arm, or with the unease of little practice.

"Cricket." Cricket smiled, standing up and holding out a hand to her. "Please, just Cricket."

Genevieve's eyes widened, her cheeks blushing brightly as her gaze flicked from him to Ignacia as if needing confirmation. Ignacia nodded, and Genevieve looked back at Cricket with more interest. Her nose wrinkled as some thought occurred to her, but she didn't let it pass her tongue.

"Please, have a seat. We just have a couple of questions. I promise we won't take long, and then you can go back to your day." Cricket moved to pull out a chair for her.

"Thank you." Genevieve took the seat, her eyes tracking Cricket's movements around the table where he sat across from her. Maybe Ignacia was right, maybe the bookish girl did see more than he'd thought. "Ignacia said there is some magical anomaly going on here?"

"Yes. How long have you been in town?" Cricket pulled Ignacia's journal from his bag. Ignacia twitched, hands moving as if to take the book from him but stopping short.

"Oh, I just arrived last night. I've been traveling all week from Mahin, and I plan to leave in the morning." Genevieve's fingers tapped at the table as if nervous, but her words came easily enough. Quiet, but measured. "I was invited to study at the library in the capital by one of the librarians."

"And what day did you plan to leave Tochtli for the capital?"

"Tomorrow," Genevieve repeated looking confused.

"What day is that?" Ignacia asked gently.

"Monday?" Genevieve asked more than said, her tone unsure. She clenched the book to her chest, knuckles turning white. "Why? Have I been affected?"

Cricket looked to Ignacia, and she shook her head. He sighed, scrubbing at his face. "You might have been. We'll know more soon."

"But you're going to fix this, whatever it is." Genevieve looked determined. "I can help. I know a lot about curse magic. I want to help."

"The best thing you can do to help us right now, is let us get back to questioning the others." Ignacia's tone was gentle as she held out a hand to Genevieve to help her from her chair. If she had only been there the day the event began, there was likely little she could tell them about the lead up to it. It was best they move on to other subjects, Cricket could see that Ignacia knew it too. "I promise to let you know if there is anything else you can do to help."

"What is it? What kind of curse?" Genevieve refused to move from her chair. Her eyes fixed on Cricket's; mouth set in a serious line.

"It looks like the town is stuck in a loop. Tochtli disappears every day at around 6:30 and reappears the next morning at the same time. And everyone repeats Sunday again." Cricket felt tired saying it, frayed at the edges, knowing there was little he could do at that point to help. He didn't have any answers. He didn't have any solutions. He just had more questions.

"That's... That's preposterous!" Genevieve slammed her chair back, her face livid. "There isn't even a spell that can do that! That's the silliest thing I've ever heard!"

"Genevieve, please." Ignacia reached for the other woman. "Let's just sit down and talk this through. Maybe you can—"

"No. I'd... I'd know! I'd *know* if I was repeating the same day over and over!" Genevieve stormed from the room, and then out of the inn. The door slamming behind her in her hurry to get away from them.

"I told you not to mention it to them." Ignacia leaned forward, pressing her forehead to the table. "I told you they get mad."

"Yes, but we didn't know if it was just the locals, or if it was everyone. Now we know it's everyone." Cricket scratched more notes into the journal. He ran a hand over his hair, pushing small loose strands back from his face. "That's useful information to have. It means it's not just in the town."

"We knew that when it happened to me." Her voice was muffled by the table, but he could still hear the upset in it.

"We *thought* that, when it happened to you." Cricket corrected gently. "We didn't know for sure, now we do. But hey, look on the bright side."

"If you say I still have a chance with her because she won't remember tomorrow, I am going to stuff you face first into what's left of the pot pie." Ignacia didn't lift her head, but she didn't have to, to point a vaguely threatening finger in his direction. "Don't test me."

"No. No testing, ma'am." Cricket bit his lip to keep from laughing.

Ignacia lifted her head to glare at him, auburn hair falling into her eyes where it had come loose from the two braids she kept it in. Cricket did his best to look innocent. Her gaze narrowed further. Cricket smiled, and then a flash of white caught his eye and he looked up to see a white clad man, being led to an empty table.

"That's him," he said more to himself. His gaze was fixed on the elegant young man. White-blond hair, the color of the sun at its hottest, pulled back into a messy short tail at the crown of his head, with feather soft waves falling loose to brush high set cheekbones. Smooth brown skin stretched over a stately jaw. Two amber stones—darkening from pale gold to the deep reds of the rising sun—hung from long chains in his earlobes. He was...he was...well he looked rather put out to be in the inn. But even with that, he was lovely.

"Him who?" Ignacia asked, turning to look at the man at the table. "Oh, so I get teased for flirting but you—"

Cricket shook himself, fixing his eyes back on Ignacia. "No, I chased him yesterday. He was running down an alley trying not to be seen. It was very suspicious. This has nothing to do with—"

"With how devastatingly handsome he is?"

"Absolutely."

"Mhm. Sure." Ignacia eyed him. "So, should I get him or..."

"No, I'll go talk to him. Why don't you grab that messenger and see what he has to say?"

"And this has nothing at all to do with how—"

"Ignacia." Cricket glared at her.

"All right. Statement retracted. I'll just go handle the

messenger, shall I?" She stood from her chair, offering Cricket a knowing smile. "Try not to put your foot in your mouth yeah? Remember the last time you—"

"Ignacia."

"Right. Good luck." She gave him a cheerful wave, shoulders shaking with laughter as she ducked out of the room.

"And she calls me a brat," Cricket muttered to himself. He tucked the journal back into his satchel, waited for Ignacia to find her place with the messenger, and then made his way across the room toward the figure swathed in white.

CHAPTER 8

Was dropping into the seat across from the white knight unceremoniously without first asking if he could, a good idea? As it turned out, no. No, it was not.

In Cricket's effort to look casual his knees bumped the table leg, jiggling the knight's teacup and sloshing liquid onto the table. The knight, who was just moving to pick up his cup, lifted eyes as golden as the first rays of the sun on a midsummer morning, to glare coldly at Cricket.

"Hi," Cricket said, going for smooth as he leaned forward to press one elbow onto the table, chin resting in hand, and... missed entirely. He yelped, scrambling back into his seat to keep from toppling to the floor. When he'd gotten himself situated again, he shot the knight a crooked, dimpled grin. "Umm... Hi. I'm Prince Cricket."

The knight looked him up and down, measuring Cricket's worth in the quick motion. He found Cricket wanting, if the annoyed press of his lips was anything to go by. Instead of responding, he grabbed a napkin to sop up the mess, and poured himself another cup of tea.

"So... That could have gone better." Cricket cleared his throat, feeling awkward. He looked over to see if Ignacia was having better luck, and sent a silent 'thank you' to the Lady Selene that Ignacia was too wrapped up in her own conversation to see Cricket making an ass of himself. "Anyway, like I said, I'm Prince Cricket."

"I heard you," the knight said, lifting his gaze to fix Cricket with another annoyed expression.

"Right umm... I could... I can order you another pot?" He nodded to the tea pot, folding his hands carefully into his lap to keep from knocking anything else over. If Uncle could see him, Cricket was sure he'd have something to say about the mess he'd made of things already.

"No need."

"Oh." Cricket frowned. His fingers fiddled with the end of his long braid, needing something to keep him distracted under the other man's scrutiny. "You know, it's common practice when someone introduces themselves to introduce yourself."

The man's face remained the same, fixed in that expression of mild annoyance. Cricket couldn't tell if he was considering giving his name, or not. Maybe he was trying to figure out if introducing himself would make Cricket go away or keep talking. (Likely keep talking, Cricket was always one to take an opening when it was presented to him.) Cricket fought the urge to fidget more under that penetrating stare.

"And your name is?" Cricket tried again, holding his hand out to the man.

Those golden eyes flicked down to Cricket's outstretched hand, but he didn't even twitch to take it. He stared long enough that Cricket let out an awkward laugh, letting his hand fall to the table.

"Yoshi," the knight finally said, his voice soft but stilted, like he had to force the word out past something blocking it.

"Yoshi?" Cricket asked. He dragged his hand back to his side of the table, and into his lap.

Yoshi nodded.

"Well, it's very nice to meet you, Yoshi." Cricket smiled brightly again.

Yoshi didn't return the sentiment; he just sipped his tea.

"So, um...you're from Helio right?" Cricket's own eyes fell to the sun crest sewn with gold thread into Yoshi's white cloak.

"Yes."

Cricket perked up a little more. He leaned forward to brace his elbows on the table, letting his eyes move over Yoshi quickly. Yoshi had been inspecting him too, why not return the favor? Besides, Cricket needed more information. Knights from Helio didn't just meander around Lunette for the fun of it. Yoshi's cloak was nice, lined in soft fabric, but light enough for the summer months. He had to have left Helio recently then. The sword resting on his hip was well maintained, the grip freshly polished. Combine that with the upright posture, and the steady look Yoshi was giving to a prince...

"You must be really high up in the ranks," Cricket concluded, rejecting the urge to pat himself on the back for the conclusion.

Yoshi just looked at him blandly as if that were obvious. Which... he supposed it was.

"What's a white knight from Helio's ranks doing so far from the mountains? I mean Tochtli is no hop skip and a jump. Or were you heading to the capital to see me?" Cricket couldn't help the teasing smirk that pulled at his cheeks. He wanted to, he did, but he *couldn't*.

Something shifted on Yoshi's face, but before Cricket could catch if it'd been a pull of his lips, a raising brow, or a wrinkled nose, it was gone again. "No."

"No? To which bit?"

Yoshi stared some more, but didn't say anything else.

"Well, you're in luck then, aren't you? Because I seem to have come out to meet you instead!"

"Nonsense." Yoshi broke his stare to flag down a waitress with a restrained wave that still seemed to catch her attention. Likely because Yoshi was so handsome. "More tea."

She bowed, and scurried away.

"Nonsense? Which bit was nonsense?" Cricket puffed out his cheeks, pouting. This would have worked on anyone else. But Yoshi was immovable. He simply poured the last of the tea into his cup, and waited for Cricket to be through his tantrum. Which was very annoying. Cricket deflated, letting the air out of his cheeks in a huff. "Fine, not to see me. Then why are you here?"

"To help," Yoshi said plainly.

"Oh, that's brilliant! Me too! Ignacia and I are here to help too. Have you heard the same reports we've heard about the town disappearing? We think it must be some kind of curse, but we can't figure out on what yet. Is it on a person? Or is it on the whole town? Or is it just a cursed object? Honestly, I hope it's not an object because finding it could take forever. And I have at least another oh...twenty odd towns suffering from curse magic I should probably see to. Although, I doubt Anstice will send us to them all. She'll probably just send us to the most imminent threats."

Yoshi let him babble. When the new pot was brought, he poured a cup for Cricket and shoved it into his hand.

"Thanks." Cricket blinked down at the cup for a moment, as if confused, and then took a slow sip.

"I am not here to help Tochtli ," Yoshi clarified.

"No?"

Yoshi shook his head.

"But what about the town disappearing?"

"I had not heard of that."

"Then why are you here?"

"To rest."

Cricket hummed his understanding, pulling the journal from his satchel again, and setting his tea carefully aside so he could write this down. "So, you were on your way to somewhere else? Where?"

"There are reports of a dragon in Ilkay."

"Really? Oh, stars, that's not good. We haven't had a dragon in...at least five decades." Cricket frowned, writing that down as well. They would need to head to Ilkay next. Or maybe they should go now? Which was more dangerous: a disappearing town or a dragon? No. If Anstice had thought the dragon was more dangerous, they'd have been sent there. She wouldn't neglect something like that. Unless she hadn't heard? No, Anstice knew everything, and Cricket trusted her to plan this mission. "You haven't noticed anything strange around here?"

Yoshi's eyes flicked down to the journal, then back up to Cricket, then back down. He seemed to be deciding something, and when he'd made up his mind, he pursed his lips just a little. "I will handle it."

"Excuse me?" Cricket's hand stopped where it was scratching words that only he'd be able to decipher into the page.

"I will handle it," Yoshi repeated, tone calm, and measured.

"No. You won't." Cricket clenched the pencil in his hand tighter, his mouth pressing into a hard line. "I am here to take care of my people. If you'd like to help, that'd be great. But you aren't handling this, not on your own. Not in my kingdom."

"I will handle it." Yoshi left no room for argument. He

stood from his chair, setting some coins on the table. "You would get in the way."

"Get in the... Get in the *way*?! Look here, I am the prince, and—"

Yoshi walked to the door without giving Cricket a backward glance.

"Hey! You come back here!" Cricket stood abruptly as well, his chair scraping hard against the floor. Everyone looked at him; Cricket felt their eyes like heat on the back of his neck. But he wasn't done yet. He followed behind Yoshi out into the street. "You can't just end an argument by walking away from me!"

"Were we arguing?" Yoshi asked. Mild. Calm. Annoying.

"Yes! Yes, we were!"

Yoshi stopped and turned around to face Cricket. "I work alone."

"Not this time you don't. This is my kingdom, and I'm here to help my people. I appreciate your concern, but if you're going to do anything, it is aid me." Cricket stood up taller, puffing out his chest.

"Aid you?" Was that incredulity in his tone? It sounded like it was, but Cricket opted to ignore it.

"Yes. Aid me."

"You will only get in the way." It didn't sound like Yoshi was saying it to be hurtful, but merely stating the facts as he saw them, and it chafed far more than Cricket would like to admit.

"I will not."

"You will."

"I will not."

"You will."

"Cricky!" Ignacia called. Cricket turned to her, only just then realizing that he'd been chasing Yoshi through the streets. Ignacia was out of breath, looking a little frazzled.

"Oh, thank Selene, I thought I'd lost you. You said we had to stick together. Remember?"

"I remember. I was just..." Cricket turned back around to motion to Yoshi, but the knight was gone. He growled, stomping his foot.

"You were just?"

"We are not done, white knight!" Cricket called after the man, his fists shaking at his sides. "Not by a long shot!"

"What's going on, Cricket?" Ignacia asked, worry pinching her brows together.

"Nothing." Cricket forced the word past a tongue that wanted to scream. "Let's finish up our lunch and get on with questioning. Someone other than that impossible, rigid, ridiculous, white knight has to know something."

Ignacia nodded, but the wrinkle between her brows was still there. They returned to their table in the private room, and Cricket wrote down everything Yoshi had told him. Silent rage made his handwriting even worse than normal, but he could still read it, so it was fine.

"What did your messenger say?" he asked when he was finally able to breathe through his nose without exhaling like an irate bull.

"Not much. He said he was sent here by a lord some towns over in search of healing herbs from the local witch. She's apparently very well known. What about your knight?"

"He was of very little use, unfortunately." Cricket grabbed a roll from the still too-full table and tore it with his teeth. "He's from Helio, and was just passing through on his way to deal with a dragon in Ilkay."

"A dragon?"

Cricket nodded, chewing hard enough to grind his teeth. He wasn't even sure why he was so angry. He'd come up against plenty of arrogant people in his time, and they didn't usually set him off like this.

"Should we maybe head that way instead? I mean if it's a dragon..." She frowned, holding out her hand to him. "Show me the map."

He pulled it from the satchel and handed it to her before stuffing the last third of the roll into his mouth.

"Ilkay would be a half a day's ride. We could get there and deal with that before coming back here." Her fingers traced the route they could take.

All they needed to do was cross the river and they'd be halfway there. But... But that would leave Tochtli to Yoshi. The idea of leaving this problem to the haughty white knight felt like losing to Cricket. And he was not about to lose to some puffed up, vain—

"Cricket. Hello?" Ignacia waved her hand in front of his face. "What's going on with you?"

Cricket sucked in a breath, squeezing his eyes shut. He found his center again, shaking off what Yoshi had said to him. "I'm sorry. What were you saying?"

"I said, we could make it there and back in three days. You could go on and I could keep investigating here."

"No. Anstice sent us here. She knows what she's doing. We stay here." He shook his head.

"Let's call her and check in? Maybe the dragon is new. If it is, that should take precedent over this. I mean this isn't hurting anyone."

"That we know of."

"That we know of," Ignacia agreed.

"We'll call Anstice and see if any news has come from Ilkay. After we see the witch." Cricket held his hand out for the map, and Ignacia rolled it up again before handing it back. "I'd rather get a better handle on this first."

Ignacia's gaze flicked over his face, searching. But she didn't ask, and so long as she didn't, Cricket wasn't going to tell her. Because there were more important things to worry about than how Yoshi's words had rubbed Cricket raw, exposing insecurities he'd buried deep under hours of sparring, lessons in diplomacy, and so many books on strategy. Tochtli needed a prince with a clear head, so Cricket cleared his. Then pulled the watch from where he'd hooked it to the outside of his bag.

"It's only two. We still have plenty of time," he said, tucking it back inside, letting the chain dangle for easy access. "Let's ask the innkeeper where the witch is."

The witch—as the innkeeper told it—lived above a small shop on the west side of town, nearest the lake. Hers was an old, crooked building, perhaps the oldest in all of Tochtli, that sat on the boundary line between town and not-town. Which was a strange place for a building to be, but Cricket supposed that perhaps there had been more buildings there at some point and they'd all just fallen where the witch's had remained.

Magic hung in the air like petrichor, earthy, and damp. Different from the magic that had always clung to Cricket which seemed to smell a little cleaner, a little less muddy, more like the river at midnight.

"Well, this is the place," Ignacia said, and moved forward to peek in through the front window. Cricket stepped up beside her, his hands cupped around his eyes to cut the glare, but it did nothing to help them see inside. For in front of the window was a bookshelf that was so full he'd be surprised if any light got through at all.

Cricket pulled back and smiled at the crooked open sign,

swaying on the door. "It looks like they're open, we should just head in."

"What if she's dangerous? What if she cursed the town?" Ignacia crossed her arms over her chest, her hip cocking out to the side.

"Then we'll go in slowly?" Cricket asked. It did nothing to move Ignacia, who stood firm, an unimpressed look on her face. "Iggy, it's already three. We really don't have time for this."

"Fine." She sighed. "But I'm going in first."

"Right. Right. Of course." Cricket rolled his eyes.

Ignacia held up one hand, the other resting on her sword at the ready, and then stepped inside. Cricket watched as she looked this way, and that, the hand she'd held up to keep him from following urged him forward. He followed behind her, his own hand falling to his sword just in case. What he found inside was piles upon piles of books. All stacked to the ceiling, and teetering just enough that one wrong move would bring the lot of them down onto Cricket and Ignacia's heads. In the center of the room right under a skylight (which was strange because wasn't this building two stories?) sat a rough wooden work bench littered in glass jars of varying shapes and sizes. Some of them were glowing, others bubbling, and others still seemed as if perhaps they weren't wholly there at all.

"Hello?" Cricket called softly, his eyes darting this way and that, searching for any sign of movement aside from the gently swaying stacks of books. There didn't seem to be anyone there. "Maybe they're upstairs?"

The door, finally reaching that particular point which all doors reach before they inevitably give up staying open, slammed shut behind them. Someone yelped from behind the workbench. Then the hat, which to this point Cricket had just assumed was sitting on a stool, jerked upwards. A young face peered at them, a boy, not more than thirteen with dark circles under his eyes.

"You're not the town witch," Ignacia said, accusingly as she sheathed her sword.

"I am." The child sat up straighter, jutting out his chin in offense.

"No. The town witch is an old woman." Ignacia's eyes narrowed on the child, and Cricket stood up straight to get a better look at the youngster. He certainly looked like a witch. He had the pointed hat, and the cloak, and all. But the hat didn't fit quite right, it kept sliding down over his brow, and he was swimming in the cloak.

"Who told you that?" His voice cracked, lips pursing almost in a pout.

"The innkeeper." Cricket stepped closer, his hands folding behind his back, and a winning smile splitting his lips. "You must be her young apprentice."

The boy's shoulders sagged, and he slid from the stool. When he came around to greet them the cloak, which was being held around his neck by a rather ugly brooch, dragged the ground. It looked like he hadn't yet hit his first teenage growth spurt, Cricket wagered if they gave it six months he'd sprout up like a beanstalk. It was hard to see his eyes under the wide brimmed hat in the low lighting, but Cricket knew he was assessing them. Cricket could feel keen eyes looking them over and trying to decide if they would cause him trouble.

"You're the prince," the boy said, tipping his head back so he could look up at Cricket and meet his eyes properly.

"I am." Cricket chuckled. "And who, may I ask, are you?"

"I'm Abner." Abner's tone said that this was an obvious fact, and that Cricket had obviously been living under a rock for not knowing it.

Ignacia snorted, rolling her eyes.

"I'm Saoirse's apprentice. And who are you?" Abner asked, scathing. His head tilted up and down as if he were looking Ignacia over, the hat wobbled and nearly covered his eyes in the process.

Ignacia opened her mouth, no doubt to say something equally cutting, but Cricket beat her to it. "It's very nice to meet you, Abner. This is Ignacia, my dear friend."

"Friend?" The word came out strange, like Abner wasn't quite sure what it meant. Like he was trying to fit two pieces of a puzzle together only they were both corners and it was a 5,000-piece puzzle.

"More like babysitter," Ignacia mumbled. Cricket nudged her, and shook his head a little. She huffed, but fell silent.

"Yes, friend. Iggy and I have been friends since I was a baby. Right, Iggy?" Cricket draped his arm over her shoulder, pulling her into a one-armed hug.

"Right." Abner sounded skeptical, which may have had something to do with the annoyed shove Ignacia gave him to end the hug. But that was neither here nor there. "What do you want?"

"Ah, straight forward. I like a person who doesn't beat around the bush!" Cricket laughed. He dug around in his satchel to pull out Ignacia's journal. He'd likely have to buy her a new one in the next town, he'd cross that bridge when he came to it.

"What do you want?" Abner asked again, annoyed. "I have work to do."

Ignacia's hand twitched for her sword, the lines of her face going pinched. Cricket had to cut her off with a little wave before she could ruin Abner's very fine hat for insulting the prince.

"Of course. Of course. But perhaps you could spare some time for the crown prince of Lunette. We only have a few questions. I promise we'll be brief." Cricket offered the boy his most dimpled smile, it always worked on people in the palace. Why shouldn't it work now?

Abner sighed the sigh of a teenager who was very bored and annoyed with old people (which was to say anyone more than two years older than themselves). "Fine. But I'm going back to my work."

"Splendid!" Cricket cheered. He followed Abner back to the bench, fingers twitching to move some of the jars aside and make a space for himself, but stopping mid-movement at a sharp look from Abner. "Right. No touchy."

"What do you want to know?"

"Where in the name of Styx is your Mistress?" Ignacia all but snarled over Cricket's shoulder. Abner twitched, shoulders straightening in irritation. But to his credit, he didn't growl back at Ignacia as some might have done.

"She left two days ago to visit her sister in the capital. I was left in charge."

"When will she be back?"

"A fortnight, she said. But I never really know with her. Sometimes she stays for a whole month. Is that important?" Abner sounded annoyed again, and that wasn't good. Cricket wanted him relaxed, open, willing. Cricket swatted Ignacia lightly behind his back.

"No, we're just curious." Cricket perched the journal on his knee and jotted all of this down. The fact that all of this had started soon after the town witch left was suspicious, but not altogether worrying. It could have been a coincidence. "There have been some reports of strange things occurring in town. You wouldn't happen to know anything about that, would you?"

Abner shrugged, but his head ducked lower, hiding his face almost entirely under the brim of the hat. "I don't know anything about all that."

"Of course. You're just being a good apprentice and

holding down the fort, right? Staying out of trouble, and maintaining whatever spells Saoirse left." Cricket nodded in understanding. "Filling any outlying orders and all that. It's a big responsibility."

"It is!" Abner brightened, looking up at Cricket and meeting his eyes. "It's such a big responsibility!"

"Of course, it is. And you're doing a fine job, aren't you?"

"I am!" Abner's shoulders stiffened. "Has someone told you I'm not? If it was those—" He stopped himself, lips pressing together.

"Those who?" Cricket pressed gently.

"No one." Abner ducked his head back to his work. "Is that all? I really have to finish up this ointment."

"Yeah, I think that's it. Thank you for taking the time to speak with us Abner." Cricket slid off the stool. Ignacia shot him a questioning look, and he shook his head before leading her toward the exit. The door slammed shut behind them again, but Cricket didn't stop. "We need to ask about smaller events. Curses on children."

"What? Wait. Why did we just walk away from him? That kid knows something." Ignacia raced after him before falling into stride beside him, frowning. "He's hiding something. It's all over his face."

"It is." Cricket agreed. "But he's not going to tell us what he's up to. We need to find out for ourselves. Yoshi said something..." Cricket frowned, shaking his head. "He said something that made it sound like he'd heard of some other magical issues while he'd been here. If that's the case, then it hadn't been reported before the town disappeared the first time."

"Which means?"

"Which means, whatever is going on here was probably caused by someone poking around into those smaller disturbances. So, we need to find out what those smaller distur-bances were."

Ignacia nodded. "Where do we start?"

"Back at the market. But this time, let's talk to the moth-ers, not the vendors."

THE MARKET WAS JUST how Cricket remembered it. He stuck close to Ignacia as they walked into the circle.

"'scuse me," a child giggled, bumping into them in his hurry to get past to the stalls.

"Jingyi! Get back here!" his mother shouted; her strides quick. "I'm so sorry." She bowed to them. "He's just so excited about the Sunday market is all."

"Excuse me ma'am," Cricket called just as she was turning to run after her son again. "Do you mind if we ask you a few questions?"

Jingyi's mother looked after the child, frowning when he tripped, and nearly toppled into the melon stand. Thankfully he caught his balance just in time. She shook her head.

"It will only be a moment," Ignacia promised.

"All right. What can I help you wi—" She stopped, her eyes widening when she finally got a good look at Cricket. "You're the... the..."

"Yes, ma'am." Cricket chuckled. "But please, the questions?"

"Of course! Of course!" She dipped into a low curtsey. "Anything His Highness needs."

"That's really not necessary." Cricket rubbed at the back of his neck, trying to make the heat that crept up it go away. He wondered briefly if he'd ever get used to people scrambling over themselves to pay him respect he wasn't sure he was due. Especially with him not being of royal blood. Without the magic of the royal line singing through his veins... Well, he much preferred it when people just acted like he was another person, as Abner, Ava, and even Yoshi had done. "We're just wondering if there have been any strange things going on in town in the last couple of days, ma'am."

"Misses Wyatt, Your Highness." She curtsied again.

"You don't have to...do that." Cricket muttered awkwardly. He looked to Ignacia for help, but her shoulders were shaking with suppressed laughter, so she'd be no use. As always. "Please, let's go have a seat."

"Of course, Your Highness."

Cricket swallowed a groan, and led her to the fountain where they sat on its edge. "So, please, if there is anything strange?"

"Not that I can think of." Misses Wyatt frowned, taking a moment to think. "Unless you count the Cyrus boy coming down with a truly terrible case of the chicken pox."

"Was there an outbreak?" Cricket pulled out the journal again. "How old is he?"

"Fourteen, too old for it really." Misses Wyatt shook her head. "Jingyi had them when he was three, it went through the school. And the Cryus boy's were..."

"They were what?" Ignacia prompted.

"Well, they were far worse than any case I'd ever seen. I don't think the scars will ever go away, and oh my, they were all over his face." Misses Wyatt tsked, shaking her head. "Such a handsome boy too."

"Handsome?!" Jingyi asked, where he'd just appeared next to his mother. He let out a loud, hard laugh. "What's handsome got to do with it?"

Misses Wyatt shushed him. "Go off and play."

"No. No, what do you mean, Jingyi?" Cricket leaned

forward to get a better look at the child. He looked to be about five, and his face was scrunched up in that expression children usually reserved for vegetables.

"Dempsey Cyrus is a jerk! He deserves those scars!" Jingyi all but spat.

"Jingyi! You can't just say things like that about people! That's horrible!" Misses Wyatt had turned all the way around to reprimand her son. "You need to apologize, right now!"

Jingyi huffed, crossing his arms over his chest.

"I'm so sorry, Your Highness. I promise he's not usually like this."

"It's quite all right." Cricket brushed off the apology only half paying attention. His pencil moved fast across the page. His mind was already working over what that could mean. Bullies very often went unpunished, but this one had gotten his just desserts. Was it possible that he could have beat up on Abner? Enough to draw the young witch's ire?

"Thank you for your time," Ignacia said when it didn't look like Cricket was going to raise his head from the journal. "Please don't let us keep you from your shopping."

Misses Wyatt nodded. When Cricket came up for air from his thoughts, the Wyatt family was gone.

"We need to talk to some more mothers," he declared, snapping the book shut, and stuffing it back into the bag.

CHAPTER 10

The trend continued with a twelve-year-old girl named Bellatrix who was suddenly too afraid to leave her room, a thirteen-year-old boy named Christos who woke up one morning with a strange allergy to water, and one teacher whose lips had been inexplicably fused together. No one said as much, but Cricket was certain that each had had something to do with Abner. What their crime had been to cause them to be punished by the boy, he didn't know.

"It's too much magic for someone so young." Cricket frowned down at his notes. "He shouldn't have that much power."

"But he does." Ignacia's hands were tucked behind her back as they walked.

"But he does," Cricket agreed. His fingers drummed against the strap of his satchel as he thought.

"It has to be some kind of amplifying magic. Doesn't it?"

"It would have to be, but where would he get something like that? I doubt his mistress would leave him with it, that would be irresponsible, no witch in their right mind would leave a thirteen-year-old with amplifying magics." He shook his head, frowning more. There was something that wasn't fitting. Something that didn't add up. "And besides, why would he curse the entire town to repeat the day?"

"Maybe we should just wait till his mistress comes back? She'll set everything right, I'm sure." Ignacia shrugged.

Cricket sighed, grabbing the watch from his satchel to check the time. His eyes widened at the hand slowly ticking away toward 6:30. They had a minute, maybe a little less. He grabbed Ignacia's wrist and started running.

"What in the name of Styx are we doing?!"

"Running!" He didn't stop. The edge of the town was in sight. Just a few more feet and they'd be safe.

"I can see that, but why?"

"It's almost time!"

"It's almost time for..." Ignacia yelped beside him when she understood. "Well run faster then! I don't want to get trapped here again!"

"I'm trying!" He growled, pushing himself faster. His heart hammered in his ears, but the line was right there. He could see it. Just a few more steps and they'd be out in the plane again. They stepped over the boundary out into the surrounding grass, Cricket let out a long slow whine, and flopped down face first into the dirt. He held the stitch in his side, wheezing to try to catch his breath. "I really need to get back into shape."

"We'll have to work on that." Ignacia scoffed. She'd turned to look back at where Tochtli had been and was frowning. "Cricket."

"What? I know. It's gone. Weird, right?" He'd squeezed his eyes shut at some point, but wasn't sure when.

"No. Cricket. Look."

"It's not weird?" Cricket asked, blinking hard against the

still too-bright light of the sun kissing the horizon as it fought to stay longer.

"No.... It's... It's not gone." Ignacia's words were soft, almost lost on the wind.

"What?" Cricket sat up abruptly and looked back the way they'd come. He was fully expecting to see fields as far as the eye could see, but no. There was the cobblestone road that led into the center of Tochtli. Someone was whistling as they pushed a cart down the street. A woman on the second floor of one of the homes had come out to take her laundry down off the line. Tochtli was still there. And its people were going about their normal routines as if nothing had changed. "But that's not...that's not right."

"Maybe you got the time wrong."

"No. I wrote it down and everything. It was 6:35 when I was finally able to write it down." He shook his head, scrambling through his satchel to pull out the journal again. Fingers fumbled as he flipped to the page, nearly ripping it in his hurry, but then he pointed. "Look? See? 6:35."

"Maybe you read the watch wrong?" Ignacia frowned, tilting her head to try to read his handwriting, and then looking away when she gave up.

"I can read a watch." Cricket shook his head. "The sun had just touched the horizon. I remember. This...this isn't right. It should be gone. It should all be gone! By this time last night this was just an empty field!"

"Well, it's not now."

"I see that, Iggy." Cricket bit out, pulling the watch by the chain to get a better look at it. 6:38. It should be gone. "Something has changed. We did something to change it."

"Do you think..." Ignacia let her words drift off, but there was a smile creeping up her lips. A dangerous, victorious thing that may very well be premature, but Cricket wasn't about to look a gift horse in the mouth.

"That it was you?" he finished, rising to his feet, the same slow and hopeful smile twitching at the corners of his own lips. "That getting someone out before it disappeared changed everything?"

"Is it possible that we broke whatever spell he put on the place?" There was hope gleaming in her eyes.

Cricket could feel his knees bouncing in excitement. "I mean we had to have, right? Look! It's still there! Tochtli is still there! We saved the town! Iggy! We did it! We saved the town!"

"We saved the town!" Ignacia cheered, grabbing his hands and bouncing with him. They both jumped, and spun, and laughed at their success until the sun had well and truly set. By that point Cricket was breathless, the stitch in his side had come back, but he hadn't been happier in such a long time, so he didn't complain.

They built a small fire on the embers of his previous one, and made a brief supper. Cricket couldn't help how his eyes were drawn back to Tochtli. The town was still there, lights flickering in the windows as people went about their evening routines. He did that. He made sure they were safe. And tomorrow they'd go back into town, and he'd have a very stern chat with Abner about misusing magic.

"We should give Anstice a call. Let her know we're done here and figure out where we should go next." Ignacia sat up from where she'd laid back in the grass to look up at the stars.

"And bring up the dragon." Cricket dragged his satchel closer so he could dig out the mirror. "Ooooh, Anstice."

His reflection rippled, and Ignacia scooted in closer as they waited for Anstice to pick up. When she finally did, Cricket frowned. Her usually neat hair had several strands pulled from the haphazard braid on her shoulder.

"What's wrong?" he asked immediately.

"It's nothing, Cricky." Anstice shook her head. "Nothing I

can't handle anyway. Your father has just come down with a little cold."

"The healer?"

"Has already been in to see him. He's been put on bed rest, and that should be the end of it."

"I should come home."

"No. You are doing important work out there, and you should continue to do that. Which...speaking of... Hello Iggy!" Anstice crowed, her face lighting up in a wide smile. "So nice to see you again, dear!"

"I was missed, I see." Ignacia laughed, shaking her head.

"Oh, so much. Our dear prince was in ruins, absolute tatters, when you disappeared last night. I don't think I've ever seen him so distraught." Anstice's face had slipped into something more relaxed. Cricket huffed at the gentle ribbing, but didn't put a stop to it. It was true enough; he had been frazzled. But more than that there was comfort in the familiarity of their teasing. "Speaking of, I presume you have news?"

"Yes! Tochtli!" Cricket brightened, turning the mirror so that Anstice could see the town where it still sat next to the river. The lights were slowly winking out as people turned in for the night, but it was still very much there. "We think we know what caused it, and it seems that pulling someone out was what broke it."

When he pulled the mirror back so he could look at Anstice her face had settled into a thoughtful expression. "And you're sure it's broken?"

"Well, the town is still there. By this time last night, it had been gone for a couple of hours." Cricket wrinkled his nose thoughtfully. "I don't see why it wouldn't have been broken at this point."

"What do you think the cause was?" Anstice was drumming her well-manicured nails on the table, making the mirror jiggle a little.

"An amplifying spell combined with an underage witch," Ignacia supplied. "We met the kid; he doesn't seem malicious."

"Just lonely," Cricket said.

"Hmmm," Anstice hummed, chewing on the inside of her cheek for a moment. Then she shrugged.

"Where to next?" Ignacia reached over to grab the map from Cricket's bag and unfurled it.

"We heard there was a dragon in Ilkay." Cricket tried and failed to keep the excitement out of his voice. He'd never seen a dragon in person, and he'd love to get the chance.

"A dragon?" Anstice tilted her head.

"Mhm. We ran into a knight that said he was headed that way to deal with a dragon." Cricket leaned in to look at the map with Ignacia. "Iggy figures it's about a half day's ride. And if it's—"

"No. No. Don't worry about the dragon." Anstice waved her hand, brushing off the idea.

"What?" Cricket and Ignacia asked as one, both heads lifting to eye their friend skeptically.

"Let's sort out where you'll go next after you've dealt with this young witch. You don't know how long it'll take you to talk him down, do you?"

"Well no. But I mean... he's just a kid... and this is a drag-on." Cricket held the mirror handle more tightly to keep from fidgeting. "Dragons are definitely more dangerous."

"They are. But I've got a contact in Ilkay I'll reach out to and see what's really going on there. If we hadn't heard about it yet, it might not be that serious."

"How is a dragon not serious?" Ignacia asked. "I mean they're huge, and they breathe fire, and they usually like to destroy things. Or are we talking about something else?"

"Look here miss, don't sass me. Who's the advisor here?" Anstice's finger shook in the direction of Ignacia, or tried to, in the little mirror it really just looked like she was wagging her finger at both of them.

Ignacia huffed, but didn't argue.

"Right. I am." Anstice looked much too pleased with herself, and Cricket sent up a silent thanks to Selene that they were not in a room together which would either descend into yelling or them picking on him instead. "It wasn't on the list that Theo brought us before you left."

"It could be more recent. I didn't get an exact date of when the knight had arrived. It could have been after we left." Waiting didn't sit right with Cricket. He'd rather know where they were headed next so he could prepare. He didn't want to go in blind as he had with Tochtli and possibly lose Ignacia again. Once had been enough.

Anstice sighed. "Trust me Cricket, I'll get an answer about the dragon."

"No. I know. I'm just..." He shrugged.

"I'll have plenty of information on your next location before you get there, I promise." Her voice had gone a little softer, like Anstice could see the upset on the edge of Cricket's mind. She probably could. She'd known him all his life, and Cricket had never been one to play it close to the vest.

"I'm not going anywhere." Ignacia slung her arm over his shoulder, giving him a tight hug and then she pressed a messy and loud kiss to his cheek. "You won't get rid of me that easy!"

"Gross! Iggy cooties!" He laughed, scrubbing at his cheek. Ignacia gave him a hard shove, and Cricket almost dropped the mirror. She snatched it from him before he could. Anstice was laughing too, he could hear it. It took a minute for their laughter to die away, and then he sat up, pressing his shoulder hard into Ignacia's to fit himself into the mirror.

"Good to see you two are getting along as well as ever." Anstice shook her head. "You should get some rest. I'm not a seer, but I predict another early start in your future."

"Noooooo," Cricket whined.

Ignacia snickered, and Anstice offered them both a wink before her image blinked out. They settled into the tent after that. Curling up and going to sleep to the sounds of the night around them.

CHAPTER 11

The sun was high in the sky by the time Cricket woke the next morning. He rolled over, swatting at the blankets beside him.

"Iggy. Iggy we overslept. Iggy. Why didn't you—" he stopped, body going rigid when his hand was met with nothing but blankets. There was no warm shoulder, no long hair. Just blankets, blankets, and more blankets. He sat up, panic seizing hold of his insides to look down at the place where Ignacia had fallen asleep the night before. She was gone. There was no sign of her there.

He scooted to the edge of his bedroll, pulling on his boots and heading for the flap to the tent. She'd just gone to get breakfast started, he told himself. She was being the responsible one of the two of them. She hadn't disappeared. He could see Tochtli through the opening, it was still there. And if it was still there, then Ignacia also still had to be there. He was just... he was getting worried for nothing.

It wasn't nothing, he realized all too quickly as he looked around their small camp. There was no sign of Ignacia. The fire from the night before had completely burned out. She'd left no note. Her horse was still there. Everything was as it had been before they'd gone to bed, only with the absence of his best friend.

"But we fixed it," he protested to no one in particular. His horse huffed at him. "No, we fixed it, Buttercup. We did. Look, Tochtli is still there. We fixed it. There's no reason for her to have disappeared again."

Buttercup pressed her face into his shoulder, nudging him. He patted her muzzle, carefully ignoring how his hands shook. Panic. He did not have time for panic. Nor did he have time for the strangled manic laugh working its way up his throat. He swallowed it down, along with the burning in his eyes.

"Maybe she just went into town to grab some scones," he reasoned. It sounded reasonable, after all. Ignacia was a grown woman; she could go into town and get them breakfast. She didn't have to check in with Cricket every minute of the day. But...but she would have left a note. She would have let him know she was going. She would have woken him up and told him, even if he was grumpy about it. Especially after everything. She'd know he'd be worried. She would have mitigated that. She hadn't.

Buttercup snorted against his hair, moving in to nibble at one pointed ear.

"Yeah, that's it. She's gone into town to grab some scones. I'll just go and find her, shall I?" He didn't know who he was trying to convince, certainly not himself because the words didn't make the hysteria clawing at his throat go away. And definitely not Buttercup and Saber (really, who named their horse Saber? Ignacia, apparently.) who were looking at him like he'd finally lost his mind, and it had been a long time coming.

"I'll just go find her." He nodded to himself and started down the hill toward Tochtli. His steps felt forced, and unsure, but he kept taking them. One after the other. Ava, the smithy was tidying up her shop, getting ready for the day's work when he reached the edge of town. "Good morning, Ava!"

Ava cocked her head at him, a waterfall of dark hair falling over her shoulder where she had yet to pin it back. "Prince Cricket?"

"Ha! Yes. We met yesterday, remember? Iggy and I spoke to you about the strangeness in the town?" Cricket stood up taller, trying to look official, but still, he couldn't hide the uncertain tone in his voice.

"Iggy?"

"Yes. About yay high," he gestured to about shoulder height. "Dark red braids, very angry looking. Iggy. Or Ignacia rather."

Ava shook her head. "No. I don't remember any Ignacia. Your Highness, you haven't been by here at all. And I'm afraid if you're looking for something, I don't have the materials to make anything half as fine as what you're used to."

"No. No. That's all right." Cricket shifted his weight back onto his heels, readying to run at any moment. He needed to find Ignacia and get to the bottom of this. He needed to understand what in the name of Styx was going on here. He couldn't lose Ignacia again. "You really don't remember talking to me and my knight yesterday?"

"I think I'd remember talking to the prince." Ava huffed, crossing her arms over her chest. "Look if this is some kind of—"

"Where is the bakery located at?" Cutting people off was rude, or so he'd been told on more than one occasion by Uncle Sunil. But Cricket was in a hurry. Judging by the sun it was 10:00 or 11:00 by now. That meant he had a grand total of seven hours to figure out what was going on in Tochtli before he lost Ignacia again. And that was if the pattern held, and he didn't do something to change it involuntarily as he clearly had the previous day.

"It's...just down the block." She pointed.

"Thank you, Ava!" Cricket said over his shoulder, already running in the direction she'd pointed.

"But they won't be there!" She called after him. "It's Sunday, they'll be at the market!"

His steps stuttered, stumbling. A missed stair in the dark. Sunday. The market. Again. It was the same day. *Again.* Cricket ducked into an alley, bracing his knees as his lungs struggled to draw in air. Again. It was Sunday. Again. It was the same day. Again. He slammed his fist against the wall behind him, and then winced. The pain brought him back to the time limit. Seven hours, max. That's all he had. He had to hurry!

Ignacia was in the center of town, talking to the apple vendor. Just where he'd found her the previous morning.

"Iggy," he all but sobbed, running up to her and tackling her in a tight hug.

Ignacia yelped, her hands scrambling to get a hold of his arms where he'd wrapped himself around her shoulders. "Cricket! Get off!"

"No. Not again. I'm not losing you again!"

"What are you talking about? Stop being ridiculous! I just saw you! You were talking to the vendors and wandered off! *You* left, not me!"

Cricket took her hand, and pulled her with him, ignoring the strange looks the apple vendor gave them. Once they were far enough away from everyone else, he pulled her into another tight hug. Pressing his face into her braids, which if he was being honest wasn't terribly comfortable, but it didn't matter. Because she was here. She was safe. And she was here.

"Are you going to tell me what's going on now?" Ignacia's voice was muffled by the fabric of his scarf and tunic, but she didn't pull back. He was glad of that, because he didn't want her to see the tears gathering at the corners of his eyes.

"You're stuck."

"Yes. Because you won't let me go." She huffed, giving his chest a gentle shove, but not enough to pull from the hug, just enough to loosen it.

"No. In the town. You're stuck in the town. We got out yesterday, before it disappeared, and then it didn't disappear. And so we thought that we'd broken the curse, but we didn't. We didn't, Iggy. I woke up this morning, and you were gone. And then I went to see Ava and she didn't remember me. And then I came here, and here you were. Again. Just like yesterday." The words were leaving him in a mad scramble now. He was sure he wasn't explaining it right, and that he likely wasn't making sense. But he couldn't seem to stop and force his brain to process it any slower. Not when they had seven hours. Just seven hours.

Ignacia snorted. "So, it's repeating?"

"Yes." Oh, thank Selene she understood! He didn't think he'd be able to explain it fully without crying.

"Let's say that I believe you," she said slowly. He pulled back enough to shoot her an offended look. "What? You could be playing a joke! You've done stupider things!"

"This is not a *joke*, Iggy!" He sniffled, scrubbing at his eyes. Traitorous things, who said they could let the tears fall? He'd be having words with them later.

She frowned at the sight of him, and then nodded. "All right. It's not a joke. Then, how does the spell work? What did we figure out yesterday?"

The emotions seeped out of him in a rush, and then all Cricket was left with was a grumbling belly. "Can we get breakfast first?"

Ignacia's lips pursed, and she shook her head. "Really? A time like this and all you can think of is your stomach?"

"Iggy. I ran all the way here. I was very upset. Growing princes must have breakfast. It is the most important meal of the day." Cricket pouted, widening his eyes in that way he had distinctly learned from Anstice (or maybe she'd learned it from him, he couldn't be sure anymore) and looked every bit the helpless damsel that he was.

Ignacia's eyes narrowed. "We'll go to the Inn for breakfast. You will talk on the way."

"Oh! That's a good idea! That's where the knight is." He perked up.

"The knight?"

"Yes, I'll tell you aaaaaaall about him, just follow me." Cricket took her hand, holding tightly as he led her back out onto the street and toward the inn. Along the way he told her about Yoshi, and the witch's apprentice, and the people who had been cursed very likely by Abner. He didn't take a breath or stop to answer questions. There wasn't time, she needed to get caught up and quick. He finished by the time the inn door opened. "I'm thinking that maybe it's not really a curse on the town at all."

"I heard from Ava that the prince was here!" The innkeeper rushed over to them, bowing deeply. "Please come. Come. I'll show you to our best table."

"No. Please. We'd rather sit out in the main dining room today, Madam Shen." Cricket bowed back, offering the confused woman a grin as he led Ignacia to a back corner where they wouldn't be overheard, but they could see the entire room.

Madam Shen bustled after them, recovering quickly from her confusion to grace Cricket with a wide smile once he'd sat. "I will have the kitchen bring out our inn's finest dishes."

"That won't be necessary, Madam Shen. If you could just bring us a menu? We'd like to order like your regular guests, please?" Cricket did not want to get stuck with the exorbitant amount of food they'd had been the previous day. It was probably that meal that had caused the multiple stitches in his side the night before (even if it wasn't, he was going to blame that anyway), and he needed to be nimble on his feet today.

"Yes. Of course, Your Highness." Madam Shen bowed, and turned away with a perplexed look on her face like she was adding one plus one and somehow getting five.

"You don't think it's a curse on the town?" Ignacia asked once Madam Shen was out of hearing range.

"No. I don't think it's just one curse, either." He drummed his fingers on the table, pulling the journal from his satchel.

"That's my—"

"I know. I'll buy you a new one. I just needed a place to keep everything together."

"You have a sketchbook," Ignacia said blandly. But she didn't reach to take it from him. "It's not just one curse?"

"Well. It is and it isn't." Cricket tapped his pencil on the notebook, his tongue poking out as he doodled in the corner. Deep in thought.

Ignacia huffed.

"What?"

"It is and it isn't? You sound like an oracle. No riddles. What does it mean?" She stood up and moved to sit beside him so she could stare down at the journal with him. Her eyes squinted, trying to make sense of his handwriting. "I see your calligraphy classes are paying off."

Cricket opted not to dignify that last comment with an answer. "It is and it isn't because it's the same spell, but it's being cast over and over."

"That doesn't make sense."

"It does when you're thirteen."

"Abner is doing it," Ignacia said, frowning. "But he's not powerful enough for that."

"I know, last night we concluded he must have some kind of amplifier." Cricket turned the journal to a fresh page to write that down along with everything he'd gathered about Abner the previous day. "What I think is happening, is that he keeps casting the same spell, to try to get a do over."

Ignacia's brows rose. "Because something is going wrong, and he's trying to fix it. But...why isn't it working?"

"Whatever spell he's using is keeping him from remembering he's doing it. He gets to start the day again, at 6:30 in the morning every day, but he doesn't remember he did it. So everything just happens over again, exactly as it did before."

"So he doesn't know what he needs to change." Ignacia wrinkled her nose. "That's an amateur mistake."

"Yeah. Well. He's thirteen."

"Fair."

"We just need to figure out what the triggering event is. We did something yesterday that pushed it off, whatever it was. It was someone we talked to." He started writing names on the page opposite of his list of facts about Abner. "There were the mothers, Abner himself, the messenger, the scholar..."

"The white knight." Ignacia added, tapping the paper. "You have lots of notes about him. It looks like he's important."

"I don't think... I mean... I think I was mistaken." Cricket cleared his throat to hide the blush that crept up his neck. "Oh look! Menus! Thank you, Madam Shen!"

Ignacia eyed him closely, but didn't say anymore on the subject until they had ordered, and their tea had arrived. Small mercies.

"Maybe we should follow the white knight, see where he goes," she suggested a knowing look in her eyes as she watched Cricket from over her teacup.

"Or...and hear me out on this because it's crazy..." Cricket leaned forward, and waited for Ignacia to give him her full attention. "We ignore the white knight and go and wait outside the witch's shop to see what happens."

Ignacia huffed, sitting back in her chair. "I'm going to see him eventually."

"Yeah, that's what I'm afraid of," he muttered.

"What?"

"What?"

CHAPTER 12

"What if I was wrong?" Cricket asked, shifting awkwardly on the balls of his feet where he was crouched in the shadow of the squat building beside the witch's crooked shop.

"Do you honestly think that, or are you just bored?" Ignacia sounded bored too. Or maybe she was tired of hearing him complain after three hours of sitting and watching as the witch's shop remained unchanged. No one had gone in. No one had come out. Nothing was happening! All right, maybe he *was* just bored.

"We didn't change anything today. We didn't talk to anyone different," he said instead of answering the question. Because he was not about to admit that he was in fact a five-year-old who couldn't sit still for more than a couple of hours without something to do, as he'd frequently been accused of.

"So, we could have waited to come here till closer to the time? Say in... three and a half hours?" Ignacia grumbled, her fingers drumming on the cobblestones underneath them.

"Probably."

"Remind me to never let you plan out a mission again." Ignacia snorted, rising from the ground, and brushing off the back of her grey-blue tunic. "You'd think I'd have learned that after the last time..."

"Rude." Cricket huffed. "Where are you going? We can't change anything. If we change anything the pattern won't hold, and I won't be able to guess the time. We could speed it up!"

"Relax. I'm just going to grab us something to eat." She patted his head. He swatted her hand away, huffing. "You can handle one knight. I know you can."

From anyone else, the words would have sounded condescending (and maybe had she said them to anyone else they would have been meant to), but they weren't. There was confidence there. Ignacia, for all her blustering, and complaining, had never once doubted his abilities. She knew what he was capable of, perhaps better than he, himself, did. If she thought he could handle Yoshi, he probably could.

"All right." He nodded. "Bring me back something good."

"Yes, Your Highness." Ignacia curtsied, a laugh on her lips.

"Go!" Cricket snickered, tossing a pebble at her. She disappeared around the corner, and Cricket slid to his bottom on the ground. It would be a long couple of hours, he might as well get comfortable.

She returned about a half hour later with fresh baked scones, and some kind of goat cheese, and sat beside him without a word. By then, Cricket had pulled his sketchbook out, and started on the base of a portrait, mindlessly drawing the lines that would help him sort out where eyes and nose went. They ate in silence, every once in a while glancing back to the witch's shop which had continued to be as stubbornly boring as it had been the last few hours.

"He can't be that good looking." Ignacia peered over Cricket's shoulder down at the sketch which had changed from a generic portrait into a drawing of the white knight at some point. He wasn't sure when, or even if he'd made that conscious decision, but what was done was done.

"What? No. He's not..." Cricket frowned down at the drawing. "You don't even like men."

"Doesn't mean I can't find someone objectively handsome." Ignacia shrugged. "And he is. Or at least this drawing is."

Cricket huffed, shutting the sketchbook, and stuffing it back into his satchel.

"Oh, don't be like that." Ignacia leaned in to bump his shoulder with her own. "I'm just teasing."

Cricket grumbled, crossing his arms over his chest, and focusing on the shop again.

"Come on Cricky, you can't—"

"That's him." He cut her off, standing quickly. A white clad figure had appeared, ducking from an alley out into the open of the small courtyard in front of the witch's shop. He looked just like Cricket remembered. Shoulders set into a hard, determined line, face impassive.

"I rescind my original statement, he *can* be that good looking," Ignacia muttered under her breath just loud enough for him to hear. Cricket rolled his eyes, bracing himself as he took long, quick strides toward Yoshi. He needed to stop him. He wasn't sure how, but he needed to. Maybe if he could just talk to Yoshi, get him to see sense. Surely as a knight, he had to be a sensible man.

Yoshi was drawing his sword, and Cricket couldn't have that. His strides quickened, turning into a run. Before he could stop himself, and think about what he was doing, he placed himself in front of the shop door, his own sword drawn. Yoshi lunged for him, white cloak turning into a blur as he swung his sword toward the obstacle (also known as

Cricket) in his way. Cricket lifted his own, metal meeting metal in a loud clank.

"You're early," Cricket grunted through clenched teeth. "It's only 5, you're not supposed to show up till at least 6."

"Get out of the way, *Your Highness*." Yoshi's face was set into a hard look. Eyes narrowed, and face alarmingly close. So close that Cricket could see specks of earth amongst the sunlight of his gaze, golden brown grounding the brightness, and making it richer for it.

Cricket didn't lower his guard. Instead, he braced his foot, and shoved Yoshi back. Yoshi's gaze widened just a touch, before he found his footing again and lunged toward the door. Cricket was ready for him, knocking the strike aside, and nodding to Ignacia to take up his post at the door as he backed Yoshi away from it.

"Out of the way."

"No." Cricket spun, thrusting forward. A smile twitched at his lips as Yoshi parried, swords singing. Cricket advanced, putting more space between them and the shop, taking them into the cobblestone street.

"You are protecting the witch." Yoshi's lips twitched, wrinkled at one side. Cricket wasn't sure if it was confusion or disappointment he saw there, but there wasn't time to think about it.

"He's a child," Cricket answered the underlying accusation. He didn't need Yoshi to say it to hear it. His foot caught on a stone, stumbling back, and Yoshi took the advantage to push them toward the shop again.

"Dangerous." Yoshi growled, his sword thrusting forward, and catching Cricket's bare forearm.

"Rude!" Cricket hissed. The blade left a thin slice behind, raw, and already welling with blood. It had been a long time since anyone had gotten a clean hit on him. "Impressive. But still, *rude* to draw the prince's blood."

"The prince is protecting—"

"The prince is protecting a *child*!" Cricket snarled, his sword meeting Yoshi's again as the man lunged for him. Locking together to keep Yoshi from advancing further. "Children make mistakes, it's how they learn!"

"You are making excuses for him." Yoshi's face was so close now. Too close. Cricket could feel the knight's breath on his cheek. Bracing one foot on Yoshi's thigh he pushed off, flipping backward to break the hold. They were getting too close to the shop, but Cricket wasn't sure if he could push Yoshi back again. He'd had the element of surprise before, that was gone now.

"I am making excuses for no one!" It was said on a hard breath, panting. It had been too long since Cricket had come up against someone other than Ignacia who could match him parry for thrust. He really was out of shape.

"What of the people of Tochtli?" There it was. The accusation. The assumption that Cricket was picking sides. That he was making a mistake. That he didn't know what he was *doing*.

"I am protecting them too." Cricket brushed his sleeve across the sheen of sweat gathering on his forehead, falling into his stance again. He could feel Ignacia watching them, but there wasn't time to think about that. Not now. "He is a child."

"*You* are a child!"

"Okay, you know what? I tried reasoning with you. I'm done!" Cricket lunged, sword flying, and just missing Yoshi's long white cloak as the knight spun out of the way. But Yoshi had taken the opportunity for what it was, braced himself against a nearby wall, and flipped over Cricket. Anger had made Cricket reckless, just as his teachers had always said it would, and provided Yoshi with the opening he needed. A mistake. One he couldn't afford to make but had made just the same. If it weren't for the movement, for the rush of running to put his body between Yoshi and the door again, he might have stopped to berate himself for it. There would be time to toss and turn over that mistake later.

"What is going on out here?!" Abner shouted from where he was trying to peek around Ignacia.

Yoshi took the opening and lunged for the child. Even with Ignacia in the way, even with Cricket racing to stop him, he wasn't fast enough. And the next thing he knew there was a flash of green, the sharp twinge of petrichor in the air, and the sound of a roaring ocean filled his ears. A tide of magic flowed from Abner, erasing first Ignacia and then the shop, and then the street.

"No! No! No! No! NO!" Cricket shouted, but it was too late, the magic had started. And all he had left was to grab Yoshi by the arm and yank him away from the spell. To save them both from being dragged into the undertow. Yoshi followed, and they ran through the street, the tide of the spell chasing them. Only a step ahead of the rushing current of magic that filled his ears. He saw it, the edge, the line, the safety. He had to make it there. His heart hammered in his chest, almost blotting out the sound of the spell following him. "This is all your fault!"

Yoshi didn't say anything, but he kept up with Cricket. Just a few more feet, and they'd be safe. If he could get Yoshi out, maybe it would stop things from repeating. If he could...

Pop.

The magic hit the border just as Cricket stepped over the line. He turned back to yell at Yoshi, prepared to scream in the man's face, but Yoshi was gone. Swallowed up by the spell just as everything else had been. The town. Ignacia. Abner. The Inn. The smithy. The market. Jingyi, and his mother. Everything.

"WHY?!" Cricket fell to his knees, and screamed to the sky, gripping hard at his hair.

He had figured it out. He knew what to do. He just... he hadn't been quick enough. He hadn't been smart enough. He hadn't...

He hadn't been *enough*!

CHAPTER 13

The waiting was the hardest part. Cricket didn't sleep. He didn't sit. He didn't rest. He dressed his wound, ate a light meal, practiced his sword forms. And he waited. For the sun to rise. For Tochtli to reappear. For the torture of that damnable repeating day to start over again.

It seemed to drag on, the moon inching across the sky little by little. But eventually, the sun peeked over the horizon, and Tochtli returned. Cricket wasted no time making his way back to the center of town to find Ignacia speaking with the apple vendor again. He grabbed her wrist and dragged her away without a word.

"Cricket! Don't be rude! I was just—"

"There isn't time. We've got to make it to the witch's shop and talk to Abner before Yoshi gets it into his head to attack early again." He didn't feel like explaining this all over again, but he knew he was going to have to. He knew that without the explanation, Ignacia wouldn't understand what was going on, and she wouldn't be able to help.

"Cricket." She dug her heels into the cobblestone street, using her weight to pull him to a stop.

Ignacia was quiet, patient, as Cricket took his time to draw in a breath. And then he spoke. He told her everything all over again. What he knew, what would solve this, what they had to do. It was a lot, and by the time he was finished his throat was dry. But that was all right because Ignacia nodded in understanding.

"We just have to convince a thirteen-year-old to give up his amplifier, and a stubborn warrior not to run him through. How hard could it be?" she asked.

"A lot harder than it sounds." Cricket laughed hollowly, shaking his head.

"How many times?" She sounded worried, and he didn't like that. He didn't want her to worry, not about him, not now. There were more important things than how he was fairing in all of this. Far more important things. He squeezed her hand, hoping to reassure her, but she just looked at him, brows knit together in concern.

"It doesn't really matter. This will be the last time. I'm going to fix this." He sighed, and then set his shoulders. "We'll deal with Abner first."

THE SHOP'S open sign swayed in the breeze, mocking Cricket as they approached. He lifted his chin, pulled out his watch to check the time, and took a steadying breath. They had eight hours to make this right, maybe less, if something changed. Cricket sent up a silent prayer to Selene that things wouldn't change. That they still had plenty of time. He knocked on the door lightly and waited for the young boy to come to open it.

Abner looked just the same as he remembered, perhaps a little more tired, with the too-big hat sliding down his forehead as he looked up to assess Cricket critically. "You're the prince."

"I am." Cricket smiled, giving the boy a little bow. "And you're Abner the witch's apprentice. I've heard a lot about you."

This seemed to take Abner off guard. He blinked, lips falling open in surprise. "You have?"

"I have." Cricket nodded. "Do you mind if we come in? We'd like to chat with you."

"Yeah. I guess." Abner moved out of the way to let them into the shop. "I don't have any seats."

Ignacia opened her mouth, likely to point out the two stools sitting beside the work bench, but Cricket shook his head. "That's all right. We'll stand."

Cricket waited, looking around the shop for anything that seemed amiss. Something that didn't fit in with the rest of the items. A book. A candle. A talisman. Something that screamed amplifier. There was nothing. He looked back to Abner, trusting Ignacia to continue searching, and smiled as the boy climbed back up on his stool to gaze at them imperiously.

"What can I help you with, Your Highness?" Abner asked, the cloak on his shoulders sliding down. He grabbed it, pulling it tighter, and there...*that* was it. How hadn't Cricket noticed it before? The brooch pinning the two sides of the cloak together. It was clearly an addition the boy had made, all gaudy and too big. The witch wouldn't have chosen it for herself. It stood out too much, and witches were known, ironically, for their subtlety.

"We heard from some of the people in town that there's

been some strange magic floating around. Chicken pox, lips fused shut, allergies to water, the like. You wouldn't happen to know anything about that, would you?" It wasn't terribly subtle, but Cricket (unlike witches) wasn't known for his subtlety. He tended to face a problem head on, and he didn't think they had time to talk in circles.

Abner stiffened, his eyes flashing to the exit as if he'd like to make a run for it.

"We aren't here to punish you," Cricket said, holding up his hands to show he meant no harm. "We just want to understand why you did those things to them. And maybe help you."

"Help me," Abner repeated, his voice hollow.

Cricket nodded. He looked to Ignacia to see if she'd seen what he had; her eyes were fixed on the brooch. Good. Now, all they had to do was get it away from Abner.

"Yes, help you," Ignacia agreed. She gave Cricket a look as if asking what his plan was, but she wouldn't move until he gave her some kind of signal. He sighed, relieved. He didn't want to set Abner off.

"You know what I think," Cricket said, walking closer to the table, his arms folded behind his back. Abner stiffened further, but then relaxed when he saw that Cricket wasn't reaching to touch or grab for anything. "I think they were bullying you."

"And what if they were?" Abner frowned, clutching the brooch more tightly. "Maybe they got what they deserved then."

"Maybe." Cricket shrugged. "But that's not really for you to decide, is it?"

"What?" Abner's dark eyes narrowed, a faint glow twisting through his fingers around the brooch. Danger. Cricket was pushing him to the edge, he needed to pull back.

"It's just been my experience," Cricket said, taking a step

back. "That bullies always get what's coming to them in the end. But by punishing them yourself, you're really no better than they are. Are you?"

Abner slumped, the glow fading away. "No. I guess not."

"And that's not what your mistress would want you to do, is it?"

Abner shook his head.

"So maybe you should lift the curses you placed on them?" Cricket let his voice flow softly, leading Abner to the right decision, not forcing him to make it. It was better that way, if Abner pulled the magic back himself. If not, Cricket worried about the kind of damage they could do to the poor child by ripping the brooch from him. They might leave him power-less entirely, and that was not Cricket's intention.

Abner nodded with a heavy sigh as if this whole thing had weighed on him more than Cricket knew. Then he murmured the incantation to undo all of his spells, the brooch glowing brighter as he worked. Once it was done, he slumped forward against the bench, breath coming in hard pants.

"It's hurting you," Cricket said, voice still soft. He stepped back toward Abner, telegraphing his motions slowly and deliberately so the boy would see him coming. "Isn't it?"

"I need it." The words were a ghost of Abner's voice. Tired, drained. Maybe drained enough that he wouldn't be able to enact the curse that would make the day start again, but Cricket wasn't going to take that chance.

"Why?"

"I..." Abner sat up, chest still moving too hard, eyes a little hazy. "Without it..."

"You're lonely." Ignacia stepped up to stand beside Cricket. She held out her hand for the brooch. "Lonely and powerless?"

Abner nodded, swallowing loudly. His eyes shimmered in the faint light now, tears sticking to the dark lashes.

"I know what that's like," Ignacia whispered, but she didn't move. She waited, with her hand outstretched, and her eyes firm.

"You do?"

"I do." She offered him a soft smile, one of the ones she reserved for children and bunny rabbits. One of the ones that Cricket rarely saw. "Why don't you give the prince that ugly bit of kit, and I'll tell you about a little girl who didn't have any friends and lost her daddy to the war."

"What happened to her?" Abner reached for the brooch, his fingers fumbling with the clasp. Cricket wanted to help, but this was something Abner had to do. He had to give it up on his own, or it might attack them all. As it was, he kept his eyes fixed on the item to make sure it didn't lash out against the boy.

"She met an idiot prince."

"Hey." Cricket grumbled. "I'm not an idiot."

"Foolish then?"

Cricket huffed, blowing a raspberry at her.

There was a soft wet laugh, and when they looked back Abner had divested himself of the brooch, and was scrubbing at his eyes. "Was he always like this?"

"Oh no, he was much worse when I first met him." Ignacia grinned. Her fingers closed around the brooch, and she held it behind her back for Cricket to take and tuck away into one of the magic sealing pouches Anstice had packed for them. "Come on, let's go grab some pastries from the bakery, and I'll tell you all about it."

Abner slid off his stool.

"You got it from here?" Cricket whispered.

"Yeah, go hunt down your knight." Ignacia gave him a knowing smile. The three walked to the door, and then they parted ways; Ignacia shooting him a wink over her shoulder, and Cricket turning to head toward the inn. It was nearly lunch time, and he knew he'd be able to catch Yoshi there.

THE INN WAS QUIET. It was past breakfast, and not quite lunch yet, so the little restaurant on the first floor was empty but for a few stragglers at the bar. When Cricket walked in, Madam Shen saw him immediately and raced to him.

"Your Highness!" She curtsied lowly.

Cricket bowed his head, offering her a dimpled smile. "You have a knight from Helio staying with you. Has he been in for his midday meal yet?"

"No, sir." She rose, cheeks a little flushed from the motion. "Can I get you a table?"

"Yes, please."

"Our private room is—"

"Oh no, that won't be necessary. It's just me, and I'd hate to take up too much space. Just a spot back in the corner will do nicely, and a pot of tea. Thank you." He waited for her to argue, but she merely nodded and led him back to the back before scuttling off to get his tea. Cricket sat, sipping his tea, and waited.

It wasn't much longer before Yoshi appeared, and took a seat at the table where he'd been when they first met. Cricket smiled a little, vowing to do better this time. He sat down payment for his drink and went over to the chair opposite Yoshi's.

"Sir White Knight," Cricket said, bowing his head a little, a playful twitch at his lips.

Yoshi lifted his eyes to glare at the mocking tone. They widened just a fraction, just enough for Cricket to know that he'd registered the long braid, and the Lunette crest embla-zoned onto the navy-blue tunic that he'd hidden under an oversized scarf the first day. "Prince Cricket."

"See? Now, isn't that a pity?" Cricket clicked his tongue, sitting across from Yoshi and somehow managing to not miss the seat (small mercies), still smiling. "You know my name, but I don't know yours."

"Yoshi." Curt. Direct. Clipped.

"Yoshi." Cricket repeated, ignoring the itching in his palm for his sword. This man had nearly bested him just the day before, and Cricket wanted a rematch for no other reason than to prove he wouldn't be outdone by some pompous knight from across the border. No other reason. "What, may I ask, is a knight from Helio doing in Lunette?"

Yoshi's shoulders pulled back, sitting up straighter, his chin tilting back. "Help."

"Are you asking for it, or looking to give it?" Cricket knew the answer, but he needed to get Yoshi to say it. They couldn't talk about this if he didn't say it.

"Give it."

"Ah. I see." Cricket nodded, tapping the side of his nose. "Well, if it's Tochtli you were intending to help, don't bother. The problem here has been dealt with."

Yoshi's brows lifted just a little, but he didn't speak. Then he rose from his chair and headed for the door in a quick but even stride.

"Here we go again," Cricket muttered to himself, racing after him. "I said it's been handled."

"I will see for myself."

"Can't take the word of a prince?" They were out in the street now and drawing attention. Cricket didn't like it. He didn't want bystanders getting in the way of the fight that was inevitable. But he wasn't going to get a choice. Cricket reached for Yoshi, hoping to stop him before he got too far.

Yoshi spun, sword already drawn, and pointed the tip at Cricket's face. "Stay out of the way."

Cricket laughed, throwing his head back, hair dangling dangerously close to the ground with the motion.

"Stay. Out. Of. The. Way." Yoshi repeated, pressing the tip to the soft palate under Cricket's chin.

"So that's how it'll be then?" Cricket stepped back, unsheathing his sword, and settling comfortably into his stance. "The boy you're after, is under my protection."

"He is dangerous." Yoshi fell into his own stance, lunging for Cricket. Cricket parried quickly, spinning away from the blade with a grin. He'd already fought this fight once; he had a one up on Yoshi.

"He's a child." Cricket felt like he'd said that a million times in just the span of twenty-four hours, and maybe he had. He'd lost count by that point. He pressed forward, cutting through Yoshi's defenses.

"He has cursed people." Yoshi stepped back, blocking his blow.

"He has made mistakes. He is a child." Cricket repeated, sweeping low to swipe for Yoshi's ankles. Yoshi's sword caught his, flinging it backward and Cricket with it for a moment. But he was quick to recover.

"And you would solve it how?"

"I *have solved* it, by speaking with him." Cricket grunted, locking his sword with Yoshi's to keep from taking the brunt of another blow to his arm. He really didn't want to have to treat another wound, and Ignacia would kill him if he came back hacked to ribbons.

"Show me." Yoshi demanded, flinging Cricket backward onto his bottom in the street. Cricket winced at the impact of bone meeting cobblestone.

"You win this one." He wagged a finger at Yoshi, his voice coming out a bit choked from the pain still lingering in his backside, ignoring the pleased tilt of the knight's eyes. "But next time..."

"There will not be a next time." Yoshi breathed, grabbing the hand Cricket had extended, and yanking him to his feet. Cricket let his fingers brush over the softness of Yoshi's gloves at his wrist... he shook himself. "Show me."

Cricket nodded, swallowing sandpaper and dust. Then he grabbed Yoshi's wrist, and dragged the knight behind him. It didn't take long to find Abner and Ignacia. They were sitting at the fountain, laughing with another boy about Abner's age. "There? See? No danger. Just a child."

Yoshi's eyes narrowed, and he made to step over to them, but Cricket steeled his grip and held him back.

"He had an amplifying brooch. He used it to curse a couple of bullies. We think he was just lonely. So, Ignacia dragged him out to make some friends. It looks like she did all right as far as that goes." Cricket grinned, proud.

"And the brooch?"

Cricket dropped Yoshi's wrist to dig into his satchel and pull out the pouch. "He handed it over without much of a fight after lifting the curses. You can ask around. The mothers in town will be able to tell you that everything is well now."

Yoshi pulled out the brooch, turning it over in his fingers carefully.

"So, you see? No bloodshed needed."

Yoshi squinted down at the brooch, then seemed to come to some conclusion before putting the offending piece of tacky jewelry back into the pouch, and holding it out to Cricket. Cricket took it and stuffed it into his bag with everything else. "I will take my leave."

"You don't want to come say hi, at least? The kid is pretty nice. Bit of a brat, but that's most thirteen-year-olds." Cricket grinned at him.

Yoshi shook his head, and before Cricket could argue, he'd turned to leave, disappearing around a corner and down an alley.

"Well. Goodbye to you too." Cricket huffed.

"So that's it then?" Ignacia asked, suddenly right behind him. Cricket yelped, clutching his chest.

"Don't sneak up on me like that!" He straightened his tunic, running his fingers over his hair. "What's what then?"

"You and him. He's just going to disappear after making our job harder."

"That seems to be the measure of it." Cricket shook his head, smiling a little to himself. "We'll see him again, I think."

"You mean you hope we will."

"You said he was handsome too!"

Ignacia snorted.

BOOK III
TIANI

CHAPTER 14

"I think his nose was a little bigger." Ignacia had taken to leaning over in her saddle, watching Cricket sketch, and making a general nuisance of herself. Neither of which did Cricket appreciate.

"You didn't even see him." Cricket grumbled. "Wider or longer?"

"Wider." Ignacia looked pleased with herself. "Abner painted a very good picture with his words."

"I should have just had Abner sit with me while I did this." Cricket huffed. He shut the sketchbook and stuffed it back into his satchel. "He would have been more reliable than a secondhand account."

"Firsthand accounts are never totally reliable."

"More so than secondhand, I'm sure."

"You're awfully grumpy, Your Highness. Does this have anything to do with the fact that the white knight put you on your ass?" He looked over to glare at her. Ignacia was of course, smirking, entirely pleased with herself. "Thought so."

"Tell me again, everything Abner told you." Cricket narrowed his eyes on her thoughtfully.

"We've gone through this three times already." Ignacia whined. She slumped forward on Saber, her shoulders hunching. "And Anstice is just going to make me tell her when she calls."

"Then you'll be well practiced, won't you?"

"You're a horrible taskmaster, Yue Cricket." She shook her finger at him, but there was a smile on her lips. She was...proud of him.... Huh. That felt weird. Ignacia glowing with pride? (Perhaps not quite glowing, but as close to glowing as Ignacia would ever get) He'd never thought he'd see the day, but there it was. He stared long and hard, vowing to sketch it later, for posterity. "All Abner said was that he bought it off some traveling trader. The guy was selling all sorts of junk. Jewelry, books, talismans. He had a big caravan of the stuff, bright blue with flowers painted on the side."

"And didn't know what he had?"

"That's what Abner thought, anyway. It seemed like the man didn't realize that he was carrying an amplifier at all. He gave it to Abner for a couple copper pieces."

"He was headed west?"

Ignacia nodded, pulling the map from her saddle bag to check it again. "You think he's the cause of all this?"

"Honestly?" Cricket sighed, scrubbing at the freckles along his nose. "I don't know. He could be innocent. He might not have known that what he was carrying could hurt people in the wrong hands."

"Or?"

"Or we have a bigger problem." They were still a few hours out from the next village, but they'd been riding for a day already and Cricket was tired. He was tired of sleeping outside. He was tired of the stress of this whole thing. He was tired of losing Ignacia over and over again. He just wanted to rest, and they'd only been gone from the capital a little over a week.

"Let's hope it was an accident."

Cricket did hope. He hoped that the amplifier was just a coincidence. That whatever magic had been used to curse the other towns, cities, and villages was just spells. Spells that would wear off when no longer in direct contact with the magic user. But if they weren't. If they were magically infused items...well...he didn't want to think about the kind of chaos that could cause. Cricket let the conversation lapse; his face pressed into a serious line.

It didn't take long before he found the silence unbearably boring. About an hour. (Beating his previous record by at least ten minutes.) There was much to think of, but he didn't want to stay in his head all day. It wouldn't do either of them any good if he got lost in there.

"Are we there yet?" Cricket whined.

"Another twenty minutes or so." Ignacia didn't even bother to look at him and see the slight pout he'd spread across his face. Which might have been for the better as he didn't think he wanted to be scolded.

"His Highness is hungry."

"His Highness can wait another half an hour until we are settled in Gülay."

"His Highness might starve by then." By that point he was well and truly sulking, poking out his bottom lip, and making his eyes round and glassy. It usually worked on others, but never on Ignacia. Still, he'd never stop trying.

"His Highness will survive longer if he does not test his handmaiden's patience."

Cricket huffed, pulling in his lower lip, and looking ahead again.

THEY MADE it to Gülay without any more mishaps, pouting, or whining. The innkeeper was delighted to have the prince staying with them and offered their largest suites for himself and Ignacia. Excessive. And Cricket didn't see the point in it. He'd never been the type to want to be fawned over, and this whole journey was leaving him frayed with it.

"Just the one, please. We don't need two rooms so long as there are two beds." Cricket smiled serenely at him, shaking his head when the innkeeper opened their mouth to protest. "Really, I mean it. We'd hate to put someone else out of a room just because we were being greedy. Right Iggy?"

The innkeeper looked back at Ignacia who was standing behind Cricket with her arms crossed over her chest, looking thoroughly displeased, as per usual. Their eyes were pleading, asking her for her help.

"There's no use looking at me, he's made up his mind." Ignacia snorted.

Cricket raised a brow and waited. He'd get his way, he usually did. It was just a matter of getting the other person to see sense. Thankfully, it didn't take the innkeeper much longer to come around.

"Yes... yes, Your Highness." The innkeeper grabbed a key from the rack behind them. "You will have a lovely view of the courtyard garden, Your Highness."

"Splendid!" Cricket clapped happily.

Cricket and Ignacia headed up to settle in, taking their time to unpack, or Ignacia unpacked anyhow. Cricket had never much seen the point in unpacking when they'd be leaving again in the morning, but he watched Ignacia hang up her cloak, and pull out her spare clothes to fold neatly into the drawer.

"I'm going down to grab us some supper. Go on and call Anstice to get her caught up," Ignacia said before turning back to head out again.

Cricket flopped onto the bed, pulling off his scarf and slinging it toward the end of the bed, then he pulled the mirror from his satchel.

"Yoohooo, Anstice," he called to the mirror, lounging back on one elbow.

"Cricky." Anstice's face appeared with a wide smile. There were circles under her eyes again, exhaustion seeming to weigh her down, but she looked happy to see him. "How was your journey to Gülay?"

"Well enough. I'm saddle sore from being on my horse for so long." He groaned, leaning back further, and propping the mirror up on a pillow so that he could lay on his belly. "I'm sure Buttercup is happy for the rest."

"I'm sure you all are." Anstice was still smiling, but it didn't quite reach her eyes. "You'll be headed out again in the morning?"

"That's our plan. Is there something wrong at home? How is Father?"

"He's still on bedrest, but the doctor says he should be fine by this time next week. Don't you worry about him, I'm taking good care of him. You worry about our people."

"Are you sure he's all right? I could come home. Iggy can do this on her own.... Or we could send someone else." A knot had formed in his stomach, he wasn't sure when, but it was there now, and it would probably remain until he had seen Father for himself. Weighing down his insides like lead.

"Cricket," Anstice said seriously, the smile falling from her lips so she could give him her full attention. "You trust me, don't you?"

Cricket nodded, fists clenching in the pillow under his chin. He did trust Anstice. He trusted Anstice with his life, with Father's life, with Uncle's life, with his kingdom. Anstice had never been anything but good to him, and he had no reason to think that she would lie to him.

"Then trust that your father will be fine under my care."

"Okay." It was a struggle to get the word out with his tongue feeling like it had stuck to the roof of his mouth all of the sudden, but he managed. "Okay."

"Good." Anstice let her shoulders relax, her face calming into a small grin. Not happy or joyous like the ones Cricket had known all his life but it was enough. "Now, you're off to Taini next."

"So you said." Cricket rolled to grab Ignacia's journal, which had become his own, from his bag, as well as his pencil. "You said you'd have more for us by the time we got here."

"And I do." Anstice stepped away from the mirror for a moment, and Cricket could hear her digging through something at her desk before the victorious crow of, "Ah there it is!"

Cricket laughed, scribbling the word Taini on top of the page. Notes were good, they'd keep him from forgetting things. Most things. Or at least he hoped they would. She moved to sit in front of the mirror again, a few sheets of loose paper in her hands. "You know it's going to take us at least a fortnight to get to Taini."

"I do. But if you could cut down on that time..." Anstice sighed. "They really need your help, Cricket."

Cricket pulled out the map again, chewing on the inside of his cheek as he plotted the road from Gülay to Taini. "We could cut it down by a couple of days if we don't travel the main road through the towns, and camp out instead. But Iggy isn't going to love that idea."

"No. She probably won't." Anstice's shoulders sagged. She looked like she'd aged since the last time they'd seen each other. Maybe it was more than just Father's illness...maybe there was something else...something... No. Cricket had to focus. If he let himself worry too much, they'd never make it to Taini because he'd turn them around and head home.

"How urgent is their need?" He had started scribbling a little bunny rabbit into the corner of his Taini page, to calm his nerves. It didn't help like doodling usually did. It was a very cute bunny, even still.

"They've had several people get hurt. Nothing life threatening yet, but it's just a matter of time." There was heaviness to her words, Anstice was worried. Far more worried than she'd been about a whole disappearing town. It settled like a stone in the pit of Cricket's stomach, right alongside the lead.

"Iggy will just have to get over it then." He scrubbed at the tip of his nose. Ignacia wouldn't like that he had made that decision without her, but he didn't see where they had much choice. People were getting hurt; it was their job to stop that from happening. That was all there was to it. "What do your sources say?"

Vaguely, Cricket heard the door creak open to let Ignacia back in with their tray of food. He waved to her to sit everything on the short table in the middle of the room, hunger momentarily forgotten.

"The citizens say it's a ghost—"

"A ghost?!" Ignacia yelped, dropping the tray. Cricket winced at the sound of dishes shattering.

"A ghost stag," Anstice continued as if she hadn't been interrupted. "It's beguiling the men, and some of the women. Leading them out on hunts at all hours of the night that end in many of them hurt."

"We're not going after a ghost." Ignacia announced, her strides taking her to the bed Cricket was happily splayed across. She snatched up the mirror to look at Anstice, her hands shaking, and her face pale. Cricket had seen her frightened plenty of times in his life (mostly when there were spiders), but this was a new level of fear. "I will not go after a ghost."

"We don't know that it *is* a ghost, Iggy. Calm down,"

Cricket soothed, taking the mirror from her tight grasp. "It's probably another curse, like the one we dealt with in Tochtli."

His words did nothing to calm Ignacia, who had begun to tremble where she stood. Cricket pulled her into a one-armed hug, pressing her face into his chest.

"I don't think it is a ghost," Anstice said, her own voice soft and soothing. "I think it's a white stag. A manifestation of someone's magic that they either don't know how to control or are deliberately using to hurt people."

"We won't make you chase the ghost stag until we're sure it's not a ghost, promise." Cricket held up his hand, fingers pressed together in an oath. He never broke a promise, ever. "Until then, I'll deal with it."

"Ghosts aren't real." Anstice rolled her eyes.

"Not helping, Annie," Cricket hissed. "You know how she gets."

"Fine. Fine." Anstice grumbled. "That's all I have for you, unless you have something for me?"

"We do. Iggy fill Anstice in on everything Abner told you. I'm going to get this cleaned up and get us some more supper." He pressed a kiss to the crown of her head, gave her another firm squeeze, and waited until she nodded to pull away and gather their ruined dinner.

AFTER SUPPER, and plenty of conversation with Anstice about everything they were missing back home, Ignacia went out into the courtyard. Cricket could see her through the window as she practiced with her bow.

"Iggy said you met a white knight," Anstice teased, her

expression soft. He hated it when they gossiped about him, but he supposed it was better than the alternative which was Ignacia letting herself dwell in her fear.

"She told you that, did she?" Cricket huffed, ignoring the blush he could feel creeping up the back of his neck, and thanking Selene for his long hair.

"She did. She said he was terribly handsome. Did this charmer who put you on your butt in the middle of the town square have a name?"

"He didn't—" Cricket growled through his teeth. "Okay he did put me on my butt. But that doesn't make Yoshi a charmer. He was just... I was just distracted all right? He won't get the better of me next time."

"Yoshi?" Anstice's neatly plucked brows wrinkled in the middle.

"Yes. That's who he introduced himself as. Which I thought was strange, usually knights are all 'I'm Lord Fancypants of the Gilder Fancypanstses.' But he just said his name was Yoshi." Cricket's eyes flicked from the mirror back out the window. Ignacia was still outside, but she'd stopped and turned to glare at the stone bench for some reason.

"Yoshi... Yoshi... Yoshi..." Anstice said as she tapped her fan to her lips. "Why does that name sound familiar?"

Cricket shrugged.

Anstice looked up suddenly, eyes wide, and mouth open. "You don't mean Takayoshi, do you?"

"No. He said it was Yoshi." Cricket didn't look at Anstice, he was focused on Ignacia who had...who had drawn her sword. Hopefully not on another innocent spider. "Anstice, I've got to go. Iggy is..."

Ignacia lunged toward the bench, presumably to end the existence of whatever she'd taken a dislike to.

"Oh no."

"Wait! Cricky, I think you ought to be nice to this Yoshi. Try not to cross him."

Cricket stopped mid-leap to his feet and crouched to look at Anstice in the mirror again. "Don't cross him? What? Why?"

"I think he might be—"

"DIE you eight-legged beast!" Ignacia's war cry carried through the open window. And that was his cue.

"No time! Tell me later! Send Father and Uncle my love!" Cricket blew a hasty kiss and waved his hand over the mirror to sever the connection. "Iggy! You leave that spider alone! He didn't do anything to you!"

CHAPTER 15

There were still two more full days to their journey when Anstice contacted them.

"Someone died. The stag led them right off a cliff in the woods," she said through panicked breaths, eyes wild and glassy with unshed tears. "You have to get there, quick."

They rode through the night after that, only stopping for brief breaks to let the horses drink. It wasn't the ideal way to travel, by any means, but they made it to Tiani just after breakfast on the second day. By that point Cricket was aching everywhere, and he was so hungry his vision was starting to grow fuzzy around the edges.

"You get us a table at the inn, and I'll take the horses to the stables," he said, not giving Ignacia a chance to respond before he'd slid down off Buttercup and grabbed both her and Saber's reins.

"Should I start asking questions?" Ignacia asked when her feet were firmly on the ground again. She took a couple of steps toward the inn, a limp to her gait. Cricket didn't have to see himself to know he was probably limping too. Somewhere around lunchtime the previous day his right calf had cramped up so much he'd be an old man before he stopped walking funny.

"No. Let's get some food in us first, and rest for a bit. We can start on questions after lunch. I doubt this ghost stag is out during the day." He shook his head, pointedly ignoring Ignacia when she opened her mouth to protest. He wasn't in the mood, and he wasn't sure he ever would be in the mood again. At least not until after he'd had a long hot bath that loosened his muscles and left his skin pink. A luxury that was unfortunately, probably not in the cards for him.

A thought that was only confirmed when he caught sight of the White Knight exiting the stables ahead of him. It just had to be the White Knight, didn't it? They just had to be on the same path, didn't they? Where had he gone wrong? What was fate punishing him for? Maybe he'd been a murderer in a past life...

"Your Highness," Yoshi said, his tone just as stiff and stilted as it was the first time they'd spoken. He bowed formally.

Cricket pulled on a dimpled smile like he'd pull on a good tunic. Letting it wash over him to hide the aches, and the weariness that had settled into his bones long before the last day of hard travel had begun. He tilted his head, making sure to keep his gait steady as he walked toward the stables.

"White Knight," he said in return. He didn't bow, he didn't duck his head, he just met Yoshi's sunshine golden eyes head on. "I thought you were headed to Ilkay to slay a dragon?"

"I was needed here." Yoshi's eyes had narrowed thoughtfully, as if he were trying to remember telling Cricket about that. And that...that was worrisome. When had Yoshi said that to him? Had it been the first conversation or the second? Ignacia didn't remember anything from the various repeats, so of course Yoshi wouldn't either. He had to think of something. He had to cover.

"Yeah, me too," was what his mouth said. Traitorous thing that it was didn't seem to want to provide anything useful these days. "I mean... I was needed...umm...I was needed here too."

Yoshi nodded, seeming to accept that as the truth. But he still looked troubled by something.

"Well, let's try not to step on each other's toes, huh?" Cricket rallied.

Yoshi just looked at him some more. It was becoming increasingly alarming how one sided it was to converse with the white knight. It left Cricket feeling unbalanced, and wrong footed. He was used to the give and take of conversation with his family. This. This was... Frustrating.

"Right. Good talk." Cricket laughed, patting Yoshi's shoulder as he walked by with Buttercup and Saber behind him.

"We should work together," Yoshi said. His voice was still just as stiff, just as stilted, but there was a hush to it then.

"I'm sorry?" Cricket turned around where he stood in the door to the stable. It wasn't that he was trying to embarrass Yoshi, for all it might seem that he was. It was simply that he wasn't sure he'd heard right. The man who had accused him of getting in the way in Tochtli was asking to work together? Cricket cocked his head, reassessing Yoshi in this new light. He looked...he looked unsure. Like he was afraid that Cricket would say no. And huh. Wasn't that just weird? The stone-cold white knight afraid of rejection.

Yoshi took a breath and straightened his spine more (as if that were possible, his posture was impeccable. Really, who taught him how to stand? Monks?).

"I would like to work with the prince and his...." Yoshi drifted off. He was struggling with the words, whatever they were. If he were a more expressive man, someone like Cricket for example, Cricket could see Yoshi waving his hand around to try to indicate what he was saying. But Yoshi was not more expressive. So he just stared at Cricket, begging him with his eyes to fill in the blank.

"Ignacia?"

"Yes. His Ignacia." Yoshi nodded.

"You can just call her Ignacia, and you can just call me Cricket." Cricket laughed.

"You are the prince." Flat. The words were flat. But there was a twitch of Yoshi's brows, as if they wanted to come together in the middle in confusion.

"Yeah. I am. And I'm saying you can call me Cricket."

"But..." Yoshi was struggling again. Trying to put words to whatever inner turmoil he seemed to be having. And as much as Cricket would have loved to stand there and watch Yoshi flounder, his stomach had started to ache from lack of food, and he really did need to sit down before he *fell* down. So, he took pity on Yoshi.

"If we're going to work together, we should call each other by our names." Cricket turned back to the stable and led the horses inside. He half expected for Yoshi to follow him and continue to voice whatever misgivings he had about being so informal with royalty, but he didn't.

Instead, Cricket found Yoshi waiting for him when he exited the stables.

"I shall accompany Prince Cricket—"

"Just Cricket."

"I shall accompany Cricket," Yoshi amended, though it looked like it pained him. "To the inn. If we are to work together, we should..."

Yoshi did that thing again, where he looked like he had more thoughts than words. He gripped the sword at his side hard enough to turn his knuckles white as he struggled.

Well, this would either be terribly amusing, or dreadfully awkward.

"We should talk about our first steps." Cricket supplied helpfully. "Iggy already got us a table at the inn. We haven't had anything to eat since lunch yesterday. You're welcome to join us."

Yoshi nodded.

Ignacia was going to love this. Now, Cricket just had to survive the inevitable teasing about the handsome white knight teaming up with them. If he died from embarrassment, he'd haunt Yoshi forever.

The tavern on the ground floor of the inn was quiet when they entered. Ignacia had gotten a table at the back of the space and ordered tea as well as a cheese tray to start. Cricket strode quickly across the space, not noticing as Yoshi seemed to hesitate, before Cricket flopped down across from Ignacia.

"Iggy, my love, you're a dream. You'll marry me, won't you?" Cricket asked, grabbing a piece of cheese, and bread off the tray and stuffing what was arguably two bites into his mouth.

"Don't be gross." Ignacia snorted. She swatted his hand as he reached for another bite to stuff in with the first. "Chew and swallow. I'm not saving you if you choke to death from your own idiocy."

Cricket pouted, but he took his time chewing the contents of his cheeks and swallowing before grabbing another bite. "So cruel to me. My own sister wouldn't save my life if I were choking!"

"You—" Ignacia stopped. Her jaw dropped, and her eyes went comically wide. Who knew they could get that wide? Not Cricket. She let out a soft croaking sound that was a cross between confused, and alarmed.

"What're you—?" Cricket turned to look up at Yoshi standing awkwardly beside the table. He looked as alarmed and confused as Ignacia had sounded. Like he wanted to sit, but didn't think he should without introducing himself, or bowing, or doing something else that decorum clearly dictated, and Cricket ignored for his own sanity. "Oh, Yoshi is going to be teaming up with us for this one."

Ignacia blinked. Shook her head. Blinked again. Looked from Cricket to Yoshi. Looked from Yoshi to Cricket. "I'm sorry, I think I just hallucinated from all the horseback riding. I thought you just said the white knight was working with us."

"Sit. Sit." Cricket grabbed at Yoshi's sky-blue tunic to urge him into the seat beside himself. Yoshi looked down at Cricket, his expression almost blank. Almost. But for a slight widening of the eyes that might have been panic. "Come on. I'm sure you're tired and hungry. You have to have been riding as long as we have. Sit."

It took another moment of tugging, and coaxing, but eventually Yoshi sat beside him. His back was straight, and he was sitting on the very edge of the chair. But he was sitting, and Cricket counted that as a victory.

"So. Like I said, Yoshi will be working with us. Stop looking at me like that, Iggy." He grabbed a grape from the tray and threw it at her. It pinged off the skin just above her eyebrow and went rolling, which earned him a glare. Progress! "I figure since someone has already died, it's probably better if we have as much help as we can get."

"Right." Ignacia sounded skeptical. She grabbed the tea pot and poured each of them a cup.

Cricket decided to ignore the skepticism and forge ahead. He'd deal with Ignacia's teasing after they saved Taini from the ghost stag. "Have you heard anything while you've been sitting here?"

"No. The only waitress working right now didn't know anything." Ignacia was all business again. She grabbed an olive from the tray to eat and chewed thoughtfully. "We might have better luck with the man who runs the inn."

"Annie did say that most of the victims were men."

"Annie?" Yoshi asked, and Cricket jumped. He'd almost forgotten the white knight was there.

"Anstice. She's the royal advisor," Ignacia said around her half chewed olive.

Yoshi lapsed back into silence sipping from his teacup.

"All right, so after we eat, let's split up." Cricket leaned forward, pulling the journal from his bag. "Iggy, you question the innkeeper while you secure rooms for us... Oh. Yoshi, do you already have a room?"

Yoshi nodded.

"Just one room then." Cricket tapped his pencil on the side of the journal. Anstice hadn't been able to provide them with much, but it was something. Enough so that he knew where he wanted to start. "You handle that, and Yoshi and I will go and speak to the victim's family."

Ignacia quirked a brow, her expression speaking louder than any words could. It asked, *Oh, is that how it's going to be?*

Cricket sighed. He didn't have the fight in him for that particular argument. "Would you like for Yoshi to go with you then? Because I can question the family alone if that's what you want."

"No. You take him. Since you two seem to be such good friends all of a sudden."

Cricket was not going to dignify that with an answer. He was not. He grabbed another grape and chucked it at Ignacia's head.

She ducked.

CHAPTER 16

While they ate, Ignacia had very helpfully formulated a list of interview questions to ask the victims and their families. And Cricket had very sensibly decided not to use them. Oh sure, he wrote them down, and nodded his head very seriously as if he might.

But the moment they were out of sight, he folded the sheet of paper up into a tiny triangle and stuck it into his satchel where it would no doubt disappear as all small things did.

Yoshi blinked at him, something close to a frown twitching at one side of his mouth. More like a wrinkle than a frown really. Like when your tunic folds in on itself oddly.

"What is it?" Cricket asked. He folded his hands behind his back as they walked toward the address the innkeeper had supplied them with.

"The questions..." Yoshi sounded conflicted. He didn't seem sure if he should contradict Cricket, or let Cricket get away with whatever harebrained idea he had in his head. Not that it would matter which he decided, if Yoshi would learn anything from this interaction it was that Cricket very often followed through with whatever scheme he had in mind. Whether people agreed with it, or not.

"If I show up with a piece of paper in my hands, all ready to ask people who just lost their son a litany of questions about it, how likely are they to throw us out of their house, prince or not?" He looked over at Yoshi who still seemed to be struggling for what was the right answer in this circumstance. When the silence stretched on too long for Cricket to handle, he answered his own question. "People in grief don't want to feel like they're under an inquisition. Trust me, it'll work out better if we let the conversation lead us instead of the other way round."

"I..."

"Do you trust me?" Cricket stopped and turned to look at Yoshi, his hands braced on his hips.

"What?" The wrinkle at the corner of Yoshi's mouth was threatening to become a real frown now.

"Do you trust me?" Cricket repeated. He didn't move. He would wait. He would wait for Yoshi's answer. Because this partnership would never work if Yoshi didn't trust him. Even if it wasn't implicit. There still had to be some trust there.

Yoshi thought for a moment, the frown-wrinkle flattening out before he nodded, seeming to surprise even himself.

"Good." Cricket smiled. His hands fell away from his hips, and he turned to head back the way they were going.

"Prince..." Yoshi stopped, shaking his head for a moment. "Cricket."

"Yeah?"

"Do you trust me?"

Cricket looked over at Yoshi. He brushed his tongue across his teeth and gave it some thought. Yoshi had wanted to use a sword on a child. So much so that he'd caused a village to be locked in a loop for at least a week. But ultimately, he was a knight. He must have had some kind of moral code. Even if it was oddly black and white. He was trying to do the right thing, it just happened that they didn't agree on what the right thing was.

"I don't know yet," Cricket answered honestly. He didn't want to lie to Yoshi. He didn't want to say something that wouldn't be true, just because it would be beneficial. He knew Yoshi meant well, but that didn't mean he trusted the other man. Still, meaning well would be enough for a start.

The frown-wrinkle was back, but Yoshi didn't protest, he just nodded. As if Cricket not trusting him was totally fair, and reasonable, and logical. Which it was, but Yoshi didn't have to agree with it.

"But..." Cricket huffed out a breath, making the loose strands of hair on his forehead flutter upwards. "Lots of things change. I don't see why this shouldn't be one of them."

Yoshi didn't say anything, but at least his mouth had returned to an impassive line. Still, there was something in his eyes, under the calm. Determination, if Cricket's guess was right, and it usually was.

"Here we are." He stopped in front of a little cabin under a willow tree. "What did the innkeeper say their family name was again?"

"Everett."

"Ah yes, thank you, Yoshi. What would I do without you?" Cricket teased, turning to knock on the door before he could see Yoshi's reaction.

An older woman with greying hair, and soft eyes opened the door. Her brow knit in confusion as she took in the prince on her doorstep, and the knight beside him.

"Misses Everett, I'm Prince Cricket." Cricket's tone was polite. He offered her a bow; his expression somber. "My companion, Yoshi, and I are here to investigate what happened to your son. Do you mind if we come in?"

"I..." Misses Everett blinked, awestruck for a moment, and then she nodded quickly. "Yes. Of course. Of course. I'll make you some tea."

"There is no—" Yoshi started.

"That would be wonderful, ma'am. We'd really appreciate it." Cricket cut him off and shook his head when Misses Everett had turned to busy herself in the small kitchen.

"Make yourselves comfortable, please," she said, waving to the sitting room.

Cricket sprawled onto the couch, slumping back into the soft cushions with a sigh. Yoshi sat beside him, back straight, hands folded neatly in his lap. He looked like he wanted to say something. Maybe scold Cricket for asking the woman to make them tea when they'd clearly just had lunch and didn't need anything. But Cricket wasn't paying him any attention. Instead, his eyes were flicking around the little sitting room. There were small masculine touches, a worn pair of boots at the door, a scratchy looking jacket on the hook, but nothing to say that a man owned the home or spent any significant amount of time there, other than visiting.

Misses Everett came back with the tea tray and set it on the table in front of them. Cricket quickly returned his gaze to her, and offered her a small, grateful smile.

"Thank you very much. It's been a very long journey." Cricket leaned in to pour his own tea, but she swatted his hands away and poured it herself before holding out a cup for each of them. "Ah, thank you."

"I had heard the prince was in town." She settled back into an old armchair, her feet dangling a couple inches off the ground. Cricket should have expected as much, but he didn't think he'd ever get used to how quickly word seemed to spread in places that were not the capital.

"We only just arrived in Taini this morning."

"You're here about the ghost stag."

Cricket nodded, setting down his teacup after taking a dainty little sip. "We are. Was your son a hunter?"

"Evan? Oh no. He never went out on the hunts." She shook her head, taking a sip from her own cup. There was something far away and a little lost in her expression, but she quickly replaced it with anger. "It was just that...that damned ghost."

"Do you know about when it started appearing?" Cricket grabbed the journal from his satchel and stopped before pulling it out. "I'm sorry, do you mind if I take some notes?"

"If it'll help kill that thing." Misses Everett frowned, swallowing around something sharp, her eyes watering with it. "Go ahead."

"Thank you." Cricket nodded again and pulled out the journal to perch it on his knee.

He ignored the way Yoshi watched him, a question in his gaze. As if to say, *oh? You won't use Ignacia's questions because you don't want a piece of paper on your lap, huh?*

"When did it start appearing?"

"About a fortnight ago," she said thoughtfully. "It just wandered out of the woods one day."

"And you've never had any prior hauntings in Taini?"

"No. Not as far as I know."

Cricket scribbled this across the page. "You said it was just the stag? That Evan had never hunted before?"

Something tired crossed her features, and she sagged a little in her chair. "Evan's father had been a hunter when we'd first gotten married. But when Evan was young, Connor had an accident in the woods. He never quite recovered, and we lost him before Evan reached his tenth name day."

"I'm so sorry." Cricket reached across the space between them, nearly knocking over his teacup in the process. But he took her hand and gripped it lightly. "If there is anything we can do..."

"Just...just make it stop," Misses Everett croaked out around a throat thick with tears. "Whatever it is. Don't let it take anyone else's child."

"We will not," Yoshi said with a certainty that threw Cricket.

"We won't," Cricket agreed, giving Misses Everett's hand another light squeeze before retreating back to his seat. "I just have a couple more questions. Is that all right, or have you had enough?"

"No. I want to help." She nodded, scrubbing at her eyes. When her hand came away, they looked sharper. "What do you need?"

"Where did Evan live?"

"He had a small cottage on the outskirts of town, near the woods. If you want to go to his place, I can give you the key." She moved to stand, and Cricket stalled her with a little wave.

"No. That won't be necessary. But the address would be helpful. I have one more question though."

Misses Everett nodded, settling back into her chair.

"Has there been a traveling trader through town lately? Maybe shortly before the stag appeared? We're told he looked a little like this..." Cricket grabbed his sketchbook to flip to the half-finished sketch of the man he'd been working on with Ignacia. He didn't move quick enough to tear the pages passing the portrait of Yoshi, but it was a near thing. "He was in a blue wagon."

"Now that you mention it... There was someone. He had a cart full of junk. I didn't get a good look at him, but the wagon was green, with flowers on it." She frowned. "I'm sorry I can't be of more help."

"You've been a huge help! Thank you, Misses Everett." He offered her his most dimpled smile, and it seemed to lighten the load on her shoulders. By the time they had finished their tea, and gotten the address, she was smiling back tentatively.

The door shut behind them softly, and Cricket started toward the address of Evan Everett.

"The trader?" Yoshi asked, keeping his strides carefully in sync with Cricket's.

"Abner bought that amplifying brooch off an old man selling a bunch of stuff out of his wagon. He didn't think the man knew what he had." Cricket shrugged. "It's a hunch."

"A hunch."

"Yeah, a hunch. I don't have any hard evidence, but two traders with wagons full of bits and bobs passing through before the town starts to experience strange magical activity hardly seems like a coincidence. I'll have someone help me draw up a..." Cricket stopped before a weathered announcement board in the middle of town. On it were stapled advertisements for town events, the hours of the weekly market, and someone selling kittens. But that wasn't what caught his eye. What caught his eye was the portrait of the beautiful blonde woman. She was smiling in it, her eyes crinkled as her long hair flitted around her. Above the portrait in big bold letters was the word MISSING.

"Another hunch?" Yoshi sounded annoyed.

"Maybe." Cricket carefully pulled the paper from its staples and folded it up to put in his bag. "We'll ask around and see who this Mister Cannan is."

"Why?"

Cricket didn't have a good answer for that. He didn't know why the picture of the young woman had stopped him in his tracks. Or why her disappearance seemed so strange. So instead of answering he turned around, walking backwards to keep his eyes fixed on Yoshi's blank face.

"Say Yoshi..."

"Hm?"

"Why did you decide to work with us?"

Yoshi's eyes flicked to him, then back to the path in front of them. He didn't look like he was going to answer.

"Not that I'm not grateful, what I said at the inn is true. We could use the extra hands, and maybe the extra sword if things get messy. But you don't seem to like me very much, so I can't see you enjoying this particular partnership." Cricket stumbled a little on a root, his steps faltering, and arms swinging out to cartwheel in an attempt to keep his balance. But alas it was no good. He was going to...

Yoshi grabbed his wrist. "Walk properly."

"Right. Thanks, Yoshi." Cricket laughed, pulling his arm back to himself when Yoshi dropped it. And that was the end of that.

CHAPTER 17

Evan Everett's home, as it turned out, held no significance other than that it was a respectable little cabin in a lush cluster of trees where Evan Everett had lived when he wasn't visiting his mother or working at the miller's. Yoshi stood next to (not leaned against because he seemed too upright and proper to lean) one of the trees in the yard while Cricket took a third lap around the cabin. Cricket scratched his chin, his steps measured as he followed his own tracks around.

"It's strange," he said by way of greeting when he'd finished his latest lap.

"Hm?" Yoshi asked. His eyes hadn't left Cricket, which would normally be enough to make Cricket self-conscious, but not when there was a mystery to solve.

"There are no tracks here. Not even his own. You'd think if he was hunting something, he'd have followed it into the wood here."

"Strange."

Cricket wasn't sure if Yoshi was agreeing, poking fun, or questioning, but either way Cricket shook his head. "There aren't even any animal tracks. This close to the forest there should be some animal tracks. Even if it's just bunnies."

"Would a ghost leave tracks?" That sounded like a genuine question, even if it was an utterly ridiculous one.

"Well. No. But you don't really think this is a ghost, do you?" Cricket frowned, tilting his head as he looked at Yoshi. His eyes flickered over the other man. Taking in his upright posture, and his firm stance that grounded him to the earth. He didn't seem the type to believe in such things.

"No." Yoshi was still staring at the cabin as if he would see something that Cricket had missed. Maybe he would, that was the good thing about having two sets of eyes after all. Sometimes one person alone could miss something that the other would catch. Usually, it was Ignacia who caught it, and she positively delighted in seeing something Cricket did not.

"Ah, so that was a purely philosophical question then!" Cricket laughed, shaking his head. "Did you notice anything?"

Yoshi settled his gaze on Cricket and nodded just minutely.

"Well? Out with it!" Cricket crowed. "Wild speculation. Off the wall theories. That's how we get to the truth of a thing in the end."

Yoshi gave him a look as if to ask: *it is?* But didn't say as much.

Cricket folded his hands behind his back, rocking back on his heels, and settled in to wait. He wasn't a very patient person, but he could wait for someone who was trying to find their words. Besides, he thought it only fair since Yoshi decided he wanted to work with them.

Yoshi pursed his lips a little, meeting Cricket's eyes. He looked like he didn't want to talk. Like he'd have sooner swallowed his words down than let them be heard. But Cricket was going to wait. Whether Yoshi liked it or not, they would stand there all day if he needed to.

"He does not seem to spend much time here," Yoshi said when it seemed that Cricket was not going to give him an out.

Cricket smiled brightly, rocking forward onto his toes, and probably getting much too close to Yoshi for the other man's liking. "You're right! So, he probably came into contact with the stag elsewhere! Maybe at the miller's."

Yoshi nodded.

"That's genius, Yoshi! Let's go check around the miller's for tracks. Then we should head back to the inn to regroup with Ignacia before dusk." Cricket leaped forward, heedless of Yoshi's personal space, took hold of Yoshi's wrist and tugged him back toward the center of town.

"Dusk?"

"Yes, from our reports the stag doesn't appear until the sun sets. So, we have another couple of hours to wait. Then we can see the thing in person, I suppose."

Cricket didn't realize he was still holding Yoshi's wrist until they were out in front of the miller's. Then he dropped it, laughing nervously. Yoshi didn't seem to notice, or if he did, he was too polite to say anything. Probably the latter. The miller, a middle-aged young woman with washed out blue eyes, and a tired smile met them out front.

"Your Highness!" she yelped and fell into a wobbly curtsy.

"Ah... Haha," Cricket laughed awkwardly, returning the gesture with a well-practiced bow. "Misses..."

"Devorah. Miss Devorah," she supplied, a hint of a blush painting her cheeks.

"Miss Devorah." Cricket smiled, dimple and all. "Would you mind if my companion and I ask you some questions, Miss Devorah?"

"I wouldn't mind at all." She returned the smile, a blush spreading across her nose. "I'd... uh... I'd offer for you to come in. But the workshop is kind of a mess with-out...without Evan."

Something lingered at the edges of her words. There was something she wasn't saying. Cricket narrowed his eyes trying to figure out what it was, and then he saw the sheen of tears on her eyes. Ah. That was it then.

"Out here is just fine, Miss Devorah." Cricket folded his hands behind his back, and relaxed his posture, his shoulders hunching a little.

Yoshi cut him a questioning look, but Cricket ignored it.

"Oh, wonderful." Miss Devorah's own shoulders loosened, and her smile became a little less pinched. It might have looked like she was hiding something, but Cricket had a suspicion all she was hiding was grief. "What do you want to know?"

"Evan's mother said he wasn't a hunter, but he hunted the stag. Do you have any idea why?"

"No." She shook her head frowning. "No one who has hunted that thing and been hurt by it has really had a reason. It just... They just catch sight of it, and off they go. We were...we were..."

"Take your time, Miss Devorah," Cricket said softly.

"I'm sorry." She sniffled, scrubbing at her eyes a little. "I'm sorry."

"There's no need to apologize. You're allowed to be sad. You're allowed to miss him."

Miss Devorah scrubbed more at her eyes. "Thank you."

"Of course." He offered her a soft smile and waited.

When Miss Devorah had control of her tears again, she sucked in a shaking inhale, and lifted her chin. "Evan and I were out for a walk that evening. We didn't usually go out after dark, but we'd had a lot of work that day, and then with clean up...."

"A little later than usual," Cricket said, and she nodded in agreement. "Go on. Please."

"And then it just appeared, or maybe it rounded a corner and came from the center of town? I'm not really sure." She frowned, her hands twisting in front of the thick canvas apron draped around her hips. "But...Evan looked at it, and it was like he wasn't really seeing anymore. He made this sound...like...like a sigh? And then he ran toward it. It turned and ran away, and he chased. I shouted after him but...but he wouldn't...he wouldn't..."

"He couldn't stop," Cricket whispered in understanding.

"I don't think he even wanted to anymore. It was like there was nothing else for him outside of that thing."

"Can you describe what it looks like? People are calling it a ghost, but we aren't sure that it is one."

"I don't think it was a ghost. It was solid. But it glowed. Maybe it *was* a ghost? I'm not sure. It just looked like a glowing white stag."

"Antlers?"

She nodded.

"Thank you, Miss Devorah. You've been very helpful."

Their goodbyes said, Cricket and Yoshi made their way back toward the inn. Yoshi was pointedly silent, his steps in sync with Cricket's. His chin was held up high, and he'd pursed his lips together just lightly.

"If you have a question, ask it," Cricket said, looking back to the street in front of them.

"You did not ask about the nature of her relationship with Evan Everett." It was less a question and more a statement, but Cricket was going to take it as one.

"Should I have?"

"It was not strictly professional."

"No, it was not. She was in love with him. I imagine if

he'd lived another six months, he might have gotten up the courage to ask her to marry him."

Yoshi looked at him, brow creasing just the slightest in the middle.

"You thought because I didn't say that I didn't notice? I noticed."

"Why did you not say as much?"

"She was already hurting enough."

Yoshi nodded, turning back to the road ahead. No more was said, no more needed be, in Cricket's opinion, until they reached the inn. Cricket gave Ignacia a recount of everything they had learned as they ordered their meals. By the time their food arrived, he'd told her everything from their conversations with Misses Everett, Miss Devorah, and what little they'd learned at Evan's cottage.

"Please tell me you had some luck with the traveling trader angle." Cricket slumped further back into his chair, lifting his glass to his lips.

"No one in the inn was here when he came through, and none of the staff purchased anything from him." Ignacia shook her head. "And I don't know that it was the same man. The descriptions I got from everyone were drastically different than what Abner gave us."

"So it was just a coincidence that both the affected towns have had a trader selling random items out of a wagon come through?"

"There are quite a lot of that kind of person, Cricket. I know we don't get many of them in the capital, but they do exist. It's very likely that it's a different person." Ignacia's tone was reasonable. It grated on Cricket's nerves. There was something connecting them, he knew there was. But he had no way to prove it. And wasn't that just a pickle?

"Yoshi. You agree with me, surely?" Cricket asked, looking

to the white knight who until then had been eating quietly. "It can't just be a coincidence."

"It can," Ignacia said, rolling her eyes. "And it probably is."

"Yooooshi."

Yoshi looked between them. The frown-wrinkle was back, tugging at the corner of his lips helplessly. On anyone else, the expression would be one of panic.

"Ah ha. No, never mind. You don't have to pick a side, Yoshi. Just finish your dinner," Cricket said, taking pity on him, and patting his hand lightly.

Yoshi ducked his head back to his food where he didn't have to participate in the conversation.

"So, what's next then?" Ignacia asked.

"Next, we go out tonight and see if we see the stag." Cricket shrugged.

"That's it? That's your grand plan? We go out, we see the stag, and hope it doesn't lead us off a cliff, or into the lake, or worse?"

"Well...it's not an exact science..." Cricket hedged.

"It's not science at all! It's a disaster waiting to happen!" Ignacia threw her hands up.

"The stag doesn't affect everyone. Odds are at least one of us won't be drawn in."

"And what about the other two? Will that one person be tasked with babysitting them?"

"Like I said, it's not an exact science."

"Ugh!"

CHAPTER 18

For all her griping, Ignacia stood beside Cricket as they walked out into the fading summer sun, ready to face the stag. She may not have thought it was a good idea (she'd made that abundantly clear), but she also hadn't proposed a better solution.

"We'll watch each other's backs," Cricket said.

"Right." Ignacia grumbled, her eyes flicking back to Yoshi who had remained eerily silent through their planning session. His silence might have bothered Ignacia more than it bothered Cricket, but only just. "Where should we start?"

"Miss Devorah said she and Evan were out for a stroll when the stag found them. The Miller's isn't far, let's start there, and walk in the direction of the center of town. Maybe we'll come across it just like they did."

"I'm hearing a lot of maybes, and ifs," Ignacia mumbled under her breath.

"I'm sorry. Do you have a better idea? I suppose we could wait until we've interviewed more victims, but by then it might have led someone else to their death. Besides, I need to see this thing for myself. It's not a ghost, but it's definitely magical." Cricket crossed his arms over his chest but didn't let his steps falter. She was right, perhaps they should have been being a little more cautious, especially after what had happened in Tochtli. But Cricket had never been the cautious type. "We'll be careful, Iggy. Don't worry."

"I'm not worried." Ignacia huffed.

"Right. Of course not." Cricket rolled his eyes.

"Shh." Ignacia gave him a little shove and pointed to a corner. They fell silent, listening to the faint murmur of voices from just ahead. With a motion, Ignacia led the little group around the side of a building to find what looked to be a small hunting party. Five men with bows and arrows stood together, talking in hushed tones. Cricket's gaze flicked between them, determination, violence, anger painted in hard lines across their faces.

"That's not good," Cricket whispered, grabbing Ignacia and Yoshi by the sleeve to pull them away. Once they were far enough that they wouldn't be overhead, he started pacing. "We can't let them get to the stag first."

"Why not?" Ignacia leaned against one of the nearby buildings, her legs crossed at the ankles. "If they kill that thing then we can move onto the next town."

Yoshi nodded his silent agreement.

"Because we don't know what that *thing* is." Cricket huffed, using air quotes and everything, because this was serious. "It could be human."

"Or it could just as easily be a cursed animal." Ignacia shrugged. "And if that's the case what's the difference in them killing it from them killing another stag?"

"The difference is we don't know the nature of the curse. Maybe it would die with the creature, or maybe it would attach itself to the next available life source. You know dark magicks have a mind of their own sometimes. Or were you not paying attention during those lessons?" Did he sound a little manic? He felt a little manic. He felt like something strange was wriggling inside his stomach, wanting to come out, and clenching around his organs in its attempts. But he couldn't let it out. Because there was too much else to do, too much else to worry about. Ignacia, Yoshi, the people of Taini, they were all depending on Cricket to do the right thing. Maybe the right thing would be to let the creature die, but that didn't *feel* right.

"What do you suggest we do instead?" Ignacia asked. "Should we go tell them that by orders of the prince they aren't allowed to hunt the creature that's terrorizing their town. That'll go over well."

"No..." Cricket sighed, shoulders slumping. "But maybe we could distract them?"

"Sure. Hey Yoshi, why don't you go distr..." Ignacia's snide tone faded off and she released what sounded like a sigh.

Cricket frowned, looking up from where he'd been watching his feet pacing back and forth on the stones to see a vacant expression on her face. "Iggy?"

Her eyes were fixed on something over Cricket's shoulder. Before he could reach out for her, she took a step toward him, and then another.

"Iggy. This isn't funny. Where are you—"

"Cricket," Yoshi said, taking his elbow and pulling him out of the way just before Ignacia broke into a run. Cricket turned back to look just in time to see a little tail of glowing fuzz round the corner, and Ignacia chasing after it.

"That's not good." Cricket groaned, leaning forward to press his forehead into Yoshi's arm. Yoshi stiffened from the closeness and patted awkwardly at Cricket's shoulder.

"Cricket," Yoshi said again.

"All right, here's the plan. I'm going to go chase after Iggy and make sure she doesn't get herself killed doing something stupid. I need you to hold off the hunters. Do you think you can manage that?" Cricket lifted his head to meet Yoshi's gaze. He didn't know what he'd do if Yoshi didn't agree. There was no time for another plan. No time to argue over what needed to happen next.

To Cricket's great relief, Yoshi nodded.

"You're great!" His mouth got ahead of him again, and he huffed, shaking his head. Then took one giant step back to put space between himself and the beauty that was the white-haired knight. "I mean that's great. I'll just... I'm going to go."

"Me too. I am going to go."

"Right." Cricket scrubbed at the back of his neck. He took another giant step back from Yoshi, stumbling a little on the path. Then he turned to jog off after Ignacia. "I'll meet you back at the inn! Be careful!"

Following Ignacia's trail wasn't hard. In spite of his fumbling, she hadn't gotten that much ahead of him. He turned the corner to find Ignacia and the stag just up ahead on the street. The stag was running as fast as it could, but Ignacia was keeping up pretty well.

"Ignacia! Iggy! You get back here right now young lady! This is not a time to go gallivanting off and chasing deer!" Cricket shouted after her to no avail. She didn't even seem to hear him. The stag kept galloping toward the center of town. Cricket kept pace, hoping they wouldn't leave the road. He looked around them. He needed to track this. He wished he'd had a map with him so that he could scribble in the path. It might not be important. It might be completely random. But the stag seemed to know where it was going.

His breath came in harder pants the longer they ran, but he didn't let it slow him down. The stag raced around a block of houses on the western end of town, leading them in a big loop, and then it jetted back through the center. Cricket heard the hunters before he saw them. Another small group.

Yoshi might have kept the others at bay, but they couldn't account for everyone.

An arrow whizzed past him, ruffling the hairs beside his ear.

"Hey! There are people up here! Watch where you're firing!" He shouted over his shoulder, but when he looked back, he found more of the same glazed look he'd seen on Ignacia's face. They weren't seeing him; all they saw was the stag. It's white down glistening in the moonlight. "I need to get her out of here."

Cricket heaved in a breath, pushing his legs to run faster. He'd regret it tomorrow, everything would hurt. But there would be time to worry about that then. At that moment, he had to get Ignacia out of the line of fire. She was just within reach when the woods came into view from between the buildings. Trees shrouded in darkness and washed out by moonlight.

He needed to get to her before they went into the forest. If he didn't, he'd probably lose her, and there was more danger of the hunters behind them hitting her with their arrows or her hurting herself. The stag disappeared into the darkness beyond, and Cricket caught up to Ignacia just as she was about to chase in after it. He grabbed her wrist, spinning her around.

Another arrow flew past Cricket's ear, just missing him. He heard the gust of air from it. Then another, this one lower. The third he wasn't lucky enough to avoid, or rather, he wasn't lucky enough to keep from hitting Ignacia.

She yelped as the point swiped past her leg, leaving a cut in her trousers, and a red gash already swelling with blood. She stumbled back from the pain. Cricket lost his grip on her wrist. Then she was tumbling over a root at the tree line, and down she went. Cricket stumbled after her. The men who'd been behind them ran past, taking no notice of the pair sprawled on the forest floor.

And then Ignacia started crawling after them. Whatever the stag was, it still had a hold on her.

"Oh no you don't," Cricket said. He scooped her up in his arms and started back out of the forest. Careful of her clearly injured ankle. "We're getting you back to the inn. I'll have Yoshi go for the healer once he's back."

"Put me down!" Ignacia snarled, kicking, and clawing at him, fixated entirely on the woods over his shoulder. Cricket tightened his grip. Ignacia swung a wild fist. It caught him on the jaw.

"That's going to bruise." He winced but didn't let go.

Making it back to the inn was quicker when they weren't chasing a stag who wanted to lead them in circles all around town. Ignacia thrashed again, an elbow digging into Cricket's ribs so hard he almost dropped her. He kicked the door shut behind them, bracing himself against it.

"Rope! I need some rope! Does anyone have some rope?" The innkeeper came out from the back room looking upset by the noise in the lobby. His scowl said he was about to yell at Cricket for shouting and waking his guests. "I'm so sorry, but I need something to tie her down, so she doesn't get out again. Please."

"I....I might have some twine in the kitchen." The innkeeper had already turned to go.

"Anything! Please!" Cricket could feel tears welling up in the corners of his eyes the more Ignacia thrashed.

She shouted, and spat, and took another swing at him which he was able to duck. But eventually Cricket and the innkeeper got her tied to a chair in the corner, as far away from any of the exits as they could manage.

"I'll go get you something for that bruise," the innkeeper

said, excusing himself before Ignacia could turn her vitriol on him again.

Cricket heard the door open, and close behind him, and turned to meet Yoshi's eyes with a grateful sigh. Already, he could feel the heaviness of the evening weighing him down. How long had it been since they had first seen the stag? Two hours? Three, tops? He didn't know, but he did know that until the sun rose, they would have to watch Ignacia.

The innkeeper came back out with some ice wrapped in a towel. "Your friend saw the stag."

"Yes, she did." Cricket took the ice and held it to his face. "Were the others like this?"

"I don't know. No one got in their way." The innkeeper hovered out of Ignacia's reach, his hands twisting in front of him. "Is there anything else I can do for you?"

"Could you get my companion and I something to eat, and some tea please? It's going to be a long night."

The innkeeper nodded, relieved to have something to do, and scurried back to the kitchen. When he was gone, Yoshi moved to stand in front of Cricket's seat. Before Cricket could look up at him, Yoshi was kneeling. His white trousers no doubt getting grubby from the floor of the dining room.

"Are you all right?" Yoshi asked, quiet. He kept his hands braced on his knees, but his fingers twitched as if he wanted to reach out.

"Yes. I'm fine. But I think Ignacia twisted her ankle, and she has an arrow wound. We need to get the healer here. I'm just... I'm worried about taking anyone else out into the town in case the stag comes back." Cricket readjusted the ice, wincing when it pressed too hard on his bruised jaw. "Stars, she's got a mean swing on her."

"I will get the healer."

"Didn't you hear me? We shouldn't take anyone else out

there in case they catch sight of the stag and go mad like Iggy did. We can't risk that. No. We'll wait till morning."

"I will get the healer." Yoshi rose to his feet and headed for the door. Before Cricket could argue with him, Yoshi was gone.

CHAPTER 19

Cricket had closed his eyes for what felt like a minute, but must have been more, for the next thing he knew the table off to his left was laden in food, and tea, and the front door was opening again. In came Yoshi, leading the healer who had a piece of cloth bound over her eyes.

"I have brought the healer," Yoshi announced, as if that weren't perfectly evident.

"Oh good." Cricket yawned into the back of his hand. Ignacia had stopped shouting, but she was still looking at him like if he got close enough, she might kick him or bite him, whichever was easiest. "I hope you have something to knock her out for a bit. Otherwise, I don't know if she'll let you touch her till morning."

The healer, an older woman with sharp features, and weathered skin, nodded. "Yes, Your Highness. I have a sedative talisman in my bag."

"ARGH!" Ignacia screamed at the top of her lungs.

"Delightful," Cricket said through another yawn that cracked his jaw. "What do you need me to do to help?"

It didn't matter that he was tired. It didn't matter that he was hurting. He was already on his feet, moving toward Ignacia. Her eyes focused on him, mistrust and hurt written in every sharp edge of her face. She'd never looked at him like that before. Nearly ten years of friendship, and she'd never looked at him like that. Like he'd betrayed her. If Cricket were a lesser man (which he was not, whatever Uncle Sunil might say) he might have sagged under the weight of that look. He might have let it and the feelings it brought on pull him down into a puddle on the floor. But he was a prince, and his best friend needed his help.

"Cricket," Yoshi said, taking quick steps to intercept Cricket in his path around Ignacia. "I can help."

"No need. You've done enough for the moment. Sit down, have a rest, let me and the healer work." Cricket shrugged him off and inclined his head to the healer.

Yoshi looked as if he might argue, then he took a step out of the way, and watched from a safer distance. He didn't say the words, but Cricket could read them in his stance. *If you need me. I'm here.*

It was appreciated, far more than Cricket would like to admit. It made something warm, and fluttery light up in Cricket's chest. But there would be time to examine that feeling later. Right then, he needed to focus on Ignacia.

"Do you think you can get close enough to stick this to her?" The healer asked, holding up a paper talisman with characters scrawled across it. "I'd do it myself, but I don't think I'm quick enough."

Cricket took the paper. It was a thin sheet. Easy to rip. Easy to turn into shreds if Ignacia had her way. Her eyes met his. Challenging him. She'd always been faster than him, even when he was in the best shape of his life under the careful guidance of Chiaki. Now he'd been lazy for a year. Only practicing with Ignacia when he felt like it. She could outmaneuver him, easy. He knew that. But he had something she didn't. He had the need to save her.

He inhaled deeply through his mouth, and out through his nose, closed his eyes, and focused. It shouldn't have been as easy as it was to slip back into the lieutenant's teachings. It had been over a year after all. But he had spent much of his life training with Chiaki, and it was simple to let his mind focus and sharpen. He let the gentle hum of magic that always buzzed beneath his skin swim to the surface. He listened to Ignacia's still labored breathing, from her injuries, from her rage. And then he opened his eyes and took a quick lunge into her space. She thrashed, one leg kicking out for him, but he sidestepped it, and placed the paper against her spine.

Instantly, Ignacia fell still. Her breathing evened, and her head sagged forwards. When Cricket came around to her front, she was asleep, and his shoulders hunched in relief.

"Good job." The healer smiled up at him, her eyes crinkling around the edges. "Now go sit out of my way with your handsome friend and let me work. Oh, and bring me some of that tea, would you?"

"Yes ma'am." Cricket bustled over to the table where Yoshi had already poured a cup for the healer and brought it to her.

"Such a polite prince we have," she said. She looked as if maybe she wanted to pat his head, but she couldn't reach. A part of Cricket longed to bend down and make it easier for her, but another part recognized that it would make him look foolish.

"Thank you, ma'am." He flushed brightly, ducking his head.

"I'll see to your wounds when I'm done with your friend.

Now shoo." She flicked her wrists to brush him aside and turned back to her work.

Cricket slunk back to the table, settling into a chair with a heavy sigh. He hadn't noticed it before, but suddenly he felt every bone in his body aching. It had been such a long night, and all he wanted was to go to sleep, but he knew that wouldn't happen. Not until Ignacia was herself again.

"I don't suppose you could help me take her up to our room when she's done being seen?" It was probably too much to ask, he knew that. Ignacia wasn't Yoshi's responsibility, or his problem.

Yoshi looked up from his teacup to blink at Cricket for a moment, then he nodded. "I will help."

"Really?" Cricket breathed, his shoulders hunching into a boneless sprawl as he gradually lost the will to keep himself upright. "You don't have to, if you don't want. She's not your responsibility."

"I will help," Yoshi repeated as if it was as simple as that. And perhaps in his mind, it was.

"Thank you."

Yoshi inclined his head. He poured them both another cup of tea and scooted a plate with cheese and fruit toward Cricket. Cricket took a few pieces gratefully. It wasn't so much that he was hungry as he needed something to keep him awake. He hoped the food would do that, though already he could feel sleep weighing on him.

"You didn't see it when you went out to retrieve the healer did you?"

Yoshi shook his head.

"Good. That's good. What about the hunting party I sent you after?"

"I convinced them to disband for the evening." Yoshi shrugged. Cricket wondered what 'convinced' meant in this context but decided he didn't really want to know.

"Hopefully the others won't get themselves hurt. I wasn't able to stop them when..." Cricket sighed heavily, biting at the inside of his cheek to try to keep his voice from shaking.

"You did your best," Yoshi said.

Cricket didn't quite believe that. But he was too tired to argue. He grabbed another piece of cheese and a grape for something to do, letting silence settle between them.

"You were not," Yoshi started, breaking the silence a few minutes later, "compelled to chase the stag?"

Cricket blinked at the question. "No... I wasn't. But maybe it was because I didn't look it in the eye? What about you?"

The frown-winkle made another appearance as Yoshi took a moment to process those words. "I did look it in the eye."

"And? You weren't compelled to chase it?"

"I was not."

"Huh. So, it doesn't affect everyone, like we thought. Wonder why that is." Cricket stuffed another piece of cheese into his mouth, chewing thoughtfully. "Do you have any theories?"

"No."

"I have some," the healer said when she'd finished with Ignacia. Ignacia was still slumped in her chair uncomfortably. Cricket was sure she'd give him an earful about that in the morning, but for the time being, he wasn't going to worry about it. "Lift your shirt."

"What? Why?" Cricket frowned, scrambling up right, and twisting to evade the healer's searching hands.

"Because you're favoring your right side," the healer said crossly. "Now, lift your shirt so I can see the damage."

"It's nothing, Iggy just elbowed me in the ribs when I was wrangling her to the inn. I'm all right, really."

The old woman crossed her arms over her chest, looking

thoroughly unimpressed. "You can show me willingly, or I can have your handsome friend help me."

Cricket felt his neck heat, and instead of letting his eyes be drawn to Yoshi (because he somehow had more control over them than his mouth), he blinked at the healer. "All right. All right. Just go easy on your fair prince, will you?"

The healer just eyed him expectantly. He lifted his shirt to let her have a look and frowned down at the bruise blooming against his ribs. It wasn't the largest bruise he'd ever had, certainly nothing compared to some of his early training injuries. But he had little doubt that it would cause him some pain in the days to come. It might even hinder his progress in hunting the stag.

"She's a tough one, isn't she?" The healer asked, conversationally. She pressed one cold, wrinkled hand to the bruise, light dancing around her fingers as she reached out with magic to assess the injury.

"Toughest woman I know." Cricket laughed, and then instantly regretted it when it pushed the bruised skin into her hand. "Ouch."

"Well, the bruise will last a bit. But it's nothing serious," the healer said when she pulled back. "I'd suggest taking it easy, but it doesn't seem as though you'd follow that direction."

"Probably not," Cricket agreed readily. "Can I put my shirt back down now?"

The healer nodded.

"You said you have some theories of why the stag affects people differently?" Cricket pressed as he tugged his shirt down into place again. He looked over to see that Yoshi had busied himself with pouring the healer another cup of tea while she'd been inspecting his ribs.

"Thank you darling, you're very sweet," the healer cooed at Yoshi, making him blush faintly at the tips of his ears.

Well, good. At least Cricket wasn't the only one uncomfortable here. She took a long sip from her cup, and then sat in a free chair. "I believe it either has to do with mental state, or it has to do with the level of magic the person possesses."

"Explain," Yoshi said.

"Well mental state, it might be that the person is looking for love. Or is missing something. Or is running from something. I'm not really sure, but many of those who've been enraptured by her were single."

"Her?" Cricket asked.

"Oh. That's the other bit, I'm pretty sure the stag is female."

"But it's a stag." Cricket felt like he was missing something. Like he was coming in halfway through a conversation and trying to catch up.

"Yes," the healer nodded, setting down her cup with a soft thud.

Cricket waited but she didn't explain further. She merely busied herself making a small sandwich out of a biscuit, some cheese, and a few of the meats the innkeeper had brought them which had mostly gone untouched.

Questions pressed at the back of his teeth, making it uncomfortable when he refused to let them out. It didn't seem the healer was going to elaborate, and a barrage of more questions about that particular subject might yield them nothing at all when she inevitably closed up entirely.

"And the magic?" Yoshi asked. Cricket looked to meet his eyes and nodded his gratitude.

"Oh, well, people with higher magic levels have higher magic tolerance. It's a simple fact." The healer shrugged. "If your charming knight here didn't yield to the call of the stag it might be because he's got powerful magic."

Metallic and sharp, Cricket tasted blood as he bit his

tongue to keep from arguing that Yoshi was not *his* anything, much less *his* knight.

"That's most helpful," Cricket said. Although he didn't really think it was. What she'd supplied was vague theories that he could not prove one way or the other. He couldn't go around checking how much magic anyone had. Nor could he ask people about their emotional state. Well...he could. But he didn't think he'd get an honest answer. "Thank you very much for your help. Yoshi, would you mind seeing her back to her home?"

"Mm," Yoshi said, rising from his chair.

"Thank you." Cricket sighed, relieved that even though Ignacia had lost her head, he still had Yoshi to rely on. He'd never been so thankful for an impromptu alliance in his life. "How long till the sedative wears off?"

The healer shrugged; she was making herself three more of her little sandwiches. Cricket didn't mind, there was too much food for just himself and Yoshi, and honestly, he was too exhausted by that point to eat anyway.

"It varies from person to person depending on magic levels. Might be a couple more hours, might be past breakfast."

"That's a pretty large range."

"It's not an exact science."

Cricket groaned loudly. Yoshi made a strange huffing sound that might have been a laugh, or it might have been a tired sigh, Cricket wasn't sure which.

"Oh, and don't let her walk on that ankle for at least a week. It's not broken, but it's twisted pretty badly," the healer said this as if it were an afterthought, and maybe it was. "If she walks on it, she's likely to make it worse."

"She's going to love that." Cricket pressed the heels of his hands into his eyes, then dragged his fingers down to tug at the skin beneath them and his cheeks.

"Let us get you home," Yoshi said, holding his hands out to the woman. She tied the blindfold around her eyes and took his hands to let Yoshi guide her back out into the street.

Cricket looked over at Ignacia. She was snoring now, her expression entirely relaxed. Well, at least one of them would be getting some sleep that night.

CHAPTER 20

Yoshi arrived back at the inn shortly after Cricket asked the innkeeper to take away what was left of the food and tea. Then it was the work of ten minutes (and lots of soft curses and grunts from Cricket) to wrangle Ignacia out of the chair and up the stairs. They barricaded themselves into his and Ignacia's room once there. Cricket tied her wrists to the bedpost, then sealed the single window with a spell before they both slumped against the closed door.

"You don't have to stay with me for this," Cricket said, drawing his knees up toward his chest. "I can watch over her until morning."

Yoshi didn't respond, he just crossed his legs into a pretzel, and rested his hands on his knees, making himself comfortable. Or as comfortable as someone as upright and stiff as Yoshi could be.

"I mean it, Yoshi. You should go and get some sleep. This is going to be an all-night thing."

Yoshi still didn't say anything. He didn't even shrug.

Shrugging was likely undignified and impolite in his book, Cricket was sure.

Cricket sighed and scooted down so his back was curved more comfortably against the door. It didn't do much. The door was hard. The floor was hard. His body was still aching.

"I'll grab us some pillows," Cricket said, hopping up. He grabbed the pillows from his bed and went back to the floor. Holding one out to Yoshi, Cricket slumped back against the door, and settled the other beneath his curved back.

"I am fine."

"Take the pillow, Yoshi."

Yoshi let out another of those gentle huffs that could have been a laugh or could have been exasperation. Cricket wasn't sure. He supposed he'd have to be really looking at Yoshi next time he did it, instead of adjusting the pillow under his lower back to get more comfortable. When he looked up Yoshi had set the pillow between his own back and the door, his posture still upright.

"You can relax. It's going to be a long night."

"I am relaxed."

Cricket huffed, sitting up to mimic Yoshi's posture. "No, you aren't. This doesn't feel relaxed."

Yoshi didn't answer.

Cricket sunk back down a little, stretching his legs out, and bumping his shoulder intentionally against Yoshi. Once he was comfortable again, he looked over at Ignacia. They'd laid her on the bed so she could be comfortable, but she hadn't woken yet. He hoped she'd stay asleep until morning. The quiet was nice, after all the screaming downstairs.

Time ticked by, and Cricket felt himself being dragged down by his exhaustion. There had been some hope of a nap earlier on in the day after they'd arrived in Taini, but it had never happened. And perhaps that was his own fault. He was the one who'd insisted they set to work right away. But there was no waiting when there were lives on the line. And how was he to know that Ignacia would be ensnared by the stag and become more of a problem than an aid?

"What do you think we should do?" Cricket asked eventually.

"Hm?" Yoshi tilted his head so he could look down at Cricket where he'd slumped.

"Well, obviously we can't let them continue to hunt it. They're going to get hurt or hurt it. And I still think it might be a person. Especially after what the healer said."

"Mm."

"We have to keep them from doing that." Cricket was thinking out loud at that point. Tapping his fingers in a steady rhythm against his thigh. "And then there's the matter of the stag itself."

"We should hunt it," Yoshi said decisively.

"But I don't want to hurt it." Cricket frowned.

Yoshi fell silent. The silence stretched for such a long time that Cricket nearly fell asleep again. He sat up, rearranged himself into the same sitting position as Yoshi, and waited.

"Hunting and killing are not the same thing," Yoshi said at length.

"No. But what you're suggesting still involves hurting it, doesn't it?" Cricket turned his body so he could peer at Yoshi more fully. "I don't want to hurt it."

"It has hurt others," Yoshi reasoned, then his eyes flicked to Ignacia. "It has hurt your friend."

"I don't think it did that on purpose." Cricket sighed. No, he was sure it hadn't been on purpose. It didn't seem like it wanted people to follow it. "It was just running. I don't think it was trying to lead anyone to any place in particular. Least of all someplace where they might get hurt. I think it was just trying to get away."

"It must be stopped." Yoshi's face had hardened a little, his jaw clenching. It was such a small gesture that if Cricket weren't sitting right next to Yoshi, he may have missed it.

"I know that. You think I don't know that? But...but there was something intelligent in its movements. It was trying to tell us...or me maybe...something." Cricket frowned thoughtfully, his fingers fidgeting with the length of his long braid as he pulled it over his shoulder. He petted it; a self-soothing motion Uncle Sunil had told him numerous times made him look like a child. But at that moment, he felt like a child. Ignacia was hurt. The stag was still out there. There were no good solutions. It felt like all of his worst fears were coming for him, and the only thing left to do was hide under the bed.

"What could it have been telling you?" Yoshi prompted after a few moments of Cricket quietly stroking his braid.

"I don't know. But it was something. There was something with those buildings at the center of town that it led us around. We went in a circle all the way around." He twisted his fingers into a loose strand of hair. When was the last time he'd brushed and braided it? Probably not since before they'd come to Taini. He must look a sight. Instead of asking Yoshi about that, he merely continued to twist the few strands around his fingers.

"Or it was just confused and looking for an easy escape."

"Then why come into town at all? The safest thing to do would be to stay in the woods, away from people. It doesn't need to come into town to eat or anything." Cricket felt that was a valid argument. It had to be looking for something, or someone maybe.

"Unless it came here to find victims," Yoshi pressed softly.

"No.... No, I don't think so. If that was the case it would

have gone looking for a bigger group than just us." He shook his head. "And I couldn't... I don't know. There was something about it, Yoshi. Something..."

"What?"

"I don't know!" Cricket groaned, slumping back against the door again, and tugging at his hair.

Yoshi blinked at Cricket, a little crease forming between his brows as if he were trying to understand Cricket, and what he was thinking, but it was not making sense.

"In the morning I want a map of the city," Cricket said once he'd calmed down a bit. "I want to see what's in those buildings we ran around."

"We can procure a map."

"And... And there was that girl. The missing one? We should talk to the man who is looking for her." Cricket felt like he was creating a mental list. To dos to handle in the morning. After he'd had breakfast, and perhaps a bath. Definitely a bath.

"We can do that." Yoshi's voice had grown soft. Like he was fighting back sleep too. Or perhaps he was afraid of waking someone.

"But first the map." Cricket yawned into his elbow. "And maybe a chat with whoever lives in that area. Maybe they've seen something."

"All right."

"You know Yoshi," Cricket said, feeling his eyes grow heavier. "You're really not all that bad to talk to."

"Good night, Prince Cricket."

"What?" Cricket struggled to draw his head up. "Oh yes, good night."

HE MUST HAVE FALLEN ASLEEP SHORTLY THEREAFTER, for the next thing Cricket was aware of was a warm but boney shoulder under his cheek, and a drool spot forming on the white fabric beneath him. A very nice white fabric. And the fabric smelled all right too. Like...like... Wait.

White fabric. A boney shoulder.

Cricket jolted upright, realizing perhaps too late that he'd somehow fallen asleep slumped against Yoshi's shoulder in the middle of the night. All he could hope was that Yoshi hadn't noticed. Maybe he'd fallen asleep too, and Cricket could play the whole thing off...

"Good morning, Prince Cricket," Yoshi said.

No such luck.

Yoshi sounded wide awake. When Cricket pulled back to look at him, he found that there were dark circles underneath Yoshi's eyes as if he'd remained awake the entire time. But if it wasn't for the bruised skin as evidence, there would be no indication that Yoshi was tired. His eyes were alert. His posture, perfect. His hair even looked like he might have combed it at some point within the last twenty-four hours. Unlike Cricket. Whose braid was rapidly becoming a wild tangle and could feel dried drool at the corner of his mouth.

"Why didn't you wake me? I was supposed to stay up and watch Iggy." Cricket scrubbed at the drool spot, hoping Yoshi wouldn't notice. He didn't seem to.

"I was awake. I made sure she did not move."

"I remember telling you she wasn't your responsibility." Cricket sighed heavily. "But thank you."

Yoshi inclined his head in acknowledgement.

"Has she woken up at all?"

"No." Yoshi's eyes had drifted back to Ignacia who was sprawled spread eagle on the bed, snoring lightly.

"All right then, I'm awake now. Why don't you go to your

room and freshen up? We can go over our plan for the day afterwards." Cricket stretched his arms above his head, trying to force wakefulness into limbs keen on dragging him back into sleep. "Maybe take a nap."

Yoshi shook his head.

"No? No nap?"

"No nap. I will go and freshen up and order breakfast to be brought to your rooms." Yoshi nodded to himself, as if this was a better suggestion than what Cricket had told him to do. He stood to his feet in one fluid motion, grabbing the pillow as he went. Once he was standing, he held the pillow out to Cricket.

"Oh umm... thanks?" If Cricket sounded unsure, it was because he was. It wasn't that he wasn't used to people doing things for him. People always did things for him. But Yoshi hadn't seemed the type to coddle anyone, and there he was letting Cricket sleep on his shoulder and offering to order him breakfast.

Yoshi held a hand out to help Cricket to his feet.

Cricket groaned, arching his spine to stretch out his back once he was standing. The floor had not been forgiving to his already sore body, but he supposed a bath might help. If he had time to have one.

"Ignacia should be waking soon. I will have enough brought for three."

Cricket smiled sleepily at him. "Perfect. Then we can eat and go over the plan."

Yoshi nodded. Then he stepped around Cricket and exited the room, pulling the door shut behind him with a soft click.

"Well. You two seem cozy," Ignacia's voice said from the direction of the bed.

Cricket yelped. "Iggy! No sneaking up!"

"How is it sneaking up on you when I'm tied to the bed? Come untie me you dolt. My wrist is chafing."

"You aren't going to go running off again, are you?" Cricket approached the bed slowly. One step at a time. The two pillows held to his chest in case she got it into her head to kick him again.

"No. I'm fine now. Just tired. And sore. And... What did I do to my ankle? Styx, it hurts." Ignacia turned her head to look at him. "And what happened to your face?!"

"You happened to my face." Cricket grumbled. He dropped the pillows on the bed beside her and untied the twine they'd used to tie her wrists to the headboard. "You punched me right in the jaw while trying to catch the stag. That was after you were shot with an arrow, fell, and twisted your ankle."

"Ah. That explains the bandage then." Ignacia sat up, rubbing at the tender skin on her wrist. She moved her foot and winced when the motion hurt the injured ankle. "Looks like I won't be walking on that. How long?"

"The healer said a week of rest." He moved to sit beside her on the bed. "You scared me last night, Iggy."

Ignacia frowned. She took his hand, and held it between both of hers, giving it a little squeeze of apology.

"What do you remember of last night?" He had to know. He didn't think he was going to like the answer one way or the other, but he had to know.

"Nothing. There's...there's impressions of things." Ignacia's nose scrunched up; her brows tugged together as she thought. "But nothing concrete. It's just colors and sounds."

Cricket's free hand lifted to rub at his face.

"I'm sorry I scared you."

"I know." Cricket leaned over, resting his head on her shoulder. They sat quietly together for a few scant minutes. Happy enough to be safe, and beside each other.

"So, like...a full seven days? Or are we just talking Monday through Friday?"

"Iggy." Cricket sighed exasperated.

"What?"

CHAPTER 21

"You and the white knight," Ignacia said, nudging Cricket's shoulder where he sat in front of her.

"We aren't doing this right now. He'll be back any minute. Just brush." Cricket crossed his arms over his chest. "Brush and braid."

Ignacia snorted. "So bossy all of a sudden. This wouldn't be because you're embarrassed, would it?"

"No."

"Your neck is red."

"It's a sunburn!"

"Yeah. Okay." She ran the brush through his damp hair, slowly and carefully untangling any knots in the midnight blue tresses. It was a long slow process, and usually it took two people to help him get all the knots out and wrangle his hair back into a braid. But it was just he and Ignacia on the road, so they would have to make do. Which is why when the door opened to a maid carrying a breakfast tray, they were still sitting there working on Cricket's hair.

"Oh, I'm sorry. Am I interrupting, Your Highness?" The maid asked. She was balancing the tray on her hip and looking uncertainly between Cricket and Ignacia sitting on the bed together. Cricket wasn't sure why, but people always seemed to assume that when he and Ignacia were sitting this close there was some kind of impropriety going on. Never mind the fact that Ignacia was his right-hand woman, sister, and very much uninterested in those of the male persuasion.

"No, we're nearly done, I think." Cricket glanced over his shoulder to check.

"Five more minutes," Ignacia grunted around the hairbrush in her mouth.

"Should I come back?"

"No. Just set it over there. Thank you. We're still waiting on Yoshi anyway." Cricket gestured to the low table in the middle of the room surrounded by flat pillows.

"The knight?"

"Yes." Cricket ignored the soft snicker of Ignacia behind him as his neck heated again, and valiantly resisted the urge to swat her.

"He went to check on the horses in the stables. He told me to tell you that he'll be with you shortly." The maid blushed a little, bowing her head.

"Oh ah... Thank you. Was there something else?"

"No, Your Highness. Will you be needing anything more?"

"No, I think we're all right. Thank you."

The maid bowed and scurried out. Ignacia waited until the door was shut to snicker softly. "Seems you have competition for your brave knight's affections."

"I swear Iggy, if you don't stop..." He glared at her over his shoulder.

"You'll what? Last I remember you couldn't best me in a duel. But you're welcome to try." She smiled back, all teeth.

"Don't you make your scary face at me. It doesn't work on me anymore. I'm all grown up now. And you aren't scary anymore!" Cricket turned to jab at Ignacia in the shoulder. His cheeks flaming in his fury.

"Is something wrong?" Yoshi's soft voice called.

Cricket yelped, turning his head to look at Yoshi in the doorway. As polished as he'd looked when they'd woken up, he somehow looked more so now. His hair neatly tied back in a ponytail, the soft wisps of bangs framing his face seeming more intentional than haphazard. And in spite of the bags under his eyes, he looked well rested. How was that even possible?! Cricket needed to know what spells he used on his skin.

"No. Nothing's wrong," Ignacia answered for Cricket while his brain seemed to spin out of control. "I'm just teasing Cricket."

"Ah," Yoshi said. He did not, as most people would, ask what about. He just seemed to accept this as a normal part of their friendship and moved on with life. Cricket was forced to wonder what kind of person didn't ask what someone was being teased about. Was Yoshi just that saintly? Or was he dull? Maybe he was dull. Dull people didn't get curious about things like that. Yes, dull. Dull and boring. That would make life much easier for Cricket. "May I come in?"

"You did order enough for all of us, didn't you?" Cricket asked, ripping himself out of his inner spiral. Because he was spiraling. And if he didn't stop himself, he wouldn't make it back out of the rabbit hole.

Yoshi nodded.

"Then please have a seat. Iggy, are you finished?"

"Yeah, help me over to the table, would you?" She tied off the end of his braid tightly with a ribbon and set the brush aside. Cricket pulled her arm over his shoulder to support her weight on their short trek to the table. Then he lowered her carefully to the pillow.

"You should probably prop it up while we're gone today.

I'll throw some of the extra pillows from my bed onto yours." Cricket grabbed at the tray, pulling the cloche off the tops of the dishes.

"Are you really going to make me stay here all day? I could come with you and help." Ignacia whined, grabbing the tea pot before Yoshi could, and pouring them each a cup.

"Healer's orders." Cricket shrugged, loading up his plate.

"Ugh. You're the worst." Ignacia flopped forward onto the table.

"I have procured a map," Yoshi said, perhaps sensing a bickering match and wishing to get ahead of it. Smart man.

"Oh! Perfect! Let's see it!" Cricket held out his hands, wiggling his fingers excitedly.

"We are eating." Yoshi had begun to pile food on his plate, and in spite of Cricket's usually very convincing grabby hands, was not making any move to hand over the map.

"So?"

"We do not work while we are eating."

Cricket narrowed his brows at Yoshi. "I work while I'm eating all the time. I do my best work while eating, as it happens."

"We do not work while we are eating." Yoshi pursed his lips stubbornly.

"Yoooooooshi. Just give me the map. I just want to look at it. Pleeeeease." Cricket whined, leaning forward so his chest rested on the table, and his grabby hands were very close to grabbing Yoshi's perfectly portioned plate.

Yoshi looked at Ignacia, his eyes just a little wider than normal. He looked...unsettled. Maybe even panicking. Like he wasn't sure what to do with a whining, pleading prince.

"If you want him to stop, you should give him the map," Ignacia said with a shrug. She then proceeded to stuff a rather large bite of egg into her mouth.

Yoshi looked back at Cricket. Although his shoulders didn't heave, and Cricket didn't hear him let out a breath, he seemed to sigh. Then he pulled the map out of his pouch and placed it in Cricket's still wiggling fingers. Cricket sat up immediately, offering Yoshi a blinding smile and then unfurled the map to inspect it while stuffing half a vegetable bun into his mouth.

His eyes traced the path they'd taken from the inn the previous night, and around the little block of buildings. The map didn't provide any real context aside from the fact that none of the buildings had little signs to indicate a business within. Logically, that would make them residences.

"That's what I thought," Cricket mumbled to himself through a mouth full of food.

"What is what you thought?" Yoshi asked.

"Swallow what's in your mouth before talking!" Ignacia ordered at the exact same time.

Cricket chewed and swallowed, then pushed several plates out of the way to clear a space to lay the map on the table. His fingers circled around the little block of buildings. "They're residences."

"You thought they were someone's home?" Ignacia frowned, her eyes looking at the map as if maybe she'd see what Cricket had found so special about them but was coming up empty.

"Why?" Yoshi asked.

"Because the last time there was an issue it was with a magical object, right? A brooch. A normal looking thing that someone would buy for their personal use. If that's the case, then whatever curse this is must have attached itself to a person, right? And that person must live here, in one of these houses. Either the object itself is still there, or the person being affected by it was there at the time."

"That's a lot of leaps." Ignacia drummed her fingers on

the table. "How do we know it's not like a cursed hammer or something?"

"You think a cursed blacksmith hammer created a ghost stag?" Cricket blinked at her blandly.

"Well...no. But it could be something else! It doesn't have to be jewelry." Ignacia huffed.

"I didn't say it was jewelry! I just said it was something for personal use. A figurine maybe. Or a paper weight."

"What should we do?" Yoshi asked, before they could descend into more bickering.

Cricket rolled the map up, sat back on his own cushion, and grabbed what was left of his bun. "First thing's first. We have to impose a curfew on Taini until we get this thing sorted."

Ignacia stopped, setting down her chopsticks to look at him through narrowed eyes. "You think a curfew is a good idea?"

"I don't see where we have much other choice." Cricket shrugged. "And I am the prince. I can mandate that kind of thing."

"And you think the people of Taini are just going to go along with that?"

"It's for their safety!"

"It's an infringement on their freedom. Besides, they want to catch this thing themselves. We saw what? Two hunting parties last night?"

"Well, yes. But Iggy, I really don't see where there is any other way to keep them safe."

"How will you enforce it?"

"I... I don't know."

"A royal proclamation," Yoshi supplied.

"What?" Cricket and Ignacia both looked at him confused.

Yoshi's head was ducked over his plate, and he spoke

slowly, but clearly. "An official proclamation. Explain to the people that this is a temporary solution, and their prince is only here to protect them."

"I don't know, Cricky. It feels a little too much like martial law." Ignacia shook her head. "Maybe you can figure this out before that's necessary?"

"No. I think this is the best way to keep everyone safe. This will leave Yoshi and I free to investigate the stag's movements without having to worry about hurting anyone."

Ignacia sighed. "All right then. I'll help you draft up the order. Grab me a pen and some paper."

Cricket jumped up to gather her supplies. Over the next hour the trio ate and worked on the order. Once it was done, Yoshi went off to have copies made, and hired some people to spread it around the town.

"You really think this is a good idea?" Ignacia asked once he was gone.

"Iggy... I wish we had a better option. But I just... I don't know how else to keep them safe. And it's only for a little while. We should have this whole thing sorted within a few days, then Taini can go back to normal."

Ignacia let out a long-defeated breath but didn't argue further.

The maid returned, knocking lightly on the door. "Your Highness, I'm here to clear away the breakfast things."

"Yes, thank you. We're done." He grinned, and then he had a thought. "Oh, but while I have you, could I ask you a question? We found this missing poster on the town board yesterday. Can you tell me where this Mister Cannan," he said reading the name off the poster, "lives?"

"He lives right there." The maid gestured with her chin to the map that they'd rolled out on the table between their three teacups.

"Right where?"

"In that circle. He's the third house in on the right. Terrible what happened to his fiancée." She shook her head, clicking her tongue softly. "He was so in love, and we thought she was too. But then she just ran off shortly after he proposed. Beautiful ring too. Had the loveliest opal on it I've ever seen."

"How long ago was this?" Cricket sat up a little straighter.

"Oh, about a month ago, I'd say. You can ask the innkeeper, he'd know better. He's Mister Cannan's brother-in-law."

"Thank you. That was really helpful, Miss..."

"Daphne, Your Highness." Daphne muttered, ducking her head as bright red painted her cheeks. "Are you finished with the tea things?"

"Yes. Thank you, Daphne. You're a gem!" Cricket flashed her a dimpled smile.

Daphne giggled, loading the rest of their dishes quickly onto the tray and making a hasty exit with her cheeks still flaming. Yoshi returned, watching her scurry down the hall with a tight expression pinching his brows.

"Something wrong?" Yoshi asked.

"No, nothing. Just Cricket flirting his way into more leads. Well, you boys have fun. I'll just be here, *resting*." Ignacia huffed, flopping back onto the bed.

"Flirting?"

"Iggy is being dramatic. Come on, we're going to talk to the innkeeper." Cricket rolled his eyes, grabbing his satchel he stuffed the map inside, and threw it over his shoulder.

"The innkeeper?"

"Yes. You'll see why in a minute. Come oooon." He clasped Yoshi's wrist and tugged him back out the door. "Bye Iggy, behave!"

"Yeah. Bye." She grumbled.

CHAPTER 22

"Your Highness!" The innkeeper squeaked, fumbling with an overturned inkwell on his desk as the door slid shut behind them. His eyes flicked nervously from Cricket to the white knight standing behind him. Cricket couldn't see Yoshi, but he could feel his presence over his shoulder, no doubt standing perfectly straight with his hands clasped behind his back. "What can I do for you and your umm... Are your rooms not satisfactory? Was breakfast not—"

"No. No. Nothing like that." Cricket waved him off, smiling gently to reassure him. He wished that Yoshi would stand a bit more relaxed, it felt like having one of the royal guards with him all over again. It made things uncomfortable and awkward. At least with Ignacia she stood beside him. "We just have a few questions about your brother-in-law."

"B-b-brother-in-law?" The innkeeper laughed nervously. His sleeve had fallen into the puddle of ink on the desk. His eyes were still firmly over Cricket's shoulder. No doubt made more nervous by the menacing looking knight.

"You have a little something...." Cricket pointed to the growing stain on his taupe sleeve. He sighed, shook his head. "Anyway, yes, Mister Cannan. I understand he's looking for his fiancée."

"Oh. Oh me." The innkeeper frowned, grabbing a handkerchief from a pocket to rub at the stubborn stain. It wasn't going anywhere. Cricket would wager not even magic could get it out of the cloth. Ink was like that, stubborn. "Ah well," the innkeeper sighed, giving it up for lost. "Yes, what about Emrys?"

"His fiancée," Cricket continued, pulling the missing poster from his satchel. "What happened to her?"

The innkeeper took the poster, looking sadly down at the blonde woman. He was silent for a few moments, seeming to choose his words carefully. "She left."

"Did she leave a note?"

"No. Not as such. But people don't just..." The innkeeper shook his head. "They don't just disappear."

Cricket had to bite the inside of his cheek to keep himself from saying that sometimes people did very much just disappear. It would do nothing to make the people of Taini feel safer to know that sometimes people were kidnapped by fairies, or by other people, or cursed, or just fell off the face of the earth somehow. That was the nature of people, they were not constant. He didn't say as much. He merely began to pace the length of the innkeeper's desk.

"Cricket," Yoshi said after the innkeeper began to fidget nervously with his now no doubt empty bottle of ink.

"What? Oh. Right." Cricket nodded. "When did she leave?"

"Shortly after he proposed. I think that was three weeks ago or so."

"And the ring?" Cricket lifted his head from where he'd been watching his boots tread lightly across the wood floor.

"What about it?" The innkeeper frowned, brows creasing. "Where is it?"

"She took it with her, of course! Probably so she could sell it." The innkeeper huffed, sounding as if it were he who'd been jilted, and not his brother-in-law.

"Of course." Cricket frowned, shaking his head. He paced a few more steps, tapping his fingers against his thighs as he pondered. "The maid said it was a very beautiful ring. An opal, I think. Where did he get it? I don't imagine you see many opals in Taini."

The innkeeper shrugged. "He had it made in town by the jeweler. She makes very fine things. You won't see anything half as pretty for at least three towns in any direction. If you go by and see her, tell her Ciro sent you." The innkeeper winked and tapped his nose conspiratorially.

Cricket nodded. "Thank you. That'll be our next stop, I think. Yoshi, did you have any questions for our friend here?"

Yoshi shook his head.

"All right then, that's it. If you could see to it that lunch is brought to my rooms for my friend, and supper if I don't make it back in time, I'd be most grateful." Cricket turned to beam at the innkeeper. "I know it's an imposition, but she really ought not walk on her ankle right now."

"Of course, Your Highness. We are happy to look after you and your companions while you're here." The innkeeper bowed low over his desk, the front of his tunic dipping into the still wet ink on his paper.

Cricket bit back a wince. "You're too kind. Come along Yoshi, let's head off to the jewelers."

Yoshi turned to open the door for him. Cricket smiled up at him as he passed. The air outside was fresh and beginning to cool with the early hints of fall. Cricket leaned back as he looked up at the blue sky.

"You have a question," he said when Yoshi remained a silent presence at his side.

Yoshi was quiet for a little longer, his expression one of concentration as he seemed to think over his words. Once he'd found them, he asked, "Why did you not tell the innkeeper that you think the stag and the missing woman are linked?"

"Oh. That." Cricket looked to the sky again. He closed his eyes for a moment, drawing in a deep breath that he let out through his mouth in a sigh. "I didn't want to get anyone's hopes up. It would be cruel to make people think perhaps she wasn't really gone, and she'd come back, only for me to be wrong."

Yoshi looked at him, head tilted a little to one side. "That is very wise."

"Ah!" Cricket laughed, shaking his head. "You sound surprised. Why are you surprised that I'm wise? I am a prince, you know."

"Not all princes are wise."

"No. I suppose not." Cricket frowned, scrubbing at his nose. "Do you know a lot of princes, Yoshi?"

Yoshi stared at him; an expression of blankness set onto his features. Cricket couldn't help but feel that in spite of the impassiveness, he was being silently judged for something. He didn't know what that something was, but he decided to ignore it lest it get him and Yoshi into another fight. He didn't want to fight with Yoshi. They had been working so well together!

"Right, of course you do! You're a knight. You probably know the queen and her elder brother. Selene, I haven't seen them since I was... Oh what was I? Seven? I think it was the prince's twelfth name day. There was some kind of celebration and Father took me—"

"We are here."

"Huh?" Cricket looked up at the sign over the shop. "So we are. Shall we?"

Yoshi opened the door, then stepped back to hold it for him.

"Ah, thank you." Cricket muttered, rubbing at the back of his neck as he stepped past Yoshi. The shop inside was small, more the front room of a home really. Probably what had once been the drawing room before the jeweler moved in. Sunshine streamed in through the bay window to highlight a velvet lined case full of jewelry along the back wall. A bell over the door tinkled softly.

"I'll be with you in a moment," a light, and high voice called from the back of the shop.

"Take your time." Cricket called back, pacing carefully across the floor to look into the case. "Ciro was right, some of these are quite lovely. The filigree work is so delicate. Yoshi. Come look."

Yoshi let the door fall behind him and walked to Cricket's side. Their shoulders brushed as he bent to look into the case. "Very nice."

Cricket shifted his weight, putting a little more distance between the warm press of Yoshi's shoulder and his own. The case was full of beautiful gold work, but nothing with a stone set into it. Cricket wrinkled his nose, turning his head. "No opals."

"No opals." Yoshi agreed, with a little nod. He stood back to his full height when the freckle faced woman came from the backroom.

"Sorry about that," she said, rubbing her hands on a rag. "I was just finishing up a commission."

"It's quite all right." Cricket looked up from the case, not moving from where he was bent over it to smile at her. "We were just admiring these beautiful pieces. Your gold work is so delicate."

"Oh well... It's nothing like what they do in the capital." She flushed hotly, ducking her head to hide behind a length of dark hair. "But umm..." she cleared her throat. "What can I do for His Highness?"

Cricket stood; his hands braced behind his back as he pinned her with the full force of his dimpled grin. "We heard from Ciro that you sold Mister Cannan his engagement ring. We just had a few questions about it."

"Ah! That was a lovely piece." She shook her head. "Shame what happened with Eniko. I always thought they were so good together. They were childhood sweethearts. Soulmates, really, or at least everyone thought so."

Cricket frowned. "That's sad. What do you think about her disappearance?"

"Well, I don't like to gossip," she said in a tone that implied she very much did like to gossip. "But as it's for the investigation... Word around town is that Eniko had a lover on the side. One of the merchants who comes through town occasionally. She disappeared shortly after the last band of them came through."

"You think she ran away." It wasn't a question. Cricket had the sinking feeling that everyone in this town thought Eniko had just left without so much as a by your leave to her fiancée. But what he couldn't understand was why. If they were soulmates, childhood sweethearts, why did everyone think so poorly of her? Or was it merely the need for sensationalism in a small town?

"That's what it looks like, doesn't it?" She shrugged.

Cricket's expression must have turned troubled, for Yoshi shifted beside him.

"There are no stones," Yoshi observed quietly.

The jeweler nodded. "We don't get much call for that

kind of thing here. Stones are expensive, and we're not like the capital, we don't have any wealthy merchants here. But that opal." She whistled rocking back on her heels. "It was something else."

"It was not from your supplier?" Yoshi pressed gently.

"Oh no, Emrys bought that off one of the traveling caravans. He said he got a great price on it, and it was a gorgeous stone. He only came to me to have me set it for him."

Yoshi hummed his understanding.

Cricket turned to smile at him, his brows raising in an expression that, to Ignacia would say very clearly, *I told you so.* "Then I guess we need to talk to Emrys."

Yoshi glanced at Cricket from the corner of his eyes and nodded.

"Where can we find Mister Cannan right now?" He turned back to the jeweler.

"Emrys will be out checking his traps. He's a hunter." She shrugged. "But he always comes home for lunch. You should be able to catch him before he heads back out around one."

"Thank you! You've been most helpful." Cricket bowed slightly.

"Ah of course. Of course. But before you go, maybe you'd be interested in purchasing something for your..." Her eyes swung meaningfully to Yoshi.

Cricket felt heat creep up his neck, and his jaw fall a little slack. "Oh um. No thank you. We're not— I'm not going to— This isn't— Let's go Yoshi!" He squeaked.

Yoshi's brows rose just a fraction as if confused by Cricket's sudden discomfort, but he turned without a word to open the door for Cricket again.

"Thanks again!" Cricket called over his shoulder, and promptly raced out onto the street. Yoshi followed him at a much more sedate pace. "We'll head back to the inn and have an early lunch with Iggy, and fill her in, before going to find Emrys."

He was talking too fast. Why was he talking so fast? And why was he walking so fast?

"Mm." Yoshi murmured, keeping pace with Cricket without seeming to have to try.

"Okay? Okay. Good? Good." Cricket laughed nervously.

CHAPTER 23

"It's so booooring here alone, Cricky," Ignacia whined as soon as the door opened to let Cricket and Yoshi into their rooms. "All I have to do is read, and we didn't really bring any books with us. I'm stuck with whatever the innkeeper could dig up from his wife's collection."

"And what's what?" Cricket asked, pulling off his scarf and dropping down onto one of the pillows around the table.

"Romance novels." She huffed, sulking.

"You like romance novels. As I seem to recall—" A pillow smacked him in the face, cutting off his words, and he chuckled darkly. "You could always just flirt with Daphne. She was pretty enough."

"Stop trying to distract me, I'm complaining here."

"Of course. Of course. Do carry on." He leaned back onto his palms, flashing a knowing smile and a wink at Yoshi who was looking between them rather strangely. Like he'd never seen two people interact the way they did in spite of already having spent a good few hours with them. Cricket reflected idly that perhaps it wasn't so much the nature of he and Ignacia's friendship, but their status as friends at all that perplexed Yoshi. It did most people. Ignacia was meant to be Cricket's servant, a lady in waiting of sorts, and a guard. But instead, he'd always considered her an elder sister.

"Well now you've ruined it." Ignacia sat back against the bedpost, crossing her arms over her chest in a sulk.

"My apologies, my lady." Cricket bowed as lowly as he could while sitting down, and then leaned back again. "Do you want to hear what your humble servant, Prince Cricket, found out while investigating today or not?"

Ignacia waved her hand vaguely, as if to say *carry on*. The gesture was distinctly royal, and Cricket was sure if Uncle Sunil saw it, he'd have flown into a rage. Good thing he wasn't there.

"Mister Cannan and his missing fiancée only just got engaged three weeks ago, shortly before she disappeared."

Cricket leaned forward onto his knees, relaying everything they had learned that morning to Ignacia as Yoshi quietly poured them tea and then they ate lunch. When he sat back with his bowl of rice, he didn't even try to hide the smug expression on his face.

"Get it over with," Ignacia said, setting down her fork to fix him with a look of utter annoyance.

"I don't know what you're talking about." Cricket blinked innocently at her, but he could feel that self-satisfied smile on his face. And he knew without a doubt that Ignacia had read it for what it was.

"Either you say it now, or you don't say it at all. Don't play this game with me, Cricky. You aren't too old to grab by the ear."

"She told me to. You heard her tell me to, didn't you, Yoshi?"

"Yes," Yoshi said, although he looked very much like he didn't know what he was agreeing to. Ah, well, probably for the best.

"Yue Akio Cricket, I am losing what very little patience—"

"I told you so." Cricket leaned away from Ignacia as she reached to smack him on the shoulder, a laugh on his lips. "I told you it was that trader. Mister Cannan probably bought the stone off the man, and then had it made into a ring."

"We do not know that it was the same merchant," Yoshi added reasonably.

"Thank you! At least one of you has some sense," Ignacia cried, throwing herself back against the bed. "I feel so much better knowing that you're there as a steadying influence, Yoshi."

"Although it does seem a rather odd coincidence if it is not the same person." Yoshi's eyes were firmly on his plate, but Cricket thought he saw a flicker of amusement as Ignacia shouted in exasperation.

"Ack! He's drawn you in. Mark my words, Yoshi, he'll have you spouting gibberish before all this is through." Ignacia shook a finger at him.

"Prince Cricket is very well spoken." The frown-wrinkle made an appearance at the corner of Yoshi's lip as he met Ignacia's eyes.

Cricket spluttered a little, trying not to choke on the over-sized bite of rice he'd just stuffed into his mouth. "I umm...thanks!" He coughed into his sleeve.

Yoshi dipped his head back to his food. He looked like maybe he was hiding a smile, but Cricket had no proof of that.

"You know what, it's better I don't go with you two idiots while you're off questioning people. I don't think I'd survive the cringe." Ignacia snorted, grabbing her fork, and taking a decisive bite of the pasta on her plate.

"We aren't cringe. We're... Well, we're... You know what? Shut up, Iggy." Cricket swatted her hard with a pillow which only made Ignacia snicker with laughter. Cricket laughed with her, unable to help himself. It was hard not to laugh when Ignacia was. She had one of those laughs that was absolutely hilarious, half snort, half chortle, all happiness. When they'd both finally settled, Cricket wiped at his eyes.

"You know what that means though," Ignacia said, grabbing her fork for another bite of pasta.

"Yeah. It means that this isn't an accident." Cricket sighed, lifting a hand to scrub at his eyes. "These are deliberate attacks."

"Did the brooch have a stone in it?" Yoshi asked. He'd been quiet during their strange interaction, but now he was looking at Cricket intensely.

Ignacia grabbed the pouch they'd stored the brooch in and dumped the clunky piece of metal on the table. The thing was gaudier than Cricket remembered it, as if it had morphed inside the pouch, which of course was impossible. But that wasn't the important bit. The important bit was the gleam of the raven's eyes. All red, and ruby, and shimmering.

"Not very big ones." Ignacia frowned a little.

"No. But it doesn't take much. Even little stones like these can hold magic for longer than the metal alone." Cricket shook his head. "Good catch Yoshi."

Yoshi inclined his head, looking pleased with the praise.

"Whoever we're dealing with has enough power to curse stones." Ignacia frowned, poking the brooch with her fork. "Cricky, I know you don't want to do this, but maybe we should send for reinforcements. I'm sure that Annie can—"

"No. We don't need soldiers." Cricket shook his head. His tone was soft, serious, an order from a prince. "They'll just come in and make everyone nervous and tip off whoever is responsible for all of this. We deal with this ourselves, and we do it quietly."

"Okay." Ignacia's shoulders sagged. "Just, promise me you'll be careful."

"I will, but whoever cursed these people isn't here now, Iggy. So there's nothing to worry about."

"I will protect him," Yoshi said softly. "You do not need to worry."

"Thank you." Ignacia offered Yoshi a little nod of approval.

"Oi! I'm not helpless! I can look after myself." Cricket huffed. Despite what Uncle (and some of the guards) seemed to think, Cricket hadn't been helpless since he was a very young child. And he hated to be treated as if he were, especially by Ignacia. She knew how he had worked, and trained, and fought to become someone who could defend himself. Someone who didn't need protection. The reminder of people's opinions to the contrary chafed.

"No. But it doesn't hurt for someone to have your back. Now does it?" Ignacia quirked a brow but didn't wait for Cricket to agree before continuing. "While you two are out, I'm going to talk to the staff and see if we can figure out what direction this merchant went in. We should follow his trail."

"Good idea." Cricket brightened quickly. "Maybe we'll be able to catch up to him. We're only three weeks behind."

"Exactly. That should give us enough time to sort out what to do with him when we catch him." Ignacia sighed, pulling herself back up onto the bed. "Or I hope so at least."

MISTER CANNAN'S home was on the second floor of his little building. The first belonged to a Misses Harrison, as Cricket and Yoshi discovered. She was very sweet. She also had five cats, and Cricket, being not fond of cats, stayed hidden behind Yoshi for most of their interaction.

By the time they'd made it to the second floor, Yoshi's trousers were boasting a very healthy layer of cat hair and Cricket had clutched a crease into his cloak.

"Sorry about that." Cricket muttered, trying to smooth out the creases with his hands.

"You do not like cats." It wasn't a question; it was a statement of fact. One that Cricket should have been embarrassed by, because really what grown man was afraid of cats? At least Yoshi hadn't said afraid, that was a kindness he supposed.

"They're all right when they're kittens." Cricket shrugged, as if that might be explanation enough. He didn't have a valid reason (not one he wanted to talk about with someone he didn't know very well) for why he didn't like cats.

Yoshi merely nodded as if that were in fact just cause to not like them. It wasn't. They both knew it wasn't. But Cricket was grateful that no further discussion was needed.

He knocked on the door at the top of the steps, and they waited. After some fumbling, and shuffled footsteps, a man with deep brown skin and a wide, friendly smile, answered the door.

"I heard the prince was stopping by. Come in! I made tea!" He moved away from the door, and over to the small kitchen to pull a kettle from the stove. "Please have a seat."

Cricket settled into a chair after a small polite bow. "Word really does get around outside of the capital."

"Well, you know, there isn't much else to talk about." Mister Cannan shrugged but there was a sadness that tugged at his lips. He wanted to say more. Perhaps something along the lines of 'there isn't much else to talk about besides my missing fiancée.'

"Yes, I suppose I'm big news." Cricket smiled, taking the offered mug between his hands, and letting it warm his fingers. "I'm sorry we have to come and dredge up something that's painful for you, Mister Cannan."

Mister Cannan shook his head, pouring another mug for himself after sliding one over to Yoshi. Then he sat beside Cricket, leaving the seat between him and Yoshi empty. Cricket turned to follow him.

"Emrys, please. If you think it'll help everyone, I'm more than happy to tell you what I know." Emrys sighed. His shoulders had slumped a little, eyes downcast into the mug in front of him, but he didn't seem be letting that stop him. "I just don't know what any of this has to do with Eniko."

"We don't either, not yet. But we want to find out." Cricket's voice was soft. He leaned closer to Emrys, reaching out slowly in case Emrys wasn't comfortable with this, and then patted his hand. "We hope you'll be able to help us understand."

"I'll do my best." Emrys clenched his cup a little tighter and then looked up to meet Cricket's gaze. "What do you need to know?"

"You bought the stone for Eniko's ring off a traveling merchant. Did anything strange happen before you proposed?" Cricket sat back with a serious look.

"No. Nothing."

"And the stag appeared shortly thereafter?"

"Yes. Almost...almost the next night after Eniko had gone." Emrys swallowed with an audible click, his knuckles turning white around the mug in his hands. Cricket could see the tea inside sloshing a little. "I don't understand it. She was... We were so happy. She..." He shook his head.

"You don't think she ran away."

"No." Emrys's shaking had stopped, his expression turning serious. "Eniko would never. If she didn't want to marry me, if there was someone else, she'd have just told me. That's how she is... was."

"Is." Yoshi amended softly.

Emrys turned to offer Yoshi a watery smile. "Is."

"If I show you a sketch I've made of someone, could you tell me if you'd seen them before?" Cricket asked gently.

Emrys nodded, sitting back, and pushing his now cold tea away.

Cricket leaned down to pull his sketchbook out of his bag, flipping through the other sketches until he found the one from Abner's description.

"I don't think I know him. He looks familiar, but... I'm pretty sure I've never seen him before. If I have, I can't place his face." Emrys frowned, tilting his head to look at the sketch from a different angle. "Who is this?"

"We believe it's the person who sold a cursed item to someone in Tochtli." Cricket sat the sketch in front of him, letting him look it over a little more thoroughly. "What did the man who sold you the opal look like?"

"I..." Emrys's brows scrunched, and lips pursed. He was concentrating, perhaps too hard. As if trying to pin down a memory that seemed to shift every time he looked at it too closely. "I don't remember. I'm so sorry."

"No, it's all right. That's normal. If he used cloaking magic to alter his appearance, you wouldn't remember. Or it would feel like you weren't remembering correctly even if you did. It's not your fault." Cricket soothed, shutting the sketch-book, and putting it away.

Emrys's shoulders relaxed, seeming to find relief in Cricket's words. "Is there anything else I can help you with?"

"Have you hunted the stag?" Yoshi asked, setting aside his empty mug. "And if you have, have you been affected by it?"

"Oooh good questions, Yoshi!" Cricket crowed, nudging him playfully in the shoulder.

"I have not hunted it. I don't..." Emrys frowned a little, his jaw working as he tried to find the words. "Those who have been hunting it are looking for a prize. They want something rare. I don't go after that kind of game. Hunting isn't a competition for me, it's a way to provide for myself, and for my family. I've been staying out of the woods in the evenings."

Cricket nodded sagely. "That's very wise. We're planning to hunt it ourselves, if you have any tips."

Emrys frowned, but he spent the next twenty minutes giving them as many tips on hunting as he possibly could. (Many of which Cricket promptly forgot as he wasn't the type to go hunting anyway.) By the time their cold tea had been drunk, and Cricket had a detailed list of all the things they should keep in mind when hunting a stag written in his untidy scrawl, it was well past time for Emrys to head back out into the forest.

They were halfway down the steps, when Emrys said, "Your Highness."

"Yes?" Cricket turned to look back at the man lingering in his doorway. The light was poor in the closed stairwell, but Cricket could see a look of worry etched across his brows.

"Don't hunt that thing. It's...it's not worth it." He shook his head.

Cricket offered him a confident smile, squaring his shoulders. "Don't worry about me. I've got Yoshi to protect me. Right, Yoshi?"

Yoshi turned to look at them, nodded once, then turned back to the steps. Cricket couldn't be sure, but he thought he saw a flicker of amusement cross his features. Shaking his head, he laughed softly.

"See? I'll be just fine."

Emrys sighed, his shoulder slumping in defeat. "Just be careful."

CHAPTER 24

What followed could only be described as a comedy of errors.

After returning to the inn Cricket and Yoshi parted ways to rest for the evening's hunt. A nap was necessary, Cricket reasoned, if they were to give their first hunt their best efforts. Yoshi agreed, although he seemed to do so begrudgingly. Hours later, after a light supper, Cricket met Yoshi in front of the inn as the sun settled low in the sky.

"We should get the horses," Yoshi suggested. He stood against the wall of the inn, hands folded behind his back, posture erect. Although he had been against their nap, he seemed to be more well rested than he'd been before. Cricket didn't pat himself on the back, but he greatly wanted to.

"No." Cricket shook his head, starting back toward the place where they'd first caught sight of the stag. Taini was quiet all over, every citizen seemed to have taken Cricket's edict seriously, and decided to stay in for the night however they may dislike the idea. He wasn't sure how long their luck would hold out, but he was willing to hope it would be enough for them to catch the stag and solve this.

Yoshi turned to follow along beside him. It was clear from his silence alone that he did not agree with Cricket's decision, but that was all right. Cricket didn't really expect them to agree on most things. Especially after their differing opinions on how to deal with Abner.

"It wasn't running that fast when we saw it last night. I think it wants to be caught." Cricket continued on conversationally as the lamps in the town began to light, magic flowing into them casting the streets in a soft yellow glow. "It could have outpaced us easy, but it didn't."

Yoshi looked over at him, eyes narrowing just a fraction, hardly enough to even be noticed if Cricket weren't actively looking for some kind of response. Which he wasn't. He most certainly was not examining Yoshi's facial expressions close enough to notice even the most minor of changes. Nope.

Cricket smiled blithely, pretending not to notice. "Why do you think it didn't affect us?"

Yoshi turned back to the path ahead. He seemed intent on not having this discussion, or any discussion at all really.

"Oi. We can't just walk around in dead silence all night. That'll be boring. I'll fall asleep walking. Don't test me. I've done it before."

"Hunting is a silent activity," Yoshi said brusquely, picking up his pace.

"But it doesn't have to be! We could chat! So long as we aren't too loud!" Cricket sped his footsteps to keep up with Yoshi. "Come on Yoshi. Talk to meeee."

"Sh." Yoshi held his fingers to his lips, crouching low as he peeked around a corner.

"Sh. You don't just shush the prince! Do you—" Cricket flapped his arms.

Yoshi turned to glare at him.

"Fine, I'll shush." Cricket grumbled, crossing his arms

over his chest. "I'll shush right up. Just you watch, you'll find no one quieter than me."

Yoshi didn't say anything, nor did his face move, but Cricket got the vague impression that Yoshi wanted to quirk his brow at Cricket and eye him condescendingly.

"Don't take that tone with me, mister. I'll have you—" He was cut off mid-tirade by the stag running past them at breakneck speed. It brushed close enough that Cricket felt the whoosh of air as it moved. He spun trying to keep his eyes on the creature, his boots getting tangled in one another, he lost his balance. The ground rose up to meet him, looming dark and hard enough to crack teeth. And then there was an arm around his waist, reeling him around until he was pressed into the firmness of Yoshi's chest.

"Are you all right?" Yoshi asked, voice soft, worried, and a little smug. How was that combination even possible? Cricket wasn't sure. And perhaps had he not almost smashed his face on the ground a moment ago, maybe he would have taken issue with the smug part of Yoshi's tone. But as he had almost busted his beautiful visage on the ground, he would let Yoshi have his smugness.

"Ah... Haha..." Cricket laughed nervously, pulling away from the hold Yoshi had on him. "I'm fine. Thanks for that. Sometimes I just...lose track of my feet."

"Mm." Yoshi continued to hold Cricket's waist for a moment longer than might have been deemed appropriate, but Cricket reasoned he was likely just worried the prince would fall again. A reasonable concern.

"We should umm... We should keep looking. It went that way." He hooked his thumb over his shoulder to gesture in the direction, and Yoshi nodded.

They headed off after the stag but saw no more of it for the remainder of the evening.

"YOU KNOW, I wonder if we could try some traps to capture it," Cricket said as he walked down the lamp-lit streets two nights later. The previous two nights all they had managed to do was chase the stag into the woods where it had promptly lost them. "Nothing too complex, of course. Just a net and a simple capture spell should do the trick."

Yoshi looked at him as if he were trying to figure out if Cricket were serious or not, or perhaps he was merely thinking the idea over, one could never tell with someone so inexpressive.

"You don't happen to have a net on you, do you?" Cricket grinned a little, his hands going behind his head as he stretched backwards. "I'd say we could set it up right on the edge of town, where those two buildings have the long overhangs."

"I have a net," Yoshi said by way of agreement.

"Great! Then let's head over there and get it set up." Cricket led the way to the aforementioned buildings, which did have a considerable overhang on either side of the narrow street, almost enough to touch in the middle. Almost enough to completely shield the stones below from rain if one were to stand under them.

Yoshi stopped beneath them, reaching into the small pouch on his waist to pull a vast net from within.

"Ooooh you have one of those bigger on the inside bags. You know, I never could get the charm work quite right for those." Cricket grinned, taking the net to inspect the size, and leaning back to look at the opening available to them. It wasn't terribly wide, a few feet across at most, but if they could get the stag right in the center, and drop the net, they'd be in business.

"It requires patience."

"Yes. Yes. And a steady hand, neither of which I really have time for when it comes to spellwork." Cricket shrugged. He took one side of the net to stretch it across the opening, looking up at where they'd have to attach it. "There always just seemed to be so much else I could be doing."

"Like?"

"Art. Playing with the bunnies. Going into the capital with Iggy. Scheming with Annie. Helping in the kitchens. Hiding in the library amongst all the history books. I don't know. Anything other than working with fiddly spellwork that half the time doesn't want to work anyway, and when things go awry could be rather embarrassing." Cricket laughed, stretching his fingers up as high as they'd go, and murmuring a soft spell. The magic lingered in the air for a moment, pale and sparkling as Lunette magic always did, then it lifted his half of the net up to attach to the underside of the overhang.

"Bunnies?" Yoshi asked, mimicking the gesture with his side, his own rainbow of magic settling the net in place.

"Yeah, you know, long ears, soft fur, a whole host of colors, hops around and eats cabbage. Bunnies. You have any chalk?" Cricket knelt on the ground under the net, holding out his hand as he examined the stones. "It won't be the smoothest trapping circle I've ever created, but it will do."

"There are bunnies in the palace?" Yoshi procured a thick chunk of blue chalk from his pouch and set it into Cricket's outstretched palm.

"Well, not inside the actual palace. Although, don't think I didn't try, but Father said they weren't indoor pets. They have their own hutch in the gardens, it's huge. Big enough to host a small tea party if you wanted, which we did a lot when

I was growing up." Cricket kept muttering, his hands making quick work of the space beneath the net. Scribbling in symbols and infusing the chalk with magic. "There. That ought to do it." He rose, wiping his hands on his trousers, and tossing the chalk back to Yoshi.

"Why bunnies?" Yoshi asked as Cricket stood back to examine his work.

"Huh? Oh, haven't you heard? I'm the bunny prince." He laughed, winking at Yoshi. "Right then, let's go chase it this way."

"The bunny prince," Yoshi repeated as if testing the words out on his tongue, long and slow.

"Long story. I'll tell you later." Cricket tapped the side of his nose grinning. "Right now we've got a stag to catch."

THE NET SEEMED like a good idea, in theory. It should have been easy, chase the stag through the capture circle, the net would fall onto it, and it'd be caught. Alls well that ends well.

Except this didn't end well, so he supposed it wasn't all well.

"Get me out of here," Cricket grunted, wriggling again which only served to tangle the net further around his body. "It's getting away."

Yoshi squared him with a look that might have been something along the lines of *be quiet*, or *stay still*, or perhaps both. Either way there was exasperation painted in the lines of Yoshi's firmly pressed lips.

"It's pulling my hair," Cricket whined.

Yoshi huffed.

It took them another fifteen to twenty minutes to free

Cricket, and his hair, of the net and by then the stag was long gone. Another night was wasted.

"I TOLD you following it into the woods wasn't a good idea," Cricket grumbled from where he sat in the middle of a gently moving stream. The water was a couple inches deep, not enough to drown anyone, but certainly enough to make him feel cold in the later summer night air.

Yoshi leveled a look at him, and Cricket didn't need to hear the words to know what he was thinking.

"Fine! *You* told *me* that following it into the woods wasn't a good idea." He huffed, crossing his arms over his chest. "But how was I supposed to know we wouldn't be able to see well enough?"

"It is a new moon," Yoshi said simply. He stepped carefully across the slick stones, the soft glow of a magic orb floating over his shoulder.

"Whatever. You can gloat later. Help me up."

"ALL RIGHT NOW I think it's just playing with us!" Cricket shouted, from where he'd fallen headfirst into the fountain at the center of town. Thankfully he hadn't hit his head, there had been some real danger there.

Yoshi held his hands out to help him out of the musty smelling water.

"Stop laughing at me!"

"I am not."

A FORTNIGHT! It had been a fortnight! And thus far Cricket had been caught in his own net, dumped into several bodies of water, and now had a bruised tailbone that he was fairly certain would make riding a horse quite difficult in the coming weeks.

"Please," Ignacia said, taking a deep breath in through her teeth. "Explain to me why *riding* the ghost stag seemed like a good idea?"

Cricket shifted on the pillow beneath his bottom, hissing. "I thought it would take me back to its den."

"And you didn't think it would buck you off?"

"Well, there was a chance of that. But I'm a pretty good rider. I figured I could handle it. Plus, Yoshi was there." Cricket shrugged.

"Yes. Yoshi was there." Ignacia's eyes narrowed on Yoshi who was sitting beside Cricket, murmuring a spell under his breath to cool the pillow as the healer instructed. "I remember very clearly saying that you were meant to keep him from doing anything stupid."

"You said to have his back," Yoshi said evenly. The soft rainbows of magic, reminiscent of sun dogs, filtered into the pillow cooling it and numbing the bruised skin to Cricket's relief. "I did have his back."

"And yet here he is. Bruised."

"I was not quick enough. I will endeavor to do better next time." Yoshi pursed his lips in his determination.

"Impossible! You're both impossible!" Ignacia flung

herself back on her bed. "Fine. What is your next wild gambit?"

"Ask me again in the morning." Cricket yawned, his jaw cracking with the motion. Then he leaned over toward Yoshi without a second thought and rested his head on Yoshi's shoulder. "The healer's pain herbs have made me sleepy."

Ignacia huffed but didn't say anymore.

CHAPTER 25

"I guess our luck has run out," Cricket panted tartly.

Yoshi turned to look at him, his expression blank as usual, but Cricket thought he saw a flickering of *be quiet and run!* written in his eyes. Then he turned back to look at the stag galloping ahead of them.

Cricket could feel the pressure of the hunters at their back. Their crazed, half-hazed stares making the back of his neck prickle with nervousness. They needed to make it to the woods and cut the hunters off or the stag would never escape. He stumbled; foot caught on a loose stone in the road. Yoshi's arm reached out lightning fast to grab his elbow and keep him from falling as they ran.

"Thanks," Cricket breathed, offering Yoshi an embarrassed smile.

Yoshi merely nodded in return.

The stag led them down an alley off the main road through town. It seemed as if it thought it could hide its light in the darkness and escape that way. But it merely glowed brighter, and as it reached the end the soft glow fell upon a dead end.

"No." Cricket skidded to a halt and spun. His hand pulling the sword from his waist and immediately falling into position.

Yoshi was quick to follow his example, settling beside him.

"How many were there?"

"Ten."

"Don't hurt anyone if you can help it, it's not their fault. They aren't in their right minds." Cricket frowned. The footsteps were growing closer. There was no way the hunting party hadn't seen them turn down the darkened alley.

"There they are!" One of them shouted, and the whole group piled into the end of the alley. It was a tight fit, of that Cricket felt they could be grateful. It meant he and Yoshi wouldn't have to take on the full crowd at once. Three at a time was manageable, if not ideal.

Battle sounds soon filled the small space. Daggers ringing against sword blades, and grunts of fists when they connected with a soft part of someone's face or body in their attempt to get to the stag. Cricket ignored the pain still radiating from his tailbone and focused on the next connection of fist to jaw.

"That's right where Iggy hit me!" Cricket groaned, rubbing at the still yellow-green bruise on his face that would no doubt be black and blue again by morning. He staggered back under another blow from the man's dagger. Then stumbled over one of the fallen hunters, falling to the ground with his legs draped over the man's back. His sword clattered to the ground, leaving him open to another swipe of the dagger which suddenly looked much sharper than it had a moment ago.

The man lunged, the blade glinting in the moonlight. Cricket yelped, lifting his hands to stop it as best he could. Another clank of metal on metal sounded before the sting of the dagger, and Cricket looked up to find Yoshi's sword holding the blade at bay. The man pulled back, and lunged again, knocking Yoshi's arm, and drawing a thin stream of blood. Cricket thought fast, magic fluttering through the air like dust motes as he whispered under his breath, and then reached out to grab the man's wrist. There was some struggle, but Cricket tightened his hold, and then the man succumbed to the sleeping spell.

"You need to go." Yoshi spun to put himself between Cricket and another attacker. "Get the stag out of here."

"They'll try to follow us." Cricket stood, searching for his sword in the gloom as he dodged a punch aimed for his nose.

"I will hold them off."

"I can't ask you to do that." Cricket's magic whispered through the air, a string of it wrapping around the man's ankle trying to sneak around them to the stag and yanking him off his feet.

"You are not asking." They'd thinned the hunting party, but Cricket could hear another in the distance. They would just keep coming, and he didn't know how much longer he and Yoshi could hold them off. "I will clear a path, get the stag to the forest. I will see you at the inn in the morning."

Cricket opened his mouth to argue again. To tell Yoshi that this was too much. That he couldn't possibly hold off two whole hunting parties by himself. That he'd get himself hurt, and that was unacceptable. But in the next moment they were both knocked from their feet by the stag. The creature stumbled, and Cricket could hear the unmistakable sound of an arrow hitting home.

"Now. Cricket. Get it out of here now!" Yoshi ordered, his tone near frantic (or as near frantic as someone like Yoshi could be) as he moved quickly in front of the creature and began to cut a path for them.

The stag bumped Cricket lightly with its hip.

"Huh? Oh. Right. Are you actually going to let me ride you this time?" He asked, meeting the creature's dark eyes curiously.

It bent its head low in a slow nod.

"All right then." Cricket hoisted himself onto its back. From that position he was able to reach down and break off the length of the arrow. "We can't remove it yet; it'll bleed too quickly. But I'll patch you up once we're safe. Okay?"

It nodded again, then turned to pick its way carefully across the fallen hunters, following the path Yoshi was clearing for them.

"We're going to have a long chat about all of this once we're safe." Cricket chided softly. He leaned forward to wrap his arms around the stag's long neck.

"There are more coming," Yoshi said. He was panting, his chest heaving just enough to make it obvious that he'd exerted himself. The last few of the hunting party had fallen under a combination of magic and quick footwork.

"You be careful, Yoshi." Cricket frowned, reaching down to grab at his shoulder. "I want you back in one piece."

Yoshi lifted a hand to give the one Cricket had rested on his shoulder a returning squeeze. Then he pulled away and led them to the mouth of the alley. The street beyond was clear, for the time being, but that didn't mean they had time to waste.

"I will meet you at the inn in the morning," Yoshi said again.

Cricket nodded. Then he dug his heels into the stag softly. "Let's go!"

The stag took off at an easy gallop. When the creature wasn't trying to buck him off, it was a lot smoother of a ride. They had made it out of Taini and into the forest beyond,

Cricket could just hear the first sounds of a sword ringing out against the second hunting party.

"I hope Yoshi's all right." Cricket whispered, leaning closer to the stag to avoid being hit with any passing branches.

THE STAG CARRIED him deep into the forest, to a cave hidden in the side of a hill by vines, and overgrowth. By the time the stag knelt to let Cricket ease himself to the ground, its flank was stained red with blood from the arrow wound.

"I don't have any bandages," Cricket said, kneeling to dig through his satchel. "Iggy usually carries that kind of thing for me. But I have a spare scarf, I'm sure we can make do with that."

The stag bowed its head in thanks.

Cricket ripped the scarf down the middle and went to hunt down some water. He returned with the wet half of the scarf, and settled beside the stag with a wince. Pulling the arrow from its flank was no easy task, but once it was out Cricket made quick work for cleaning and dressing the wound.

Brushing his hands on his trousers to clean them, he sat back on his heels. "You're not really a deer at all are you?"

The stag shook its head.

"I didn't think so." He sighed, running a hand over the loose strands of hair that the ride through the forest had pulled from his braid. "Do you stay a stag when the sun is up."

The stag nodded.

"Hmm, that's interesting. Then why has no one seen you in the daylight?"

The stag just looked at him.

"Right, only yes or no questions. Got it." He drummed his fingers on his thigh, leaning forward to put less weight on his still bruised backside. "You were trying to tell me something that first night, weren't you? Running around that block like you did."

The stag nodded again, this time faster, more eagerly.

"Well, at least you're more expressive than Yoshi." Cricket chuckled under his breath. "You don't happen to be Emrys Cannan's fiancée, do you?"

The stag nodded again, rising to its hooves to press its face closer to Cricket's. It nudged his cheek with its muzzle.

Cricket laughed a little, patting its head. "Right then we've just got to figure out how to get you human again. It was the ring, wasn't it? Or the opal rather, as Yoshi and I figured."

The stag tilted its head, it wasn't quite a shrug, but he supposed deer didn't shrug.

"Hmm." Cricket tapped at his chin thoughtfully. "Well, we'll just have to drag him out here to see you and see what we can come up with. Hopefully it's something simple."

The stag let out a puff of breath, a sigh really, and then settled back onto the floor of the cave.

"I should be getting back into town. I can't leave Yoshi to fend off all those hunters by himself." Cricket stood, brushing off his trousers with his hands. The stag rose to follow him, and Cricket held out a hand to stop it, patting lightly at its back. "No. No. If you come back, you'll just make things more of a mess. I can find my way back to town on my own."

It looked at him, its head cocked to one side as if to ask if he were sure.

"Yeah, I'll be just fine. I can follow the magic trail you left back out. It should still be fresh. You stay hidden until I come to get you. Don't come back into town tomorrow, all right?"

It nodded.

"Good. I promise you; Yoshi and I are going to get this sorted." He gave the creature another light pat on the back and then headed to the mouth of the cave.

FINDING his way back to town turned out to be the easy part of the remainder of the evening. The hard part was finding Yoshi on the outskirts of the forest. His pale blue tunic was a splatter of blood, and Cricket was sure not all of it was someone else's. He'd fallen to his knees, but not gone down entirely. Still, his chest was heaving with each breath.

"Yoshi!" Cricket fell to his knees beside him, hands flitting over his injuries as he tried to assess them in the dark. "Styx, this is bad."

"Flesh wounds." Yoshi's speech slurred a little.

"Yeah, but there's still blood loss to worry about. Don't be stupid."

"Not stupid."

Cricket sighed. "Right. Of course not. Come on, let's get you back to the inn, and then I'll have someone go out for the healer. We won't be seeing the stag for a little bit so we should be safe for tonight."

"Where is she?" Yoshi looked up at Cricket as he rose, pulling on Yoshi's arm to tug him to his feet. "Is she safe?"

"Yes. She's safe. I told her to stay put until we could go and get her though. So for now let's worry about you, yeah? I told you I wanted you back in one piece." With Yoshi on his feet, Cricket pulled his arm across his shoulders to support his weight as they made their way back through Taini.

"I am in one piece." Yoshi looked down at himself. "Mostly."

"Was that a joke? Yoshi! I didn't know you were funny!" Cricket laughed loudly.

Yoshi looked at him, and Cricket thought he caught the hint of a smile in his eyes.

CHAPTER 26

It was still too early for Cricket's taste when the hunters from the previous night showed up. Not all of them, of course, some of them were in pretty rough shape from their fight with him and Yoshi, but enough of them that Cricket could feel rage, sharp and hot, forming in the pit of his stomach. He didn't think he'd ever been so angry in his life. It wasn't like him to get angry about things, but this...this was a mistake that could have been...*should* have been avoided.

"Your Highness," a woman said, kneeling before him and holding up his forgotten sword. It took everything in him to keep from snatching the weapon. So much so that his hand shook when he reached for it.

"We deeply apologize, Your Highness." Another of the small party fell to his knees and dragged the other two down with them.

"Do you?" Cricket asked, the barely concealed fury making his voice quiver. "Are you sorry? What of this are you most sorry for, I wonder? Is it for defying a direct edict from your prince? Is it for putting your lives in danger over something I was handling? Is it for almost hurting your prince in your stupidity? Or—" Cricket stopped for a moment to look back to Yoshi. He was fine of course, as he'd said it had all been flesh wounds. A swipe of a blade here, a bruise there. But the bandages still peeked out from under his clothing, and it made something sick settle into Cricket's stomach. "Or is it for nearly slicing my companion to ribbons?!"

He waited, to see if any of them would argue with him. To see if they'd even dare open their mouths and offer an excuse. There was some excuse for their action, Cricket could see why they had taken matters into their own hands. But that didn't change how irritated he was by it, and he had to wonder if Father had been there, if the edict had been put out by Father or even Uncle and had their signature on it, would the hunters have been foolish enough to go against them? Or was it just because Cricket was the prince? Young. And inexperienced. They must think. That thought made his hand tighten around his sword, knuckles turning white.

No one spoke. They kept their eyes firmly on the ground as if afraid to meet the heat of their prince's gaze.

"Tonight," he hissed through a clenched jaw when the silence had become unbearably uncomfortable for even him. "You will stay home. If I see anyone, and I mean *anyone*, on the streets of Taini that is not one of my personal party, there will be consequences. Have I made myself clear?"

A collective nod.

"I need a verbal assurance." Cricket growled. "Have I made myself clear?"

"Yes, Your Highness," they said in unison.

"Good. Now I do not want to see any of the faces I saw last night until all of this is over. Get out of my sight! And be sure to tell the rest of the fools what I've said."

Once they were all gone, Cricket moved to his seat at the table and collapsed into the chair. There was a strange look on Yoshi's face. He could see it from the corner of his eye, but he didn't have time to deal with that just now.

"Iggy, I need you to take a message to Mister Cannan. Have him come here after his evening hunting; we need his help with this." She blinked at him, and Cricket shooed her. "Go on before he leaves for the morning."

Ignacia huffed but rose from her seat. Her ankle had healed, finally, and she rushed from the room to follow orders. When they were alone, Cricket set his sheathed sword on the chair beside him.

"That was not necessary," Yoshi said quietly.

"I gave an order." Cricket wasn't in the mood to argue about his decisions. Least of all with Yoshi, who had a long expanse of bandage wrapped around his forearm which the healer had left exposed after removing his ruined gloves.

Yoshi did not argue, but he looked as if he maybe wanted to, his brows pinched just a hair at the center, and his throat working in a rough swallow.

"You should go and get some rest." Cricket sighed, running a hand over his face.

"I am fine." Yoshi sat up straighter, lifting his chin.

"That wasn't a suggestion. Go to your room and get some rest. We have another long night ahead of us." Cricket bit the words out, teeth gnashing on them. He kept his eyes on the table in front of him. Not wanting to see the look on Yoshi's face.

"Yes, My Prince." Yoshi rose from the chair, careful of his injuries. He stood there for a moment, breathing silently, as he seemed to ponder something. Then he said, "You should rest as well. Long night."

"Yeah. I'll rest." Cricket laughed almost wetly.

Unlike Ignacia, or Anstice would have, Yoshi said nothing else. He had to know that Cricket wasn't going to rest. He had to know that Cricket was too keyed up and restless to do any such thing. But he at least gave Cricket the mercy of not calling him on it as his sisters might have done. Cricket wasn't sure how he felt about that.

He shook his head and headed out of the inn. His sword at his waist again, he tried not to notice how the people of Taini avoided his eyes. He'd failed them. Was *still* failing them. They expected their prince to ride in on his horse and solve everything, but there they were more than a fortnight later, and at least on the outside it looked like he was no closer to solving the mystery of the ghost stag. More people were hurt now than before he'd shown up, some of them even at his own hand. And he had to wonder if maybe they would have been better off had he followed Uncle Sunil's advice and sent soldiers instead of coming himself. At least then maybe Yoshi and Ignacia wouldn't have been hurt by his own lack of...whatever it was he was lacking.

"You've spent the whole day sulking, haven't you?" Ignacia asked when he returned to the inn that evening just before supper.

Cricket shrugged, not meeting her gaze as he fell into his chair and pulled a plate toward himself.

"It wasn't your fault. You know that, don't you? What happened to me, to Yoshi, it wasn't your fault." Ignacia's voice was soft, reassuring. It chafed more than anything else he'd said to himself that day. Like she thought he needed to be coddled because he was weak, and fragile. And maybe he was, but she didn't have to say as much. "Yoshi, tell him it wasn't his fault."

Yoshi, Selene bless him, said no such thing. He just

grabbed another steamed bun from the pile on the plate and said, "Emrys Cannan will be here soon."

It didn't quiet the doubt, or the fear, but it did give Cricket something else to focus on for the moment. Something he could do in the face of those emotions. He nodded. "Iggy, I want you to patrol the streets. Make sure no one is out past curfew."

"But the stag..." Ignacia frowned.

"She won't be a problem. I've spoken with her, and she's agreed to let us come to her tonight. She'll stay in her hiding place until I can reach her. You'll be safe." Cricket poured himself a cup of tea, hoping it would settle the gnawing pit in his stomach. It didn't, and he wasn't sure if putting food in it would help either.

"Then why didn't you go during the day?"

"Because we don't know what the magic would be like during the day," Cricket said simply. His teacup made a soft *thunk* as he spun it round and round on the table. "I don't want to take any chances on it affecting us differently, or what it might do to Emrys. I also don't know what the stag will be like during the day. She said she would still be a stag, but she may not know."

"She?"

"You think it's Eniko, don't you?" Emrys asked from where he was standing next to the table. There was a wild look in his eyes, and Cricket wondered how much he had heard, but he supposed it didn't matter. What was done was done, and he'd have to explain anyway.

"I do." Cricket nodded.

"When can I see her? Can we go now? How is she? Is she eating all right? Has anyone hurt her?" The words left Emrys in a rush. He reached for Cricket, seeming to want to grab him by the shoulders, and then thinking better of it and abandoning the motion halfway.

"Mister Cannan. Emrys." Cricket lifted his head to give the man a stern look. He could see the panic in Emrys's eyes, but it would do none of them any good to panic right then. "Please sit and have supper with us. We will do our best to answer all of your questions, and head out after it gets dark."

Emrys looked as if he might want to say more. To demand answers. To drag Cricket away to show him where the stag was right then. But he remembered himself quickly enough, nodded, and sat next to Ignacia.

THE FOREST WAS quiet around them. No sound of nighttime insects. No owls hooting. Just the unsettling rustle of leaves in the wind.

"It's never this quiet during the day." Emrys's worry seemed to echo in the silence.

"It's the malice in the magic," Cricket said, following the lingering trail of magic in the air. It had taken some doing to find it again, magic only lingered so long, and it had been nearly twenty-four hours. But after sitting where he'd found Yoshi on the edge of the wood and meditating for all of five minutes (he hated meditating. Who wanted to just sit still and be quiet? No one.), he'd found it again. It was faint, fading stardust in the darkness of the trees, but it was there. "Non-magical creatures avoid curse magic if they can. They've probably moved on to another part of the forest."

"They will come back," Yoshi assured. "Once we have solved this."

Cricket hummed in agreement. The cave was deeper in the woods than Cricket remembered, but as they approached the stag poked her glowing white head out of the curtain of vines. She looked at them, and then her eyes widened at the sight of Emrys and she backed away, hiding herself in the cave again.

"Eniko," Emrys breathed beside Cricket, taking quick steps to the mouth of the cave.

Cricket grabbed his arm to stop him. "Let her come out to you."

"But..."

"She is frightened." Yoshi's tone was soft, understanding. Unlike Cricket had ever heard from him before.

Emrys let out a loud breath through his nose, and then moved to sit on the ground. "Eniko, please."

The stag poked her nose out again, looking at Emrys. When Emrys just sat, and waited for her to come to him, she took first one careful step then another, and then another until she was standing before him. He reached for her, and she flinched, but didn't run again.

"You're safe," Cricket assured her.

With a little dip of her head, she bent her legs, and kneeled before Emrys, looking him in the eye.

"Eniko?" Emrys asked, his hands fisting on his thighs to keep from reaching out. "I'm so sorry. This is all my fault."

The stag sighed, stretching forward a little to lay her head in Emrys's lap. Emrys let out a wet sob, and then he was pressing his forehead to the glowing white fur of Eniko's own forehead. Cricket looked away; he didn't have to see the tears trickling down to know they were there. A crack, like thunder during a storm, and when Cricket looked back the stag had shifted into the blonde woman, her head leaning onto Emrys's knee as he cried, and ran his fingers through her long hair.

Yoshi pulled his cloak off his shoulders and offered it to her to cover up.

"Thank you," Eniko said, voice tight with emotion, and disuse. "Thank you both."

"You are welcome." Yoshi's eyes were carefully locked on the ground between them, to protect Eniko's modesty, or his own, Cricket wasn't sure.

"Let's go home," Emrys whispered a little brokenly.

"Home." Eniko sounded wistful, and soft. Emrys stood, helping her to her feet, and covering the rest of her with Yoshi's cloak. Then he scooped her up.

"Lead the way, Prince Cricket."

Cricket smiled. The way back to Taini was quiet. Emrys and Eniko in their own world, and Yoshi a steady presence at his side.

"We'll need to get the ring from them," Cricket said softly. His eyes flitting back to the couple where they trailed behind.

"They will understand." Yoshi sounded so sure, and confident it was hard not to see how this could settle itself so simply.

"I hope it's as easy as all that." Cricket scrubbed his face tiredly. The malice of the magic lingered in the air, keeping the forest silent. It was not going to be that easy, he knew it without having to see the ring.

CHAPTER 27

Famous last words, Cricket thought as he stared down at the ring which had fused with Eniko's finger. It looked like the gold had melted into her pale skin, or her skin had melted into the gold, he wasn't sure which. Not that it mattered, either way, it was stuck.

"Well," Cricket said, licking his lips nervously. "That's not good."

Yoshi cut him a look that clearly said, *you think?* in the most judgmental tone possible. Cricket thought maybe he liked it better when he couldn't read Yoshi's expressions so easily. At least then he didn't know that he was being judged ninety percent of the time.

"Maybe it's not active anymore? Maybe we broke the curse when Eniko turned back into a woman." Emrys sounded hopeful. His fingers were clasping onto Eniko's right hand tight enough to make Cricket wince, but Eniko didn't complain, she held on just as tight. "She might not turn again."

"No." Cricket sighed, letting Eniko's hand drop so he could scrub at his face. "If the curse were broken, we'd have no problem removing the ring. And because it's fused with Eniko that means it's feeding off her own internal magic to keep itself going. It won't run out on its own."

"But she's not a stag anymore." Cricket was sure Emrys's argument sounded weak, even to his own ears.

"For now." Yoshi's words were soft, as if to negate the hurt they would cause, but they both knew there was no way to soften the blow. Nor was there any way to undo what would have to be done to protect Emrys, Eniko, and all of Taini.

"Yoshi's right. Everything seems fine now but what about tomorrow night? Or the night after that? Or maybe it'll be on the next full moon? The curse isn't done with her. And we can't take the chance that it'll cost Taini any more lives." Cricket shook his head, tucking his hands behind his back to keep the others from seeing them tremble. "The ring has to be removed by any means necessary."

"Can't we just...wait, and see?" Emrys was all but begging by this point. His eyes shone glassy with tears. "And...and even if she does change again, I can bring her back, right? Eniko?"

Eniko looked up from the ring. Her expression was somewhere between confusion and upset. As if she'd gone so long without someone speaking to her that now she wasn't sure what to do with herself. She didn't know how to make this choice, and she shouldn't have to.

"No," Cricket said, soft but firm. "If it keeps using her magic like it is, one of two things will happen. Either it'll kill her, or she'll be stuck as a stag next time she changes. The madness she inspired before will continue, and the ring will feed off that as well, only becoming stronger. We can't take that chance."

"How do you know?"

Cricket sighed, shoulders slumping. "Because I know."

"I think he's right, Emrys," Eniko said, her voice soft, and still a little strained. "I can feel it feeding off of me. We have to get it off."

"Isn't there another way? A spell? Or a potion?" Emrys sounded desperate. Cricket couldn't blame him; he didn't like this solution any more than Emrys did. It was the least bad of a series of bad options, but it was still in the end, a bad option.

"I'm afraid not."

Emrys looked to Yoshi, as if hoping he would give them something else. Some other way.

Yoshi shook his head. "The prince is correct; we do not have any good choices."

"But—"

"Can we have a few hours?" Eniko asked, cutting off Emrys's protests. "Just until first light. We've been away from each other for so long, and…"

"Of course. Of course. I'll send someone by in the morning to escort you to the healer so we can get the ring sealed away as soon as possible. The healer will ensure that it's safe and painless. If you'd like we can have a guard set up outside? In case you're worried about repercussions from the rest of Taini." Cricket's tone had gone flat, he could feel it. It was like he was listing off facts from a textbook. The words themselves echoed through his insides around an emptiness he couldn't quite understand.

"We aren't. But I… I uh… I want you to be there with us." Eniko turned her head from Emrys's to meet Cricket's eyes. And oh, that was so much worse. He didn't know how he would stomach watching the healer remove the ring and the finger attached to it. He was sure that he wouldn't, but he didn't have much choice. Eniko had asked him to, and he would be there.

"Yes. I'll—I'll meet you here tomorrow morning?"

"Thank you, Your Highness." Eniko smiled, and Cricket felt his stomach twist violently.

"Of course." Bile rose hot and sharp in the back of his throat, burning, but he swallowed it down. "Of course."

"We should go," Yoshi said. He had already taken the first few steps toward the door and the stairs beyond when he turned back to look at Cricket. "To rest."

"Yes. We should. Good night you two. I'll see you at first light." Cricket bowed shallowly, and the couple returned it more deeply before he let Yoshi drag him back out into the cool night air with his expectant gaze alone.

"You are not all right," Yoshi said the words as if they were fact. They were, but that didn't mean Yoshi had to say so.

Cricket closed his eyes, letting the darkness settle into his skin, and cool the fine layer of sweat which had coated his face. "No. I am not all right."

"You did not have to agree." If Cricket didn't know better, which he did, he'd say Yoshi sounded concerned.

"I did." It wasn't an argument, not in Cricket's mind, it was another fact. Inevitable, and true, just like *you are not all right*. He could not have said no even if he had wanted to, and oh, how he wanted to. But this was not about him, and he couldn't deny Eniko what little comfort his presence might provide.

Yoshi nodded his understanding, or agreement, or whatever he was thinking when he nodded. Who knew? Not Cricket. "There was no other way."

"No. But that doesn't make this hurt less." The inn door shut behind them, and Cricket was grateful for its emptiness. He didn't think he had the strength in him to put up the front of the prince Taini needed. Not today. Maybe not tomorrow either, not that he had any choice in that. It was a relief to slide open the door to his and Ignacia's room and find that she was still patrolling. He turned to shut the door, but Yoshi was standing in the doorway. "You should go to bed."

"I will stay with you. At least until Ignacia returns."

"That's not necessary, Yoshi. I'm fine." Cricket sighed. He felt his body sag against the door, wanting to push it shut, and collapse onto the floor if he couldn't make it to the bed. The bed did look very far away at the present time. Perhaps he could just sleep on the floor.

"You are not all right." Yoshi didn't wait for Cricket to argue further, he swept into the room as if it were his own, pushed the door shut, and took hold of Cricket's elbow to guide him to his bed. He nudged Cricket gently, and then sat on the cushion beside his bed. "Rest."

Cricket exhaled deeply, and laid back, staring up at the ceiling.

IT BURNED. Why did it burn? Cricket squinted to keep the early morning glare at bay.

"You didn't have to come," he said, frowning at Yoshi.

Yoshi gave no reply.

"Really, Yoshi. Iggy could have come with me."

"Ignacia was patrolling all last night, as per your orders. Which you did not retract." Yoshi did not sound as annoyed or judgmental of this oversight as Cricket might have thought he'd be. It had been an obvious lapse in Cricket's leadership, but no one had chided him for it. It must be because of how terrible he looked after a night of tossing and turning. Perhaps he should have looked in the mirror before leaving after all.

"Then I would have been fine on my own," Cricket tried to protest.

"You are not all right," Yoshi said. It was the third time he'd said those words in the span of twenty-four hours, and Cricket wasn't really sure what they meant any more now than he'd been the first time. Of course, he was not all right. He was asking one of his subjects to have her finger amputated just because there was no better solution to a curse.

"No," Cricket agreed. "I'm not."

"We will find who is responsible for this. They will be punished for hurting your subjects."

Cricket wondered if Yoshi heard how those words sounded coming from his lips. It was as if they'd been carved into stone, an inevitable, immovable, force of nature. Yoshi would see to it that whoever did this was punished. He would make this right.

"Thank you," Cricket said softly, knocking on the front door of Emrys's residence.

"Mm." Yoshi ducked his head to look down at their feet, as if perhaps he were embarrassed by the sincerity in Cricket's tone. But no... that couldn't be right.

THE WALK to the healer's was silent. Not that Cricket had expected anything different. He was just glad that Eniko seemed on board with this plan and wasn't fighting them. It would make things so much worse if she were to fight. He didn't want to feel like he was forcing her. He wanted to feel like she understood the why behind this horrible thing. And she did.

"Eniko! It's so nice to see you dear girl!" The healer

moved a little too quickly for someone so old, gripping Eniko in a bear hug that caused Eniko to inhale sharply. "I've missed you."

"Yes, I've missed you too, Granny." Eniko smiled, hugging the healer back.

"I told everyone you'd be back. Didn't I tell everyone, Emrys? I told them that you hadn't run away to find another man. Why would you when you have Emrys?" The healer laughed, punching Emrys playfully in the arm. When he didn't smile back at her, she frowned. "What is it? What's happened?"

Loud exclamations and fussing followed the question. In the end, they deferred to Cricket and let him explain everything that had happened, and how he'd learned of the stag's true identity.

"I... I don't know what else to do." Cricket faltered. The healer had brought out a large lens so she could get a better look at the cursed object in question. She'd been humming and haww-ing over it for a good two minutes at least.

"No. No. You're quite right. The only way to sever the magical tie the curse has made with Eniko is to remove the finger entirely. You're lucky it's not worse." The healer tucked the lens into a large pocket on her apron and went to a dark wooden cabinet full of tiny drawers. From one of them she pulled a small green vial and returned to the examination table that she'd set Eniko up on. "Take this dearie, it'll keep you from being too lucid during the procedure."

"Thank you." Eniko downed the whole vial in one quick gulp.

"Wait. Worse?!" Emrys asked at the same time. He moved to take Eniko's free hand and held it tightly.

"Oh yes. Much worse. If the prince hadn't suggested you come here and get this taken care of right away it may have infected the rest of her arm. Magic like this never just stops, it has to *be* stopped." The healer grabbed a knife from another cabinet and sat on a small stool next to the table. Cricket could see the knife already buzzing with magic. To make it a clean cut. To seal the wound after. To heal as much as to harm. "Prince, do you have your sealing pouch ready? None of us should have contact with this thing for any longer than we need to, lest it get it into its head to latch onto someone else."

Cricket nodded. Bile rose hot and angry in his throat again, making his eyes burn.

"Well bring it here, boy, I don't want to have to rush it to you." The healer pointed to the spot beside her rickety stool. "Lay back dearie. We'll make this quick."

"Yes ma'am." Cricket forced his voice to be steady, even as his hands shook, and knees wobbled. What followed either happened too fast for Cricket to follow, or his vision swam too much. Either way, there was a scream, and a soft thud, and then he was scooping the finger up into the bag and running from the room on trembling legs to keep from throwing up on Eniko. Cricket didn't hear the footsteps behind him, but he felt the firm grip on his elbow that kept him from toppling to the ground as the edges of his vision grew dark.

"Breathe, Cricket. Breathe." Yoshi's voice was far away, like at the end of a tunnel. It echoed off the walls of Cricket's head, making it sound distorted and strained. Or maybe it was actually strained? He didn't know. "Count with me. In. One. Two. Three. Out. One. Two. Three."

Cricket wasn't sure what he was saying, but he took in a breath, and held it for the count, then let it out again in a soft whoosh. It made the darkness recede, but his legs refused to straighten again. Cricket wondered when it was that Yoshi had wrapped him up tight in his arms. Not that it mattered. It definitely didn't matter.

"Good. That is very good. Come, let us head back to the inn and get some water."

"Water sounds nice."

"I am sure it does. And perhaps some breakfast—if you think your stomach can handle it?" Yoshi was already half-carrying Cricket back down the slowly busying streets of Taini. No one was looking at them, and Cricket couldn't tell if it were because they were trying to give him his privacy in a moment of weakness, or if it were because Yoshi was shooting every one of them a death glare. Either way, he appreciated it.

"What about Eniko and Emrys?"

"The healer sent them home already."

"I'm fine," Cricket protested.

"You are not. We will get breakfast."

"Pancakes?"

"If that is what My Prince desires."

Cricket nodded, swallowing against his dry tongue which rubbed coarse against the roof of his mouth. My Prince... that sounded nice. Almost as nice as pancakes... "Yes. It is."

"Then there will be pancakes."

CHAPTER 28

As promised, there were pancakes. A fluffy stack of sugary goodness drenched in enough syrup to, if not erase the events of the morning completely, at least dull the ache of them. Cricket had never been so happy to see pancakes in his life. Yoshi sat across from him, a soft pleased lilt to his mouth, as he nibbled a piece of toast.

"Are they good?" Yoshi asked when Cricket swallowed another bite so big that it made a sharp gulping sound.

"Very." Cricket offered him a powder sugared smile, and then ducked his head back to his breakfast. He polished off half the stack before the sugar cleared his head enough to think again. "We need to sort out where we're going next."

"We do," Yoshi agreed easily. Cricket didn't want to think too much about how he'd just assumed that Yoshi would be coming with them to their next destination, and Yoshi hadn't bothered to correct him. It was probably better if they traveled together anyway, since they kept bumping into one another. That sounded reasonable, and not at all like he was enjoying Yoshi's company perhaps more than was appropriate.

"We?" Ignacia said, dropping into a seat beside Yoshi. Yoshi glanced at her from the corner of his eyes, giving her a look that could only be construed as irritated at her sudden arrival. Cricket could relate, especially as she was so loud, and well rested. "What is this 'we'?"

"Yoshi is coming with us. He's been a lot of help in Taini, and since he's trying to help with the curses too, I don't see any reason why we shouldn't travel together." Cricket shrugged. Nonchalant. Or at least he thought it was. But the skeptical look Ignacia was giving him said he probably wasn't pulling it off as well as he'd hoped. Well...damn.

"Uh huh. And who's idea was that?" Ignacia reached over to grab a half-finished pancake from Cricket's plate with her bare hands, because she was a heathen. She then rolled it up, and bit off the end, murmuring appreciatively before she swallowed. "Did you even ask him if he even wants to come with us?"

"It was my idea," Yoshi said, setting his toast down carefully.

Ignacia narrowed her eyes at him. She could tell he was lying; Cricket knew that. Ignacia was a human lie detector, it was her special brand of magic, passed down from her mother, or so she'd said. Cricket just thought she was really good at intimidating people into telling the truth. A tact that wouldn't work with Yoshi who continued to look forward impassively.

"Uh huh," she said skeptically around another bite of rolled up pancake. Then, seeming to decide it didn't matter one way or the other, she stuffed the rest of the pancake into her mouth, wiped her hands off on her napkin and clapped them together. "Right then, which way did he go?"

"We'll have to ask around and see if anyone can tell us. Maybe the innkeeper will know? He seems to pay pretty close attention to the comings and goings of Taini."

"What about the map? Didn't Anstice rig it to update when a new town was affected by the curses?" Ignacia flagged down one of the wait staff. "Can I get some pancakes too? And coffee please." Then she turned back to Cricket. "Let's see the map."

"I know she set it up so we could tell which were most dangerous based on brightness." Cricket pulled the rolled-up map from his bag, and unfurled it onto the table between glasses, and plates, using his orange juice, and Yoshi's tea to hold down each end. "Yeah, see, this won't help. I don't think it's updating at all."

"No, look, it is. Tochtli has been cleared." Ignacia pointed a finger at the small town on the map, leaving behind a powdered sugar fingerprint. Cricket glared at her, and she shrugged.

"The question is, is it self-updating or is Anstice updating it?" Cricket's fingers drummed on the table; his other hand occupied with stuffing another bite of breakfast into his mouth. "An whip of dese—"

"Swallow before you speak! Great Selene, Cricket, did your etiquette teacher instill no manners in you?" Ignacia shook her head, her expression souring.

Cricket looked across at Yoshi, helplessly, and caught a glimmer of amusement in his eyes. Or what Cricket thought might be a glimmer of amusement. It was hard to know when he'd never seen Yoshi smile, much less laugh before. What would that look like? Would his whole face light up with it? Or would it be a small, restrained thing, like the frown-wrinkle? Cricket had to know! The pancakes stuck to the roof of his mouth a little, but he peeled them away with his tongue and swallowed, his eyes flicking back to Ignacia.

"Do we know which of these are new? Do you remember which were here, and which weren't before?" he asked before grabbing his juice to take another healthy gulp more to busy himself than to distract from the heat crawling up his neck. Or so he told himself anyway.

Ignacia shook her head. A thoughtful frown knitting her brows as she began to cut up the pancakes that had just been delivered to their table. "There were so many. I couldn't... But maybe Anstice would know?"

"Let's ask the innkeeper first. Then if he doesn't have any answers, we can check in with Anstice."

"We should split up," Ignacia said, pointing her fork at Cricket for no particular reason that Cricket could see. "There are three of us, let's split up. Yoshi can speak to Emrys, I can talk to the innkeeper, and you can call Anstice."

"I don't really think that's—"

"It would be the most efficient," Yoshi interrupted, looking almost apologetic at having done it.

"Right. Cover all of the possibilities, and hopefully get the best answer. We want to make sure we're on the right track, right?" Ignacia ducked her head to take a bite which would arguably not be called a bite, and more be called a quarter of her pancakes. Really. And she called Cricket rude.

"I want to get ahead of him."

"Of course, you do," Ignacia said, somehow managing to move all of her food into her cheeks like a squirrel so she could speak around it. Clearly, she'd learned nothing from his etiquette lessons either. "This way we'll know what direction, and maybe can cut him off more easily. If we can get ahead of him, we can stop him from hurting anyone else."

"If you're sure," Cricket said, his eyes meeting Yoshi's.

"I'm sure." Ignacia finally pulled the food from her cheeks and went back to chewing it. Gross.

Yoshi cut her another look which would have frozen ice, but Ignacia seemed immune to it. Then he looked back to Cricket, and nodded once, slowly. "I am sure."

AND THAT'S how Cricket ended up on a call with Anstice all by his lonesome in his room. It wasn't that he didn't miss seeing her—because he did. It was nice to see her face, and to know she was still back home looking after Father. It was also nice to lay down and let the weariness of the morning melt from his bones. Maybe that was the real reason they'd suggested it. Maybe they had seen how wound up he'd been and were looking to give him a break. He'd have to remember to thank them later.

"Taini is safe," Cricket announced with a slow, tired smile.

"You don't look particularly excited by this victory." Anstice noticed, of course she noticed. She'd known him longer than even Ignacia. She had probably noticed the minute the mirror revealed his face.

"It doesn't really feel like a victory." He forced the words around a tightness in his chest he wasn't sure how to explain. It was clenching, but also hollow. How did that work? He wasn't sure. "It feels...it feels... I don't know how it feels, but it doesn't feel like a win."

"What happened?"

"I don't really want to talk about it, Annie. It still...it still hurts." He pushed the words past that strange restrictive feeling in his chest. "Let's just say there was some bloodshed."

Anstice nodded. Her expression was still curious, but she didn't press for answers. Small mercies. "I'll mark it off the map."

"Thank you. How's Father?" He needed some good news, any good news. Even if it was something as small as Father getting over a cold.

"On the mend. Sunil has been fussing over him non-stop

all this last fortnight. It's particularly annoying when I'm trying to meet with Jaxith about pressing matters of state." Anstice rolled her eyes.

"Good. That's good." Cricket breathed a little easier. "Now, with Taini squared away, where should we head to next? I think the responsible party is this traveling trader I keep hearing about. I want to get ahead of him, if I can. Any ideas how?" Cricket sat up on his elbows, trying to look like he was taking this more seriously. It didn't do much but make his lower back ache, but he felt he looked more alert.

"I don't have anything for you on how to cut him off. But let me talk to some of my sources and see what I can dig up. In the meantime, I need you in Nishi. They have a... Oh, what was it they called it..." Anstice shuffled some papers on her desk, cursing under her breath when she didn't find the note she was looking for right away. "Ah ha!" She held up the little scrap of paper victoriously. "Haunted mist."

"Haunted what?"

"Haunted mist. Or evil mist? Or... I don't know something with the mists. Don't use the word haunted when you tell Iggy, you know how she gets."

"Yeah... I do." Cricket wrinkled his nose, unrolling the map on the bed next to him. "That's at least a week and a half ride, if the weather holds out."

"Then may Selene bless you with clear skies." Anstice winked at him. "But enough about work. Tell me more about this white knight. You did run into him again, didn't you? Were you rude again? Please tell me you weren't."

Cricket laughed, the feeling in his chest loosening a little at the gentle ribbing from his dearest friend. "How did you know I'd run into him again? Are you psychic?"

"Lucky guess." Anstice fluttered a fan that she must have grabbed from the desk where the mirror sat, but Cricket hadn't seen before. "Tell me you've been more polite to him."

"He helped...a lot with this one. Iggy was out of commission for a fortnight with a sprained ankle. Yoshi was the only other person I could find who wasn't affected by the stag's pull. So..." Cricket shrugged, not sure he wanted to say much more than that.

"Oh, come on, that can't be all there is to it!" She huffed, swatting the fan at the mirror, and nearly knocking it from its perch. "Is he good looking? Dashing? Tell me everything!"

"I suppose that he is rather dashing... But look, Annie, as much as I love chatting with you. I think Iggy and Yoshi meant for me to get some rest. I'm going to take a nap while I wait for them to get back. Then we have to get on the road before sunset."

"Fine. Fine. Stiff me on the details. But I want all the juicy bits when you get home. Am I clear? And... and pictures! I want pictures," she demanded.

"Right. Pictures. Goodbye Annie. Give a kiss to Father for me." Cricket blew a kiss to the mirror.

"Yes, Your Highness," Anstice replied in a tone of faux seriousness, and then waved her hand over the glass. A moment later Cricket's tired reflection stared back at him. And ah... Styx, he did look just as bad as he thought he did. Sleep. Sleep was definitely in order.

BOOK IV
NISHI

<h1>CHAPTER 29</h1>

As it turned out, Selene was not in the mood for blessing anyone with anything, especially good weather, and least of all the prince and his small traveling party. They were several miles between Taini and the next town when the skies opened up to pour rain down upon them. And that was only the first of the disasters to befall them on their way to Nishi.

"It's flooded," Cricket said, his voice flat for once in his life. Rain trickled cold down the back of his tunic, the late-summer season doing nothing to keep the chill away when it had been overcast and raining for days by that point.

"Flooded? How can a bridge be flooded?" Ignacia asked, pulling Saber to a stop beside Buttercup. Cricket pointed toward the submerged bridge, and she squinted through the downpour, before nodding. "Yup. That's flooded."

"How long will it take us to go 'round?" Cricket slumped forward to hug Buttercup around the neck, ignoring how his tunic stuck to his back.

"It will add two days to the journey," Yoshi said from Cricket's other side. His majestic white horse, and his majestic white self didn't look bothered at all by the water for all it had turned them all into drowned rats. Cricket wondered how long it would take his hands to stop being pruney with things the way they were.

"What if we make camp, and try to wait it out? The water might recede?" It was false hope, Cricket could feel it even as he said the words. They were too high, forced into brightness by a warmth he wasn't sure he'd ever feel again. Still, someone needed to try, and he knew it wouldn't be Ignacia or Yoshi. Buttercup was a good choice, but she couldn't talk, so that was out.

"I think we should keep going," Ignacia said. "If we don't go around now, and the water doesn't recede we'll still have to go around in the morning, and then we'll be behind."

"But it's already getting late, Iggy. We'll lose what little light we have soon." Was Cricket begging? He didn't think he was begging. But he was pretty close to it at this rate. He just wanted to get out of the rain, just for a little bit. Even if they couldn't manage a fire in this muck.

Ignacia turned to eye him. He couldn't tell if she was squinting to keep the rain from dripping into her eyes, to be able to see him through the fading light, or because she was genuinely annoyed with him. Not that it mattered. He was used to being squinted at by her. Cricket smiled winningly and stared back. Normally, this would be a question of who would blink first, but with water pelting them there was quite a lot of blinking to go around.

"There is a forest to the south. Perhaps we can find some cover there for the night," Yoshi said, breaking their standoff. He made it sound like they had already decided what to do, and Cricket had to wonder at that. Why was Yoshi agreeing with him? It certainly couldn't be because Cricket was the highest ranking.

Selene smiled upon them long enough for them to find a

cave, and then Cricket heard a crash followed by more rushing water.

"I don't want to know what that is, do I?" he asked the darkness of the cave, hoping no one would answer.

"Likely not." Yoshi responded from somewhere closer to the mouth where he was rolling out his bedroll. "I will go see what it was."

While he was gone Ignacia and Cricket managed to scavenge some brush from the back of the cave and get a small fire going. It wasn't much, not near enough to dry their clothes, and they'd all have to lay very close to it and together to stay warm, but it was something.

Yoshi returned a half hour later, his hair had come unbound, and it hung limply around his face, his breath coming in visible puffs. "The bridge was washed away."

"Stars!" Cricket cried sprawling dramatically on his bedroll. "What else could possibly go wrong?!"

As it turned out, quite a lot. For Cricket had broken the cardinal rule of bad luck; one never asks what else could possibly go wrong, without expecting an answer.

The following morning brought a bout of the sniffles for all of them, which quickly turned into a coughing fit for Cricket. Ignacia discovered that she had set her bedroll, as if by bad fairy magic, upon a plant which caused uncontrollable itching. And Yoshi had lost his hair ribbon, which arguably was the least of their problems because it was still raining! All of these events transpired before they had even left the (relative) safety of the cave.

It continued to rain.

It continued to rain for the entire first half of their journey.

When the rain finally, blessedly, stopped, there was the mud to contend with.

"Come on Buttercup," Cricket groaned, tugging at her reins from where he stood in front of her, shin deep in mud, trying to pull her with him. "We'll get to dry ground soon. I promise. I know you hate the mud. But come on!"

Buttercup neighed unhappily at him, clomping her feet hard enough in the mud to splatter them both in the muck.

"What'd you do that for?! It just made everything worse!" he shouted, cheeks burning with irritation. Yoshi and Ignacia had gotten their horses through the lowlands no problem, but Cricket's... well, Buttercup had always been a bit of a brat.

"Come on Cricket! You're holding us up!" Ignacia called from where Saber was munching happily on some soggy grass.

"Look Buttercup, Saber is eating. Don't you want to go eat with him? Pleeeease, Buttercup, we have to go n—" just then his grip on the reins slipped and he fell backwards on his backside in the mud. Cricket threw back his head and screamed a loud and unintelligible "AAAAARGH!" at the sky.

He felt tears pricking at his eyes, wet seeping into his last dry pair of trousers, and a dark feeling clenching in his chest. He wasn't sure what it was, but he was sure he was about two seconds away from cursing up at the sky and asking Selene what he'd ever done to her to deserve such a fate.

"Here, let me help you," a soft, deep voice said from above him, and then a dark elegant hand was hovering in front of his face. Cricket looked up at Yoshi's face, a manic laugh gripping his throat so tightly he couldn't speak as his brain supplied the word *angel* for the way the sun had haloed around Yoshi's pale hair. Probably better he didn't say anything if that was what his mind was going to give him. "Let me help."

Cricket nodded, took the hand, and let Yoshi help him to his feet. He tried for a thank you, but his tongue remained stubbornly stuck to the roof of his mouth.

If this bothered Yoshi, he didn't show it. Instead, he turned to Buttercup, and clicked his tongue softly, holding out a handful of the sweet grasses from up on the hill, guiding her out of the mud puddle calmly. And somehow managing to only get traces of mud on his boots.

THEY WERE two days out from Nishi when their bad luck hit again.

It was late one evening. Late enough that visibility was low, and they should be stopping for camp soon. A deep, dark wood was off to one side of them as they trotted along another river. It would feed into the lake that was at the heart of Nishi, but for the time being the narrow road was all they had to travel on.

"We should stop soon," Cricket called, narrowing his eyes to peer ahead and see if there was a good camp area. He didn't want to set up camp just off the main road, but it didn't seem as if they were going to have much choice. They would make do, they always did. He was just about to say as such, when a howl filled the air.

"Great Selene, not now," Ignacia whispered beside him.

"Just stay calm. Maybe they're far off."

First one. Then another. Then a third, a fourth, a fifth. A pack. A whole pack. The sound grew louder as the wolves made their way toward the edge of the forest.

A shrill whinnying sound preceded a soft curse, and a thud. Cricket looked back just in time to see Yoshi's horse buck. The straps on the saddle gave way as if they'd been cut, and Yoshi was thrown off.

"Styx," Cricket cursed, steering Buttercup around. "Create a distraction," he ordered over his shoulder as he bolted back down the road toward Yoshi. It was the work of a few seconds, but the wolves in the forest were close enough that their galloping footsteps were loud in his ears. He slid off Buttercup, to his knees to check on Yoshi. The white knight was conscious, but dazed. "Can you stand? Is anything broken?"

"No. I can stand." Yoshi let Cricket help him to his feet. Then he turned a dismayed look down at the ruined saddle on the damp ground. "I cannot ride with that."

"No, you can't," Cricket agreed, already grabbing the heavy leather saddle, and throwing it over Buttercup's hind end. "You'll have to hold onto it, we'll get it fixed when we get to Nishi."

Yoshi nodded.

"Cricket! They're not following me!" Ignacia shouted from up ahead. Saber was kicking up enough earth and noise to draw the whole packs' attention but... but they weren't... Wait. Was that blood? One flick over Yoshi turned up nothing, but when he looked back to the white horse, there were several cuts where it looked as if the horse had nicked herself somehow on their journey. Nothing serious, but enough to draw the attention of wolves.

"Get on the horse!" Cricket ordered. He bent down, his hands making a basket to throw Yoshi into the saddle.

"But Lily," Yoshi protested.

"Let me worry about Lily!" He didn't wait for Yoshi to agree. He practically threw the other man onto Buttercup's back. Lily was still bucking. Her eyes wild with fear. "Iggy, check his head. I think he hit it."

"Got it," Ignacia said. Cricket turned and gave Buttercup a light smack, sending her into a gallop in Ignacia's direction, ignoring it when the ruined saddle slapped to the wet ground. To safety, for both of them. At least for the time being, until the wolves were done with Cricket and Lily.

"All right, Lily girl," Cricket crooned, holding his hands up. The wolves howled again. A nervous prickle lifted the hairs on the back of Cricket's neck. Calm. He needed to be calm. If he wasn't calm, Lily couldn't be calm. "Shhh. Shhh. I know. Those big mean doggies. Don't worry. I'm not going to let them get you."

Another loud whinnying, but at least she'd stopped bucking up onto her back legs, and Cricket counted that a victory. And then the wolves breached the tree line, and everything went to Styx in a saddlebag. Lily bucked, stumbling closer to the river. Cricket grabbed her reins in time to keep her from going further, but then he could feel the heat of the whole pack at his back.

His heart pounded in his ears so loudly he couldn't hear Ignacia or Yoshi if they were shouting, which he was sure they were. He turned slowly, making direct eye contact with the lead animal. A mistake, he knew, for the creature would see it as a challenge.

"Shoo. Go away," Cricket said in a voice that he prayed to Selene didn't shake. They didn't stop. At the front was a large grey wolf, big enough to take Cricket to the ground if it got it into its head to lunge for him. A surge went through Cricket, confidence, or magic, or what, he couldn't tell. But it flashed like lightning, electric, and hot through his veins.

Stand down. The words boomed out of him though he didn't feel them pass his lips. It was like one moment they had been thought, and the next they had been something else. Not sound necessarily, but command.

The wolves stopped immediately. Then with a whine, they turned tail and ran back into the woods. When they were gone, Cricket's shoulders slumped, and he let out a long low breath. The air smelled of the sharp, bitter, scent of ozone that always went along with his magic. Lily had stopped fighting and stood behind him with her head lowered.

"Well, that was some trick," Ignacia said by way of greeting when she and Yoshi had returned.

"Let's make camp here. I don't think they'll be coming back." Cricket turned to brush his fingers over Lily's muzzle. She leaned into the touch hesitantly. "You'll ride with me in the morning, Yoshi."

Ignacia and Yoshi looked at each other, Cricket could see the gesture from the corner of his eye. Like they weren't sure. Or they were nervous. Or they just didn't know what in the name of Styx they'd just seen. He didn't particularly care which. He was tired. Without another word they made camp, and although they took shifts keeping watch, the wolves did not return.

WITH ALL THEIR TROUBLES, the journey, which should only have taken a week and a half, took a full fortnight.

CHAPTER 30

They had ridden through the night to reach Nishi early on the fourteenth day.

The mists still clung heavily to the small city surrounding the lake for which it was named. But that was not what stuck out the most about Nishi to Cricket, no, it was the silence. Quiet hung heavy in the air with the early morning fog. While many cities, and even the villages, woke and came to life before the sun rose, Nishi had not.

Nishi was as silent as the grave.

Cricket peered through the haze to try to find some sign of life, but there was none. Not a soul on the streets. Not a flicker of movement through the fog. Not a sound. Not a breath.

What was more, as they rode into the city, they found the windows boarded up on every building that they passed. Nailed-in boards pressed so close together that Cricket would be surprised if even air could get in past them.

"Where is everyone?" Ignacia hissed, but even her hushed tone bounced off one building and then the next turning into a ghostly whisper.

"I hope we aren't too late." Cricket nudged Buttercup on, eyes flicking around them for any sign of movement. There was none. Stranger still, the place did not look abandoned per se. It didn't seem as if people had dropped everything in a frantic bid for escape. No. Things were where they ought to be. Market carts propped against their respective shops, tools in their rightful places, gardens well-watered. It looked as if everyone had just put their things away the night before and hadn't come out of their homes to use them yet. Nothing amiss. Except, these were the sights of a much earlier time, not of an hour, nearly two, past dawn. The baker, at the very least, should have had his windows open and be filling the streets with the smell of freshly baked bread. But there was nothing. Not even any horses tied up outside.

"Should we split up?"

"No." Cricket shook his head, and then his eyes caught on one of the boarded-up windows. There were scratch marks. Evidence of tiny talons trying to rip into the wood to get inside. "And don't get off your horse. If we have to make a quick getaway, I don't want to waste time mounting."

They continued on, the fog growing thicker the closer they got to the lake at the center of Nishi. There, Cricket could see more evidence of creatures trying to get inside. Not just tiny talons, but hoof marks, and claws, and maybe even a fingernail or two. It sent a shiver up his spine. Yoshi's hands tightened a little where he'd perched them on Cricket's waist.

"I think we should head back." The words were hardly out of Cricket's mouth before he heard the frantic buzzing of at least a dozen tiny wings. He felt the hum of magic in the air, an undercurrent of rage in it. "Fall back!"

"Why? What is it?" Ignacia was already wheeling Saber and Lily around to head back to the edges of Nishi. It was too late; Cricket knew it was too late. Not even horses could outrun raging pixies. Especially horses that had been carrying riders all night.

The buzzing turned into a thundering beat just before the swarm descended on them. Iridescent wings, gnashing teeth, and wicked talons ripped at Cricket's hair, at his clothes, catching on his face to draw blood. Ignacia had nudged Saber into a run, and she was steering the two horses and herself away from danger as the swarm focused its efforts on Cricket and Yoshi.

Yoshi drew his sword and slashed at them. Cricket grabbed at one of the little beasties as it tried to rip away his satchel. He squeezed it around the ribs and got a good look at its eyes right before it sank its teeth into the tender skin between thumb and forefinger. All pupil. No iris to be seen.

"Ouch!" He flung the creature away, but it had been enough for him to understand. "Don't hurt them if you can," Cricket ordered, kicking at Buttercup's side. The broken saddle fell to the ground with a loud *thwap*.

"They are attacking us," Yoshi commented dryly, but he stopped trying to slice through the pixies and instead used his sword like a club to bat them away.

"They're enchanted!"

"They're what?!" Ignacia shouted over her shoulder, switching her grip on Saber's reins to one handed so she could bat off the small group of pixies who had just taken notice of her.

"Someone or something has cursed them!"

"Well, that's nice, and all, but what are we going to do?! We can't outrun them!" Ignacia yelped as one of the creatures ripped at her ear. Yoshi wasn't faring much better behind him.

"Oi! Over here!" someone called from up ahead. "Hurry up, before the goblins see you!"

"Goblins! What goblins?!" Ignacia shouted, kicking Saber to run faster. Lily galloped along behind her.

"Hold on," Cricket muttered to Yoshi, and waited until he felt Yoshi sheath his sword, and wrap his arms around Cricket's waist. Cricket ducked his head to keep the pixies from attacking his face as best he could, and pressed Buttercup to move faster.

The doors to the blacksmith slammed shut behind them. Talons scrabbled against the wood for their prey to no avail. Cricket slumped forward, pressing his face into Buttercup's neck as he tried to catch his breath.

"What in the name of Styx are you all doing out there at this hour?" The blacksmith asked, hands moving to slender hips as he eyed them with a frown. "Don't you know all of Nishi is under curfew until at least 8?"

"No. We have just arrived," Yoshi said, somehow not out of breath.

"You just arrived?" The blacksmith moved to light a candle in the corner. "Why would you just—" He stopped, jaw dropping as he got a better look at the trio crowded into the small open space of his shop. "You're the prince."

"Yes. I am." Cricket swallowed against the cotton at the back of his throat. He pressed himself to sit up straight. "I'm here to figure out what's going on in Nishi."

"The magic has gone crazy, that's what's going on in Nishi." The blacksmith threw his hands out wildly, nearly knocking over the candle on his work bench. Cricket's eyes fell to the candle for a moment, and then to the magical lighting perched behind him on the wall. "All the lower fae have..." He flung his hands again, gesturing as if to try to explain. "Well, you saw."

"*What* exactly did we see?" Ignacia asked. She'd slid from Saber's back, and was leaning against her horse, arms crossed over her chest as she eyed the blacksmith suspiciously. "Lower fae never act like that."

"And what's this about a curfew?" Cricket added.

The blacksmith sighed heavily and sat on his stool abruptly as if the breath leaving him had let all the life out of him as well. "The lower fae, they're all possessed, or mad, or something. It started a month ago, with just a few of them attacking here or there. But gradually it became swarms. And then..."

He was silent for a time, long enough for Cricket to listen for the scraping of talons outside. They were still out there. Scratching at the wood in a mad attempt to get in. There were more now, and something bigger too. He wondered, what was it about his group that was attracting them? No. That was a question for after they figured out what was going on here. For after they got their questions answered.

"And then?" Yoshi prompted. He was glaring at the blacksmith, or as close to a glare as Yoshi ever got. There was a rip in his sleeve where he'd used his sword to stave off the worst of them, and his light hair had fallen into his face when they'd tried to tear at it.

"And then it got worse. It started with the pixies, and moved up to the goblins, now we've got red caps... red caps! Attacking us all through the night." The man sounded exhausted. His shoulders slumping inward as if he were trying to protect himself from the hordes outside clawing to get in. "Don't worry about the doors. They'll hold."

"Are they shored up with magic?" Cricket turned to walk toward the heavy oak doors which had slid into place and then been barred with another long piece of timber. The sounds outside stopped, all movement stilling. He lifted his hand to the wood, pressing his magic into it to feel the creatures outside. They started back up, frantic to get at him, doubling their efforts.

"Magic? Styx, no!" The blacksmith shook his head. "They thrive on the stuff. We haven't been able to do any magic within the city limits for a month."

"My prince," Yoshi said softly, suddenly at Cricket's side. He reached for Cricket, dark fingers wrapping warm around his boney wrist to pull his hand away. A look of concern had wrinkled Yoshi's forehead in lines so shallow only someone as close as Cricket was, could see them.

"That's why they were attracted to us then," Ignacia concluded.

The scratching continued. And then something slammed against the doors making them shudder. Yoshi pulled Cricket back, tucking him behind himself to stand between him and the door. Cricket couldn't see the wood anymore, just the clean white of his cloak.

"And the curfew?" Yoshi asked, voice thoughtful.

Cricket's eyes were locked on the space where the door had been. He didn't know why, but he couldn't look away, and he was having trouble focusing on anything else. He could hear the words, process the answers, but he couldn't get any questions of his own to come out. He didn't have any questions of his own. All he could think of was... was... a soft humming. Not even really a sound, more a feeling. It was in the air here. It called to the magic thrumming through his veins asking it to... to... what? Give in? He shook himself.

"They come in with the evening mists," the blacksmith said. "By eight in the morning the mists have dissipated, and they've gone."

"Where do they go?" Ignacia moved to grab Cricket by the back of his tunic and pull him bodily away from the door. Cricket dug his heels in, but when Yoshi followed the retreat, his back still to them and his sword drawn, Cricket slumped and let Ignacia tug him along. The distance from the outside made it easier to breathe past the humming, but only just.

"Back to the forest, I guess." The blacksmith had risen from his slump and was now sliding around the horses to get his shop ready to open up. "We thought it was maybe in the ley lines, so we stopped using magic entirely. No lights. No hot water if you don't boil it. No... modern conveniences."

"But?" Cricket asked, the first question he'd been able to get past the strange haze in his mind for a while.

"But they keep coming. No matter what we do, they keep coming. And they're getting bigger. Two days ago, we found selkie tracks up near the inn."

"So they're not just coming from the forest then. They're coming from the lake too." Ignacia reached into Cricket's bag to pull out the journal and started taking notes. He probably should have been offended at her doing so without asking him, but he wasn't. He could still feel... No. Wait.

"They're gone," Cricket breathed, his mind clearing almost suddenly. It felt strange to come back from the haze. Like seeing the world through magic glasses for the first time and realizing all the crisp lines you'd missed all your life. "The mist is gone too."

"How do you know?" Ignacia asked at the same time that Yoshi volunteered, "I will check."

Before anyone could stop him, Yoshi moved the timber and slipped outside, shutting the door behind him. A scant few minutes dragged on forever as they stood in silence, waiting. Cricket's shoulders hunched up a little each second that ticked by.

When Yoshi returned, he looked just as put together as he had been before, and he nodded. "The mist has lifted."

"Oh good! Then I can open up shop!" The blacksmith smiled, moving to slide the doors open, and shoo Lily, Saber, and Buttercup out of his shop. "The inn is at the center of town. Big building, you can't miss it. They have a stable. I don't mean to sound rude but..."

But he was sounding extremely rude, Cricket thought, even as the man began to shoo Cricket and his party out as well. He also didn't sound overly apologetic about it. Like he was pleased to have them out of his shop, and off to ask someone else questions.

"Thank you, for your help," Yoshi said, offering the man a slight bow. Although he didn't really sound thankful. If anything, he sounded slightly annoyed, maybe even a little petty. Cricket swallowed back a dry laugh.

"Of course. Of course. Anything to help the prince and his... his uh... friends!" The blacksmith laughed. "Please feel free—"

"We might have more questions later," Cricket cut him off, his eyes flicking over the man as he ushered them out.

The blacksmith's Adam's apple shifted in his throat nervously, and his smile grew more strained around the edges. "Yes, Your Highness. But I assure you, I've told you all I know."

"Mhm." Ignacia didn't sound convinced.

"I'm sure you have," Cricket offered him a forced smile, complete with dimple. "Still, if we have any more questions..."

"I'd be happy to help in any way that I could, Your Highness." The blacksmith bowed. "Now, like I said, the inn is at the center of town. You can't miss it."

"Yes. Thank you." Cricket turned and led Buttercup, and his little group along with him toward the inn.

CHAPTER 31

The innkeeper, a spritely, curvy older woman named Miss Calais, was absolutely "pleased as punch" to help them.

"We haven't had any visitors in Nishi in nigh on a month," she babbled on happily, her bun bobbing through the air as she put together their beds. "And here we are, with the prince as a guest. The prince!"

"If you don't mind me asking ma'am—"

"Oh, just Susan will do, dear. No need to be formal, especially as you're the prince." She cut him off, shaking her head.

"Susan," Cricket corrected. "Where is your staff?"

It had been strange, when they'd knocked on the inn door, Miss Calais had answered, and no one else had been in sight. Ignacia had seen to stabling their horses while Cricket and Yoshi picked out rooms when normally there would have been someone on staff to do all of these things for them. Yet, there Miss Calais was, turning down a bed as if she were a maid in her own inn.

"Oh, they don't come in until a bit later. We haven't had many guests, and with the..." She hesitated for a moment, perhaps about to reveal more than she ought, then shook her head and continued on as if nothing had changed. "I don't ask them in until the afternoon unless we have guests. But I can fix you some breakfast, no trouble."

"If you wouldn't mind, we'd really appreciate that. Our provisions ran out yesterday around lunch and we haven't had anything since." It wasn't so much a lie as a stretching of the truth. Their provisions had run out, but they hadn't exactly gone hungry. For Yoshi was an excellent forager. Yoshi was excellent at everything, it seemed.

"You poor things! Well, I'll just hop down to the kitchen and get breakfast started." She smoothed her hands over the turned down quilt, nodding happily to herself. "If you should need anything, don't be afraid to give me a holler."

"Thank you so much." Cricket gave her his best dimpled smile as he ushered her to the door of the room she'd proclaimed was 'the best in the house' and thus would be his. It was a very nice room. A tall four-poster canopy bed, and a beautiful view of the lake. But for as tired as he was, there was little time to rest. Even if the pillows did look especially soft. Which they did.

Cricket waited until he heard the faint creak on the landing that he'd noticed on the way up, and then poked his head out his door.

"Yoshi," he whispered into the empty hall. When no answer came, he repeated himself, a little louder, drawing out the name, "Yoooooshi."

"My Prince?" Yoshi asked, opening his own door to look out into the hall. He did not poke his head out, because he was too dignified for all that. No, he took one step out into the hall, and turned his body to face the door at the end where Cricket had stuck the top half of his torso out, clinging to the doorframe so as not to topple over.

"Come here."

Unlike all of Cricket's other friends, and many of his acquaintances, Yoshi did not ask why. He did not ask what the prince might want. He merely nodded, stepped fully out of his room, turned to shut the door, and strode toward Cricket. In his surprise Cricket nearly lost his balance and fell face first onto the floorboards.

"Really? You're just gonna—" Yoshi pushed the door open behind Cricket and stepped around him to enter the room. "Well, okay then."

He nudged the door shut with his hip and turned to see Yoshi, standing in the middle of his room, regarding him with what could only be curiosity. Because what else could it be?

"Yes?" Yoshi asked when the silence stretched on for too long.

"Yes. Right. Okay." Cricket nodded, moving to sit on the edge of the bed. There was no place else to sit. Why weren't there chairs in this room? There had been a table and cushions in Taini! "The innkeeper is hiding something."

"She is," Yoshi agreed.

"So was the blacksmith."

Yoshi nodded.

Cricket frowned, curling his legs up onto the bed with him so that he could drum his fingers against his knees. "I doubt we'll be able to get either of them to answer any of our questions. We'll have to venture out and hope someone else will."

"We should split up." Yoshi had moved to stand at the corner of the bed. His shoulder pressed into one of the long pieces of wood that framed it, but he wasn't leaning. "Someone should stay here."

"Yes! That's what I was thinking. To listen, to see if anyone says anything once they've let down their guard and think no one is around to hear it." Cricket smiled suddenly, his eyes widening as he sat up straighter. "You'd be good for that, you're so quiet!"

"They might be more at ease with someone they consider a servant."

"You think we should leave Iggy here, and let her spy?" Cricket tapped at his chin thoughtfully. "They also might feel less intimidated by another woman."

"Yes."

"But Iggy isn't my servant." Cricket huffed. "And she's going to be really angry if we label her as such."

"Then do not label her. Let people make assumptions." Yoshi looked as if perhaps he might shrug—if it would be polite to do so. It wouldn't be, or at least Cricket had been told it wouldn't be. So Yoshi did not. "She was tasked with seeing to the horses. I cannot be mistaken for your servant as I bear the Helio crest."

"That is... very true. All right, I should fill her in on the plan, right?"

"Do as you wish. I am going to get breakfast." Yoshi turned and strode from the room without another word.

"She's not going to like this Yoshi," Cricket called after him, but received no response.

"I don't like it," Ignacia said, picking at the skin under her fingernails. She'd traipsed into Cricket's room without so much as knocking, and dropped onto her back on the bed, getting dirt all over the coverlet.

"This is what I told Yoshi."

"But I see his point. It'll be easier for me to just pretend I'm doing things like unpacking and making sure your rooms

are ready for you. I can talk to the staff like I'm one of them."
She was still picking the dirt from under her nails and wiping
it on her trousers. Gross. That was gross.

"No flirting."

"Oh, come on Cricky, don't take all the fun out of my
day."

"Minimal flirting."

"Fine. Minimal flirting. And while I'm doing that you can
use your princely pull, and Yoshi's death glares to get answers
from the rest of the people in the city. I'd start with business
owners, they're more likely to have dealt with any merchants
that came through."

"I know how to conduct interviews, Iggy." Cricket
nudged her with his foot. "Get off my bed, you're getting it
dirty."

"You already got it dirty with your own dirty ass," she
pointed out, shoving at his shin to keep his boot away from
her. "Besides, aren't I supposed to be all 'woe is me, my liege
is such a horrible taskmaster. Look at the horrible mess he
made which now I have to clean up'?"

"I am not."

"Aren't you?" A smirk played at Ignacia's lips.

"I'm going to get breakfast." He stood up and headed for
the door, not giving her a backward glance, but he felt her rise
behind him.

"But your highness, shouldn't I have that brought up to
you? Wouldn't you like to have breakfast in bed?" Ignacia's
jeering followed him down the hall.

"You know, this is why working with Yoshi is better, at
least he judges me quietly." Cricket huffed. She cut off the
comments as they made their way down the steps, but he
could still feel her smug energy targeted at the back of his
neck. Yoshi looked up from his table in the corner, where he
was eating some eggs over rice. "I told you she wouldn't like

it," was all Cricket said as he grabbed a bit of toast and stuffed it into his mouth.

"Hmm," Yoshi hummed. Cricket wasn't sure if it was agreement, sympathy, or sheer indifference. He figured it was best not to ask. "I have asked that Susan join us for some tea when she is finished in the kitchen. I thought you might ask her some questions."

"Good thinking," Cricket said around a mouth full of dry toast. To his credit, Yoshi only cringed a little at the sight of Cricket's half-chewed food. They fell silent, filling their bellies that had been only mostly empty since the previous day. Which is how they knew Miss Calais was coming before she announced herself.

"So, what can I do for you, Your Highness?" Miss Calais asked as she came to sit beside Yoshi. He slid over to give her space, or perhaps to give himself space, and she poured herself a cup of tea.

"Cricket, please." Cricket smiled, brushing his fingers off on the napkin draped over his knee. "And this is my traveling companion, Yoshi. And my handmaiden, Ignacia."

Miss Calais gave each of them a nod, and a too-wide smile.

"We've been through some other towns and villages in the area suffering strange occurrences. Someone told us that Nishi was also, and well... we witnessed it this morning." Miss Calais's eyes sharpened. The smile remained, but it was tighter around the edges, forced. She didn't want them to know that something strange was going on in Nishi, and Cricket had to wonder how she thought she was going to hide that. Either way, he needed an answer. "We're wondering if a vendor in a painted wagon has been through? He's older, selling a number of different items ranging from jewelry to books. All at very reasonable prices. Has anyone like that come through Nishi?"

"Not that I've seen," Miss Calais said in a nonchalant tone. "But then, I'm the owner here. I was left the place when my mother passed, and so I don't get out much."

"Ah, of course." Cricket nodded. "Well, Yoshi and I will just have to ask around then. Ignacia, you're in charge of getting us settled. Could you have a bath ready for me when I come back this evening?"

Ignacia kicked him hard under the table, leaving if not a bruise than red skin all along his calf. Which he wholeheartedly deserved. "Of course, Your Highness," she forced out through gritted teeth.

"Perfect." Cricket bowed his head to hide his wince. "We will see you this evening Susan. Thank you for your time."

"No trouble. No trouble at all. Do make sure you're back around supper time, that's when I start locking up for the night. And you won't want to be on the streets when..." She shuddered.

"Yes ma'am. We'll be back in plenty of time. No need to worry about us. Right, Yoshi?" Cricket rose from his chair, straightening his tunic. It would be nice to change. To take a bath and put on fresh clothes. But there were no fresh clothes to be had, and there was too much else to do. They were on a time limit. They would have to do all of their investigating during the day until he could determine exactly how dangerous the creatures in the mist were.

Yoshi nodded, and rose from his own chair. "Thank you for breakfast Miss Calais."

Miss Calais laughed, and blushed, and waved them away. Ignacia watched them go with a carefully crafted disinterest. Cricket knew better. She was going to punish him for this little stunt, he just didn't know how yet. And he didn't have the time to bother with it. There was too much else.

"Businesses first?" Yoshi asked, walking beside Cricket with his hands tucked behind his back.

"That was Iggy's thinking. Let's start with the baker, and the cobbler. Everyone in the city has to see them at least once a week. They're in a prime position to get all the gossip." Cricket stretched his legs out in a couple long strides, his knees popping from disuse. "Then this afternoon we'll go grab your saddle from the stable and see about getting it fixed."

"Will they speak with us?"

"Oh, they will, I just don't think they'll actually give us anything worth hearing." Cricket sighed.

Cricket could see Yoshi turn to look at him out of the corner of his eye. An expression like annoyance drawing his brows together. "Then how will we learn anything?"

"By what they don't say, I expect." Cricket laughed, keeping his steps light. "Or maybe we'll just get lucky, and the right person will overhear us asking, and we'll get answers that way."

"That seems," he paused to think of the correct word, and then continued with, "inefficient."

Cricket shrugged.

CHAPTER 32

They did not, as it turns out, get lucky. By the time Yoshi and Cricket dragged themselves back to the inn they were no closer to understanding what was going on in Nishi than they'd been that morning, and Cricket's feet were sore. So in his mind they'd been doubly unlucky.

"No one knew anything," Cricket announced from where he'd perched himself with his knees to his chest on the edge of the blanket they'd laid out in front of the fire in his room. It was nostalgic eating picnic style inside, reminiscent of better days curled up giggling with Ignacia and Anstice and even on occasion Marwa and Father. Yoshi managed to make it awkward by insisting on sitting with his back ramrod straight. Still, it was the only privacy they'd get, and for this conversation, they needed privacy.

"No one saw our phantom merchant?" Ignacia asked around a bit of roasted duck.

"Depends on who you ask. The baker saw the caravan. The tanner says no such person came through Nishi at all. The chocolatier, they have one of those here, he's very good,"

Cricket said, stuffing a bit of tofu and rice into his mouth. "I got you some in my bag for later."

"Get on with it." Ignacia rolled her eyes.

"The chocolatier gave us a brief description of the man. The varying accounts are enough to make me almost believe that they don't know what's going on at all." He took another too-big bite, and chewed thoughtfully around rice and spongy well-seasoned tofu.

"But," Yoshi supplied, prompting him to continue.

"But." Cricket swallowed loudly around his mouth full of food. "But they all were so adamant that whether there was or was not such a person no one bought anything off them. It's the one thing every story has in common."

Ignacia pulled a face.

"Weird. Right?"

"It's not much to go on."

"No, but it's weird."

"They're all in on it then. The whole damn city?"

"Probably not. We were able to question at least half of the merchants today. We'll look in on the other half tomorrow. Till then I want to chat with Annie about what kind of magic can warp low level fae like that." An image of inky black pixie eyes flashed in his mind, and Cricket frowned down at his half-finished plate. Suddenly, he wasn't very hungry.

"Will she have answers?" Yoshi asked softly.

"She might. She always took magical theory a lot more seriously than I did."

"You mean she didn't sleep through your lessons," Ignacia said, a knowing smile tugging at her lips. He wasn't sure if she was doing it to get a rise out of him, or if she thought it would make him feel better. It did neither.

"I always thought she'd be around when I needed advice for something like this," Cricket whispered down to his plate.

He wasn't sure where the mood had come from. Maybe it was memories of sitting on a blanket around a fire as they were now, but long ago, with more people. Maybe it was thinking of Marwa, and how she should have been there to help them with this. How she would have known the solution right away before Cricket had finished the question. Anstice was whip smart, but no amount of book smarts could make up for experience. Or maybe it was something else. There was just...something hanging in the air, making him sag under the weight of it.

"Let's give her a call then." Ignacia's voice was all forced brightness and excitement, and he appreciated it. One of them had to be, and he didn't feel up to the task.

Yoshi nodded his agreement and rose from his careful seat on the floor to retrieve Cricket's satchel. From which he pulled the mirror and held it out to Cricket, a soft look about his eyes, or maybe Cricket was imagining that. Maybe he just wanted to think that Yoshi had warmed to him in some way. No matter. Now was not the time.

Muscle memory made the task of waving his hand over the mirror easy as Yoshi returned to his seat. The glass rippled, and a moment later Anstice appeared. She was sitting at her desk, as she seemed to always be these days, and there was a soft smile on her face. The familiarity of it eased something inside Cricket he hadn't realized was knotted.

"Cricky," she waggled her fingers at him. "You've reached Nishi in one piece I see."

"Mostly," Cricket said on a breath which turned into a self-deprecating laugh.

"Long journey?"

"Annie, you have no idea!" Ignacia said, jostling Cricket's shoulder to get into frame with him. "Honestly, I thought crickets were supposed to be good luck for traveling."

Anstice huffed a laugh. "Not ours, I suppose?"

"No! Not ours at all! We had the worst journey from Taini to here. So much rain. And washed-out bridges. And mud. And broken saddles. And wolves! There were wolves, Annie. I've never even seen wolves up close before." Ignacia stuffed another bite of food into her mouth, managing to dribble sauce on Cricket's tunic. But he could not possibly care less about it. For *this* he understood. This was familiar. The ebb and flow of Ignacia and Anstice teasing, and laughing, and being far too loud for anyone else.

"Or maybe I am good luck, because we somehow got here safely," Cricket argued, tapping at the side of his nose as his shoulders relaxed away from his ears. He felt himself leaning back into Ignacia. Letting her companionable warmth seep into his shoulder under his clothes. It wasn't old times, but it was close enough to take some of the edge off.

"I don't think that's how that works, Cricky." Anstice laughed.

"Oh, it definitely is!"

Ignacia snorted loud enough in his ear to make it prickle, and he jerked away to rub at it as she chortled more.

"Ugh gross! Swallow your food before you start laughing with your mouth open like that." Cricket shoved her away, and then sat up straighter so he could look at Anstice. He lifted his chin, mimicking a posture he'd seen Father use so often. "Anyway."

"Yes, by all means, tell me what you called for." Antice's eyes twinkled with teasing. "I am a very busy woman. I have advisor things to do, you know."

"Of course. Of course. You're both very important people. How dare I intrude with my blatant tomfoolery." Ignacia nodded sagely, but her eyebrows wiggled. She leaned back against Cricket's side, sharing her warmth with him. "Well? Get on with it. She doesn't have all night. You heard her. She has advisor things to do."

"If you'd shut up for more than two seconds, I could," Cricket griped.

"Children. Children." Anstice's voice wobbled with a giggle, but she'd managed to hide her smile behind one of her fans. She cleared her throat to clear the laughter. "What can I help you with?"

Cricket nodded, taking a deep breath to calm himself. "What magic do you know that can possess lower fae?"

Anstice's eyes sharpened behind the fan, and she lowered it to reveal her mouth pressed into a firm line. "What do you mean when you say possess?"

"I mean their eyes were black, and they attacked us. They weren't... they didn't seem to be fully cognizant. We used to play with pixies out in the gardens. They were never like this. But it's not just pixies, the blacksmith said there were goblins, and selkies too."

"Only lower fae so far?" There was a soft scratching noise from Anstice's end as she wrote this down.

"That we saw." Ignacia supplied.

"And the blacksmith said they worked up to the selkies and goblins. It started with pixies. But if it's spreading by order of magical potency—"

"Then it won't be long before it starts affecting Nishi's elven citizens," Anstice finished for him, nodding seriously. "I can't think of anything off the top of my head, but I'll do some digging. Till I have some answers, avoid them. Whatever is affecting them seems contagious, and if we don't know how it's spreading..."

"Then we could easily be infected." Ignacia frowned, her eyes flicking down to Cricket's hand which they'd bandaged somewhere between breakfast and now.

"Exactly. Keep me posted on anything weird going on. Stay safe." Anstice's words were soft. "I love you. Both of you."

"We love you too, Annie." Cricket smiled and waved over the glass as Ignacia blew a kiss. He slumped, setting the mirror aside, and falling onto his back on the floor. "We should get some sleep. I'm exhausted."

"Someone should stay with you," Yoshi said from where he was still perched on one lonely corner of the blanket. Cricket lifted his head just enough to see him. Yoshi wasn't looking at him, his gaze was on the fire, the frown-wrinkle marring his handsome features. "In case you are infected."

"No need for all that. You're both right down the hall. You'll hear if I start flinging myself at the walls." Cricket flopped back again, shaking his head in a way that made him dizzy from where it was pressed into the floor.

"Yoshi's right." Ignacia leaned over him to obstruct his view of the ceiling and meet his eyes.

"And what will you do if I am infected?" Cricket rubbed at his nose. "If I am then I'm a danger to you more than I am to myself. It's safer if you don't stay with me."

Ignacia glanced over to Yoshi, and they exchanged what could only be described as A Look.

"I'll be fine. Really you two. I just want to sprawl out in that big bed and pass out. Get out of here, leave me to it."

"If you need us," Yoshi said. He still hadn't moved from his spot on the blanket, and Cricket was beginning to wonder if he'd just stubbornly refuse to leave.

"You're just a shout away." Cricket lifted a hand and waved them both off. "Honestly, I'm fine. I promise. Go to bed."

Another shared Look, more assurances, and one change into his sleep clothes later found Cricket sprawled across the four poster, staring out into the slowly fading daylight. It was almost meditative to watch the sun sink on the lake, and the moon rise to dance across its surface.

Some time later, long enough for the fire to have died

down to nearly embers, and the moon to be obscured by the fog which had drifted through Nishi, Cricket shifted in his sleep. There was a scratching sound. Like something sharp against glass. He pulled the pillow over his head, blotting out the noise as best he could to keep from waking. And muttered something unintelligible which was probably meant to be, 'go away I'm sleeping' but really sounded like, "gerrway eepin'."

More scratching slowly dragged him into the world of the waking. Too slowly for, a moment later, the scratching turned into the thuds of small bodies against the windowpane.

"Shut up, Iggy," Cricket whined, piling a second pillow onto his head. He squeezed his eyes shut tight, trying to will himself back into a deeper sleep. It didn't work as one body turned into two, turned into five, turned into what sounded like the sky raining birds to pelt against the glass. Cricket threw off the pillows, and sat up in bed fully prepared to scream at whoever was interrupting his much needed—

Crash!

The window gave way. Glass flew across the floor, glittering like water in the moonlight. A second later dozens of tiny bodies rushed through the window at him, carrying with them the mist from outside. Cricket opened his lips to scream and sucked in a mouth full of the damp air. The haze settled in immediately. It made everything else seem far away, and indistinct. The tugging of tiny taloned fingers at his bed clothes toward the window. The press of glass into his feet. These were all distant sensations that didn't quite register. Not past the fuzziness of the world around him, and the beauty of the watery moon through the fog outside his window.

A sharp *thud* didn't register to him but did draw the attention of the pixies dragging him toward the outside. He turned to follow their movement, and saw Yoshi rushing toward him.

My door, he thought belatedly staring at where it rested against the wall beside the frame, *must have been what made the noise.*

Yoshi swung wildly. Smacking at tiny, winged bodies so they thumped against the wall until he reached Cricket. Cricket's feet went out from under him in one dizzying, fluid movement. Then he was over Yoshi's shoulder, running back toward the door. It slammed shut behind Yoshi, his shoulder the only thing keeping it closed as a dozen little creatures slammed themselves against the thick wood to get it open.

"My Prince. Wake up. Wake up." Yoshi was saying, his voice strange and warbly through the water that swam in Cricket's ears.

Somehow (don't ask Cricket how, he doesn't know) Yoshi managed to get a table from the wall to the door, and wedge it closed. Then he strode quickly to his own room, dropped Cricket unceremoniously onto the bed, and moved to shut and latch the inner shutters of his windows. With that done, fresh air wafted slowly into Cricket's senses, bringing him to the surface of whatever he'd been drowning in.

Cricket didn't realize he was shaking until Yoshi's arms looped around him to hold him still. "What... what happened?"

"Your eyes were black," Yoshi said simply, but he held Cricket tighter when he trembled. "They are back to normal now."

"It's the mist. Whatever it is, it's in the mist. It... it gets into your head. It makes everything so far away. Like you're drowning." Cricket still hadn't hugged Yoshi back. Instead, he was staring at the spots where his bleeding feet were soaking into Yoshi's rumpled bedding. "You heard me."

"I said I would."

They stayed that way for a while. Cricket didn't know

how long, but by the time Yoshi pulled back his feet had stopped bleeding for the most part.

"I should get back to my room." Cricket pushed himself toward the edge of the bed.

"Your window is shattered. You will stay here. I will treat your wounds." Yoshi left no room for argument. He rose from the bed and went to dig around in a pouch until he came up with bandages and salve. "In the morning we will find you a new room."

"Okay." Cricket nodded, letting himself slump against the pillows. He was very tired, and it would be nice to not be alone. Especially as he heard the creatures outside scratching now at Yoshi's windows.

CHAPTER 33

Cricket realized that after the events of the night he should have jumped at every sound. He should have heard the scratching at the windows, and the banging at the walls from his rooms, and he should have been unsettled, frantic. But...he was not. He found it easy to settle down. To let the warmth of someone he trusted, and even liked most of the time, put him at ease. He'd shared a bed with Ignacia and Anstice a few times growing up, and always found he slept better that way. Squashed in between someone else and a wall of pillows brought comfort, and safety.

There was no squashing with Yoshi, of course. There was plenty of space between them, and when Cricket woke, there was no Yoshi either. The white knight had made his half of the bed, and quietly left Cricket to wake up on his own. Likely to go get breakfast.

Cricket sat up, stretching. His toes curled and he winced at the feeling of the cuts on the bottoms of his feet. That would be a problem. He wasn't sure how much walking he'd be able to do with his feet cut up as they were, but he'd have to make do.

"Maybe Ignacia has something to numb it in her saddle bag," he said, standing from the bed and moving to remake the bed albeit not as neatly as Yoshi's side was and with a noticeable wince.

"You are awake," Yoshi said as the door creaked open.

Cricket whirled, his hands bracing the bed to hold much of his weight as he laughed. There was Yoshi, in the door, looking like an angel with a tray laden with breakfast. "Oh yeah, I was just going to go looking for you, and Iggy. We need to go into the woods and—"

"You should rest, you did not sleep well, and your feet need to be treated by a healer. I have sent for one." Yoshi moved toward Cricket, setting the tray on the bedside table, and grabbing for the blankets to pull them back again. He held them up and looked at Cricket expectantly.

"Yoshi, I'm all right. Really. I just need to go get some of the numbing ointment Iggy sometimes keeps in her saddle-bags. Then I'll be right as rain, and we can go and check out the—"

"The healer will be here in a half hour. There is omurice. Ignacia is out for the moment."

"Iggy's out? Where did Iggy go?" Cricket didn't feel like fighting him further, that's why he was climbing back into the bed and letting Yoshi set the tray over his lap. That was the only reason. It most certainly was not because his feet were beginning to sting, and the feeling made him dizzy.

"She said she had errands to run. She will be with us presently. Eat your breakfast."

"I'm only doing this because I'm hungry, and I don't want it to get cold. My feet aren't bothering me," Cricket insisted. He lifted one foot to wiggle his toes for emphasis and winced when it made the cuts gape open.

"So I see." Yoshi's tone sounded skeptical, but he didn't press Cricket further. He took the small pitcher from the tray and poured Cricket a glass of juice. "What is this about the forest?"

"Oh!" Cricket tore off a piece of egg and blew on it as he spoke. "The mist has to be coming from somewhere. Stands to reason it'd be coming from the forest."

"The mist?"

Cricket stuffed the food into his mouth, hardly tasting it as his stomach growled for more. "Yeah, the mist. That's what's possessing them. Didn't I say last night? I was sure I said."

"You were unwell last night." Yoshi sat on the edge of the bed at Cricket's feet, carefully removing the bandages so he could inspect them.

"Oi. You don't have to bother with that. You said the healer will be here soon." Cricket kicked his foot a little when the gentle touches tickled. "And I wasn't unwell when I said it. I was coherent. I knew what was going on."

"I just want to make sure I removed all the glass." Yoshi's hands were gentle as he started on the other foot. "It was the mist?"

"That's what I just said, isn't it?" Cricket huffed. He wasn't sure if Yoshi wasn't listening, or he was intentionally trying to distract Cricket from what he was doing. Either way, he didn't appreciate the tactic. "There must be a magical object in the forest producing it every evening. Maybe something our suspect left behind on purpose when he couldn't get anyone in the village to buy anything. Or something the pixies stole off him and took back to their nest. That's where we should start."

"You believe they did not purchase any items from him?"

"That's what they said." Cricket shrugged. "I'd rather rule this out than start calling people liars. They tend to take offense to that."

"People tend to take offense to your overall..." Ignacia

waved at Cricket as a whole from where she stood at the door, her other hand behind her back.

"They do not! People love me! I'm very lovable! Lovable and cute. Tell her Yoshi." Cricket poked Yoshi in the side with one of his toes, careful to avoid brushing the cuts on his tunic.

"Yes, My Prince is very cute," Yoshi agreed, ducking his head back to examine the wounds more closely.

"There? You see!" Cricket squeaked, stuffing another bite of food into his mouth to stave off any further commentary that might be embarrassing. No. Would *definitely* be embarrassing. Yoshi had called him cute!

"I see, all right." Ignacia's eyes were keen on Yoshi, as she said it, tone a little smug. Cricket wasn't sure what that was all about, and he decided he didn't want to know. There were other things to handle.

"What's that behind your back?" he asked instead.

"What's what behind my back?" she countered, her lips turning up at the corners.

"Iiiiiiiggy," he dragged out the word dramatically. "I'm injured. Have sympathy on your poor little brother." Cricket slumped back into the bed, pouting spectacularly.

Ignacia snorted, but she took several steps into the room to stand by the bed. "Do you know what day it is, Cricky?"

"Tuesday?" It was a silly question, she had to know as well as he did, that he'd lost track long ago of what day it was. Way back in Tochtli when the day repeated over and over again. The countless days on the road. The constant running. The fighting. The struggle. What were days of the week when... Oh. Oh, it couldn't... No. He looked up and Ignacia was holding both hands in front of her, carefully cupping a cupcake. "It's the twenty-first?"

"Happy name day, Cricket!" Ignacia cheered, waggling the cupcake. "I know it's not half as exciting as a celebration at home. In the capital they're probably lighting lanterns and drinking in honor of our prince coming of age." She shrugged, a little flush spreading across the bridge of her nose. "But I thought—"

"It's perfect, Iggy! Come here so I can give you a hug." Cricket held his hands out to her, closing and opening his fingers in rapid succession, and ignoring the pinprick of tears at the corners of his eyes. Cricket pulled Ignacia in close, nearly toppling the tray to the ground if not for Yoshi's steady hand and pressed a kiss to her cheek. "Thank you for remembering."

"Yeah, well," she said, clearly embarrassed. "I knew you'd forget so..."

He laughed and gave her a playful shove.

"So, what's this about the mist?"

Cricket settled in to explain again, stuffing bites of omurice into his mouth in between his thoughts. Ignacia and Yoshi listened carefully. And by the time the healer joined them Ignacia had moved onto the bed beside him and was scooping frosting off the top of the cupcake she'd brought, while Yoshi remained on the foot of the bed watching them impassively. Quite the sight, Cricket was sure, but he didn't mind. It was his name day after all.

"It seems you're well taken care of, Your Highness," the healer, a shy young man named Finn, said softly. "There is no remaining glass, and your feet should heal well enough on their own, provided you have plenty of rest."

"I need to be able to walk today. What can you give me so I can go into the forest?" Cricket asked, leaning closer as he looked at the wrappings on his feet. They'd be a struggle to fit into his boots, but if he didn't lace them as tightly, the backs rub at his heels. He'd have to make a choice about which was more important.

Finn frowned, his hands stopping where he'd been packing

up his supplies. "Your Highness, I just said you needed rest." An uncomfortable look crossed his unlined face. "You cannot go walking about on them or they won't heal as quickly."

"I can't stay trapped in bed for the next week," Cricket said, sitting up straighter, and tilting his chin back to project the same air Father did when he wanted something done. "The people of Nishi are in danger and I'm here to figure out why. That takes precedent."

"Over your health, Your Highness? Surely your companions can handle that while you heal," Finn hedged.

"Healer Finn, this is not a debate. I will go into the forest to inspect the surrounding area today. Whether I do it in pain, or comfortably is entirely up to you." His hands clenched into fists on his night clothes. He'd need Ignacia to go and get some fresh clothes from his room if they hadn't cleaned it up yet. He'd need Yoshi to provide support if he stumbled. He'd need... He hated having to rely on them like this. He was their prince. Not their burden. "You will give me something to dull the pain enough to walk, and I will go and inspect the forest. Have I made myself clear?"

"But Your—"

"I heal much faster than you'd think. And I'll rest much better knowing Nishi is safe. Please." The word grated on Cricket's tongue. He was glad that Yoshi and Ignacia had excused themselves to prepare for the day. They no doubt would have had something to say about this. "And you will not, under any circumstances, tell my companions that you've told me to stay in bed."

"Yes, Your Highness," Finn breathed. He reached into his pack and pulled out an ointment. "This is a surface numbing agent. It should give you a few hours reprieve. You may apply it as needed."

"Thank you."

Finn ducked his head and finished his packing. He left without another word. Cricket made quick work of peeling back the bandages, ignoring their tug on his skin, and applied the ointment himself. He had just finished rewrapping the bandages when Ignacia stalked in with a set of clothes over her arm.

"You'll let me come with you into the forest today," she said. It was not a question. Not a request. It was an order from his sister, his best friend, his protector.

"I need you to stay here." Cricket stood from the bed, clenching his teeth to hide a wince as his weight shifted while he got undressed. "You didn't hear anything yesterday, but that's not to say that they won't let their guard down the longer you're here. The innkeeper knows something."

"You need protecting. Clearly, you're too foolish to do the job yourself," Ignacia spat, bending to hold his trousers so he could step into them.

"I'll have Yoshi. He'll be enough." He bent to tug on his boots, bracing himself on his heels to keep from putting pressure on the cuts. He hoped the numbing ointment would kick in soon. He didn't want to be wincing with every step. Then they definitely wouldn't let him leave the inn. "Besides, it's my feet. I can still hold a sword just fine."

Ignacia eyed him narrowly, but she didn't put up any more arguments. A soft knock sounded from the door. "That'll be your white knight, won't it?"

"I'm dressed, you can come in," Cricket called, sticking his tongue out at Ignacia. "All right Iggy, you know what to do. We won't be all day again, probably just until lunch. I don't plan on searching more than a mile out."

"We will be safe," Yoshi promised, bowing his head slightly.

"Yeah, yeah, yeah. You had better be." Ignacia brushed

past Yoshi, bumping him hard with her shoulder. "If his feet get to be too much, you bring him straight back."

"Yes, ma'am." He bowed again.

Cricket rolled his eyes. "Let's go. We're wasting daylight."

He gritted his teeth and headed for the door. By the time he got to the bottom of the stairs the pain had mostly dulled, enough that he didn't feel like he needed to tiptoe through the inn. He just had to hope it would last until they could find the pixie's nest.

CHAPTER 34

"I wish to make an inquiry," Yoshi said as they picked their way over the undergrowth of the forest surrounding Nishi. Yoshi stepped carefully as if he were afraid to disturb the forest and by extension its creatures too much.

"You what?" Cricket turned to look at him, a little smile playing teasingly at the corners of his lips.

Yoshi looked at him, unblinking, as if to say *you know perfectly well what I just said to you. Stop being obtuse.*

"All right then, ask your question." Cricket shrugged, and then returned to scanning the trees around them for signs of the pixies. He'd followed the trail as far as it would lead, but it got harder to follow the further into the woods they got. Partly because the pixies stopped hovering around ground level once the mist had set them free. They'd taken to the trees again, as flying creatures are wont to do. And that's where the nest would be. He squinted up into the dappled sunshine flickering through the leaves, looking for signs.

"How does one..." Yoshi stopped, taking a moment to organize his thoughts, and phrase what he was asking correctly, Cricket supposed. That seemed to be the way of Yoshi. He put words together as children did blocks. Trying his best to make a tower that others wouldn't immediately knock over. Cricket was not going to knock over his block tower. Probably. At least not on purpose anyway. "How does one procure friends?"

Cricket stopped, his jaw slack. "Did you just..." He shook his head, a hand lifting to scrub at his face. Okay, maybe he *was* going to knock over Yoshi's block tower. "Did you just ask me how to make friends?"

Yoshi nodded, his lips pursed in displeasure, as if he thought perhaps Cricket were making fun of him. He wasn't. Cricket was in fact trying very hard not to make fun of him. It was a Task.

"Don't you have friends back home in Helio?"

Yoshi shook his head, the frown-wrinkle making another appearance. Only this time it was much deeper, bordering on a real frown now.

"Someone you can just...talk to? Who you can ask things, and laugh with? Someone who you have fond memories of spending time with?"

"I have Sister," Yoshi said. "But I do not think that is what you mean."

"Well. It could be. I mean, I consider Ignacia and Anstice my sisters." Cricket shrugged. "We've been friends since we were little brats. I guess that makes it easier to make friends, being young. Didn't you have anyone like that growing up?"

Yoshi looked thoughtful for a moment. "There was one boy who I thought of as a friend. But it was only for a few weeks during the summer."

"And you didn't keep in touch?"

"No." Yoshi frowned "We were very young. And then I was sent to the monastery for schooling."

Cricket's shoulders slumped. Yoshi hadn't ever had

friends. He didn't know how to make them because he'd never had any. And the one he did have had left him behind. That was... That was so sad.

"Well, I'm your friend," Cricket declared, holding out a hand to Yoshi.

Yoshi's mouth fell open, a look of surprise and perhaps delight playing across his eyes. Then he took Cricket's hand and gave it a firm squeeze and nodded.

Cricket smiled back at him, eyes scrunching up into crescents, and head tilting. They stayed that way for a moment, until the soft thrumming of wings reached Cricket's ears, and he looked up to see a pixie fluttering through the trees. "Duty calls. We better follow it; it'll lead us back to the nest."

"How do you know?"

"I don't. But it's not headed toward town, so it's got to be headed home, right?" Cricket wrinkled his nose, and then took off at a run through the trees, dragging Yoshi behind him by the hand. He ignored the uncomfortable rub of boot on his torn up feet and pushed away any thoughts of how much worse that might be making his injuries. Now was not the time.

The little creature led them on a mad chase through the trees. By the time they reached the nest, Cricket was panting, and he'd long forgotten about the discomfort of his injuries in favor of the fun of running. He peered up through the leaves to see the collection of twigs, tied together with wishes and hopes that spanned the branches of no fewer than five great trees.

"There it is Yoshi. The nest." Cricket laughed breathlessly, brushing loose hairs back from his face.

"Yes," Yoshi said from beside him, not out of breath. Because that would be undignified. Cricket didn't mind though; his eyes were focused on the twinkling lights coming from the nest.

"All right, help me up." He dropped Yoshi's hand and moved to the base of a tree to reach for one of the lower hanging branches. He stretched, fingers not even managing to brush the underside of it.

"You are not going to tear down their nest." Not a question, but Cricket was sure Yoshi had meant it as one. There was concern in his tone.

"Great Selene, no!" Cricket gasped in horror, shooting Yoshi a disgusted glare. "That's their home! I'd never tear down someone's home. I'm just going to go up and talk to them. If I can get up close enough maybe I can coax their queen out to have a chat. You know, monarch to monarch."

"You speak pixie?" Now Yoshi sounded impressed, and Cricket wasn't sure which was worse. That Yoshi thought him so cruel and callous that he'd tear down the home of an innocent flock of pixies, or that Yoshi thought he wasn't smart enough to know one of the more basic mythic languages.

"Yeah. Doesn't everybody? It's easy. It's just a whole lot of chittering really fast and holding onto your head in the hopes you keep up. It's mostly facial expressions really." Cricket shrugged. "Now, are you going to give me a hand up, or what?"

"You do not think they will lie?"

"Pixies can't lie! The more condensed your magic is, the harder it is for you to lie. They might not tell me everything, though, but I'm sure they're as eager to figure out what's going on here as we are. I..." Cricket breathed, letting his hands drop to his sides, and turning to face Yoshi fully. "The feeling of whatever that was in my head last night. I didn't like it. It was like I was drowning. Like at the time everything was happening somewhere above water, and I was below it, and I couldn't get to the surface. But once I had surfaced, I remembered it all. Maybe more vividly than if I hadn't been under at all. I doubt they enjoy that feeling. No one would. It was more than just unset-tling, it was suffocating." He huffed, looking off over Yoshi's shoulder.

Yoshi moved toward him, reaching for Cricket's hands. And oh, he was well and truly frowning now, concern making his face look tight. Cricket wondered vaguely what other emotions would look like on Yoshi's face. If a smile would crinkle his eyes or his nose, or both. Then he shook the thought aside. Yoshi gave his hands a firm squeeze. "We will not let you be exposed again tonight."

"I'll be all right, Yoshi, swear." Cricket pulled on a smile, tilting his chin up, and forcing his shoulders back. "Just give me a boost, yeah?"

Yoshi nodded. He bent, bracing his hands together. Cricket stepped into them, and Yoshi lifted him up toward the branch. He scrambled for a moment to get his fingers around it, but once he had he was able to pull himself up to sit and start to sort out his next move.

"Thanks Yoshi! I shouldn't be long," Cricket called down.

"Be careful. Do not fall." Cricket couldn't quite make out the expression on Yoshi's face from where he'd moved onto the next branch, but he imagined Yoshi must look worried.

"Oh, no need to be concerned about that! I was climbing trees before I could walk!" Cricket laughed merrily, as he braced himself and reached for another branch. Just a little higher and he'd be close enough to the pixie nest to demand an audience with their queen. It would be easier without boots, and sore feet, but Cricket had never let a little injury stop him from climbing a tree when he wanted to.

Soon enough, he was able to stand on one of the lower branches and be face to face with one of the many entrances and exits to the nest. He inhaled deeply, sent up a silent prayer to Selene that pixie dialects weren't regional, and braced himself on the trunk of the tree. Then he cupped his hands around his mouth and chittered his teeth together in greeting.

"Hello," he called in pixie, and settled back to wait.

The first creature that poked their head out was a child. Skin pale green, and eyes too wide for their face. They blinked at him, gauzy wings fluttering behind them, and then disappeared into the nest again, chittering too fast for Cricket to understand.

"I'm not here to hurt you," he assured. "I just want to talk."

There was more chittering, soft now, but just as quick, as the flock talked, and came to a decision. When it was all done, a taller pixie—roughly about the size of Cricket's hand from the tip of his middle finger to his wrist—stepped out onto the branch to look down their nose at Cricket. The creature was a faded lilac, less pastel, closer to grey, showing the signs of their age, and wore an elegantly tailored suit. Not their queen, no, but this was a high ranking official in their court.

"What can we do for you, Your Highness?" They asked, giving Cricket a bow that was only just low enough to be polite. He was not welcome. Not surprising given everything going on in Nishi. They probably thought he was there to blame them for the attacks.

"I wanted to ask about a man with a caravan that might have come through Nishi a month ago. He was selling a..." Cricket stalled, trying to think of the correct word in pixie. It'd been a long time since he'd had a lengthy conversation with a pixie, and they'd never been in-depth. Always just little dares to see if he could get the garden pixies to turn Uncle red as a tomato. "A lot of things. Different things."

"We saw this man. We did not hurt him. Just as we have not intentionally hurt the people of Nishi," came the pixie's reply. Diplomatic. Imperialistic. Cutting to the quick of why Cricket was there.

"I'm not accusing you of that," Cricket assured. He tried to hold his hands up in an offer of peace, but nearly lost his balance, so he had to brace himself against the trunk again. "I was wondering if anyone bought, or..." He couldn't say stole. Because pixies did not steal. They always intended to return the items they took. It wasn't their fault if the people weren't there anymore because it was decades later. "Or borrowed something from him while he was here."

"We did not buy or borrow anything from this man." They sniffed as if put out by the insinuation that they'd have anything at all to do with elves, least of all the traveling kind that sold junk.

"Has any of the other clans in the forest? The goblins maybe? Or the will-o-wisps?" Cricket wrinkled his nose. If it weren't the pixies, then he was running out of options. They were the first infected, so it stood to reason that it should have been them.

"None of the clans of Nishi bought or borrowed from this man."

Cricket nodded, scrubbing at his nose in thought. "If you didn't buy or borrow from him, did you see him leave anything behind? Have you come across anything..." He faltered again, trying to think of the word. "Anything that didn't belong in the forest?"

"No such item has been discovered in our forest."

"I see. Thank you very much for your time." Cricket bowed his head in respect. He turned carefully, making to clamber back down the tree when the clearing of a throat stopped him. Looking back up he saw the pixie noble shifting their wings, unsettled. "Yes?"

"Our Lady wants to know what the Prince of Lunette plans to do about the crisis in Nishi."

"Oh." Cricket tilted his chin up, puffing up his chest as he'd often seen Father do. "I'm going to find what's causing this. And I'm going to fix it."

The pixie frowned, looking as if this answer did not suit them.

"Is there something..." He frowned, wrinkling his nose. "Something more?"

"Will the guilty be punished?"

Of course. Of course, they would want whoever was responsible to be punished. But he didn't think he could punish the people of Nishi. Whoever had bought the cursed item and was now harboring it, wasn't responsible. They had just been foolish enough to fall for the traveling trader's scam. It wasn't their fault.

"Will the guilty be punished?" the pixie noble asked again.

"I'll find the man responsible for the pain, and terror he's brought to my people. And he will be punished."

The noble bowed, again just low enough to be polite.

Cricket inclined his head, and then scrambled down to the lowest branch. Yoshi was waiting for him, his hands held up to catch Cricket as he lowered himself to the ground, setting him lightly on his injured feet.

As they made their way back to Nishi, Cricket told Yoshi everything he'd learned from the pixies. He knew he'd have to tell Ignacia again once they were back to the inn, but he didn't mind telling them twice.

"They did not steal from him?" Yoshi asked.

"They didn't." Cricket sighed, scrubbing at his face. His feet were beginning to hurt again, and he couldn't wait to sit down at the inn.

"They were being honest?"

"I told you, pixies can't lie."

"They can mislead."

"Well the pixie I spoke to was very straight forward."

Cricket shrugged. "Whatever it is, it's not in the forest. Which means..." He looked around the busy street. The people of Nishi were milling about, trying to get their shopping, and business done during the hours of daylight available to them so they could be home in time for curfew. It was hard to believe it was them, but it had to be. "It means someone here is hiding whatever it is."

"How will we find them?" Yoshi walked along beside Cricket, and Cricket appreciated that he either hadn't noticed yet, or wasn't going to mention that Cricket's pace had slowed significantly.

"I don't know yet. We'll have to brainstorm with Iggy."

"Hm." Yoshi took Cricket's hand, pulling him away from a cluster of people to avoid having his feet trod on. Cricket breathed his relief. The pain was making him hot. He was sure the color had washed from his face.

"Thanks."

Yoshi nodded. "How did you learn to speak pixie? It is not a commonly taught language."

"No, but our garden had a pretty big pixie nest in it. They loved the rabbits. I even caught them racing them a couple of times." Cricket laughed, shaking his head at the memory. He was grateful for the distraction. "And pixies already have a penchant for mischief. It's almost easy to get them to help you play pranks. Especially on Uncle Sunil."

Yoshi turned to him; eyes widened just a touch. "You played pranks on your uncle?"

"What? No. The pixies did. I just...you know...helped them along." Cricket tapped the side of his nose and winked at Yoshi.

Yoshi let out a huff of breath, that might have been exasperation, or it might have been a laugh. Cricket liked to think it was a laugh. The thought buoyed him along as they made their way to the inn.

CHAPTER 35

"They're as tight lipped as they've ever been," Ignacia said, chewing the crust of her flatbread viciously.

It was nice to finally be sitting. Even if that meant Cricket had to watch Ignacia gnash her teeth on chewy bread, and grumble bitterly at being left behind while he and Yoshi had been "off playing with pixies". Her words, not his.

"Well, these things don't happen overnight." Cricket sighed, leaning back on the heels of his hands. He had wriggled out of his boots and socks the moment they'd returned to his room. The innkeeper hadn't had the window fixed, but she'd cleaned up the glass, and boarded it shut. She said it should keep. But Cricket was sure he wouldn't be sleeping alone. "They don't know if they can trust you yet."

"What's not to trust?"

Cricket snorted and shook his head.

"What?"

"Nothing." He reached for a piece of the flatbread to chew on it thoughtfully. "If it's not in the forest then it must have a point of origin here in the city somewhere. It's probably visible just before it starts."

"Let's say it is." Ignacia swallowed noisily around a bite that had to scratch her throat on the way down. "Let's say you'd be able to pinpoint whatever house or shed or whatever it was coming from by sight alone. How will you get your eyes on it?"

"That is..." Cricket said, pointing at her. "A very good question."

Ignacia rolled her eyes.

"Perhaps," Yoshi said, setting down his fork demurely. He was using a fork and knife to eat flatbread while Ignacia and Cricket ate it with their hands like heathens. Because of course he was. "If we could get above the city. The fog likely clings to the ground, meaning if we got up high enough, we would have a view of where it came from."

"That's all well and good. But how are we going to get above the city? None of the buildings are tall enough, and last I checked we don't have a pegasus in our envoy." Ignacia's sarcasm and pessimism was really starting to annoy Cricket. He wasn't sure what bee had gotten into her bonnet, but he wished she'd get it out already.

"Then what would you suggest?" Yoshi asked, tone rigged and cool.

"We'll just have to search the town for clues." Ignacia shrugged, tearing off another piece of cheese coated bread to pop in her mouth. "Only option really."

"That is inefficient."

"Nothing for it, I'm afraid."

Yoshi glared at her, and Ignacia glared right back. Cricket sighed, pressing the heels of his hands into his eyes hard enough to see stars. He wasn't sure why, or when the pair had become so hostile toward one another, but it wasn't making their job any easier.

"Enough, you two," he said from behind his wrists. "We're supposed to be coming up with solutions, not more problems."

"He started it," Ignacia mumbled under her breath. Cricket dropped his hands from his face to give her a stern look, and she had the decency to avert her gaze. "Sorry."

He turned his eyes to Yoshi. Yoshi dropped his head, looking appropriately ashamed for someone who only ever showed a hint of what Cricket was sure he was feeling. Cricket nodded, satisfied.

"Right. So short of getting twenty or so pixies to grab onto me and fly me up, we can't get over top of this thing. And before you ask, no, they would not do that. These are not the friendly pixies from the garden, and they don't seem likely to want anything to do with humans, much less touch them." Cricket held up a hand to stave off the question from Ignacia. "We'll have to come up with another way."

"How are your levitation spells?" Ignacia suggested.

"Not strong enough to get any of us up that high." Cricket picked a pepper off the top of his flatbread and popped it into his mouth. "Too heavy."

"What about a tree?" Yoshi asked.

"Too far from town. I mean yeah, they go round Nishi in a circle, and there are some pretty tall ones on the perimeter. But there's no way I'd be able to see all the way across the lake from the center to the other side if the mist was coming from there." He chewed thoughtfully. "We don't have the manpower to search all the houses in the city, and that isn't really something I want to do anyway."

"No. It would give people the wrong impression." Ignacia nodded.

"A royal decree didn't keep the people of Taini from doing something dangerous. And they're already—"

A knock thudded softly against the door. "Your Highness," a soft voice followed it in through wood. "I have brought fresh tea."

"Oh, thank you, you can just leave it by the door we—"

The girl pushed in without another word.

"Or bring it in. That works too."

She balanced the tray in her hands, carefully nudging the door closed behind her. A tight expression pinched her lips at the corners, her eyes flicking from Cricket to Ignacia to Yoshi and back to Cricket. "I didn't realize you had company."

Cricket raised a brow, looking between his two friends then back to the girl. She hadn't moved from where her heels were pressed into the bottom of the door yet, fingers gripping hard enough on the tea tray to make it tremble just a little. Her lips opened, and closed, and pressed into a tight line as if silencing herself. "I can come back."

"No need," Cricket rushed to say. "Please, have a seat."

She nodded and moved to kneel at the edge of the blanket. The porcelain jangled softly as she settled the tray to the blanket they'd lain out again like a picnic. She opened her mouth again, closed it, pursed her lips, and then busied herself with the tea things.

"If you have something to say," Cricket started, voice low and soothing. "You are safe to say it here. These are my friends, and they're here with me to help Nishi."

"You can't tell anyone I told you." Her voice was barely above a whisper, only just loud enough to be heard above the crackling of the fire. "If the miss finds out..."

"We won't tell anyone." Ignacia sat up straighter, setting aside what was left of her half-eaten piece of flatbread. "You can trust us."

The girl nodded. She took her time, pouring tea for each of them, seeming to need a moment to ruminate on her thoughts. Cricket felt himself vibrating with anticipation.

Whatever she knew, it would be vital, he could feel it. Otherwise, what need would she have for secrecy?

Once everyone had a cup in hand, she sat back on her heels. Her eyes were still downcast, watching pale fingers open and close around a gathered bit of her skirts. "They lied to you."

"About what?" Cricket asked, voice soft to match hers. He wanted to say that he knew that already. He wanted to tell her that they hadn't been subtle. But he didn't want to scare her. "Who lied?"

"The...the whole town." She swallowed, hands fisting in the cotton on her thighs again. It was rapidly becoming wrinkled. "They lied about the man. He came through, and they bought things from him. Lots of things."

"Who bought things from him?" Yoshi asked, his voice sharp. The girl looked up, alarmed at the hard tone. Cricket reached out to pat Yoshi's shoulder lightly, and Yoshi nodded at the silent communication to speak more kindly. "Who bought things?" he tried again.

"Lots of them." Her eyes flicked back down to her hands. "I umm... I have a list." She hesitated a moment before digging into the depths of one billowed sleeve to procure a rumpled bit of paper. "Some of the other assistants, and maids helped me gather the names of the people seen at his cart. We don't know if everyone bought things but...this...this should be a good place to start."

She held it out with shaking fingers, and Cricket took it gently from her, grasping her hand for a moment before pulling himself away. "Thank you. This will be a big help."

She ducked her head and rose to her feet again. "I need to get back to work."

A moment later the door shut behind her, and the group visibly slumped. Except Yoshi, of course, who remained as upright as he always did. Cricket unfolded the paper, smoothing it across his thigh. "This is a pretty big list."

"She said they don't know which of them bought from him and which didn't." Ignacia scooted closer, pressing her shoulder into his to look down at the list. "We can't just go and search their homes. Like you said, we don't have the manpower."

"Then how will we find out which item is causing this?" Yoshi had leaned forward just a little to get a better look at the list. "Should we call Anstice and ask for assistance?"

"No." Cricket shook his head. "That would defeat the purpose of me coming out to do this instead of the army." A smile inched up his face as a thought struck him. A strange little thought. The kind of thought he was sure Anstice would love, Ignacia would roll her eyes at, and Yoshi would probably groan about. "What if we created a talisman to track the items? We already have two, so we've got his magical signature. We should be able to reconfigure a traditional compass talisman to react to that."

"Can you do that?" Yoshi's eyes had widened just a little. He wasn't groaning, he looked...he looked...excited? Impressed? His brows lifted just the slightest bit.

"It won't be easy," Cricket said, running his fingers over the paper to flatten out the wrinkles, and distract himself from the way the look made his heart slam against his rib cage. "And it'll take a good bit of magic to power it, even with that it'll be pretty short range. We'll need to be in the same building as the object. But yeah, I think I can do it."

Ignacia snorted, and predictably, rolled her eyes. "What do you need from us?"

"Ummm..." Cricket wrinkled his nose, grabbing the long strap of his bag to drag it closer before digging into it for his sketchbook. He jotted down a list of things he'd need, ripping the page out, and dropped the sketchbook carelessly onto the blanket again. "Linen paper. Natural inks, or as close to natural as we can get. Any magical altering will mess with the ability of the talisman to recognize the signature. And chocolates."

"What're the chocolates for?"

"Well, if you get the coffee ones, that should keep me up all night so I can get this thing done." Cricket's lips stretched into a closed mouth grin, eyes crinkling.

"Ugh, you're impossible," Ignacia spat, climbing to her feet. She didn't even glance back once as she pulled the door shut behind her.

"Right. While she's at that, I need to set up a barrier so the magic from these things can't muck about with the—"

"Cricket," Yoshi said.

"—magic that's already in the air here. Selene only knows what havoc it could wreak. Oh stars, where did I put my chalk?" He dug through the bag, searching for it.

"Cricket... Is that me?" Yoshi's voice was soft, almost uncertain, the tone so unlike anything Cricket had heard from him to that point that it stopped Cricket short.

"Huh?" Cricket looked up suddenly, and then followed Yoshi's eyes to the sketchpad laying haphazardly open on the blanket. "Oh uh. Umm..." Heat crawled up his neck, making the wisps of hair from his braid stick to his skin. "Yeah. I guess it is."

Yoshi reached for it, but before he could, Cricket scooped it up. Shutting the pad with a soft *clap* and tucked it away again. He didn't meet Yoshi's eyes as he dug around some more for the chalk.

"Ah ha! There you are, you pesky little thing." Cricket moved over to the other side of the bed, where the floor was clear, followed closely by Yoshi.

"Is this safe?" Yoshi's tone was cold, detached, again. And Cricket thanked Selene that he wasn't going to insist they have a conversation about the sketch. He didn't have a good explanation for it, and he supposed it was better he not think too hard about it.

"As safe as it can be. There's some minor chance that the curses will attach to me, but I'm not too worried about it," Cricket said offhandedly as he scratched the blue chalk across the wood in a haphazard circle. It didn't have to be perfect, it just had to be round and closed.

"You should allow me to handle them."

"Do you know how to find and record magical signatures on paper?" he asked scribbling symbols around the edges to protect, to bind, to restrain, but to remain permeable if only to him.

"No." Yoshi moved to kneel beside him, watching with rapt attention as Cricket's fingers made fast work of the little protection barrier. "But you could teach me."

Cricket sat back on his heels, dusting his hands off on his trousers. "As much fun as that sounds and believe me it does sound fun. I love teaching obscure magical knowledge, especially stuff like this that doesn't do any damage but can be spectacularly annoying when used the right way. We don't have time for that." He shook his head, rubbing at his nose as his eyes flicked over the symbols to make sure they were in the right order, and legible enough to work. "It's probably going to take me all night just to get the signature infused into the ink. And I'd rather we not find out what will be infected after selkies."

"What can I do?"

"Keep an eye on these nasty little buggers, and make sure if they start looking like they're even thinking about latching on, I get out of the way before they strike." Cricket smiled cheerily at him. "That's not too hard, is it?"

"No."

"Great! Then, let's get started." He rubbed his hands together. The brooch made a soft *thud* as Cricket dumped it into the circle and yanked his hand away quickly before the object could react to him. "All right you ugly little thing, tell me your secrets."

CHAPTER 36

Cricket had been right about one thing, it did take him all night to infuse the signature into the ink, but not for the reason he'd thought. He'd thought it would be because he was out of practice, or that the ink Ignacia brought him wouldn't cooperate the way his own stores did, or that the objects themselves would cause a problem. But no. It was because the signature on the magic was encoded. Hidden like one of those damn dolls that stacks one within another within another. Except he couldn't find the tiniest doll!

By the time he was able to wheedle the actual signature out, Ignacia had long since curled up in his bed to snore, the coffee chocolates were gone, and Yoshi had switched out his tea for something with more caffeine to help him focus.

Yoshi was still awake, sitting in a proper lotus pose, his eyes fixed on Cricket as he worked.

Cricket rubbed his wrist against his eyes in an attempt to swipe away the dry crusty feeling that came with keeping them open too long without blinking. He couldn't blink. There wasn't time to blink. Not when so much was at stake.

Not when they had so little time. What damage had the lower fae wrought overnight? Who else had been infected? Who else *would* be infected? No. There was no time.

The feeling was almost audible. He could almost hear it when the magic clicked into place, the signature finally binding fully to the ink with a sensation of two unmatched puzzle pieces being forced together. It would hold, not for more than a day or so. Soon the piece would wriggle free, and the ink would evaporate into nothing as the magic fizzled away to return to the earth where it came from. But until then, they had time.

"There she is," Cricket laughed hoarsely to himself.

"Hm?" Yoshi asked, looking at the inkwell skeptically. It didn't look any different than regular ink. It didn't glow, or shimmer, or smell like magic. But Cricket could feel the way the ink recognized the brooch still sitting in the protection barrier.

"I got it. Where's that paper Ignacia brought?" He shifted back to stretch out his legs, mindful of the inkwell as he tried to wake them up and shake the tingling from them.

Yoshi moved quickly to the side table where Ignacia had sat the paper, and returned with it, holding a clean sheet out to Cricket.

"Thanks," Cricket said around a yawn as he moved to lay on his belly on the floor.

"A desk would be better suited," Yoshi reprimanded softly.

"We don't have a desk, Yoshi. We have the floor." Cricket's tone was peevish, and he knew Yoshi didn't deserve it. But he was tired, and all he wanted was to have this done and out of the way.

"You should rest."

"Should. Can't." Cricket wrinkled his nose, as he twirled a calligraphy brush between his fingers, thinking over the symbols he'd need. He didn't want to waste paper, and ink. It'd be better to do it right the first time. "In a day or so the magic will burn up the ink and leave us with nothing. I'll have to start the whole process over."

"Even if we stopper it?"

"Even if we stopper it." Cricket rolled his eyes. "Magic doesn't care about bottles. Did the monks not teach you Helio children about this kind of stuff?"

"We learned theory."

Cricket looked up from the paper to frown at Yoshi. "Just theory? That's all the training you had?"

Yoshi nodded, his brows pinched together just a little.

"Why?"

"Magic is dangerous." Yoshi's eyes were on the inkwell still. Watching closely as if he'd be able to witness the ink slowly disappearing from the bottle. He wouldn't be able to. When the magic burned it off, it'd do it all at once. Did it make sense? No. But magic rarely did in Cricket's experience.

"That's exactly why you have practical lessons, so you know how to use it without hurting people." Cricket chewed on the tip of the brush.

"We had practical lessons on..." Yoshi thought for a moment, trying to come up with the right phrasing, Cricket was sure. "I believe you would term it, household magic. The spell on my pouch. Clothing repair. Stain removal. Keeping my blade sharp. Nothing that could... Nothing we could use to fight."

Cricket's mouth hung open for a moment, then he snapped it closed with a click. "Well, that's just... Well." He cleared his throat, looking back down at the paper and dipping his brush into the ink. "When we get all this stuff settled, I'll teach you some. My specialty is talisman work, I like being able to put magic to paper. I'm sure I could teach you some useful character configurations."

"And you are inventive."

The brush faltered, nearly dragging a long useless stroke against the paper, but Cricket managed to steady his hand in time. He shrugged, and continued on as if it hadn't happened. "It's like painting. The same basic principles apply. Scale. Negative space. Balance. Contrast. When you think about it that way you know where to put what symbol as much as you know which shade of pink you need to mix to paint a cherry blossom."

Yoshi didn't say anything. Cricket thought perhaps he had nodded, but Cricket was focused on the talisman, and so he didn't notice.

"Do you draw?" Cricket asked. His nose scrunched as he worked on a neat row of characters down the right side. His handwriting was awful, but he'd practiced his calligraphy since he was old enough to hold a brush. Not that he'd tell Uncle that. Calligraphy was a "dignified" skill, and so Cricket couldn't be seen practicing it.

"No. Art is a frivolous pursuit."

"Ha!" Cricket laughed so hard one of his lines wobbled a little. He had to still his hand and focus to straighten it carefully by thickening one side just a little, his tongue poking out of the corner of his lip. "Funny," he said conversationally as he moved onto the next row on the left side. These were smaller, scrunched closer together. "Uncle says that about talisman work. Foolish, he calls it."

"It seems very practical to me."

Looking up from his work, Cricket offered Yoshi a dimpled smile, his eyes crinkling with the warm feeling that swelled in his belly at the compliment. "Careful hero, you're getting dangerously close to paying me a real compliment," he teased, and turned back to his work. "I'm glad you think so."

Yoshi nodded, and then ducked his head back to look at the slowly drying ink.

One final row of characters went down the center, written from the very middle of the paper and then spreading out, unfurling like a flower does in spring. "So, if you don't paint, what do you do? Like, as a hobby. And don't say sword fighting, that's not a hobby. That's practice."

"Music."

"Play or compose?"

"Hm."

"Hm. That's not an answer, Yoshi." Cricket huffed. He put the final stroke on the final character and sat back rubbing at his tired eyes. "There she is. Now... to test her."

"How?"

Cricket stretched his hands above his head, his joints cracking as he tugged them to loosen them up. "I need to break the protection barrier, and it should respond to the brooch."

He moved to do just that, fingers reaching to brush away the thin line of chalk between them and the curse that amplified magic to a disastrous extent. Yoshi grabbed his wrist to stop him. Cricket tried to pull free, but Yoshi just gave it a little squeeze. "Let me. You step back."

"That's really an unnecessary precaution," Cricket said, pointedly ignoring the way the sword-worn callouses of Yoshi's hand rubbed at the sensitive skin of his wrist. It tickled. In a weird, funny, gut fluttering kind of way.

"It is a precaution we are taking," Yoshi said firmly. "Step back, please." Then he released Cricket's wrist and waited expectantly for him to do just that.

"All right. All right." Cricket moved onto his knees, taking the talisman with him, and skidded across the floor until he was backed against the far wall. "Is this far enough?"

"It will do." Yoshi nodded. One elegantly calloused finger slid through the messy chalk outline, before he leaned back away from the brooch hastily.

The reaction was instantaneous. One moment the paper lay limp in Cricket's hands like any other soft sheet would, and the next it grew warm. It jerked in his fingers, growing rigid, and pointing in the direction of the brooch like a kite on a string. "Looks like it works. Put that thing back in the bag before the paper makes a run for it."

Yoshi scooped the brooch up carefully and sealed it away in its pouch. "We should wake Ignacia. Her and I can—"

"No," Cricket said, and then rolled his eyes. "I mean yes. Let's wake her up. But you two aren't going off on your own to do this, I'm coming with you."

"You should rest. Your feet—"

"Are much better now, thank you." Cricket should have felt bad about cutting Yoshi off twice in a row, but he couldn't be bothered, not really. He knew he wouldn't get any sleep if they left him behind at the inn, all he'd do was worry. And his feet did feel better. He hadn't unwrapped them to apply anymore ointment, but the discomfort had passed sometime in the night. He'd thought it was because he was so focused but... He shook his head. That was impossible. It was the adrenaline. "I'll go with you. I'm the only one who knows how the talisman works."

Yoshi stared at him, brows tugging down in the center just the slightest. Cricket stared back. He was not going to back down. Yoshi could death stare him all he liked; Cricket had dealt with worse.

"We're wasting time." Cricket lifted a brow, a smug twitch of his lips tugging them upwards at one corner.

"I will go get breakfast. You wake Ignacia," Yoshi said, averting his eyes as he headed for the door.

"Good choice." Cricket waited until he was gone to scoop the brooch pouch off the floor and dump it back in his satchel on his way to the bed.

He hadn't even flopped down beside her before Ignacia

lifted her head and asked, "Are you two idiots done making eyes at each other?"

"Making eyes! Who's making eyes? What does that even mean? How old are you, Granny Ignacia?" Cricket laughed nervously, tugging his long braid around in an effort to hide the way his fingers felt fluttery, like fidgeting. "Just get up already. We've got a long day ahead of us."

Ignacia's only answer was a derisive snort, and a roll of her eyes as she moved to climb out of bed. "Where do we start?"

"I only made one talisman, so we're going to have to stick together."

"I have to investigate...with you two?"

"That's what it sounds like."

"Yeah. No thanks." Ignacia tilted her head one way, then the other to stretch out her neck. "I'm going to investigate the tracks; see if anything new was out last night."

Cricket scrubbed at his nose, watching her stretch out her limbs. "And more witness statements? Maybe someone saw something."

"Right. You boys have fun playing detective. I'll go do all the grunt work." She winked at him. "Just don't get caught holding hands again."

"How did you even hear about that?!" The heat from his neck spread up to burn his cheeks. He pressed cold fingers to them trying to hide it.

"Just because I'm not upbeat, and bubbly all the time like some people." She cut him a knowing look, lips twitching into a self-satisfied grin. "Doesn't mean people don't tell me things. If you're not careful you're liable to break the hearts of all those pretty lords and ladies vying for your hand."

"ARRGH!" Cricket shouted and threw a pillow at her. Ignacia ducked, and the pillow smacked the wall beside the door just as it opened for Yoshi.

"Good morning, Ignacia," Yoshi said with a quick glance down at the pillow.

"Morning," Ignacia said, her voice warbling with a laugh as she grabbed a scone from the tray on her way out the door. The last Cricket saw of her was her hand through the door frame, wriggling her fingers playfully. "I'll see you boys later."

"Ignacia will not be joining us?" Yoshi sat the tray on the bed beside where Cricket was still clutching the second pillow, readying himself to chuck it at Ignacia's head.

"No. She will not be." *Pouff.* Cricket slammed the pillow back into its place at the head of the bed and sat back on his heels with a huff. "She's going to investigate the tracks from last night to see if any new creatures were affected."

"This is not a good idea?" Yoshi held a plate with a scone out to Cricket.

Cricket snatched it, ripping off a piece with his teeth to chew like a rather sullen cow. "It's a brilliant idea. I just wish I'd thought of it," he lied. Like a liar. Like an embarrassed, childish liar. "Hey, why don't we take breakfast on the road? We've got a lot of ground to cover."

"Walking and eating at the same time is bad for digestion," Yoshi said. And that was that.

CHAPTER 37

reakfast was a brief affair, during which Cricket twitched the whole time. Either from nerves, or frustration, or excitement, or far too much caffeine in the span of an evening, he couldn't tell. Maybe it was all four. That jittery energy carried him through to the bakery where their handy list said that the baker's wife—who was in charge of creating some truly splendid looking cupcakes—had been seen with the traveling trader.

"And you live above the shop?" Cricket asked, trying to get as close to the back stairs that led up into their home as he could without looking suspicious. He wasn't so sure it was working.

"Oh yes. It's quite convenient," the baker's wife—Mrs. Huckleberry—said with a wide smile as she loaded the cupcake he'd ordered into a neat little box. Then she turned to give Yoshi a curious frown. "Are you sure we can't interest you in anything, sir?"

Yoshi stared at a point just over her head, almost visibly uncomfortable with the attention he was receiving. "I do not eat sweets."

"We have more than just sweets here! We have plenty of savory items too. Our ham and cheese tarts make an excellent travel food," Mrs. Huckleberry continued undeterred by Yoshi's aloofness.

Yoshi shifted just slightly on his feet, and Cricket let out an awkward cough, drawing Mrs. Huckleberry's attention back to him.

"How long have you lived here? Did you say?" Cricket asked with a sunny smile.

"All our lives, Your Highness. We inherited the place from my old auntie Edna. She was such a sweet woman; you would have liked her. Always wanting to put a smile on people's faces, you know? And she made the best dang apple fritters you've ever tasted. Shame she took the recipe with her to the grave." Mrs. Huckleberry shook her head, clucking her tongue sadly.

"Ah, that's too bad." Cricket nodded, plastering on an expression of commiseration. The hand in his pocket fidgeted around the inert talisman. It hadn't grown warm, or so much as twitched since they'd entered the shop, in spite of him walking around the space to remark loudly on the generic paintings of the capital that hung along the walls. "Thank you, Mrs. Huckleberry. It's been a pleasure chatting with you."

"No. Thank you, Your Highness. Your patronage and care mean the world to us. It's good to know that our future king cares so much for his people. I look forward to hearing news of your coronation soon." She slid the cupcake across the counter to him. "And maybe a marriage not too long after. Huh? That can't be too far off. Can it?" She wiggled her eyebrows conspiratorially.

Cricket choked and forced out a too-loud too-high laugh. "Who knows!"

Then he grabbed his cupcake and made a beeline for the

door. Yoshi followed behind at a much more sedate pace. Cricket felt his shoulders slump once they were out in the open air again.

Yoshi fell into place beside him, shooting Cricket what could have been a curious glance, or a worried one. Cricket wasn't sure. Either way he waited for Cricket to speak as they walked along the street. And Cricket didn't keep him waiting long.

"Why is it that people are so interested in when I'm getting married? I just turned eighteen for Selene's sake! I've hardly left the palace, much less the capital. Let a man breathe!" Cricket groaned scrubbing at his face.

"They just wish for their prince to be happy," Yoshi said, very reasonably. Too reasonably. Why did he always have to be so *reasonable*? "To the tanner's next?"

"Yeah, Lily's saddle should be ready. We can pick it up while we're there."

Yoshi nodded, then steered them in that direction.

"Do people ever ask you when you're getting married?" Cricket asked, hand behind his head as he leaned back a little. "I bet they don't. I bet they leave you alone because you're all aloof and stern. They probably think you've already been matched. Oh, stars, you're not betrothed, are you?" Cricket stopped in his tracks to shoot Yoshi a worried look. He wasn't sure why it mattered if Yoshi were betrothed or not. But it did.

Yoshi stopped beside him but didn't look at him. "I am not betrothed. Despite Uncle's best efforts," Yoshi said and his tone almost sounded irritated. Like he couldn't believe his uncle would have the audacity to dare hire a matchmaker for him.

Cricket laughed, surprised, and probably too loud. "Sorry. Sorry," Cricket said, still snickering.

Yoshi didn't say anything to stop him, he just shook his

head. But Cricket would swear to Selene that he saw Yoshi's mouth twitch for a half a second into a smile.

THE TANNER'S WAS A BUST. Cricket spent a good half hour just walking around the shop, poking at anything within reach, and generally getting on the man's nerves as Yoshi watched impassively. But the talisman remained still in his pocket.

In fact, it remained silent at the stables, the chocolatier's, the blacksmith's, the miller's, the candlemaker's, the weaver's, the mason's, the cobbler's, and even the tailor's. All that was left was the Butcher's, and Cricket stood outside the large glass window doing his best to not think about what those cuts of meat used to be.

"We do not have to go in here," Yoshi said. He was standing next to Cricket, his face turned toward him instead of looking in the window at the display. Cricket could just see his reflection in the setting sun, and it looked...it looked sympathetic. Which was nice.

"It's the only place we haven't checked other than the residences." Cricket swallowed, trying to make his throat feel less raw, but it didn't work. Instead, he felt the warm saliva burn all the way down. "We won't be able to check the residences inconspicuously."

"Still. We do not have to go in," Yoshi insisted. And it was kind. It was too kind. It made Cricket's eyes burn.

"I'll have to enhance the next talisman so that we can check residences through the walls." Cricket's hands fisted at his sides, and he closed his eyes, drawing in a breath through his nose to try to calm himself down. Stars, he felt so weak. "I know this is a part of life, especially rural life."

"It is."

"But Father and I have been vegetarians since..." Since forever, he wanted to say. Since a fluffy bunny rabbit with long ears had led Father to a baby in a tree and made his life complete. It seemed the least they could do to thank the creatures who'd brought them together.

"There is nothing wrong with not wanting to see other living creatures killed. Even if it is for food." Yoshi's tone was gentle, dipping the most out of that monotone voice he'd been speaking in since they first met that Cricket had ever heard. It made Cricket's heart clench a little. Without another word, Yoshi reached down, and threaded their fingers together. Grounding Cricket in a way he hadn't realized he needed. Then with a gentle tug, he pulled Cricket away from the butcher window and out toward the piers that lined lake Nishi.

A cool breeze blew off the water, brushing against Cricket's face. He inhaled deeply the scent of water, and lingering traces of magic in the air. Let it wash over him and calm him. Yoshi, for all his uprightness, hadn't let go of Cricket's sweaty hand yet. He just stood there, waiting. When Cricket had control over himself again, he let his shoulders relax.

"Thanks for that." Cricket turned to smile at Yoshi.

"There is no need." Yoshi shook his head. His face was cast in a soft pink glow by the fading sun. He didn't look at Cricket, and Cricket almost thought he was smiling. At least on the side of his face the Cricket couldn't see. Probably his imagination, but it was a nice thought. "We should return to the inn. The sun will set soon, and Miss Calais will want us in by then."

Cricket nodded. "Yeah. I wouldn't want to put her out."

"Or get stuck out in the mist."

"Or get stuck out in the mist," Cricket agreed.

They walked back to the inn in silence, still holding hands. Cricket didn't have it in him to let go, and as Yoshi hadn't tried to, he figured he didn't have to. Ignacia was waiting for them just outside of the door, leaning against an exterior wall with one foot braced behind her, and her arms crossed. Her eyes flicked down to their joined hands, one auburn brow raising on her brown face, but she didn't comment.

"Did you find anything?" she asked instead.

"No. All of the places on the list were clean. Unless they have the items stored in their homes, we've hit a dead end." Cricket moved toward the door and nodded when Ignacia grabbed it to hold it open for them.

Ignacia said no more as they made their way up the stairs toward Cricket's room without a second glance. They'd have to call for dinner, just as they had every other night.

"Did *you* find anything?" Cricket let go of Yoshi's hand, ignoring the way it felt cold without the touch, and dropped down onto his bed to eye Ignacia. She'd been too quiet. He watched her lean against the wall. Watched her press her hands down to her sides as if forcing them to not cross protectively over her chest. Watched her chew on the words.

"There were gnome tracks out there today," Ignacia said, her words soft, but no less terrifying.

Cricket stood up quickly, his head spinning with the rush of blood. "What?"

Ignacia wouldn't meet his eyes. She was staring at the tips of her boots. Her jaw clenched as she forced down her own fear.

"How many? And how old?"

"Old enough." The words were vague, but he knew what they meant just as well as she did. "Enough."

The raw feeling was back in his throat, and Cricket felt

like he was swallowing glass just trying to breathe. "That means...that means..."

"The children will be next." Ignacia nodded, her hands fisting at her sides. Cricket's mind flashed back to twins, pressing their faces against the bakery window to get a good look at the prince and his companion, their noses smooshed so much against the glass they left fog trails behind. He shook himself.

"How long do we have?" Yoshi asked. He'd stayed by the door, whether it was to follow the volley of conversation more easily, or to make sure no one snuck up on them, Cricket wasn't sure.

"It'll depend on how much exposure they've been getting. The houses are sealed up pretty heavily, but no place is airtight. We're all still breathing it in, even if it's just a little." Ignacia scuffed the toe of her boot against the floor, leaving a little mark behind, and then did it again to remove the mark.

"We have a week, at most," Cricket said. His fingers moving to brush at the tip of his long braid, trembling a little. Once step, then two to the end of his bed, and then he was pacing across the length of it as he let himself think. "Maybe not more than a couple of days. *Probably* not more than a couple of days," he corrected. "Whatever is in the air doesn't totally dissipate with the mist, it'll cling to things like dew. It'll leave traces. The longer they spend outside, even during the day, the more likely they are to be affected."

"What will we do?" Ignacia asked, and her voice sounded small. Like she wasn't the one with the most practical battle training. Like she wasn't the oldest. Like she hadn't been the one taking care of Cricket for much of his life. If she didn't know what to do, how was Cricket supposed to know?

Cricket stopped suddenly, his eyes fixed on the floor as he took one breath, then two. Then he looked up and met two pairs of searching, uncertain eyes. "I need to go back out there. I need to see it when it comes in and figure out where it's coming from. Maybe try to trace it back to its origin."

"Cricky, no." Ignacia shook her head. "It's already affected you twice. We can't take any chances that it'll do it again. If you go under like that, you won't be any good to any of us."

"I'll wrap my scarf around my face. I won't breathe it in directly. I won't be long. Just enough to see it coming in, and then I'll make it back to the inn—"

"No," Ignacia growled. "You can't be everywhere at once to see where it's coming from. We aren't taking that chance."

"Then we'll all go. We should be able to get a pretty good view of the entire city if we're all out there, right? We can do this, Iggy. We can—"

Someone shouted from downstairs.

"It is already here," Yoshi said softly. He'd moved to peak through a crack between the boards across Cricket's window.

More shouting came from downstairs, and then there were footsteps, heavy and hurried on the creaking stairs. A moment later someone banged on the door.

"Your Highness," someone said from the other side, their voice harried and desperate. Ignacia shot him a questioning glance, and Cricket nodded. The door opened to reveal the maid who'd brought them the list, her face red, tear tracks glittering down her cheeks. "You have to come quick. Please, Your Highness. It's my sister. It's got my sister!"

"Lead the way." Cricket grabbed an extra scarf from his satchel, throwing it to Yoshi. He pulled the one around his neck up over his nose and wound it a second time. Ignacia had already pulled the cowl of her cloak up over her own.

The maid let out a soft sob, and then spun to lead them down the steps and out of the inn into the waiting misty streets.

CHAPTER 38

All Cricket could hear was his harsh breaths puffing against his scarf as they ran. No sound of footsteps. No pounding of his heart in his ears. No scrabbling claws as the creatures infected by the mist chased them through the streets. Just the steady in, out, of one pant and then the next. He focused on it, let it ground him, and remind him who he was, *what* he was. Used it to keep away the fuzzy haze that had already begun to threaten his consciousness. There was no time for that. Not when a child needed him.

He wasn't sure what he thought he'd find when they reached the room where the maid and her younger sister were living, but it wasn't what he found. The small girl, no more than eight or nine probably, was sitting up in bed staring out the window with coal black eyes. She didn't even flinch when the door shut behind them. Her small dark hands relaxed on the blankets beside her. Unlike how Cricket had been, she wasn't scrambling to get out, or putting up a fight. She was just looking.

Ignacia helped the maid stuff some blankets under the

door to seal it up. Cricket tilted his head one way, and then the other, taking a careful step toward the girl, making sure to telegraph his movements not to startle her. Another step toward her, and Yoshi's hand whipped out to grab his wrist and stop him.

"We should not get too close. In case she is dangerous," Yoshi whispered.

"She's not dangerous, Yoshi. Look at her, she's just looking out the window at the moon." Cricket shook Yoshi's hand off and stepped forward. "What's her name?"

"Isabeau." The maid was still standing with Ignacia, her back to the wall as she watched her sister, eyes wide with horror. "She's been sick the last few days, so I was making her some soup. And when I brought it to her, she was like...like this."

"Has she moved at all, since you noticed it?" Cricket took another careful step toward the bed. His foot pressed into a creaky floorboard, filing the silent room with the sound, but Isabeau remained still.

"No."

"My Prince," Yoshi warned, making an aborted movement to stop Cricket from approaching any further. Cricket moved, too quick, and sat on the edge of the bed next to the little girl.

"How old is she?" he asked, reaching for one of her wrists. Fingers closed around it, pressing his index and middle fingers into Isabeau's pulse to feel it. She didn't flinch at the contact, hardly even seemed to notice.

"She's eight," the maid said. "Is she... Will she be all right?"

"She should be. In the morning, once the mist dissipates, she should be better," Ignacia said, her tone soothing.

Cricket focused on the heartbeat under his fingertips. It wasn't erratic, nor too slow. It was steady, firm. It felt like the heart of a healthy young girl. He closed his eyes, reaching out with his magic to feel the vein of moon-drenched power that ran through all of Lunette's people. It took him longer than it should have to find it, especially in a child so young, so in tune with the natural power of the earth around her. And when he did find it, it was wrong. Where the bright glow of the moon should have been, there was only a shadow of its warmth. A new moon in a starless sky. Inky, and cold. Like a film had lain itself over top of the brightness and hidden it away.

"Your Highness?" the maid asked, her voice soft, and worried. A note of panic lingering around the edges.

He reached for the film with his own power, tried to peel it away. It reached back, threatening to latch onto him and drag him down with it. Where to, he wasn't sure, just *down.* Cricket tried to pull back, yank his consciousness away before the film—no, it was too alive to be a film, it was a thing, a creature in its own right—could pull him under. He felt it sink its teeth into his power, take a bite out of it. Leave behind a gaping hole where once energy had been.

There were voices—no, shouting—somewhere far away. Like people were yelling at him, but he was underwater, and couldn't get to them. The thing latched on tighter, digging in its teeth, yanking on his power. The sound of rushing water filled his ears like someone was thrashing, drowning. Cricket didn't think he was breathing anymore. Maybe if he did all he'd inhale was water, suffocating himself completely. Or maybe he'd be able to breathe under the surface. He wasn't sure. He didn't think he wanted to find out.

He sank deeper, and deeper under. The thrashing died down. The sounds grew quieter, more distant. He was sure he'd drown. Sure that the water would slip into his lungs and leave no room for air at all. Or maybe it already had, and this is what the end felt like.

A yank. A shout. A pain in his shoulder as he slammed to the floor.

It brought Cricket back, and he gasped for breath. Then blinked hard as he fought to adjust to the light of the room that burned his eyes. Sound came rushing back, too loud and disorienting all at once. But there was someone saying his name. A soft, worried voice.

"Cricket," Ignacia sobbed, struggling to pull his shoulders into her lap. "Don't you ever do that to me again!"

"I'll try not to," Cricket said, voice shaking around another gasp for air.

"Don't joke!" she growled, smacking his shoulder hard enough to make him wince. Oh Styx, that was going to bruise.

"My Prince," Yoshi said. There was a tremble in his tone, like he was scared, or maybe Cricket was imagining that. He wouldn't be surprised if he were, he did almost drown in dark magic after all. Cricket should be allowed some auditory hallucinations that tricked him into believing Yoshi cared more about him than he did.

"I'm all right," Cricket assured them, sitting up. He ignored the way his vision swam, and his body protested the movement. All it wanted was for him to lay on the cold hard floor and wait for the room to stop spinning, but that wouldn't make his friends feel any better. So, up he got. "There's something attached to her magic. Something dark. I tried to pry it off, and it took a chunk out of me."

"A chunk?!" Ignacia asked, her hands already working furiously to try to find the wound. Pushing aside fabric and trembling over bare skin.

He shook his head, brushing her seeking hands away. "Out of my magic, I should say."

Cricket still felt that missing piece. Like when he'd lost his baby teeth and would spend hours at time running his tongue along the gaping hole where once a tooth had been. It felt like that, only instead of his tongue it was Cricket's magic rushing over the place that had once been full and trying to smooth it away. It would take time. There would be no replacement tooth. It would leave a scar.

"Your magic?" Yoshi repeated, already reaching for Cricket's wrist as if he'd be able to tell the difference. He wouldn't. Cricket was reasonably sure Yoshi had never taken a baseline of his power to know what it was supposed to feel like, feeling it now wouldn't tell him anything.

"I'm all right. I promise." Cricket brushed their worry aside and rose to his feet. It was a struggle not to stumble, but he managed it through sheer force of will.

"My sister?" The maid had moved to sit beside Isabeau on the bed, her fingers brushing through the girl's dark curls soothingly.

"If she's not better in the morning, once the mist lifts, I need to know right away. You must tell me and let me return to examine her again." Cricket knew it wouldn't ease her mind, but he had no reassurances to give her, and he wasn't going to lie. Until he knew what was infecting the people and creatures of Nishi, he couldn't do anything about it. "So long as she doesn't become violent, you both should be safe."

The maid nodded. Her eyes were still on her sister, her fingers trembling as they fell to rest on Isabeau's slight shoulder.

"We can stay with you," Cricket offered, softly. "Until she wakes in the morning."

"No." Yoshi's voice was hard. "I will stay. My Prince must rest. Go back to the inn."

"Yoshi, I'm really—" Cricket tried to reason, but Yoshi sent him a cold look, and his lips snapped shut. And then he opened them again, anger swelling on his tongue. He wasn't sure if he was actually angry, or if he was just tired, or if it was the black magic, or some combination of the three. But he felt it rise like bile in his throat. "You know what! You don't get to talk to me like that!" He jabbed a finger at Yoshi. "You arrogant. Cold. Unfeel—"

"Yoshi's right." Ignacia grabbed his wrist and spun him around before Cricket could say anymore. "Let's get you back to the inn. We'll check in on Isabeau and Jovienne in the morning." Ignacia took his hand and led him to the door.

Cricket stayed quiet, all the way back to his room. He let Ignacia lead him through the mist and ignored the feeling of it scraping at his skin, threatening to get inside and suffocate him as it had before. He didn't want to worry Ignacia more, and if she knew how sensitive he was to it, they'd be out of Nishi before the first rays of sun lit the horizon.

Once he and Ignacia were alone in his room, he threw himself onto his bed and into a sulk. "You know I could have stayed with them. I could have helped. I'm not defenseless. He didn't have to talk to me like that. I'm not a child."

Ignacia snorted, rolling her eyes.

"What?"

"Nothing." She shook her head. "Only you would mistake someone caring about you for them being condescending," Ignacia muttered. She moved to gather up the supplies they'd left on the floor that morning and put them away. "Get into your pajamas. Yoshi's right, you need rest."

"He *was* being condescending!" Cricket argued, toeing off his boots, and moving to wiggle out of his trousers. "He was being... He was being... He was being..." He stopped, mouth working over the words. Had Yoshi been condescending? Had he been trying to talk down to Cricket? Or had he merely been worried? It was... Cricket wasn't sure.

"He was trying to protect you," Ignacia said, bland. She threw his sleep shirt at him, smacking him in the face with it. He pouted, looking down at the shirt cradled in his lap.

Maybe she was right, maybe Yoshi had just been taking care of Cricket. Oh Styx, he shouldn't have said those nasty things.

"Aww poor baby, Cricky. Did you hurt your own feewings again?"

"What? No! I don't even care what he thinks!" Cricket scoffed, tugging off his tunic to get changed.

"Yeah. Sure." Ignacia shook her head. "We should look at your feet before you go to bed. Make sure the wounds are still clean."

"No. It's all right. I'll handle it."

She stood, eyeing him for a moment longer, then seemed to decide that whatever else she was going to say wasn't all that important and left him to finish getting ready for bed. Once he was changed into his pajamas, he sat in the middle of the bed, crossing one ankle over his thigh to begin unwinding the bandages. They had come loose a little while he walked, and he was sure they were soaked in sweat, but he hadn't felt pain all day so they must have done—

He stopped. One long white strip of bandage dangling from his fingers.

"That can't be right," he muttered. His free hand lifted to scrub at his eyes, squeezing them shut for a moment then open again. When he looked down the skin on his foot was free of cuts. There was some blood on the bandage where they'd been, but the wounds themselves were gone. He rushed to unwrap the rest of his foot, and then the other, finding both completely unblemished. Not just healed, but as if there had been no injuries at all. "I... what did that healer give me?"

It was a mad scramble to find the bottle of ointment in the bottom of Cricket's satchel, during which he dumped everything else onto the bed. The glass was cool under his fingers, and it popped softly as he un-stoppered it. Dipping his pinky into the goopy cream, he pulled it to his nose to sniff. When that didn't yield any results, he closed his eyes to feel for the hum all things infused with magic sang with. None.

Hair fell into Cricket's eyes as he shook his head. "Weird. It's just a normal numbing agent."

It didn't make sense. None of it made sense. Even with magic, his feet should have taken longer to heal. Especially with how little sleep he'd gotten.

Sleep. That sounded nice. He yawned, long and loud.

"Ah well. Time for bed." There would be time to think about the mysteries of his healed feet in the morning.

Huffing a breath to blow the loose tendrils of hair from his face Cricket placed the bottle, and everything else, into his bag and then flopped back into bed. With the blankets pulled up to his chin, their comforting weight pressing down on his chest, and the exhaustion of nearly a full 24 hours without sleep pressing on him, Cricket crashed into sleep immediately.

But for all the tiredness that had been threatening to drag his body down for hours, it was not a restful sleep.

Black water.

Something dragged him by the ankle, deeper, deeper, deeper, until no light came from the surface at all, and all was darkness. The sound of rushing water. The greasy feeling of dark magic. The burn of his lungs begging for air.

None of it was enough to drag him from this nightmare.

CHAPTER 39

Cricket startled awake. Heart racing. Vision swimming. Breath ragged.

How long had he been under? How long had he been holding his breath? What time was it? He coughed, trying to draw out what he was sure was imaginary water from his lungs. It sounded wet, and a single cough didn't clear the tickle away. Another cough. Then a third, and fourth. And then he was hacking, hacking, hacking, until he had to scramble from the bed to the bathroom.

Crouched over the sink, Cricket tried to breathe through the cough, but couldn't. There was something crawling up his throat. Something wriggly, and slimy. Another hard cough that had him seeing stars, and scraped at the inside of his throat, preceded a splat of something wet into the sink below him. He opened his eyes to look down at the inky black water as it drained away.

"What in the name of Styx was that?" he managed to rasp before another bout of coughing took over.

By the time the knock on the door announced Ignacia's

arrival, Cricket had split his lip, and one look in the mirror told him that he'd burst a blood vessel in his eye.

"Cricky?" she asked as she came into the room and found his bed empty.

"I'll be out in a minute Iggy. Just a minute." He breathed in through his nose, hoping to bypass the parts of his throat that ached the most. No use. Cricket shook his head, looking down at the sink that he'd plugged up to contain the water. It wasn't a terrible lot, not even enough for a glass, but it had felt like a lot when it was coming out of his lungs. He grabbed a towel to scrub away the remnants on his lips, and the sweat at his temples.

"Where did you come from little beastie?" he asked, reaching out a finger to poke at the puddle.

It didn't respond. In the warm light of day, it didn't even reach back for him. But it hummed, loud and threatening, with dark magic.

"I wonder if I can track you back to your source." Long fingers drummed against the metal wash basin as he pondered. "Iggy," he called, ignoring the way his voice sounded raw and choked.

"Yeah? What's wrong?" She'd come to stand by the door. He hoped she wasn't worried about him, but he knew better than that. She was, she had to be. He didn't have time for worry. Not when there was a puzzle to solve.

"Nothing." He shook himself, looking up at his face in the mirror again. Cricket's freckled cheeks were red from the strain of coughing, but everything else was pale, and there were dark circles hanging under his eyes. He looked like a mess. He couldn't let her see him like this. Not if he could help it. "Nothing's wrong," he lied, and he was sure she heard the falseness in it, but she didn't argue. "Can you see if you have any empty stoppered bottles in your pack?"

Ignacia let out a breath on the other side of the door, and

Cricket heard her clothes rustle as she likely reached for the knob to force it open. But then she stopped and took a step back. "I'll be right back. I'm sure I have something."

Cricket waited until he heard her footsteps retreat back to the door and then he looked down at the water again. It wasn't doing anything. No glowing. No roiling. Nothing. It sat there, looking harmless. If he hadn't coughed it up out of his own lungs, he would have thought it was just a product of the pipes needing to be cleaned. But no, this had crawled up out of his body. He didn't know how long it had been inside of him. If it had been from the first day in Nishi, or when he touched Isabeau and that strange darkness latched on, or if it was from his dreams. But it had been inside of him, doing Selene only knew what.

"I got a bottle," Ignacia announced, knocking softly on the door. "Can I come in?"

Cricket sighed. He supposed it was too much to hope that he'd start to look normal before she returned. Not after the last few days he'd had. He reached over and pulled the door open. She was holding out a small vial, and he took it from her limp fingers as her mouth fell open, eyes widening.

"What happened?"

Cricket shrugged. "Rough night? I don't know. I just... Well." He shook his head. "I coughed this up this morning." A gesture to the little puddle in the sink finally made her look away from him, grateful for the respite from the searching look, Cricket relaxed.

"Where did it come from?" Ignacia's sharp eyes narrowed on it as she leaned closer.

"The mist? Maybe? I don't know. I just know I woke up this morning coughing, and when I came in here to hack up whatever it was. It was water. Not a lot of water, but still, water."

"More than just from breathing in some mist. That's...

Cricket that looks like that time you tried to learn to swim in the palace pond." Ignacia's dark eyes flicked back to him; concern written across her brow. For as often as he saw that look, Cricket would think he'd get used to it, but he never did. He hated worrying her. Especially when there were bigger things to be focusing on, like the fate of all of Nishi.

"Help me get it into this vial, would you?" He dipped the bottle into the sink, pressing it down to the water.

She opened her mouth to say something, but shook her head, and instead helped him scoop the water little by little into the vial. Once inside, Cricket pushed the stopper in to seal it, hoping it'd be enough to keep whatever was in the water from getting out. Not that that had ever stopped dark magic before.

Another knock came from the door.

"I'll get that, you get yourself cleaned up. You look like death warmed over." Ignacia shut the bathroom door behind her and went to let whoever it was in.

"Thanks for that," Cricket muttered sullenly. He looked at himself in the mirror, taking a steadying breath. His cheeks weren't red anymore, making the freckles that dusted them and his nose stand out harshly against his sickly pale skin. Stray hairs clung to his clammy temples. And the whites of his eyes looked pink, making the blue irises look garishly bright. There wasn't much he could do to hide all that. But he supposed he could brush his teeth.

Murmured voices came through the door as he washed up, and tried to make himself look presentable, but Cricket couldn't make out any of the words. When he emerged from the bathroom, he was surprised to find Yoshi and Ignacia deep in conversation.

Cricket looked from one stricken expression to the other, and asked, "What's happened to Isabeau?"

It was the only thing he could think that would cause

both Ignacia and Yoshi to look so serious. Well, perhaps not the only thing. But at that moment, she was the only person he could think to be worried about. Not himself. Not them. But that little girl who'd looked so small in her bed the night before.

"It is not just Isabeau," Yoshi said softly. "There were other children affected last night."

"How many?" Cricket tucked the vial into his pocket and went to grab the notebook from his satchel.

"A dozen. Maybe more. We don't have reports in from everyone yet." Ignacia shifted on her feet, her lips pursing.

"Ages?"

Yoshi shook his head.

"Have they woken from their trance?"

Yoshi shook his head again, his lips going pinched at the corners.

"Right." Cricket nodded, snapping the journal shut and bracing his hands on his hips. "We need to see as many of them as we can before the mist rises again. And we need detailed notes on their ages, if they've been sick recently, how much time they've spent outdoors. All of it. Hopefully their families can tell us. It'd be best if we split up. Iggy, I know you can check for magic veins, but I'll need you to come with me to see Isabeau so I can show you what to look for."

"What about the water?" Ignacia asked, her eyes flicking down to the pocket where Cricket had stuffed the vial.

"I'll deal with that after we've seen to as many of the children as we can." Cricket slung his satchel across his body, and took a deep breath, nodded to himself. He felt better knowing that they had a plan of action. Even if it was just information gathering. It was something. "Yoshi, do you know how to check for the vein of magic?"

"No." Yoshi frowned.

"Well then you're about to get a crash course. Let's

move." Cricket headed for the door, not waiting for the other two to follow. "We'll grab something to go from the kitchens downstairs."

"Walking and eating—"

"Is bad for digestion, I know. But we have at least twelve children to check before the sun sets, and only three of us to do it. I'm sure our stomachs will forgive us this once?"

Yoshi looked like he wanted to argue further, his jaw grinding together, but he said nothing else.

"Right. Great. Let's go."

ISABEAU WAS STILL SITTING up in her bed when they reached her and Jovienne's home. Her eyes still locked on the window, watching the world pass it in a warm blur of morning sunshine.

"No change," Jovienne said, ushering them over to the girl's bedside.

"Did she lay down at all last night?" Cricket sat on the bed next to Isabeau, reaching for her wrist to check her pulse again. It still thrummed steadily away, but he didn't know how long that would last with the darkness eating away at her magic and keeping her awake.

"No," Yoshi said, the mattress dipped under his weight as he sat next to Cricket.

"Do you think she's getting any rest this way?" Jovienne was wringing her hands, pacing the one room apartment. "She's never had any trouble sleeping before, and she's always been a healthy child. But children can't go without sleep like this. Not like adults can. And when our parents died, I said I'd take care of her. But now I just don't know what to do."

She stopped only to let out a harsh sob, and bite down hard on her lower lip. "I'm sorry."

"It's all right," Cricket kept his voice soft, tone gentle. "I understand you're worried about your sister. Right now, I don't see where it's hurting her." Jovienne relaxed. Cricket frowned. He didn't want to lie to her, but he knew he would need to put her and the other families at ease as best he could. "We are doing all we can to figure out why this is happening."

Jovienne nodded.

"I know it's hard, but if you could just sit down for a moment, and breathe, that'll calm you down a little." Cricket offered her a soft look, not quite a smile, but an expression of understanding. He knew what it was to have a loved one sick, and not be able to do anything about it. "And if you can, please be quiet for a few minutes. I need to show Yoshi and Iggy what to look for so we can check on some of the other children."

Jovienne visibly swallowed, and then moved to sit in one of the chairs at the little table. Her hands fisted in her lap, but she pressed her lips together to keep herself silent.

"Thank you." Cricket turned back to the task at hand. "Ignacia, we're going to need you as a baseline."

"Why can't we use you as a baseline?" Ignacia grumbled, but held her wrist out to him like a good little patient.

"Because I've probably already been infected and wouldn't be a good example of what Yoshi should be looking for." Crisp. Matter of fact. Curt. Cricket didn't have time for games, nor for examining his own feelings on being infected with what was eating away at Isabeau's magic. "All right Yoshi, here's what you do. It's a lot like feeling for a pulse, only instead of counting heartbeats you reach out with your magic and touch the other person's. You shouldn't have to think too hard about it, like calls to like."

"You have been infected?" Yoshi asked, reaching for Cricket's free wrist to press his calloused fingers into the tender skin of Cricket's arm.

"Probably. But that's not the point of this discussion." Cricket huffed, tugging at his wrist. Yoshi tightened his hold. "Yoshi," he said sharply. "Now isn't the time. Let go."

Yoshi released him, but his lips pursed just a little into something that almost might have been a pout. *Cute.* Cricket shook himself. "I am from Helio."

"I know that, but it won't make a difference. We're all descended from the same folk, even the pixies. Though don't tell them that; they'd sooner go extinct than admit they're related to us elves," Cricket teased. He forced one corner of his lips up into a smile. It did nothing to lighten the mood, everyone around him, apart from Isabeau, who wasn't aware of anything, seemed to know that it was fake. He cleared his throat. "Right. Like calls to like. So your fingers go here," he adjusted Yoshi's grip carefully on Ignacia's wrist. "Now, close your eyes, and reach. It's kind of like meditating. only instead of reaching out to the ambient power of the earth, you're reaching out to another person's."

"Bright," Yoshi said after a moment.

Cricket snorted a real laugh. "Yeah, sometimes. Did you find it?"

Yoshi nodded.

"Good. Now we're going to do the same to Isabeau, only when you reach for hers what you'll be looking for is not the brightness, but the absence of light." Cricket watched with fascination as Yoshi repeated the process, his face set in determination, and concentration.

Cute.

No. No. Now was *not* the time for that!

Yoshi's brows furrowed in upset, and he dropped Isabeau's wrist suddenly, as if it'd stung him.

"Is that how it felt when you were infected?" Yoshi didn't wait for an answer, he reached for Cricket's wrist again, clamping down hard enough on the tender skin and bone that Cricket felt it grinding. Then he slammed his eyes shut, and Cricket felt him reach. It tickled and tingled all up the length of his arm. Cricket closed his own eyes against the feeling and sighed as the heat of the sun flooded into him. Rushing warm and liquid into his veins, brushing against his senses.

Then like a cloud passing over the sun, it was pushed back. Chased off by that dark thing that Cricket hadn't been able to cough up that morning. Cricket yanked his arm away, hoping Yoshi hadn't noticed it. When he looked up, Yoshi's eyes were open and sharp. He was trying to understand something, but Cricket didn't know what.

"All right Iggy, your turn," Cricket said looking away from the assessing gaze.

Once Ignacia and Yoshi understood what Cricket needed them to do, they parted ways. And Cricket did his best to ignore the lingering look of...something Yoshi gave him just before they did. Now was *not* the time.

CHAPTER 40

There were more than twelve.

A lot more.

Every child in Nishi under the age of thirteen had been infected. Cricket, Yoshi, and Ignacia spent the entire day rushing from one home to the next to make sure they got all the information Cricket needed. Cricket skipped his midday meal in favor of continuing the investigation and doing what he could to calm the people of Nishi.

By the time Cricket returned to the inn he felt the hours of sleep he had missed, the night of tossing and turning, and an ache in his chest he didn't want to look too closely at. He slumped into a booth in the main dining area and ordered tea and soup for himself while he waited for his companions to return.

Drawing his knees up, Cricket pressed himself into the corner of the booth, letting his head list to one side, and his eyes fell shut. The quiet sounds of clinking porcelain and gentle chatter lulled him. It was nice. Relaxing.

He must have dozed off because he didn't even hear Ignacia come in (and she by no means did anything quietly) before she flopped herself down on the bench next to him. Gasping awake made Cricket choke on air, and soon he was coughing again. No. Not coughing. Retching. Choking. Hacking.

Ignacia thumped on his back, trying to help him get whatever it was up. But it was still there, squirming in his lungs, and up his throat. He pulled his scarf up to cough into it and when he was finally able to breathe again, he looked down to find the fabric damp with black water.

"It's getting worse, isn't it?" she asked, her eyes on the wet scarf.

"I'm not sure," Cricket said, voice hoarse from coughing. "It still feels like it's in there."

"Maybe you just didn't get it all out the first time."

"Maybe." He looked up to offer the waitress a watery smile as she delivered his tea and soup. "This should help."

"You should be in bed." Ignacia frowned, watching as his hands trembled in their reach for the spoon. "We should call the healer."

"Is something wrong with Cricket?" Yoshi asked, his lips pressed into a hard line.

"Nothing is wrong with Cricket. Cricket does not need a healer. He just needs a full night's sleep, and some soup. That's all. Now, both of you better give me your findings before this bowl of soup is finished so I can go to bed. I'm exhausted."

Yoshi and Ignacia shared a Look, and Cricket half wondered when they had begun to conspire against him in such a way.

"I'm fine! Really!" Cricket huffed, picking up his spoon in a hand that was definitely threatening to tremble, but he managed to keep still long enough to take a decisive slurp. "There. See? Nothing to worry about."

Another Look travelled between his two friends, but

neither said any more on the matter. Instead, they sat down to fill him in on everything they'd learned, which was admittedly, not much. The children's ages ranged from six to twelve, the years when a child first started showing signs of magic and when it was arguably at its most volatile. None of them had been outside during the mists. None of their parents could tell them how many hours each child spent outside during the day. Some had shown signs of a minor cold or infection before falling into the trance, others had not. It had come on quite suddenly, in all of them, on the same night.

Cricket let that information breathe for a moment. None of it told him anything, not really. Or at least not anything he hadn't already suspected. It didn't make the puzzle pieces fit together. Not yet anyway. He was still missing something. The center was starting to be filled in, but most of the edge pieces were still hidden away.

Pushing away his soup bowl, and drinking the last dregs of tea, Cricket nodded to himself. "If you'll both excuse me then, I'm going to bed. I've had a long couple of days."

"We'll see you in the morning," Ignacia said with a curt nod, and then went back to her food.

"Good night to you too." Cricket braced himself on the table and pushed to his feet, ignoring the way his knees wobbled a little. He could make it up the steps into his bed, that's all he cared about. That and sleep. Boots scuffed against the floor as he made his way to the stairs. Cricket wasn't aware of Yoshi until the white knight reached to take Cricket's elbow. "Yoshi, I can go up the steps just fine."

"I will see you to your quarters."

Cricket lifted his non-Yoshi-held arm to scrub at his face, paying particular attention to the bridge of his nose. Great Selene, he was tired. So tired. He didn't even really have the energy to fight Yoshi on this.

"No. You won't. I'm fine. I just need some rest, and I'll be fine. Now, go back to your dinner before it gets cold." With a yank Cricket pulled his elbow from Yoshi's grasp and marched up the steps perhaps a little more vigorously than he should have considering he was still having trouble breathing. By the time he made it into his sleep clothes, and into his bed, he was panting.

"It'll be all right. I just need sleep." Another cough wracked his chest and lungs so hard it nearly brought tears to his eyes.

SLEEP WAS NOT THE ANSWER. Cricket was not all right. He didn't know how long he had been asleep, but he woke up coughing again and had to return to the sink to spit more water into it. This time when he looked down at it the liquid writhed and hissed at him before slinking down the sink like a sullen cat.

"I don't know what you're so angry for, I didn't ask for this either," he rasped, clearing his throat. Then went back to bed.

But he didn't stay in bed. Cricket lost count somewhere after the third or fourth time that he had to rise to go to the bathroom and spit water into the sink.

It was getting worse. Whatever it was, was getting worse.

And by the time someone knocked on his door to wake him, he couldn't have gotten more than a couple of hours of sleep consecutively.

"Come in." A rasping mimicry of Cricket's voice called, and he wheezed around his ruined throat.

On creaking hinges, the door opened to reveal Yoshi

holding a tray with soup and tea. "I have brought My Prince breakfast."

"Oh, umm... Thank you." Cricket cleared his throat, trying to sound more like himself. It was no use, he knew that. It didn't make the frown-wrinkle, that Cricket was beginning to associate with concern for his well-being, any less upsetting. Yoshi was too pretty to be—

"Cricket, you need to get up. Now." Ignacia rushed into the room, nearly toppling the tray from Yoshi's hands. An urgency lined her voice, bordering on panic, Cricket knew that tone well. Too well, as of late.

"We were just about to have breakfast." Yoshi's hands tightened on the tray, knuckles turning white. But Cricket was already struggling with the blankets.

"What is it? What's wrong?" He swallowed down a cough and kicked the covers aside to climb to his feet.

"Breakfast," Yoshi said, firmly.

"It's Isabeau. She's... She's... You have to see for yourself." Ignacia moved into the room to help Cricket get ready as quickly as possible. The door creaked on the hinges again, he looked up to see that Yoshi had shut it behind him and turned his back toward them as Cricket stumbled into his clothes. Cricket thought maybe Yoshi's ears were a little pink, but the next moment Ignacia was yanking his tunic down over his head.

"Breakfast," Yoshi argued again, as they headed for the door.

Breath caught in his throat when Cricket heaved a sigh and let his shoulder bump lightly against Yoshi's in front of the door. And he must have been a little delirious from lack of sleep still, because Cricket moved onto his toes, closing the couple of inches height difference between them, and kissed Yoshi's cheek. "It was very sweet of you to bring me this."

The tray trembled in Yoshi's grasp, bowls clanking together, disguising what might have been a sharp gasp from Yoshi. Cricket did not have time to examine that, unfortunately.

Ignacia made a disgusted scoff that was probably accompanied by a roll of her eyes, grabbed Cricket's wrist, and pulled him out the door with a hurried, "Come on!"

Cricket let Ignacia tug him down the street, ignoring the catch in his lungs that seemed to beg for another coughing fit. It wouldn't do them any good. Not now. By the time they reached Jovienne, and Isabeau's home, he felt clammy and feverish all over. His breath was coming in sharp gasps, struggling past the water still in his lungs.

"Just give me a minute." Bracing himself on his knees, Cricket wheezed in a breath to steady himself, and then stood up.

"It's gotten worse. You should have stayed in bed." Ignacia's voice was doing something weird. It had surpassed worry. Surpassed concern, and pity, and sympathy. It had warbled into something like fear. "Why didn't you say anything?"

"It's not important." Cricket shook his head, hoping to shake off that tremble in her voice with it, and lifted his hand to knock on the door. Ignacia looked like she wanted to argue, but she didn't. He was sure she'd give him the dressing down of a lifetime once all this was through, and they'd left Nishi behind them. But that could come later.

Jovienne flung open the door just as Yoshi had caught up to them. Exhaustion bruised the skin under her eyes, and her face had been drained of color. She didn't say anything, she just stepped aside and let them in.

They heard the coughing before they saw Isabeau. She was still sitting up in bed, just as she had been. Her eyes looking out the window. But her chest moved in labored breaths, and as Cricket stood watching her, she inhaled sharply and then coughed. Water dribbled from the corners of her mouth, dripping onto the blanket.

"The others?" Cricket asked, his hands clenching at his sides. While he'd been struggling to sleep, the mist had been doing this.

"Many of the parents sent someone by the inn to tell us this morning that it's the same all over. Everyone is coughing up black water," Ignacia said, her hands going behind her back to curl into fists where Jovienne wouldn't see them. "Should we get samples?"

"No. It'll be the same." Cricket shook his head.

"Why is this happening?" Jovienne whispered, voice breaking somewhere in the middle.

"I think their magic is fighting back against whatever is infecting them. They're trying to cough it up." Cricket scrubbed at his face. He should check Isabeau's vein of magic again. He should reach out to that writhing shadow and try to force it back while it was weakened. But he was afraid. Afraid of what he'd find. Afraid of what would happen to him if he let himself be touched by it again. He was already sick. How long before he was under its spell—unable to move—like they were?

"What do we do?" Ignacia turned to him, that fear in her eyes again.

"We use the water to find the source."

"Do you have the power to do that right now?"

"Not like this." Cricket clenched his fists at his side, hating every word of that sentence. He hated feeling weak, and he was weak. He was sleep deprived. And feverish. And sick. Weak.

"Not on your own, but with help," Yoshi offered.

"Yeah, with help, we'll have enough." Cricket nodded, breathing through another squirm of the water in his lungs. "I don't think a standard tracking talisman is going to do it though."

"Then what are you going to—" Ignacia's face paled as it dawned on her what he was thinking. "No. No. No. *No.* Absolutely not."

"It only makes sense." Cricket bowed to Jovienne. "We're going to solve this, don't worry." Then he went back out into the street. He was going to need more ink.

"Cricket. I *forbid* it. You are not doing this." Ignacia chased after him.

"What is he doing?" Yoshi asked, speed walking to keep up with them.

"We don't have time to play around with talisman paper, Ignacia," Cricket said, tone firm. "It doesn't have the power we need for this. Even if we all infused magic into the ink and paper, it wouldn't be enough. Not to get us the answers we need quickly. The best thing to do is use a canvas already teaming with magic."

"Then let me do it."

"What is he doing?" Yoshi asked again, his voice strained with something close to fear. Probably brought on by the expression of abject horror on Ignacia's face. Really, and she said Anstice was dramatic.

"You don't have the water already living in your lungs. I do. It's in there, and it's multiplying. The longer we wait, the worse I'll get, and the less likely it is that it'll work," Cricket said. And what he didn't say was that it was less likely he'd survive this wild gambit of his. He knew he could survive it this time. He was weak, but he wasn't that weak. His magic hadn't been blackened to the point of it being dangerous. But give it another couple of days, and the blackness in his lungs would eat away at his power enough that he wouldn't be good for much other than telling Yoshi and Ignacia what symbols to use in the talisman.

"What. Is. He. Doing?" Yoshi's words were clipped, annoyed, bordering on manic. Or as close as Yoshi ever got.

"He's going to use himself as a tracking talisman." Ignacia scowled at Cricket who was ignoring her in favor of hunting down the stationary store.

"That is not safe?"

"Probably not the safest thing I've ever done." Cricket shrugged. "But we're out of options here."

"You've never even done it before! No one has! It's just a wild theory you've posited to your magics professor. And even they told you that you were an idiot for thinking of it!" Ignacia growled.

"Yes. Well. Professor Qiren lacks imagination. They never want to do anything outside of what has already been done and rigorously documented. Ah! Here we are!" Cricket wheezed around an overexcited breath and headed into the stationary shop.

CHAPTER 41

"You will eat a proper meal before we do this." Yoshi's voice was firm, commanding, as he slid a bowl of congee across the table to Cricket. He had taken possession of Cricket's ink stores the moment they'd been purchased under the guise of helping to carry them. Then refused to relinquish the bags even after they'd settled into a booth in the dining room of the inn. Where he'd ordered food, and tea. "Now."

Cricket looked down at the bowl of slippery rice porridge and swallowed around that slimy feeling crawling up his throat again. "I'm not really hungry."

"I did not ask." Yoshi held out a spoon to him, looking completely uninterested in Cricket's complaints. "Before it gets cold."

Cricket turned a plaintiff frown to Ignacia, and she shrugged. "He's right. You're going to need what strength you've got. It'll work better with something in your stomach."

"Couldn't I have something...else?" It wasn't that he hated congee, really it wasn't. When the weather was cold, and Youta made the squash congee he liked so much, he especially liked it. It warmed him from the inside out and settled into his bones enough to keep him warm throughout the day. But the heat of summer was still clinging to his neck, even after they'd passed the beginning of autumn. And all he could think about was that slimy water wriggling and multiplying in his lungs.

"You need something hearty that'll stick with you," Ignacia said simply.

"But..."

"The sooner you eat, the sooner we can get to work." Yoshi sipped his tea, expression impassive.

"We're not letting you do this without something in your stomach. Eat up." Ignacia nodded firmly.

They were ganging up on him, and he didn't like it one bit. It was going to make things so much harder in the future. But he didn't have much choice. So he swallowed down any further complaint, and shoveled the food into his mouth hoping to get it eaten as quickly as possible. It squirmed all the way down, but he managed to keep it there without gagging, and he had to admit that it coated his throat in a way that left him hardly feeling the urge to cough at all.

"ARE YOU SURE ABOUT THIS?" Ignacia asked for what had to be the tenth time since Cricket had sat down in front of the hearth and pulled off his tunic. Yoshi was staring carefully into the middle distance, and Ignacia was staring directly at Cricket's face. As if she could detect any hint of uncertainty merely by looking.

"It should be simple enough," Cricket said, wearing on his lip, his eyes tracing over the sketch he'd done up of his front and back. He was still trying to figure out exactly where to put the character for mind. Too far from his face and it'd do nothing at all. But his upper back and chest were already scrawled in other characters that couldn't be moved. They had to be in the exact order they were in.

"What will this one do?" Yoshi asked, pointing to the sketch of the mind character he'd scrawled in the margins. It was sloppy. Yoshi probably couldn't read it; most people couldn't read Cricket's handwriting. His character work was usually more precise, but he'd hastily scrawled everything he thought he'd need into the margins just to make sure there was space.

"It'll keep me conscious. Without it I'll probably fall into a trance, just like the others." Cricket chewed on the end of his pencil frowning. There was nothing for it, it'd have to be on his face. He drew a quick smiley face in the corner and put the character just to the side of one eye.

"You could still fall into a trance," Ignacia huffed. Then her eyes caught the sketch. "You want to put a piece of it on your *face*?"

"I don't see where I have much other choice." Cricket shrugged, twirling his pencil as he went down the list of characters one more time. Yes. This would do it. This would twist the water in his lungs and force it to show him the way. It wasn't the cleanest talisman he'd ever written, and there might be a lot of unnecessary characters, but better too many than not enough. And it would work. That—he was sure of.

"And if it backfires, and... Oh, I don't know... Makes you lose your mind?" Ignacia's eyes had squinted to slits, her mouth twisting into fury. "Then what?"

"Calm down. It's just a consciousness character. If anything, it'll just act like a really big cup of coffee and keep me wired for a couple of days." He nodded at his work. It was solid. He knew it was. It was also perhaps one of the most beautiful talismans he'd ever written, even in its sloppiness. Really, he should write a paper on it, for posterity. Not for his ego. Definitely not for his ego. It'd send Professor Qiren into fits, for sure. He shook himself. Later. He could daydream about that later. "All right, the consciousness character has to be the point of entry."

"Why?" Yoshi asked. He was still looking down at the diagram, with a strange expression on his face. Cricket wasn't sure if it was horror, interest, or something else.

"Because it has to be activated first. So we write it first, and it acts as the point of entry. If not, then I might lose consciousness before you've activated the others." Cricket grabbed the first inkwell and opened it up before offering Yoshi a brush. "You two will have to put them on for me. We can't risk them ending up distorted by an odd angle."

Yoshi took the brush, and the inkwell. He looked down at them in his hands as if he'd never seen them before. Then he looked back up at Cricket.

"Will you do the honors of doing the mind character?" Cricket grinned, dimpled and lopsided at Yoshi, ignoring the racing of his heart and likely blush crawling up his neck.

Yoshi's eyes widened a little, and his nod was more of a slow up and down motion of his chin than anything else. But it was consent.

"It's this one." Cricket held up the sketch, tapping at the symbol so Yoshi could see it better. "Make it small if you can."

"Why?" Ignacia asked, her fingers twisting into her tunic on her lap.

"Because it doesn't need to be big." Cricket shrugged, biting back the words he knew they wouldn't want to hear. They wouldn't want to know that there could be consequences. That sometimes, powerful characters leave a mark on their canvas more than just ink. Ignacia would know that

—she'd seen Cricket practically set his room on fire trying to create a traveling talisman (it hadn't worked, of course), but she clearly wasn't thinking about that.

Yoshi tilted his chin back, and lifted the brush. The first strokes tickled, and Cricket had to clamp his teeth together to keep from laughing and ruining Yoshi's careful work. When it was done, he leaned back on his heels to eye his work. "You should check it."

"No. I trust you, both of you. All right, now that that one's done, let's get to work on the others." He handed Ignacia the sheet for his chest, and Yoshi the one for his back and they both set to work. They worked silently, and Cricket closed his eyes, focusing on keeping himself from snickering every time bristles brushed some place particularly ticklish.

They were halfway through, he could feel that both Ignacia and Yoshi had moved to about mid-torso, and they'd already gone through several inkwells.

"I don't think we're going to have enough ink!" Ignacia looked down at the row of characters for different types of water that she'd drawn across his diaphragm. Ink stained her fingers, and her nose where she'd rubbed it.

"There will be enough," Cricket said. He hadn't done any calculations to make sure there would be, but he knew they'd have enough. Something inside of him said as much. "Just keep working."

"My wrist is twinging." Her lower lip poked out, but she ducked her head to get back to work.

Cricket looked down to survey her progress. "You're almost done. Just a couple more rows."

"What do we do when we are done?" Yoshi asked. He'd been strangely silent throughout this whole process, so much so that if it weren't for the gentle sweep of his calligraphy brush, Cricket would have forgotten he was there.

"Then you'll both pump the ink full of magical energy, and

hopefully we won't have long to wait for it to start working."
He glanced at the fire; it was burning lower than the last time
he'd opened his eyes. They'd probably been at this a couple of
hours. "Preferably before the mist rises again."

"We still have a few hours till that." Ignacia's hand worked
steadily, her lip between her teeth as she focused. "We should
get you some more food before we start that process."

"That's a good idea. It'll give the ink a chance to dry."

Ignacia nodded.

IT WARMED. It heated. It burned! Oh stars, how it burned!

Cricket whimpered against the pain, tears itching at his
eyes as he squeezed them shut. The small character sitting at
the corner of his right eye burned like a star. A searing point
of pain that threatened to divorce him from all sense. Threatened to make him jerk away and cower.

"We are hurting you," Yoshi said, voice breaking. He
twitched his hand, making to pull his fingers away from
Cricket's face, but Cricket reached out to clasp his wrist hard,
digging blunt fingernails into the tender skin.

"Keep going. It'll only get worse...if.... if we have to start
over," he said the words around the pain, and the heaving
breaths.

"My Prince."

"You heard me!" Cricket growled, his fingers tightening
on Yoshi's wrist. Ignacia looked between Cricket and Yoshi.
Her own fingers threatening to shy away at the obvious pain
twisting up her friend's face. "Do not stop."

"But—" Ignacia's eyes had gone glassy with tears.

"I won't be able to do it if we have to start over," Cricket said through a clenched jaw. He forced himself to breathe in through his nose, out through his lips. To swallow around the bile rising in his throat. "We have to keep going."

"It is burning you."

"I'll be fine!" Anger slithered like a snake up Cricket's throat, making him lash out. "Just finish it!"

Yoshi's face settled into something carved from jade, and he kept pushing. Sunlight met moonbeams as Cricket stared at him, unable to bear looking at Ignacia who was no doubt livid and terrified all at once. But Yoshi's eyes held a kind of resigned determination. It was comforting, in a strange way that Cricket couldn't explain. Like Yoshi understood him, and what he was doing, and was going to make it work in whatever way he could.

They kept pushing, the character below his eye blistering like a brand, until Cricket felt the other characters warm, one by one. Not to the point of burning, not like the one on his face. But once each of them was warm with the hum of magic, he gave Yoshi's wrist another squeeze.

"My Prince?"

"It's done. That's enough." The words came out broken and wet.

Ignacia and Yoshi nodded, and immediately the rush of power stopped. Shutting off like a tap. When the pressure from their magic was no longer pushing at him Cricket pitched forward, face bumping against Yoshi's chest. Yoshi steadied him, with gentle hands on his shoulders.

"How long before we know if it worked?" Ignacia asked.

Holding up one trembling finger Cricket squeezed his eyes shut and focused on breathing. The smell of travel, and sunshine, and sandalwood lingered in Yoshi's clothing, unfamiliar but comforting, and pushing away the smell of burned flesh that tinged the air.

Once Cricket had caught his breath against the pain of his

burned skin, he could focus more on the rest of his body. There was a tug, somewhere low in his gut. Like someone had wrapped string around his insides, and pulled it taught. It wasn't a yank yet, nothing so violent as that, just a gentle pressure. A guiding gesture. And if he focused on it...

He sat up abruptly, the invisible line pulling him to his feet.

"Put a shirt on first!" Ignacia shouted, grabbing his tunic, and tugging it down over his head even as the string pulled him to the door.

"I thought that symbol meant you would have control." Yoshi rose to his feet, following behind them.

"Yes. Well, no." Cricket headed out the door and down the steps. "I can turn it on and off. Look," he shut his eyes and flicked an invisible switch and though the string remained taut it didn't pull him forward against his will anymore. "But when it's on it's all go."

"Well turn it back on and let's go! We've got a couple hours until the sun sets." Ignacia scowled from where she was three steps above him.

Cricket nodded, let the switch flip back on, and followed whatever the magic wanted from his body. It led them out onto the street, in the fading early autumn sun, and toward the center of town.

CHAPTER 42

A handful of minutes later, the string tugged Cricket onto a long pier. Boards stretched like fingers out toward the middle of Nishi Lake. The closer he got to the end, the harder the string pulled, gaining power and momentum as he got closer. Cricket slammed his eyes shut and turned it off—almost too late. It would have been if Yoshi hadn't been right behind him and grabbed the back of his tunic before he tipped headfirst into the water below.

"The lake?" Ignacia panted from his other side; her hands braced her knees as she struggled to catch her breath.

The lake. Of *course*!

"The lake! The lake! Yes, of course, the lake!" A laugh left Cricket, high and forced. He shook his head, taking a step back from the edge of the pier, but leaning over dangerously to peer down at his reflection in the water.

"Of course?" Yoshi sounded skeptical.

"Of course!" Cricket repeated, throwing his hands up, and wobbling a little on his feet. "Where else would a haunted mist come from if not the lake?"

It all seemed so clear now.

"Oh, how could I be so stupid?" Long fingers raked tracks down Cricket's face, skimming the blistered skin near his eye and making him wince. "The mist itself isn't magical, Nishi has probably always had mists. It's something *in* the mists. Something in the water, that's what's making everyone sick."

"So, there is a cursed object in the lake," Ignacia said as if she were trying to make sure she was hearing him correctly.

"Yes. Well... maybe, no?" Cricket frowned.

"Cricket. Which is it?"

Boots padded softly against the wood as Cricket paced first one way and then the next, his head ducked to watch his feet, his fingers scrubbing at his nose and chin in turns. "A singular object couldn't hold this much power. Not through water," he muttered. "It'd have to be a whole hoard of them. Unless the water itself is... No. No. No. I'd have been able to feel it if such a large thing was cursed. It has to be acting as a conduit for the magic, not be magicked itself. That's the only thing that makes sense..."

"My Prince?" Yoshi asked.

"Let him talk himself through it," Ignacia said.

"But if it's a whole bunch of things, then how did they get into the water in the first place? Did the traveling merchant dump them in? Wouldn't the people of Nishi have noticed? Surely, they'd have noticed if some stranger was dumping things into their waterways. Then that means...that means...that means *they* did it."

"*They* did it?" Yoshi had much more than the frown-wrinkle this time. His entire expression had morphed into one of disgust; nose curled up just slightly, lips twisted, brows pinched. He looked positively furious, and something about it made Cricket's heart stutter in his chest. "*They* who?"

"They who?" Cricket repeated, blinking rapidly, and then the words sunk in. Oh! "The people of Nishi. Likely everyone we talked to, and then some."

"They did what?" Ignacia huffed. She'd slumped onto one of the pilings and was sitting with her arms crossed over her chest looking about two words from shaking Cricket.

"They dumped everything they bought from the trader into the water. A place this big, the chances are high that more than one person bought something. And we know everything the trader was selling was cursed. So..." Cricket gestured to the water.

"So all the curses are just interacting with each other, and creating a feedback loop." Ignacia looked down toward the water, her own features pinching nervously. "That means any minute it could..."

"It could blow, yes." Cricket nodded. "It wouldn't take much, one more curse and this whole lake would become a black hole. That's why they've had problems with their lighting, and hot water, and everything else, it's a power vacuum."

"How do we solve this?" Yoshi had taken up Cricket's spot, leaning over the edge of the dock to look down at the water as if he could see the cursed objects lying at the bottom.

"How well can you swim?" A grin had spread Cricket's lips, dimpling his cheeks, and crinkling his eyes. He could feel the edges of it, manic, and far too excited about the prospect of deep diving for cursed objects.

Ignacia let out an annoyed breath. "I suppose you'll want me to do a bubble charm for you, won't you?"

"Unless you'd rather let me drown?"

"Don't test me, Cricket. I just might." She pulled the pouch tied around her belt into her hands, and began digging around in it, mumbling to herself in search of the things she'd need.

"So, Yoshi, how well do you swim?"

Yoshi's face had smoothed over, the fury from before erased, and replaced with another impassive expression.

Cricket missed that charged emotion instantly. "Helio is in the mountains. We do not learn to swim."

"You can't swim?" Cricket pouted.

"I said we do not learn; I did not say I could not." Yoshi's shoulders heaved in something between a huff and a pout. "Just not well."

"You stay up here then and let us know if things start to look hairy. Ignacia and I will go down and see what we've got to haul up." Cricket toed off his boots, setting them aside on the dock, and began to tug off his tunic. He was suddenly grateful for the way summer clung to Nishi Lake. Deep diving would be cold enough without the added chill of autumn.

"You will be safe?"

"Of course! I'll have Iggy with me." Cricket turned to look at Ignacia who had pulled two necklaces from the pouch and was glaring at them rather pointedly as she muttered to herself. "All right, Iggy?"

"Almost done." She didn't look up from her work, just kept pumping power into them until they shone bright enough to be stars. "We'll need light down there too."

"Good thinking."

"One of us has to use their head for something other than growing hair," Ignacia murmured under her breath.

"What was that?"

"You heard me!"

"Do you see this, Yoshi? Do you see how she treats me? My sister. My own flesh and blood—"

"I'm not your flesh and blood."

"So cruel! So unkind! How ever shall I go on?" Cricket flopped himself onto the dock, crowing miserably.

Yoshi watched all of this with an expression of impassiveness, or even mild annoyance.

Ignacia watched it all with *extreme* annoyance. "Get up and come on. We've got another hour, maybe, before the sun goes down. And I don't want to be in that water when the mist starts rising."

Cricket leaped to his feet gracefully and snatched one of the necklaces from her fingers to slip over his head. Then without another word, he dove headfirst into the lake. He felt the water ripple behind him when Ignacia dove in after. He waited, treading for a few moments below the surface as a bubble of air inflated around his head, and his eyes adjusted to the dark.

Just below the surface it wasn't too terrible, but the deeper they swam the darker it would get. He'd need his eyes to adjust quickly. He looked over at Ignacia and waited until she nodded before they dove down deeper.

The water grew darker, and cooler around them as they kept going down, down, down, toward the bottom. Cricket wasn't sure how deep Nishi Lake was, that wasn't in any of the textbooks he'd read, but he knew it had to be pretty deep otherwise someone would have noticed the buildup of malevolent magic.

Just as that thought struck him, Cricket saw light up ahead, or down below rather. Kicking his feet harder, he propelled himself closer. He had to blink a few times. His eyes, which had adjusted to the dankness of the depths, were blinded by the glow. When they had grown accustomed to it, and could focus again, he saw a heap of things sitting on the floor putting off the light. There was a comb, a hand mirror, a chest, a lamp or two, and so much more. Items buried under items. Each sinking into the mud at the bottom of the lake.

Spinning in the water, Cricket found Ignacia looking just as stricken as he was. The people of Nishi had certainly been busy making a mess of things.

Ignacia pointed up to the surface, and Cricket nodded before they both kicked off, propelling themselves upwards.

The air was cooler than he remembered, the light beginning to fade as Cricket sucked in grateful breaths. They'd come up a few feet away from the dock, and he started his swim back without waiting for Ignacia.

"We're going to need more hands," he said as Yoshi helped to haul him up onto the dock.

"A lot more hands," Ignacia agreed, scrambling up beside him.

"Many items?" Yoshi asked, holding out his cloak to a grateful Cricket who could feel his teeth beginning to chatter, and wrack his chest with coughs. He curled the sun warmed fabric around himself, and took a deep inhale of sandalwood, and outdoors from it, before pulling himself back to the matter at hand.

"A lot more than I thought there would be. It looks like Nishi's people have been dumping in this lake for a long time." Cricket brushed some wet hair back from his face so he could look back at the sun. It was getting closer to the horizon now, dangerously closer. "We should move this indoors. We can sort out what to do with these people at the inn."

"Your father is going to be livid." Ignacia's boots squelched, and she left a trail of water behind her on the dock from wringing out her hair as she went.

"He will." Cricket pulled the cloak more firmly around himself. He pressed his lips together, wanting to say more, but knew it wouldn't be safe to do so. They wound their way through the city streets, and when they reached the inn, Ignacia stopped to order them supper while Cricket went up to put on clean clothes and begin the task of brushing out his long hair so it would dry. Yoshi built up the fire extra hot to keep Cricket from coughing.

"Will they be punished?" Yoshi asked. He sat facing the fire, pointedly ignoring Cricket's struggles with a particularly feisty knot about halfway to his ear.

"The people of Nishi?"

Yoshi nodded.

"Ah, that's a tough question." Cricket sighed, setting down the comb in his lap in favor of stroking at the ends of his hair. "We don't have any way to prove exactly who did this, and without a way to find the true perpetrators we can't very well punish everyone, can we? Plus, what if some of it just drifted down river?"

"You promised the pixies that they would be punished."

"So I did." Cricket tapped the comb against his knee thoughtfully. "Well, Father will want to post a military presence here to make sure it doesn't happen again. And to oversee the clean-up."

"That is punishment?" Yoshi looked displeased with this, and Cricket wasn't sure what he expected. It wasn't as if Cricket could throw them all in prison, that wouldn't be fair to those who were innocent.

A chill ran up his spine when the door opened, letting some of their carefully hoarded heat escape, and Cricket coughed raggedly into his fist. When he finally got control over his breathing again, it rattled.

"He'll raise the taxes," Ignacia said, flopping down beside them on the floor. "He'll have to, to account for the soldiers that will need to be posted here."

This seemed to appease Yoshi, and he nodded.

"Till then, we have to get the most cursed objects out of there." Cricket took tea from the tray Ignacia had brought with her and sipped it to ease the raw feeling in his throat. "If we leave them there, it'll only get worse."

"They are not all cursed?" Yoshi had made some aborted movement toward Cricket, but he wasn't sure what it was, so he shrugged it off.

"No. Some of them are just unwanted things. Unwanted things can take on a life of their own too. It's probably those things that really drove the attack. Their negative energy combined with the curse magic is what is making the mist dangerous. If we take the curse magic out of the equation, then the rest of the clean-up should be a breeze."

"And the children?"

"The children should be all right once we remove the malevolent objects, and seal them away." Ignacia grabbed a towel from the stack Yoshi had retrieved from their respective bathrooms and started wringing out her hair again. "Just like in Tochli and Taini, once it's not being fed anymore, the effects will dissipate."

"Right." Cricket nodded. "So, I need to come up with something to help us detect which items are cursed and which aren't. Does anyone have a compass?"

"Do I want to know?"

"Probably not."

"I have a compass." Yoshi pulled one from the pouch at his waist and held it out to Cricket.

"You're not terribly attached to this, are you? It's not a family heirloom or anything, right? Because I'm probably going to destroy it and put it back together again." Cricket took the little metal thing and twisted it between his fingers.

"No. Please use it."

"All right then. I need coffee, tea, and talisman paper. And probably something to help me cough up more of this water."

Ignacia groaned, flopping onto her back, but Yoshi rose ready to collect the things Cricket would need for the spell.

CHAPTER 43

It was early the next morning when Cricket finally hammered the arrow gently back into place on Yoshi's compass. Ignacia had wandered off at some point to go to bed; she'd said that she wasn't sleeping in Cricket's again. And Yoshi sat watching with rapt attention as Cricket drank his tenth cup of tea and tapped the compass lightly. It made a soft sloshing sound in response.

"Is it working?" Yoshi asked, his tone getting dangerously close to eager.

"Hmm," Cricket hummed, ignoring the tickle in his throat from the previous night's coughing fits. He reached over to dump the brooch into the protection array Yoshi had scrawled for him. The compass arrow twitched, pointing to the gaudy bit of jewelry, and its tip glowed faintly. "Looks like."

Yoshi nodded. Cricket almost thought he saw a look of impressed smugness tug at his lips, but that may have been the lack of sleep talking.

"Now we just need to get as many people down to the lake as we can to help us drag everything up." Cricket leaned back onto his hands, looking down at the compass. It should have taken him much longer to siphon magic into the device. Especially with how sick, and tired he felt. But there it sat, humming faintly with his power, and identifying cursed objects with ease. "The question remains, how will I get people to help us?"

Cricket had thought about it the night before. He'd thought about the list from Jovienne, and the parents of children who felt helpless and useless in the wake of their children's illness. He'd thought about how the whole city was to blame, but Cricket couldn't sit there and point fingers. No. It would all have to be handled differently. So much differently than he'd like. Cricket would have to be political, and tactful, two things he generally didn't see himself as.

"This would all be much easier if Annie were with us. She'd have the whole city lining up to dive headfirst into the water." Cricket sighed, rubbing at his nose self-consciously. He needed his advisor. That's what she was supposed to do for him, provide him counsel, and guidance.

"Can you not simply order them to help?"

"I could." Cricket frowned. He flopped all the way onto his back, closing his eyes against the crusty feeling lingering at the corners. "But that's not really the kind of king I want to be."

"What kind of king do you want to be?"

"The kind of king that people want to work with to make Lunette better. The kind that doesn't strong arm, or order people to do things they don't want to. The kind of king Father is." Cricket's voice caught on the word 'father'. He missed Father. He hadn't realized exactly how much until that very moment. How long had he been on the road? Almost two months. Too long.

"The kind of king," Yoshi began, voice soft, dragging

Cricket from his thoughts back into the stiflingly warm inn room. "Who leads by example?"

"What?" Cricket's eyes burst open, and he stared up at the beams in the ceiling with his brows drawn together in confusion.

"You want to be the kind of king who leads by example."

Cricket sat up quickly, a sharp gasp catching in his throat and making him cough roughly. Yoshi reached for him, patting his back lightly to dislodge some of the water from his lungs. Yoshi had said the words as if they were the most true thing he'd ever known. Simple. Direct. A fact. As if he'd been watching Cricket all this time to cut to the heart of him. And this was it. This was the heart of Yue Akio Cricket. He wanted to be a king who people would look up to and strive to be more like, and in doing so become better for it.

"I'm all right. I'm all right." Cricket waved away the care as he got his coughing under control.

Yoshi eyed him skeptically, his hand still outstretched to pat Cricket's back again if he needed it. But Cricket didn't pay it any mind, he was on to other things now. More important things.

"That's exactly it, Yoshi! Oh, you're so smart." Cricket laughed, pitching forward to hug Yoshi tight around the shoulders. He pulled back almost as quickly as the hug had begun and leaped to his feet. "What time is it?"

Yoshi pulled a watch from the folds of his tunic to check. "Seven."

"Right. Then let's do breakfast first. Something hearty. I'll go get Iggy, trust me, you don't want to be the one to wake her up. Do you think you can order us breakfast? I'd like to be ready to head down to the lake within the hour, so we have all day to start dragging stuff out." Cricket was halfway to the door already, looking back at Yoshi expectantly.

Yoshi nodded, and rose. At the door they split off, Yoshi

heading down the creaking stairs, and Cricket went to knock loudly at Ignacia's door.

A low grumble came from the other side, and Cricket took that as permission to enter as loudly as possible.

"Iggy! Iggy! Iggy! I've got it! I've got it all solved! I know how we're going to— what? Stop looking at me like that."

She'd pulled down the covers just enough to look up at him through the nest of blankets with murder in her eyes.

"I thought you were a morning person." Cricket grinned cheekily.

Thwack. A fluffy lump of feathers smacked him in the side of the head—thankfully the side that wasn't still healing from the burn mark—nearly knocking him over where he sat on the edge of her bed. Cricket giggled long, and loud, and cheerful. His eyes squeezed shut with the sheer joy of it. They had a plan. They had a plan, and the people of Nishi would be safe again very soon.

While he'd gotten over his giggle fit, Ignacia sat up in bed, rearranging her hair and giving him a bland look. He'd take that over murder any day.

"You've got *what* all solved?" Her fingers twisted and turned, re-braiding her auburn locks quickly and efficiently.

"How we're going to get people to help us clear out the lake. It was all Yoshi's idea. He's really quite smart. Who'd have guessed it with how little he speaks. Come on, we have to get breakfast and head down to the lake. We don't have a moment to spare!" Cricket was already on his feet again, pacing to the door. His mouth moving a mile a minute right along with his hands which were making broad sweeping motions in the air.

"Do you know what time it is?" Ignacia still hadn't gotten out of bed, but she looked more awake now, and he'd count that a victory.

"Seven." Cricket shrugged.

"Did you go to bed at all last night?"

"Nope!" He popped the *P* and ducked out of the door into the hall. Then he poked his head back in, gripping onto the doorframe to maintain his balance. "I'm being serious, Iggy, get up. I'll meet you in my room!"

He heard the pillow smack against the wall and then *flump* to the floor as he headed back toward his own room. Followed shortly thereafter by an annoyed groan, and Ignacia thumping around in her room to get ready for the day.

Cricket found Yoshi laying out the breakfast things in their usual spot before the fire. He looked up at Cricket, and then behind him, before asking, "Where is Ignacia?"

"Oh, she's coming. She's just got to finish throwing a tantrum first." Cricket flopped down beside the tray, and grabbed a bowl of chilled soba and dug in. The sound of a door slamming echoed down the hall to them. "That'll be her now."

Yoshi shook his head and settled back onto his heels to eat his own bowl of noodles.

Ignacia stormed in a second later and fell into a graceless heap beside him. She held out her hand expectantly, and Cricket rolled his eyes before leaning forward to grab her food and hand it to her without a word. Then he waited as she took a mouthful of noodles, her eyes barely open.

Once it was swallowed down, she asked, "All right, what's this ingenious plan of Yoshi's?"

"THIS IS A STUPID IDEA," Ignacia griped for what must have been the tenth time. She'd said she wouldn't leave the inn, but she was chasing after Cricket and Yoshi, complaining the whole way. "We'll catch cold trying to pull everything out by ourselves."

"It won't be by ourselves. Other people will come to help," Cricket said for the tenth time in response.

"You will not catch a cold. It is a warm day. I have brought plenty of towels." Yoshi held up the stack of towels he'd begged (well, more like stared until they gave him what he wanted) off the inn staff. The maid had even cast a warming charm on them to keep them toasty and fluffy all day long. It was going to be a good day for a swim, Cricket could feel it.

"And how come he's not going to help?"

"He will help. He'll drag the junk the rest of the way to the shore so everyone can see what we're doing, and then seal it away." Cricket rolled his eyes.

"But he's not going swimming."

Cricket didn't bother to answer that. Instead, he moved to the edge of the lake, shucked off his boots, and tunic, and waded in. There wasn't any point in arguing with Ignacia when she got like this. All he could hope was that she'd follow along behind him to continue to complain.

He looked back when he got to the edge of where he could stand, and sure enough she was toeing out of her own boots and throwing her tunic at Yoshi who huffed in response. Ignacia huffed back, and then followed behind him.

"Yoshi," Cricket called, and smiled widely at the white knight when he looked up from where he'd been carefully setting their things aside to slip out of his own boots. "This is the edge of the sandbar. It drops off after here. Do you want me to wait for you?"

"He's not a baby," Ignacia muttered as she passed him, and dove into the water.

"No. Thank you. I will be fine." Yoshi reached down to tug the pale blue tunic off and set it aside with Cricket and Ignacia's things. Cricket tripped on something in the lake. It wasn't just the bottom, there was something down there. Or maybe Ignacia had grabbed his ankle. Or maybe it was a fish. It was not him stumbling because Yoshi's torso was well-defined and beautifully bronzed in the sunshine. It was a *fish*.

"Hey! *You* have the compass! Get a move on!" Ignacia popped her head out of the water to see what was taking him so long.

"Uh. Right. Right!" Cricket nodded, swallowing against sandpaper in his throat, and spun around to dive after her. It was easy to find the hoard of junk under the water now that they knew what they were looking for. Ignacia and Cricket pulled sacks from their pockets and began loading them up as the compass pointed them to the cursed items. Once each was loaded to the point where it would almost be too heavy to drag to the surface, they kicked off and headed back up.

Yoshi was waiting for them, the water up to his waist, his arms crossed over his chest as he watched for their ascent. At the first sign of them he moved as deeply as he could without treading water and helped drag the heavy sacks back to shore.

"This is going to take all day." Ignacia heaved her sack onto the ground far enough away from their clothes and towels to keep them safe.

"Then it takes all day." Cricket shrugged. "Yoshi, can you start packing these away in the sealing pouches? Just be careful not to touch anything for too long."

"Yes, My Prince." Yoshi pulled a stack of folded bags from his own pouch and set to work. Cricket and Ignacia turned back to the water and took another dive.

By the time they'd brought up their second load there was a couple of young ladies hovering around Yoshi, looking as if they wanted to talk to him but unsure where to start. Yoshi rose from his work to help them haul up the next load.

"Your Highness! Your Highness!" The young women

called, waving to Cricket. Ignacia cut him a look out of the corner of her eye, and he winked at her.

"Yes?" Cricket helped Yoshi set the two bags next to the half empty one he was working on.

"What are you doing?" One of the women asked, curiosity coloring her tone. At an elbow nudge from her friend, she added a belated, "Your Highness."

"Well." Cricket rocked back on his heels, handing the compass off to Ignacia so she could get back to work while he worked a different kind of magic. "We went for a swim yesterday after noticing some weird residual magic coming from the water, and we found all these cursed items down there."

"Is that what's causing that horrid mist?" The other woman asked, her nose curled up.

"Seems to be. So we're clearing it out. You two wouldn't happen to be decent swimmers, would you? We've got some extra sacks, and we could use the help. Couldn't we, Yoshi?"

Yoshi looked up at him, his hands still working, an expression of vague annoyance knitting his brows. He knew what he needed to say, but he didn't look like he wanted to. "Yes."

"Oh, I'm no good in the water, but I'm happy to help store the items away," the first woman said, her eyes flicking down toward Yoshi appreciatively. Cricket swallowed down a bitter retort. They needed help. That was all this was. "If that's all right with you, Yoshi?"

Yoshi made eye contact with Cricket, and Cricket gave him a tiny nod.

"Yes. Thank you," Yoshi said, stiffly.

"I'll help in the water!" The other woman volunteered and started to shimmy out of her dress to reveal a camisole and breeches beneath before wading in behind Cricket.

And it really was as simple as Yoshi had suggested. The people of Nishi came out in droves to help Cricket dredge the lake. By the time lunch came around all of the cursed items had been cleared out and stored away. But they didn't stop there, no, the people of Nishi helped Cricket, Yoshi, and Ignacia continue to clean until it was nearing supper time. And Cricket knew... he just knew they'd be all right then.

BOOK V
HOME AGAIN

CHAPTER 44

The atmosphere in the inn was brighter, more cheerful the next day than it had ever been. All of the children who had been sick had recovered—Jovienne had even brought by a ribbon Isabeau wanted Cricket to have, it was pastel, and purple, and very sweet—and the mists had come and gone without any trouble. The people of Nishi breathed a collective sigh of relief. As did Cricket, who had had his first full night's sleep in what felt like ages.

Susan hummed happily, bustling about to prop open every window and door, letting in the late summer breeze as Cricket, and Ignacia sat at a table in the corner where one window met another behind them. A tray of sweet teas, mochi, and ice cream lay invitingly before them.

"This is not breakfast," Yoshi said, staring down at the tray as if it were something stuck to the bottom of his shoe.

"No," Cricket agreed, popping a mochi into his mouth and chewing with a happy murmur as the chill of it made his gums tingle. "But we're celebrating, Yoshi!"

"Celebrating."

"Yes! Celebrating. We saved Nishi." Cricket smiled widely at him, all dimples. Ignacia was studiously ignoring their exchange in favor of shoveling a scoop of purple yam ice cream into her mouth.

"There are more places to help." Yoshi stood behind the chair across from Cricket, holding the back of it in a white knuckled grip. As if it was the only thing keeping him from running out the door that very moment to go save all of Lunette single handedly.

"There are." Cricket nodded, his eyes flicking from the hand up to the expression on Yoshi's face which was decidedly...complicated. He wasn't sure when vague impassiveness had given way to emotion, or maybe he'd just gotten better at reading Yoshi, but there was something below the surface now. Something... He couldn't figure out what. "And they will be there tomorrow, when we ride out."

"We." The word seemed to leave him on a breath, and then a moment later Yoshi's hands loosened from the back of the chair.

"Yes. We." Cricket slid a plate of mochi toward him. "Sit down. We can afford to celebrate, if just for the day. Tomorrow we'll be off again. For today, let's rest."

Yoshi nodded, and pulled out the chair to settle into it. He didn't slump, or flop, but Cricket had a feeling that if Yoshi were the sort of man to do such a thing, he might.

Cricket looked around the room, letting the hum of happiness from the people of Nishi wash over him for a moment. They'd done good work there. They'd helped in a way that likely only they could have. And now it was time to move on. To head off after the next big mystery. But that left just one thing to think of.

"If we can, I'd like to get ahead of this trader." Fingers cooled as Cricket twirled a soft ball of dough between them, watching how the powder coated the tips slightly.

Ignacia's spoon made a soft *tink* against the bowl she'd been using for her ice cream. Cricket looked up to meet her eyes, one brow raised in question.

"You want to face that mad man head on?" She swallowed down a truly impressive mouthful of ice cream that ached all the way down if the twinge at the corner of her eye was anything to go by. "He's powerful."

"Clearly." Cricket shrugged, popping the little orange ball into his mouth. Tangerine. Yuck.

"And he's not worried about using dark magic to hurt people," she added as if this fact weren't also evident by what they'd seen of him.

"I'm missing your point, Iggy." He flicked his gaze back up to meet hers, noting the worry in her eyes. Of course. Of course, she was worried for his safety, and for her own. But... They had to do this. No matter what. He knew it was the logical next step. They couldn't spend the rest of their lives chasing this man around Lunette while he wreaked havoc on Cricket's people. She knew that as well as he did, he was sure of it.

When all he got was a shake of her head in reply, Cricket sighed.

"Iggy," he started, reaching out to take the hand that had been holding her spoon, "we can do this."

"How do you know?"

"Because I know." Cricket nodded firmly, giving her hand a squeeze. "You, me, and Yoshi make a good team, and we can do this. When have I ever lied to you?"

A snort. "Are we talking in the last week or...? Like that time, you told me that there was a spider in my room, and so I needed to trade with you because you found the wardrobe spooky? Or the time when you said that you didn't kiss that pr—"

"When have I ever lied to you about something important?" He cut her off pointedly.

She smirked. "Point taken."

Cricket glanced over at Yoshi to find the white knight calmly sipping his tea and looking at the tray of slowly melting ice creams in front of him as if they were the most interesting thing in the room. But if Cricket didn't know better, which he did, he most certainly did, he'd say Yoshi looked a little flushed.

"Point made." Cricket nodded and slouched back in his seat again.

"How do you propose we find him?" Ignacia grabbed her spoon and took a slurp of soupy ice cream.

"Isn't predictive magic your thing? You should be able to take the points he's already visited and figure out where he's headed. Right?"

Dark blue eyes squinted at him, Ignacia's nose curling up in distaste at the lackadaisical way he'd just suggested she use her magic. He knew there was more to it than that. He knew it wasn't something that was even always accurate. But Cricket didn't see where they had any other choices. It was either Ignacia gave them a heading, or they stick around Nishi and hope someone would talk to them. Which he didn't think was likely. Now that the people weren't under the imminent threat of death, they weren't going to be so forthcoming.

"You know full well it's not that simple," she said needlessly.

"We could ask Jovienne." Yoshi sat his cup down. "She may know something."

"She could tell us what direction he went from here, but that won't tell us where he went after that. He's got at least a month on us now; we can't afford to be this far behind him." Cricket shook his head, sighing.

"You know what we should do." Ignacia grinned, leaning forward, her hair dipping into her bowl to slip into the soupy ice cream. Cricket didn't think he liked that look in her eye, but he'd take any suggestions, even bad ones if they led him in the right direction. "Use the rumor mill!"

"Gossiping is in poor taste." Yoshi huffed, tilting his chin up just a touch.

Ignacia cackled. Cricket shook his head.

Yoshi eyed Ignacia with annoyance and turned to Cricket. "What about the compass?"

"What about it?" Cricket gave Ignacia a hard shove to quiet her cackling, and it died off in choked chortles.

"Could you not use it to pinpoint his location by tracking the dark magic he's carrying?"

"Hmm..." Cricket hummed, tracing symbols with his fingers into the smooth wood of the table as he thought. It wasn't completely outside of the realm of possibility. It would be difficult, yes. But as he'd told Yoshi before, like called to like. It wouldn't work with the compass. That could point them in direction and only up to a distance away. But... "If we can siphon enough of the signature off into a scrying tool, we might be able to use it to pinpoint his location."

"Scrying?" Ignacia asked, still choking on a snicker. "You've never been any good at scrying! That was always—" She cut herself off, sobering immediately.

"Marwa's specialty. I know." Cricket huffed out a breath, the fine hairs that had come loose from his braid fluttering around his face. "But she gave me a few lessons. I think I could manage it, especially with the massive energy signature he's probably giving off."

"What will you need?" Yoshi finished off his tea, and set the cup aside, his hands steepling before him on the table.

"A full moon would be helpful, but we can't get that. So we'll just have to work with what we've got." Cricket scrubbed at his nose, trying to remember everything Marwa had told him.

"If you use amber then you could draw on Helio's power instead of Selene's." Ignacia's bowl scraped across the table.

"But wouldn't that work like a negative magnetic force to my own magic?" Cricket wrinkled his nose, pulling out the ever-present journal to start jotting down symbols he knew would help. "Plus, where am I supposed to get Helio amber?"

Yoshi pulled an earring from his ear and settled it onto the table in front of Cricket.

"Oh," Cricket said dumbfounded.

"You'll need Yoshi in the circle, and a little of his blood." Ignacia had continued on her train of thought as if nothing big or emotional had happened.

Cricket shook his head, his throat tightening as he held the earring delicately. "Are you...are you sure?"

"I can also provide blood." Yoshi nodded. "It is no trouble."

"He says it's no trouble." Ignacia grinned at Cricket cheekily.

"We need everything set up by midday, if we can." Cricket looked down at his watch. Two hours wasn't much time to set up the complicated array they'd need, but they'd make it work.

"These won't work. You'll need Helio hieroglyphs." Ignacia tapped the paper Cricket was writing on.

"Ugh. Right." Paper rustled as Cricket flipped to a fresh page. "Yoshi could you—"

Yoshi rose and came around to their side of the table, scooting in on the end of the bench, and crowding Cricket in between himself and Ignacia. "Tell me what you need."

"Uh. Okay." Cricket swallowed, studiously ignoring the press of Yoshi's leg against his own.

THEY WERE CUTTING IT CLOSE. Too close, in Cricket's opinion. But at least the circle was drawn, and between him and Yoshi they were almost finished scrawling the characters into the pier below them. An audience had gathered to watch them work on the shore end of the dock, and Ignacia had had to go hold them off to keep the array from being trampled on by spectators.

The people of Nishi whispered worriedly from the shore.

"What're they doing?"

"What's the prince making?"

"What kind of magic is that?"

"Is this about the curse?"

Ignacia fielded all of their questions with her usual brusque nature. Quick, and simple replies to get everyone to be quiet as quickly as possible.

Cricket stood up, running the back of his wrist across his forehead to clear away the sweat threatening to drip into his eyes. He rocked back on his heels, looking down at the array with his head tilted to make sure everything was right. Then did a little spin in place and nodded to himself.

"That'll do it." Chalky hands left streaks on Cricket's tunic where they moved to rest on his hips in satisfaction. "Yes. That will definitely do it."

Yoshi stood up. A smear of chalk had been brushed across his cheek, and Cricket's fingers lifted seemingly of their own accord to wipe it away with his sleeve. Yoshi nodded his thanks.

"You know you're a much better assistant than *some* people," Cricket said loudly, turning away from Yoshi to hide the blush crawling across his nose. It was just the heat. Just the sun beating down on them. Nothing more. "Who complains the whole time, and whose character work is sloppy at best."

Ignacia made an inappropriately rude gesture at him behind her back where the people she was keeping at bay couldn't see, and Cricket snickered.

The sound of metal on wood drew Cricket's attention back to Yoshi who had retrieved the knife from the safety of outside of their circle. He was rolling up his sleeve to reveal a long expanse of skin. One pale scar slashed across his forearm, and drew Cricket's eye long enough for him to almost jump when Yoshi asked, "How much?"

"A few drops should do it." Cricket jerked his eyes away to kneel in the middle of the circle, wrapping the end of Yoshi's earring carefully in the fishing line they'd bought. He looked wearily down at the opening between the slats of the dock and sent up a silent prayer to Selene that he didn't lose the earring in the lake below. He'd never find it if he did.

"You two need to get a move on. The sun is almost at the midpoint," Ignacia called from where she stood at the end of the pier.

Yoshi nodded, and cut a neat slice across his arm, dribbling blood into the center of the array where Cricket knelt.

The earring gave a gentle twang in Cricket's fingers. "That's enough."

Yoshi pressed a bandage to his arm and moved to kneel next to Cricket to hover over the map. The earring swayed gently, as if the wind were blowing it like a pendulum. And then it began to spin. Wide circles at first, slowly, and then gaining momentum, spinning, and circling faster and faster before it stopped. The rounded end of the little teardrop piece of amber pointed like a magnet to a small town just outside of the capital. Luna.

"No." Cricket breathed, his hands beginning to shake. "No."

"What is it?" Yoshi reached out to take Cricket's hands, holding them to keep them from trembling too badly.

Cricket shook off the hold, stuffing the earring into his pocket thoughtlessly, and rising onto shaking legs. "Iggy, get our things from the inn. We're leaving now."

"What? Why?" Ignacia turned to gape at him. Cricket heard Yoshi brush his boot against the boards to clear away the array and gather up the items they'd used to track the signature. But he didn't care. He couldn't think past the need to get on the road. Now. Today. Before the sun set. To ride until his body gave out, and beyond. There could only be one reason why he'd be in Luna.

"He's headed for the palace."

CHAPTER 45

"We can't keep going like this," Ignacia said, leaning all of her weight against Saber where he had his head ducked in the river, drinking heavily. "We can't keep riding without proper rest, Cricket. It's been three days already. We need sleep, the horses need rest."

"Two and a half." Cricket's fingers drummed on the reins in his hands. He hadn't dismounted as Yoshi and Ignacia had to give themselves a break from the saddle. There wasn't time to rest. There wasn't time to sleep. They had to keep going.

"What?"

"We've only been going for two and a half days. We just left Nishi the day before yesterday. Luna is still another day and a half ride." His fingers tightened around the leather in his hands.

"Cricket." Ignacia sighed.

"No!" His eyes widened in alarm at his own shout, and he cleared this throat. "No. We have to keep going. We don't know how long he stays in one place. He could have already moved into the capital by now. He could be preparing to launch an attack on Father and Annie. We have to get there."

Cricket hated how his voice shook over the words, almost as much as he hated how he'd lost the feeling in his calves hours ago. He knew if he dismounted now there would be no getting back on his horse to ride again, at least not until he'd knocked feeling back into them. And they didn't have time for that.

"We've warned Annie, she has the castle on alert," Ignacia said, her tone reasonable. *Reasonable*, at a time like this.

"I don't care."

"Yoshi." Ignacia turned her eyes to the knight, wide, and pleading.

"He doesn't give the orders. I do." The words left Cricket's lips, all ice and steel. He was the prince, he was the one who made this choice, and he'd made it. They would keep going until they reached Luna. They would only take the necessary breaks, not more than an hour at a time, if they could help it. That was final.

"You will not be much good to your father or Anstice if you cannot walk," Yoshi said softly. His hand rested on Cricket's knee, and Cricket wasn't sure when he'd moved. Had it been before when he'd shouted? Or just now? Yoshi's long calloused fingers felt hot through the fabric of Cricket's trousers. "We should rest, at least for the night."

"I can't!" His voice broke on the words. Tears hot at the corners of his eyes, threatening to overflow and trickle burning paths down his cheeks. "We can't stop. We have to keep going. We have to stop him before... before..." He couldn't even finish the thought. Whatever horrible thing the trader could do to Cricket's family, he couldn't think it. Not now. If he did, then they'd never get there. He'd break down right here, and never move again. Moss would grow over him like a golem, and that would be the end of that. He cleared his throat. "We have to keep going."

Yoshi nodded, seeming to understand. "You should eat

something, and dismount for a few minutes, at the very least." He squeezed Cricket's knee again through the fabric, a comforting gesture. "I will help."

"Okay." Cricket swallowed thickly around the unshed tears and let himself slip from his saddle with Yoshi's help. His knees wobbled under him when his feet hit the ground, but Yoshi kept a steady grip on his waist until he could help Cricket sit along the river's edge. "Not long."

"No. Not long." Yoshi moved to his saddle bag to pull out one of the buns the innkeeper had given them, and then returned to hold it out to Cricket. "Eat this and have some water."

Ignacia came to sit beside him with a bun of her own. "We'll get there, Cricket. Jaxith and Anstice have the whole palace guard there. They'll be safe until we can reach them."

"We don't know that."

Ignacia sighed, taking the water skin from Yoshi to sip and then held out to Cricket with a muttered, "thank you."

"We do not," Yoshi agreed, settling on Cricket's other side. Close enough that if Cricket wanted to, he could lean into Yoshi's side, rest his head on his shoulder, let himself drift off to sleep. He didn't want to. "But we are moving as fast as we can. It will not help anyone to run ourselves ragged."

"Fine. We can stop and sleep for a couple hours tonight. But no more than that."

Yoshi nodded.

THEY DID SLEEP THAT EVENING. Curled onto bedrolls with a tiny fire to ward off the chill of early fall. Cricket, for all he had been tired, had not slept hardly at all. He had lain there, staring at the dying embers of their fire, waiting for the others to rise so they could be on the road again. And before the moon had even reached her zenith, they were.

By the time they reached Luna he could feel panic beneath his skin like a swarm of buzzing bees. What if they were too late? What if he had already moved on? What if they couldn't find him in Luna? What if he was too much for them? What if. What if. What if. It all rushed through him in a swarm.

"We will find him. The town is not very large." Yoshi's words were a steadying force, and Cricket nodded. He clutched Buttercup's reins more tightly and urged her on through the town.

"We should go to the inn and ask around." Cricket slid off Buttercup, leading her toward the largest building in town, hoping it was the inn.

"And get some food," Ignacia mumbled. "I'll get us a table, can you two see to the horses?"

Cricket nodded. "Maybe the stable master will have some information about the trader."

Cricket took Saber's reins and led the horses and Yoshi toward the stables. A young boy sat outside on a little stool, whittling away at what seemed to be a duck. When he saw them approach, he leaped to his feet, almost cutting himself with the knife.

"Sirs!" he squeaked. Then bowed low over his feet.

"Afternoon." Cricket pulled on a smile, hoping it hid how tired and travel worn he felt. "We need stable space for these three beauties, if you have it."

"Yes, sir! Of course, sir!" The boy scrambled to put down his whittling on the stool and open up the stable doors. He led them to three open stalls and gestured inside. "Will these do, sirs?"

"These will be perfect, thank you. We also have a couple of questions." Cricket stepped out of the way, letting Yoshi move to pull the saddles from their horses while Cricket talked to the boy. "If you don't mind."

"No, sir. I mean... Yes, sir. I mean..." The boy folded his hands behind his back and rocked onto his heels presumably to hide his nervousness. "What can I help you with?"

"We're looking for a traveling trader that probably came through here a couple of days ago. You wouldn't happen to know which way he went, would you?"

"Oh! In the red caravan with the flowers?" The boy perked up a bit, a smile splitting his face.

"That's the one." Or at least Cricket hoped it was the one. He had no way of being sure as the trader seemed to change the appearance of the wagon for every town. But flowers, at least, seemed consistent.

"He's staying just outside town. He comes in every morning to try to sell stuff to the locals. But no one's bought anything yet."

Cricket met Yoshi's eyes over the side of the stall, and saw his own relief reflected there. Good. That was good. No one had been cursed. Yet.

"If there is anything else I can do for you, sirs."

"Just take good care of these three." Cricket patted Buttercup's muzzle affectionately as she ruffled at his hair with her nose.

"Of course, sir!"

With all three horses settled, Cricket and Yoshi headed for the door, leaving them in the boy's care. Just as Cricket reached the outside, a thought struck him, and he turned back to the boy.

"Which side of town did you say he was on?"

The boy looked up from where he was shoveling hay into the stalls. "Oh. Over on the south, sir."

"Thanks again." Cricket smiled, offering him a little wave. Looking up at the sun, Cricket turned his steps toward the south side of town, fully intent on confronting the trader right then. One step, then two, then something latched on hard as iron around his wrist and pulled him to a stop.

"First, we will eat, and rest. Tomorrow we will deal with the merchant." Yoshi's voice was soft, but firm.

"Yoshi. Come on. I can just go and—"

"First, we will eat and rest." His grip tightened around Cricket's arm, almost bruising force. "You have not eaten or rested properly in days. It is dangerous to face him now."

"But what if he—"

"If he leaves, we will give chase. For now, we will prepare."

"Yoshi." Cricket sighed, but he didn't pull away from the tight hold on him. He didn't have it in him to fight about this. He was exhausted and hungry, and his legs ached. He needed rest, and a proper meal before he went off to face the villain. But that didn't mean there wasn't a part of him that wanted to run off and face the problem head on. Because he did. That's what he wanted to do more than anything. No matter how right Yoshi's assessment of him was.

"Please, My Prince." Yoshi's tone turned pleading, his brows drawing together in an expression of distress. And how could Cricket say no to that? He couldn't.

"All right. But in the morning." He wagged his finger at Yoshi.

"Yes. In the morning we will see the trader together, and we will get answers."

Cricket relaxed and let Yoshi's hand slip from his arm down to his hand, their fingers interlocking before Yoshi led him in the other direction to the inn.

Ignacia was waiting for them, fresh water, and tea spread out before her. Her elbow was propped up on the table where she leaned forward, a Cheshire Cat grin spread across her lips as she spoke to the waitress.

Cricket rolled his eyes. Yoshi cleared his throat.

"Cricket! Yoshi!" Ignacia looked up, her smile slipping from sultry to bright. "I've ordered us some supper."

Yoshi hummed his approval and moved to pull out a chair across from her. He looked from the chair to Cricket, then back to the chair for a long moment. Then he waited for Cricket to settle into the seat.

"Thank you." Cricket shifted a little, trying to get comfortable, suddenly unsure what to do with his hands. Should they be on the table? Should they be in his lap? Would it be weird if they hung limp by his side? No. That didn't seem right. He settled for folding them in front of him on the table.

Yoshi sat down beside him and poured a cup of water from the pitcher before forcing it into Cricket's hands.

Ignacia's eyes flicked from the glass of water to Yoshi, her mouth opening, and then closing before she shook her head. "What did you two find out?"

"According to the stable boy, he hasn't sold anything to anyone in town yet. He's staying just outside of town on the south side. Yoshi wouldn't let me confront him." Cricket sulked, spinning the glass of water noisily on the table.

"We should have a full night's sleep before we confront someone with powerful dark magic." Yoshi's words were wise, calm, even logical. But that didn't help the voice in Cricket's head that said he should go after the man now. Now. *Now.*

"Yoshi's right. He'll be there in the morning." Ignacia reached over to give Cricket's hand a squeeze. "I know you want to run off half-cocked and fight this battle now. But let's play it safe for once, eh?"

"Oi. This is what I was afraid of. You two ganging up on me." Cricket huffed.

"Not ganging up." Yoshi shook his head. "Taking care of."

"Yeah. Well. Same thing." Cricket grumbled. Their food came a moment later, and the three settled into silence to eat. Cricket hadn't realized exactly how hungry he was until there was a table of food spread before him, all of it mouth wateringly delicious. He found himself shoveling it in without any thought at all to talking more about their plans.

It was because of this quiet. Because of this lull in the conversation. That Cricket heard something that made the food sour in his stomach, and his heart stop.

"I heard the king is dying."

Cricket's world tilted on its axis.

CHAPTER 46

"I heard the king is dying."
Dying.
Dying.
Dying.
The word echoed in his head so loudly, Cricket almost missed the next part of the conversation.

"They say Prince Cricket isn't even *there*. He's off gallivanting somewhere."

Something shattered in the distance. The glass in Cricket's hand that had slipped from his fingers, maybe. Blood pounded in his ears, pushing away any other sound, even whatever Ignacia was saying. Her lips moving faster, and faster, her hands already reaching for him. A sharp thud, and pain in his right side. The floorboards coming up to meet him. The earth spinning and shifting and tilting so quickly Cricket had to close his eyes, because the dark was better than this. The dark was better than watching his world spin out of control and being unable to figure out how to stop it.

Then... Nothing. Darkness. A cool, quiet place that didn't make sense of the madness around and inside of him. The riotous noise of the world pounded in his ears, deafening Cricket to anything and everything else. Not even the quiet was a blessing, for that word, that damnable word, kept echoing in Cricket's mind.

Dying.

Dying.

Dying.

Cricket jerked awake, sitting up in bed fast enough to bump his forehead against Yoshi's.

"Ow!" Cricket yelped, rubbing at the surely already reddening skin between his brows. His nose wrinkled up in disdain, gaze flicking around to take in Ignacia, Yoshi, and someone who must be the village healer surrounding his bed and looking different levels of worried. Well. Yoshi looked pained as he rubbed at his own head, but also worried. "What happened?"

"You fainted." Ignacia's eyes narrowed on him, accusing. "Right in the middle of the tavern. Like some kind of blushing damsel."

"I'm not a damsel!" Oh. Oh, that was too loud. Cricket winced rubbing at the spot on his head again which had begun to ache. Stars.

"If Yoshi hadn't caught you, you would have busted your head wide open on the corner of the table." Her arms crossed over her chest, but he knew better. For all her disgruntlement, this was worry. True concern for what had almost happened to him.

"I didn't—"

"You did," Yoshi said with a nod. "We brought the healer to have your condition assessed. They say that you need to rest for at least the next twenty-four hours before taking on any more strenuous activity."

"Are you quoting them verbatim?"

"I am."

"Don't do that, it makes you sound like you're reading out of a medical textbook."

Yoshi huffed, pursing his lips a little. "Regardless. You are to stay in bed until at least the morning after next."

"But the—"

"No!" Ignacia pointed her finger at him, her face livid. "No more buts. You will rest. You never got proper rest after being sick in Nishi, and that's my own fault. We can't have you falling out like that again. You could have really hurt yourself."

"Iggy, I'm f—"

"Don't say *fine*. Don't you dare tell me you're fine! If you don't take time to rest, you'll get sick again, and I won't have it. I won't. Yoshi and I are going to stay in this room with you for the next twenty-four hours, and we're going to make sure you don't move. Not until you've rested." Her extended finger shook with her fury.

"Iggy. Really this isn't—"

"Not. Until. You've. Rested."

Cricket pressed his lips together and nodded.

"Don't make us tie you to the bed. We will."

"Okay, Iggy. I'll behave." Cricket's hands fisted in the bedding in his lap, shame crawling up his neck. He hated being spoken to like an errant child. She knew that, but it didn't seem to stop her. And then there was the issue of Father. Of having to get to him. Of having to know what was happening to him. Cricket swallowed that worry down.

"Good. Now. I'm going to go and get some supper. Yoshi, you're on first watch."

Yoshi nodded firmly.

The door slammed behind Ignacia and the healer, leaving Cricket alone with the determined looking white knight.

"Yoshi. Let's not be silly. I'm fine. I don't need you to watch me like a toddler." Cricket leaned forward, taking

Yoshi's hand in his and squeezing it. He met those sunshine eyes with his own, forcing on a dimpled, self-deprecating smile. "Come on. You can leave me alone. I'll behave."

Yoshi just looked back at him, seeming rather unimpressed by the obvious ploy.

"I'm not going anywhere. I'll stay right here in this bed." Cricket patted the blankets with his free hand. "I won't move."

Yoshi pulled back, taking his hand with him as he went to sit in a chair in the corner of the room.

"Yoshi. Please."

"No," was Yoshi's simple response.

"No?"

"No. Get some rest. I will be here." Yoshi sat upright in the chair; his hands folded in his lap as he watched Cricket in the bed. The distance between them was a deliberate message, and suddenly Yoshi felt more like a jailer than a friend.

Cricket flopped back against the pillows in a sulk. He poked out his bottom lip, eyes narrowing on Yoshi who remained impassive in his corner of the room. "I'm a grown man, you know. You can't just make me stay in bed if I don't want to."

Yoshi looked at him with an expression that said, *grown man?* And *can I not?*

"Yes. An adult. And a prince to boot. So really, you can't keep me here. If I want to go, then I'll go."

"No. Rest. I will be here." Yoshi pulled a book from his traveling pouch and settled in to wait Cricket out.

AND HE WAS THERE all night. Ignacia returned with a tray of food at some point. Cricket ate slowly, deliberately, and as sullenly as possible as he refused to speak to either of them. Then when it was time for him to go to sleep, he laid down, closed his eyes, and waited. They would both have to sleep. He was sure of that. Even if they did plan to take shifts, the exhaustion from traveling for four days would catch up to them. He would have a moment, perhaps not more than ten minutes, to sneak out.

That moment came in the wee hours of the morning, long before the sun even thought to rise over the horizon. Cricket peeked his eyes open to see Ignacia slumped on the floor near the window, and Yoshi leaning back in his chair, the book sitting lax in his lap.

Cricket slid soundlessly from under the covers. He grabbed his boots from the foot of the bed, and padded on tiptoes across the floorboards, praying to Selene none of them creaked. The door shut behind him on silent hinges, and next was the stairs. He had little doubt that if any of the staff saw him, they'd want to talk, and they'd use up what little time he had to escape. Thankfully, the whole inn seemed fast asleep.

He slid into his boots once he was outside and took off at a run for the stables where Buttercup slept in her stall. Lily chewed on the end of his braid as he put Buttercup's saddle on. Saber stared judgmentally at him from her stall on the other side.

"Look, Saber, I don't need the lecture. I'm sure I'll get an ear full from Ignacia once they catch up to me. All right?" Cricket's fingers fumbled a little in the dark on Buttercup's bridle, but soon enough she was ready to go. He looked up at Saber, but the horse was still glaring at him, not mollified in the least by his words. "Glare all you like. It won't change my mind."

Lily whinnied from her stall.

But Cricket just huffed and led Buttercup out into the early morning dark.

EVEN IN THE MOONLIGHT, it was easy to see the bright red caravan from a distance. A light hung outside the door, a beacon, guiding Cricket closer across the flat land outside of Luna toward it.

"That's it, Buttercup. Let's go get him," Cricket whispered to the horse, nudging her lightly to move faster toward the caravan.

The stairs up to the door creaked under his weight, and an irritated grumble answered his knock before the door swung open to reveal a bedraggled looking young man.

"Whatsit? You know what time it is?" he asked, voice scratchy with sleep.

Anger flared sharp and sudden in Cricket's chest. He grabbed the man by his wrinkled collars then dragged him out into the night.

"What's going on?! Who are you?! What do you want?! If you're a robber, I don't got anything worth stealing!"

The man's back hit the side of the wagon with a hard thud. Cricket growled, the sound more animal than man. Another hard shove. Cricket stepped back, his hands flexing at his sides. A soft sizzling sound came from them, and he looked down to see steam floating from his hands.

"Who... Who...? Who...? *What* are you?!" The man yelped, cowering.

"I am Prince Yue Cricket Akio." The words didn't seem to leave his mouth at all, they seemed to appear in the air.

Vibrating through it on a snarl. "And I have had enough of you hurting my people!"

The man shrank in front of him. Becoming smaller, and smaller. Cricket's breath came in hard puffs, turning into vapor once they left his nostrils. How dare this man hurt his people. How dare he come to Lunette and think that he could get away with it. Cricket took one swipe toward the man, who ducked, leaving behind deep, jagged claw marks in the wagon's side. Debris rained down on the man where he cowered with his arms protecting his head.

"Please! Please! Great dragon! I didn't mean to hurt anyone! I was just... I was just doing what I was told. He gave me money. So much money! And he said I could keep anything I made off the items." The man whimpered.

"Dr-Dragon?" Cricket frowned, looking down on the tiny man and his tiny wagon. His eyes caught on something shiny, the glass of a skylight, and he looked down at his own reflection. No. Not *his* reflection. Because the creature that stared back at him from that glass was not Cricket. It was not the young man with the dark freckles, and starlit eyes. It was all midnight blue shining scales, and pale antler that reflected the moonlight. Long whiskers trembled at his muzzle as he tilted his head to get a better look.

"Dragon," he repeated, and the jaw of the creature moved with the words.

"Yes! Yes! Dragon, sir! Please don't eat me! Please. I'll tell you all about him, and you can... You can punish him! You can eat *him*!"

Cricket lowered himself to the ground again, four great clawed feet—*his* feet, Cricket corrected—braced the earth. His long body twisting and turning around the man and his wagon. It wasn't a struggle to ignore the strangeness of the situation. Not when there was finally, *finally* someone to question. "Speak."

"It was... It was... I need protection. I need you to promise to protect me. He'll kill me if he ever finds out I told you."

"SPEAK!" Cricket's face lowered to meet the man's, eyes narrowed to slits.

"It was the king's brother!" the man squeaked. "Lord Sunil! Lord Sunil hired me to do this. To lead the army away from the palace."

"Why?"

"I don't know. I don't know." The man shook his head, eyes glistening with tears now.

"WHY?!"

"Cr-Cricket?" A voice sounded from his left, pulling Cricket from his crouch to scan the landscape. In his fury he hadn't heard the approaching hoofbeats of Yoshi, and Ignacia. "Cricky?"

"Yeah... It's me," Cricket breathed, settling back onto his haunches in the dirt. Ignacia raced to him, flinging her arms around his thick scaly neck, while Yoshi went to check on the man from the wagon. Cricket could hear the tremble in Ignacia's breaths, panic, as she pressed her face into his scales. "I didn't hurt him. I wouldn't hurt him."

"No. Of course not," Ignacia agreed, but her voice shook as if she wasn't actually sure. As if she didn't actually *know* that he wouldn't hurt someone. Ignacia squeezed his neck once more before stepping back. "Yoshi?"

"Mm," Yoshi said, seeming to say that the man was all right. Even as his hand moved to his sword to grip the hilt.

"He says it's... He says it was Uncle. Uncle did this." And like that, all the fury washed out of Cricket. He felt it that time. Felt the change as his body rearranged itself, shrinking from dragon to normal human size. Scales shifting back into wherever they'd come from, smoothing into skin. He shifted uncomfortably at the strange sensation of a long whip-like tail being tucked away.

"Cricket. What was that?" Ignacia asked, her hands had taken hold of his, squeezing them tightly. "You were... That was a dragon."

The anger was gone, but what replaced it was panic. Blind fear, clenching at his insides and making him cold. He had to get there. He had to reach them. He had to know if they were safe. He had to...

"Not now, Iggy. There isn't time. We have to call Anstice. We have to warn her and Father!"

CHAPTER 47

The mirror trembled in his fingers, Cricket's own face reflected back at him, shaking with the movement. He'd scattered everything from his saddlebag in the process of finding it. Spare clothes littered the ground, gathering dust. His bedroll had landed in a patch of dew-covered grass. And the journal with all its careful notes on his adventures, was sprawled pages down alongside everything else. None of it mattered. None of it was as important as the mirror in his hands.

Cricket's knuckles turned white as he clutched the frame, breathing sharp in through his nose, and out through his lips. Cricket was trying to calm down. He didn't want to seem frantic when he finally saw Anstice. He didn't want to worry her if there was no need.

"I will go into town, and get the local authorities," Yoshi whispered by way of excusing himself. Cricket didn't bother nodding or looking at him.

"Cricket. Maybe we should wait." Ignacia's voice was soft. Her hands reached for the mirror as if she might pry it from his fingers.

"Wait for what?" Cricket asked, voice low against the swelling tide of panic in his veins. It was better, he supposed, this panic. Better than the anger that had ripped through him without warning or any recognizable cause. He'd rather this, than the dragon. If he could control his rage maybe he could control whatever curse had been cast on him to turn him into that beast as well.

"What?" She stopped mid-reach for the mirror. Her hands outstretched between them. Cricket swallowed down the urge to clutch the cold metal frame to his chest and hoard it away from her like something valuable and precious. The palace was still hours away, this was the only thing that linked him to his family at that moment. And he needed to know.

"What should we wait for?" His hands had stopped shaking, when had that happened? He didn't know but when he looked down at the mirror in his lap, they were steady, and his face was calm. It was as if the inner turmoil roiling away in his guts wasn't showing on his face. Good. That was probably for the best. "Should we wait for word that Father is dead? Or maybe we should wait for an execution date for Anstice? Or maybe we should wait for Uncle to declare himself king in my absence and Father's failing health? Is that what we should *wait* for?"

Ignacia jerked, stricken. "Cricket, you don't really think he'd hurt them..." She frowned, her eyes flicking across his face. "Do you?"

"I don't know." And that was the terrifying part about all of this. He didn't know. Uncle had never been overly affectionate or kind, and often Marwa had even called him cruel. But he was Uncle. He was Father's brother. He was... He would be king if Father died, and Cricket was not there to take the crown. Would his ambition outweigh his familial relations? Cricket didn't know. He also didn't think he wanted to find out, but he wasn't going to get much choice in that.

"But I'd rather act as if he would, and be wrong, than act as if he wouldn't, and lose them."

Ignacia nodded. "I'll gather your things."

"Thank you."

She rose silently, turning her back on him to give him the privacy she likely thought he desired for this conversation. Cricket wasn't sure he did desire privacy, but he certainly wasn't looking for an audience.

"Anstice Dresden," he murmured to the glass, and waited.

The glass rippled for a moment, and when it cleared there was Anstice. Only...only she didn't look like the Anstice Cricket had always known. The kohl that usually lined her eyes was smudged and left dark tracks down her cheeks as if she'd been crying. Her long brown hair hung limp around her face, greasy, and unbrushed. And there were dark circles under her eyes.

"Cricket," she whispered, her brown eyes flicking over his face and then up over the edge of the mirror to something he couldn't see. "You shouldn't have called."

"What?" Cricket's heart leaped into his throat, threatening to choke on the words. "Why not?"

"It's Sunil, he's..." She jerked, her eyes widening as she stopped to listen to something. Cricket glanced at what was behind her. She wasn't in her room. She was in one of the linen closets. Fresh white sheets and towels stacked high around her. The light overhead dim enough to not give away that someone was hidden inside. The linen closet nearest the guest quarters on the east side of the palace. That's where she was. The linen closet they'd hid in as children when her father had died, and she'd needed an escape from the pitying looks.

"He's what?"

Anstice shook her head, frowning.

"Anstice, what is he doing?" Cricket's hands were shaking

again. He tightened his hold on the mirror, the metal creaking in warning at him. "I caught the trader. He told me Uncle hired him to bring the army away from the palace. Anstice. Is Uncle trying to take the throne?"

Anstice's expression shifted. She didn't have to say anything, he saw it.

"Has he hurt you or Father?"

"Your father is..." She started and then she stopped, seeming to chew on the words for a long moment. As if she wasn't sure that she should say what she originally intended to. "We will be all right."

"I'm in Luna now. I'll be there by tomorrow."

"No. You can't do that. You have to go and get help. Go to Helio, or Hermes. Gather your allies and come for us then." The words left her in a rush, her eyes flicking back up to what he assumed was the door of the linen closet. Someone knocked on it hard enough to shake the wood on the hinges. "Don't come here, Cricket. Sunil will—"

The door burst open before she could finish her warning. It banged loud against the hinges. Cricket could see the shadows of two hulking figures make their way into the room just before Anstice whispered a hurried, "Off."

The glass rippled and Anstice was gone. All that was left was Cricket's own face, and his eyes glowing with a fury that threatened to rip him apart. Rough pants left his nose in tendrils of steam. The glass cracked under his tightened grip, and when he looked down into the splintered surface, he saw scales replacing his freckles.

"ARGH!" Cricket threw the mirror, sending it soaring through the air to shatter somewhere far enough away that he'd never have to look at it again.

"She's right." Ignacia's voice was small. She'd obviously heard the whole thing, or most of it at least. "If Sunil means to do you harm, if he's taken control of the palace, we can't go. We should travel North and get help."

"No." Cricket growled, his talons closing into fists tight enough that he felt their sharpened edges break the skin of his palms. The pain was enough to keep him grounded. To keep from letting the rage completely take over, and hopefully stop the transformation before it got too far. He didn't have time to deal with this... Whatever this was. Not when Father and Anstice were in danger.

"Cricket, we can't put you—"

"I SAID *NO*, IGNACIA!"

"Okay," Ignacia said, holding up her hands. "Okay. Then what do you want to do?"

"As soon as Yoshi gets back, we're heading to the capital. We'll assess how to get into the palace from there." He took a deep gulp of air, letting it calm his senses, and looked down at his clenched fists. The talons were gone, all that was left was his short blunt nails. Good. That was good. He needed to be level headed for this.

"And what are you going to do when we get inside?"

Cricket lifted his head to glare at her. She held her hands up higher in surrender. "I'll sort that out when we get to that point. Right now, we just need to get there."

"All right."

Yoshi returned shortly after with the town magistrate. They left the trader in the brusque woman's hands with the promise to send soldiers back for him shortly. They passed the next hours as the sun crept above the horizon and made his way across the sky in silence. Cricket could tell that both Yoshi and Ignacia had questions about the dragon, and about what his plans were. But he was in no mood to answer either of them, and one sharp look had been enough to keep them from asking.

He could still feel the scales on his cheek. Scraping dryly under his fingers anytime he lifted a hand to brush his hair from his face. Scales and a scar. Yue Cricket was not returning home the same boy who had left, and if Uncle thought he would be cowed into submission, he had another thing coming.

They crested a hill in the forest around noon, and the capital came into view. Cricket had crested this same hill many times when traveling with Father, and each time the sight of the capital below had inspired awe and wonder. The sheer joy and life that burst from its seams had always made him feel at home amongst his people. But that city, and the one that sprawled in front of him now, was not the same.

"Where is everyone?" Ignacia asked with a scowl as she lifted her hand to squint into the streets below. They weren't quite high enough to see all the way to the palace, but at this distance, and this height they could see a fair bit of the city along the river.

"The market should be set up," Cricket whispered, his hands tightening on his reins. "It's noon. The market should be set up just there."

"And where are all the grannies and aunties out shopping? There's just...there's no one."

"I'm going to get a better look. Yoshi, come give me a boost." Cricket slid from Buttercup's saddle and moved to one of the thicker trees. With a quick glance he assessed the branches above him and how far he could go before he'd have to worry about their stability. Yoshi moved without a word, crouching to hold his hands into a basket so Cricket could step into them and be hoisted up to the lowest hanging branch.

Cricket scrambled up onto the branch, and then up another, and another until he was as high up as he thought he could safely go. Once there he moved out onto the branch, slowly using the nearby limbs as a means to steady himself, and then turned his focus to the city. His heart clenched, stomach dropping through his feet and down to rest on the forest floor. It wasn't just the main street of the capital where the market usually set up, it was everywhere. The whole city was empty of people. And the ones he could see, the rare few who ventured out, they walked quickly as if someone were chasing them.

"Do you see any patrols?" Ignacia called up to him.

"No. But that doesn't mean they aren't there." Cricket shook his head. "I'm coming down, we need to make a plan."

Yoshi was waiting for Cricket when he got to the lower branches, hands extended in the air to catch him and lower him carefully to his feet.

"Thanks." Cricket beamed up at him, wincing a little when the movement of his cheeks made the scales shift uncomfortably. He frowned, lifting a hand to rub against them self-consciously.

"You are welcome." Yoshi offered him a soft look in return, something almost like a smile. It caused something strange to flutter in Cricket's throat. He cleared it and looked away.

"Do we have a map of the capital, Iggy?" Cricket turned to head to where she was digging through her bags looking for something.

"Why would I have a map of the capital?" Ignacia growled, digging her arms deep into the saddle bag, which would have looked strange to anyone else as her arms were up to her shoulders in a bag that should hardly have reached her elbows. "We weren't going to the capital; we were going to the villages and towns outside of the capital. We were leaving the capital. Why would I pack a map of the capital?"

Cricket cocked his head at her back. "Then what are you looking for?"

"A map of the capital!"

"But you just—"

"That atlas Marwa gave me for my birthday, the magic one." Ignacia huffed as if this should have been obvious to him. "It's supposed to give a map of any place so long as you have the name for it. I know I packed the stupid thing."

"We should have lunch." Yoshi had moved to his own bags to pull out miniature pies from somewhere and held one out to Cricket. "Vegetarian pot pie."

"Uh... Thanks." Cricket took one and took a bite.

"Ah ha!" Ignacia crowed, pulling a thin book from the bag. It couldn't have been more than ten pages, but she dropped immediately to the ground and spread it out on her lap to inspect the blank inner pages. "The capital of Lunette," she told the book, drumming her fingers against the hard backing.

Like ants, black ink crawled across the page, forming alleys and roads. At the center of it all was the walls of the palace, and the small compound that made up Cricket's home. Cricket flopped beside her, pressing his shoulder into hers so he could get a good view of the map.

"Marwa always gave the best gifts." Ignacia smiled softly, her fingers lightly stroking the pages.

"Yeah." Cricket nodded his agreement. Then he shoved the rest of the pie into his mouth, rubbed his hands on his trousers and leaned in to get a better look of the map. "Ow bes wa—"

"Chew and swallow." Ignacia grunted, through clenched teeth.

"Right. So." Cricket swallowed down the half-chewed pie and continued. "It looks like our best way in will probably be through this series of alleys." He tapped his finger on the page, running a line from where they were up to the eastern palace wall.

"Why the eastern wall?" Yoshi asked from where he stood behind them, looking down at the map.

"I always left one of the library windows open. It's tucked away in the stacks, so no one is likely to notice it was left unlocked and cracked. That'll be the best entry point without being noticed. We just have to worry about making it across the yard to the window."

"And making it from the end of the alley to the wall," Ignacia reminded, pointing to the gap between the two.

"Will there not be patrols in the yard?"

"Probably, but not as many, I'd wager." Ignacia chewed on her lower lip thoughtfully. "He'll expect you to come in through one of the main entrances."

"Why would he expect that?" Yoshi had the frown-wrinkle again, as if he didn't truly understand what was going on. And Cricket supposed that was fair, he and Ignacia had enough experience with Uncle to know what to expect, but Yoshi was looking at this from a logical perspective. From the outside perspective of someone who would treat Cricket like a true enemy invader, not a flighty prince.

"Sunil thinks Cricket is arrogant. He'll expect Cricket to come in sword blazing, making a scene. We'll have the element of surprise at the very least." Ignacia shrugged.

"I mean, he's not wrong. I am arrogant. I'm just not stupid." Cricket tilted his head back to grin wickedly up at Yoshi and offer him a wink.

Yoshi shook his head. "We should go in at night. If we are concerned with being seen when going from the alley to the wall, the cover of night will be our best ally."

"But what about Annie and Father?" Cricket frowned, his nose wrinkling.

"He's right, Cricky. Going in at night is our best chance at getting them out safely without too much of a fuss. And it gives us time to rest." Ignacia snapped the book shut; her mind made up.

"Hm." Yoshi hummed, and turned to begin unloading something from the horses. "My Prince should rest. I will set up your bedroll."

"Yoshi. You don't have to.... I'm really all right... I'm not even..."

But it was too late. Yoshi had gone to retrieve it and lay it out on a soft patch of moss. Then he stood expectantly, waiting for Cricket to climb in and get some sleep. Cricket looked from Yoshi to Ignacia. Ignacia shrugged.

So, he'd lost that particular battle.

CHAPTER 48

The walls surrounding the palace looked so much more imposing like this, with Cricket on the outside of them, not meant to be inside. More like a fortress than like the home he'd always known it as.

He remembered climbing over this wall two months ago, letting Ignacia lift him up and tumbling down on the other side. This was nothing like that. That day seemed like years ago now. He'd been happy then. Even as he knew that Uncle would be furious with him. Even as he knew that he'd have to justify his actions. He'd been happy. Carefree in a way he no longer felt with the events of the past two months and the knowledge that Uncle had been responsible for them weighing on his shoulders.

"We could still go back," Ignacia whispered. She wasn't looking at the wall across from where they were tucked into the dark alley, her eyes were fixed on him, flicking over his features as she assessed him and his thoughts. "We can still do like Annie said, and go for help."

"No." Cricket shook his head, his hands closing into tight fists as his sides. Yoshi was silent behind them, his eyes watching the mouth of the alley, sword drawn, and ready to attack if a patrol noticed them. "There isn't time for that."

"Why not?" Ignacia sounded frustrated. Cricket knew she would support him, whatever his choice, but she didn't like the idea of risking his safety, not like this.

"The people of Helio would help you," Yoshi said with a certainty that Cricket didn't understand and didn't have time to inspect.

"We have to get Anstice and Father out first. If we leave Father when he's sick like this..." Cricket closed his eyes to keep his emotions in check. He couldn't let the anger at Uncle's actions take over. They didn't have time to deal with the dragon.

A patrol passed them. The first they'd seen since they'd made their way through the capital toward the palace. They ducked deeper into the darkness of the alley.

"They are only patrolling the wall, not anywhere else in the city." Yoshi's voice was flat, but Cricket thought he heard a sense of underlying annoyance there. "Is he not worried for his citizens."

"He knows I won't hurt them." Cricket opened his eyes again. "We should go now. Before more guards come through, or they make it back around."

"More like he's just worried about protecting himself," Ignacia muttered to herself, ducking her head around the corner to look both ways along the length of the wall. "I don't see any more yet. Could be they just have the one group."

"That would be a foolish tactical decision." Cricket definitely heard annoyance in Yoshi's voice now.

"Not if he *wants* me to get in." Cricket shrugged.

"Why would he— My Prince, wait."

But Cricket didn't wait. He stepped out into the open and moved quickly to the wall. It was smooth, just like the wall inside, but he wasn't going to let that stop him. Yoshi moved swiftly to his side, looking up at the wall with him.

"It's so there are less witnesses," Ignacia said from behind him. "Then he can say that Cricket was either killed by mistake, or some disloyal faction in the palace did it."

"He'll probably blame one of you. Or maybe Anstice," Cricket murmured thoughtfully to himself. He jumped at the top of the wall, his fingers skidding off the stone, scraping skin from his fingertips. He hissed, glaring down at the reddened skin. "Give me a boost, Iggy."

Ignacia looked around them again before crouching to form her hands into a basket. Cricket stepped into it and let her hoist him up to the top of the wall. Once on top, he turned to look back at them thoughtfully, and then shook his head.

"Help me up." Ignacia held her hands up for him to grab on and pull her over with him.

"No. You both should stay here. Where it's safe." Cricket crawled across the width of the wall and peeked over to watch the patrol set around the inner perimeter.

"Cricket. Don't you *dare*. Come help us up." Ignacia hissed.

"I'll be all right." Cricket slid down to his feet in the grass on the other side with a soft thump, his breathing heavy in his ears.

A long stretch of yard was between him and the east wall of the library. He'd have to make it around the corner to get to the back half where the window was open. Dark eyes flicked around him, waiting for the guards to be well and truly out of earshot, and then he took off across the open yard. The moon was bright above him, and he realized perhaps he should have prayed to Selene for an eclipse of some sort before all of this, but it was a little late now.

Ducking into the shadow of the eaves of the east wall of

the library, Cricket pressed his back to the rough stone, ears straining for any sign of guards. What he heard instead was the thump of two sets of feet landing on the soft grass. He looked over the way he'd come and frowned deeply at the sight of Ignacia and Yoshi rushing across the yard toward him. Idiots.

"I thought I told you to stay behind. Where it's safe," he chastised in a hush.

Ignacia shrugged, and Yoshi gave him a pointedly mild look.

"Fine. If you two insist on putting yourself up for the noose, it's this way." Cricket huffed. He stuck close to the wall, letting the shadow hide them as best it could from prying eyes. "I swear it's like talking to a wall with you two."

"Shut up and help us find this window," Ignacia hissed. She pushed herself in front of Cricket, ducking her head around the corner to check for any guards. Then with a motion they followed her around the corner to where the windows ran along the back of the library. "Which one is it?"

"This one." Cricket moved to a window just like all the others in the row. It was far enough off the ground that he had to move onto his toes to peek inside the darkened library, but just as he'd thought there was a tiny crack between where the bottom of the window met the frame. Just enough space for his fingertips to wedge and widen the gap. "We're lucky it's still warm enough out that there was no draft."

Yoshi moved to his side and wedged his fingers in beside Cricket's to help him wiggle the window open.

"Even with a draft they probably wouldn't have noticed." Ignacia had her back to them, to keep an eye on anyone approaching. "You've been leaving this window open for how long?"

Cricket shrugged, moving onto his toes to start wiggling through the gap. Yoshi grabbed his ankles and helped to shove him through the rest of the way, and Cricket rolled to his feet on the other side perhaps a little too loudly. He stilled, listening for any sign that someone had heard his entrance. When he turned back, he saw Yoshi starting to wiggle through, and he held up a hand to stop him.

On silent feet, Cricket made his way to the end of the long row of bookshelves to peek around the corner. There was a light on somewhere near the door, not bright enough to read by. It was likely something the librarian left on all the time, so no one tripped when they entered. He turned back to gesture for Yoshi and Ignacia to follow.

Once they were all inside, Ignacia slid the window back down and they crept through the library.

"We'll go to Annie's room first." Ignacia moved into the lead, her hands reaching to pull the library door open and check the hall for guards. "She'll know if there are any guards we can trust, and what Sunil is planning."

"But she is also a captive." Yoshi frowned.

"Doesn't matter. Anstice has a way of finding things out." Cricket nodded his agreement, and they made their way into the corridor beyond the library.

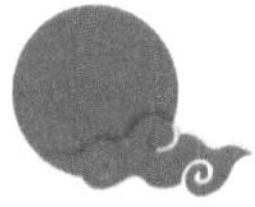

CRICKET WAS SURPRISED to find that there were only two guards posted outside of Anstice's rooms. Neither of which put up much of a fight as Ignacia and Yoshi knocked them out quickly and dragged them to the side to be tied together out of the way.

Perhaps Ignacia was right, perhaps Uncle was more worried about his own safety than anything else. But the halls of the palace had been strangely silent and empty, even for evening time. They'd seen no servants passing by, no scholars in the library, no soldiers chatting. Nothing. It was deeply unsettling. Cricket's home had always been loud, and full of life, and now it was empty and cold.

He pressed Anstice's door open and ducked inside. "Annie?"

She was sitting in a chair near the window, her body covered by a heavy blanket. When she looked up, Cricket saw the dark bruises, and unkempt hair still present. As if she hadn't been sleeping much at all. As if everything had weighed on her as it was currently weighing on him.

"I told you not to come," Anstice whispered, shaking her head.

"Get dressed, we're leaving. We're going to go get Father, and we're leaving. Iggy and Yoshi are in the hall, we're going to—"

The sharp edge of a blade pushed to his throat, and Cricket glanced over to see the captain of the guard's fingers bone white around his sword hilt.

"Your uncle has been waiting for you," the man said, his voice cold.

"Well, let's not keep him waiting then, Captain Dashiell." Cricket smiled, leaning back on his heels, subtly putting as much distance between his neck and the blade as he could.

Dashiell sneered at him, jerking his chin toward Cricket's sword at his side. "Leave that here. We wouldn't want you getting any stupid ideas."

"Oh Dashiell, you forget. I'm full of stupid ideas." Cricket winked playfully, and before Dashiell could react, he dropped into a crouch, kicking out at the man's ankles and making the man stumble. It was a second of weakness, but that's all Cricket needed to grab his sword, knock Dashiell's out of his hands, and hold the blade to the other man's throat. "Now, as I was saying, Annie, get up and get dressed.

We're going to see Father, and then we're going to get you both to safety."

"That really won't be necessary, Cricky," Anstice breathed too close to his ear. He felt the sharp prick of a dagger against the soft underside of his jaw. Without moving his head, he flicked his gaze down to look at where Anstice had pressed the point into his skin. "Captain, I believe you were going to get the guards and take the prisoners down to the cells?"

Dashiell scrambled to his feet and threw open the doors so he could dash out into the hall. Yoshi and Ignacia turned from where they'd clearly been keeping watch. Ignacia's mouth fell open, but Yoshi was already reaching for his sword. Taking the handful of steps toward Cricket and Anstice.

Anstice pressed the blade in closer, and Cricket winced. "Not another step, Prince Takayoshi. I know you've grown quite fond of my big brother here, and I wouldn't want to see the guilt you'd be wracked with should his blood be on your hands."

Yoshi faltered, the sword lowering slowly. "Release him."

Cricket squeezed his eyes shut, taking in a shallow breath not to press the sharp point further into his skin. *Takayoshi. Prince.* No. There was too much else going on. He'd have to parse that out later. Preferably when he didn't have a knife pointed at his jugular.

"Anstice, what are you doing?" Ignacia's voice was hard, her hands clenched into fists at her side. But she, like Cricket, hadn't made a move to hurt Anstice. They couldn't. They just... They couldn't.

"What I have to." Anstice's voice was sad, and soft, but no less resolute. Cricket didn't know what the words meant, but he felt there was more Anstice wasn't saying. Before he could ask Dashiell came running with more guards.

Anstice kept the blade pressed to Cricket's skin. Yoshi

and Ignacia were forced to hand over their weapons and were put in shackles. Then he, himself, was divested of his sword, and anything else that might be used against the guards. Only once the shackles snapped closed on his wrists did Anstice finally release him.

He had but a moment to look back at her as they were being dragged down the corridor, and what he saw made his stomach twist. Anstice's face was composed, a careful mask, but her eyes...her eyes looked sad. She really was just doing what she felt she had to. Even if what she had to do hurt the people she loved the most.

CHAPTER 49

"You absolute idiot," Ignacia growled her arms crossing over her chest as she cut a look at Cricket. "You got us caught! I can't believe you got us caught! You couldn't even—"

"How was I supposed to know that Anstice was working with Uncle? I didn't even know Uncle was scheming behind my back. How should I have known?!" Cricket threw his hands up in the air. He knew Ignacia wasn't really angry with him. She also wasn't really blaming him. She was angry with the situation. She was hurt by Anstice's betrayal, just as he was, but Cricket was the closest person to yell at. And maybe she should blame him... how couldn't he have known? How could he have missed Uncle's blind ambition?

"We could be halfway to Helio by now if it weren't for your foolish, self-sacrificing need to—"

"I told you not to come! I told you to wait for me outside of the walls! I told you that I would be all right."

"But you were not all right," Yoshi chimed in from where he'd been not leaning against the cell wall, watching the two of them shout at each other. "You were not all right, and if we were not—"

"Oh, I don't want to hear *anything* from you *Prince* Takayoshi," Cricket spat back, raising a finger to point at Yoshi. "How long were you planning to lie to us about who you really were?"

"I did not lie." Yoshi's voice was even, impassive, but Cricket could see that he was annoyed and hurt by their situation as much as Ignacia was. Cricket had hurt them both. He had gotten them both into this, and now he wasn't sure how he'd get them both out of it.

"But you didn't tell the truth, either. Did you?" Ignacia scowled at him, her fury turning toward Yoshi now.

"I did not lie." Yoshi's jaw tightened, his eyes flicking to stare at the wall across from him instead of looking at either Ignacia or Cricket.

"Who cares if you didn't lie?!" Cricket smacked the wall hard enough to cause a wince. "You didn't tell the truth! You traveled with us for *months*, and you never told us who you were! We trusted you!"

"You can still trust me." Yoshi's words were quiet, but Cricket heard them fine in the echoing silence of the surrounding cells. "Unlike your sister."

Cricket jerked, his eyes widening as if he'd been struck. "You don't know Annie. You don't get to pass judgement on her."

"Why not? She lied."

"Because she's our friend!" Ignacia snarled.

"Is she?" Yoshi's eyes had turned cold, his lips pressed into a thin line.

"You will not speak about my sister—" Cricket narrowed his eyes threateningly.

"I didn't expect to come down here and find you all at each other's throats," a soft voice said from the other side of the bars. Cricket stopped; he'd lifted his fist. He wasn't sure what he meant to do with it, but he was sure that had Youta's voice not interrupted him he would have struck Yoshi. The dark-haired woman shook her head.

"Youta?" Cricket moved to the bars gripping them as he looked out at her. She was holding a tray of sandwiches, her lips pressed into a hard line instead of the soft smile he'd known for so many years. Beneath her warm brown eyes were bags, hanging heavy and dark. And she looked thinner. He didn't like it. Cricket was meant to protect her, just as he'd been meant to protect all of them, and instead he'd left.

"I came to bring you a snack." Youta lifted the tray a little so he could see the sandwiches better, she'd cut the crusts off all of them, and cut them into neat little triangles. Just how Cricket liked them. She stepped closer to the bars, holding Cricket's eyes meaningfully as she whispered, "And a message."

"Thank you, Youta." Cricket nodded and took one of the triangles to take a small bite. He wasn't hungry. But he was grateful for a friendly face, and any information she could provide.

"I brought enough for everyone," Youta announced, nodding down toward the tray in her hands. "Come. Come. You must be hungry."

Yoshi and Ignacia made their way over to the bars a little more slowly, but they each reached for a small triangle just as Cricket had. In the silence of their chewing, Youta flicked her eyes down the long hall that led out of the dungeons. Whatever she saw must have settled her, for her shoulders relaxed.

"Your father is well. In spite of Sunil's attempts, we have managed to keep him sick enough to avoid Sunil's notice, but he will make a full recovery once all of this is over." Her voice was soft, and Cricket found himself leaning in closer to make sure he caught every word. "Anstice and I have been keeping him well."

"Anstice? But she—"

Youta shook her head quickly. "All is not as it seems."

"But Anstice..."

Youta pursed her lips, and Cricket knew that to be a sign that she would not explain further. Not this. Whatever Youta and Anstice had been working on together, Youta would not betray the other woman's trust. At least not yet. She must know how it looked, and still she refused to speak on the matter. Cricket would let her keep her silence, for now.

"Was that all?" Ignacia asked, her voice soft.

Another glance down the hall, and a silent moment passed as Youta listened to the comings and goings further up the corridor. "Tomorrow morning you will be summoned to the throne room to face your uncle." She kept her voice low, hardly more than a murmur, and if Cricket weren't standing close enough to touch her, he wouldn't have heard the words. "The kitchen staff will be preparing a special breakfast for your uncle and his men."

Cricket cocked his head, the little sandwich in his hand now forgotten.

"We will provide you a window during which they will be at their weakest. Whatever offensive plan you have to enact, you must do so in that window." Youta held out another sandwich to him, and Cricket took it even though he hadn't yet finished the last.

"What about weapons?" Yoshi asked. His own triangle of bread was between his fingers completely uneaten.

"What's taking so long down there?" Someone shouted from the door to the dungeons. "You were just supposed to take them sandwiches. Leave them on the floor for all I care and get back up here!"

"Yes, sir." Youta called back, pasting on a pleasant smile.

She bent, setting the tray within reach so they could take what they liked off it. When she stood, she gave them another meaningful look, and a nod, before heading up the hall without another word.

The door to the dungeons slammed shut behind her, and Cricket was left holding a triangle of sandwich in each hand, staring down at the tray she'd left behind. On it was a letter opener smeared with peanut butter. It was clear it was what Youta had used to make the sandwiches, or at least was meant to look that way.

Ignacia swiped it from the tray and tucked it into her boot without a word.

AN HOUR later another maid arrived with a jug of water and cups. When Ignacia grabbed the jug it jangled, and in the bottom, they found a small knife which Cricket tucked into his own boot.

EARLY IN THE MORNING, with little sleep, and only minimal planning, a young serving boy came down with a tray of food for them. It wasn't more than a large bowl of rice and several smaller bowls. But once the large bowl was emptied, they found another small blade in the bottom. Yoshi took this one.

AN HOUR later Dashiell was back with his guards. They were loud, and belligerent. If Cricket didn't know any better...

"Uncle lets his men drink wine with breakfast?" Cricket asked where he lounged against the wall of their cell. Ignacia shot him a worried look at the casual tone, but he shook his head. He knew what he was doing. "That hardly seems wise."

Dashiell snorted, giving Cricket a look of sheer disgust. "Who are you to criticize the future king's wisdom?"

One of the other guards had moved to fumble with the keys in the cell door. They clanked loudly, and Cricket could feel a headache pressing into his temples at the combination of lack of sleep and the noise. But he wasn't willing to back down now.

"The future king? Funny. I thought I was the future king." Cricket shrugged and gave the expression of one who is deeply unconcerned about how his words might be perceived. "But then Uncle did always think himself mightier than he was. Didn't he, Iggy?"

"You idiot child!" Dashiell snarled. "Get him out of there. His uncle wants to see him!"

The door flung open, and the guard who'd been struggling to open it stepped inside in one quick motion, reaching for Cricket as if to throttle him. Yoshi stepped between them, bodily blocking the guard from getting to Cricket. Cricket patted his shoulder, trying to tell Yoshi to stand down, but the white knight wouldn't move. He remained, back rigid, his body blocking Cricket entirely from the other men.

"Get out of the way boy. We only need Cricket. You both would do better to mind your business." Dashiell stepped into Yoshi's space, his nose practically touching Yoshi's as if to intimidate him into moving. Yoshi refused. Dashiell lifted his hand and backhanded Yoshi hard enough to jerk the white knight's head to the side. Still, Yoshi did not move. Dashiell raised his hand to strike again.

"I'll go! I'll go! Just leave them alone. Don't hurt them." Cricket grabbed Yoshi's shoulder hard, pulling him away and tucking him safely into his side. Yoshi shot him a glare, but Cricket ignored it. "They don't have anything to do with Uncle and I."

He held out his wrists, and let the guards shackle him in spite of the silent fury from Yoshi. They dragged him from the cell, Cricket hung his head, taking deep breaths, and reminded himself to be calm. To not fight back. To wait for his—

"Bring the others as well." Dashiell sneered down at Cricket whose eyes had widened. Cricket jerked back to try to get to Ignacia and Yoshi, but Dashiell's grip on the shackles was too tight. "You'll behave yourself, boy, or I'll recommend the future king make an example out of your little friends," he whispered low enough for only Cricket to hear.

"You're disgusting," Cricket snarled back.

Dashiell jerked his head to one of the guards behind him. Cricket didn't have to see it to hear the blow, and the quiet grunt of pain from Yoshi as he doubled over from the punch to the stomach. "No lip either."

Cricket's teeth squeaked as he ground them together, jaw ticking in frustration, but he didn't say anything. Not yet. Now was not the time. He'd get his opening. Youta had promised him that.

CHAPTER 50

The throne room looked just like Cricket remembered it with one minor exception. The smaller throne, the one meant for himself, had been removed. All that was left was the large high-back chair that had been Father's. The throne of the king. And in that chair, sat Uncle. His head tilted languidly onto one fist as if bored. Anstice stood at his side, doing her best to not make eye contact with Cricket. He tried not to think about what that meant. There would be time to deal with those emotions later.

"Good morning, Uncle. Anstice." Cricket lifted his shackled hands to wave cheerfully at him, a wide dimpled smile forced onto his face. He just needed to distract Uncle long enough for whatever Youta and the other kitchen staff had done to work. Just long enough to use their advantage when it came. Just long enough to find an opening. For that he needed to get Uncle talking, but then, that would be the easy part.

"Kneel before your king," Anstice said, tone flat. Dashiell forced Cricket to his knees on the stone floor. Cricket heard movement behind him, a brief struggle, and he didn't have to look back to know that Ignacia and Yoshi weren't happy with the rough treatment.

"If anyone should kneel, it's Uncle Sunil." Cricket continued to smile, knowing it would infuriate Uncle further. Uncle's eyes sharpened, his hand falling away as he sat up. Fury flickered across his features. That was it. That was what Cricket needed. "After all, if Father isn't well enough to see to his duties, they fall to his son. His son who is of age. And who is that again? Oh right! It's me!"

"You're not his son," Uncle spat, fists clenching on the arm rests of the throne.

"No? I'm pretty sure that's my title. I'm pretty sure we have the documentation somewhere and everything. It's probably in the hall of records." Cricket tilted his head to look up at Dashiell as if confirming something. Dashiell was starting to look dazed. Not long now. "It's in the hall of records, isn't it? Should we go get it?"

He made to rise from his knees, and Dashiell smacked him upside the head before forcing him down to the floor again. Another sound of struggle stirred up behind him, but Cricket just shook his head. *Not now. Not yet.* Uncle's face had gone an interesting shade of pink. He was angry, but not enough. Not yet. Cricket needed him fuming. Cricket needed him angry enough to leave his throne and come handle his errant nephew himself.

"You are not his son." Uncle's voice shook with rage. "You are an orphan. A nothing. Abandoned by your own parents and foisted upon my brother by Selene as if she had any right."

"I believe that makes me his son." Cricket laughed. "I was adopted, remember? You were there for my ceremony. It was all very official."

Dashiell smacked him again, and Cricket tasted the sharp

tang of blood where he'd bitten his tongue. He did not hear any movement behind him, and thanked Selene that Yoshi and Ignacia had gotten the message to wait for his signal.

"You are not blood!"

"Blood does not equate family. You never did learn that. That's why you're a *duke*." Cricket snorted and spat the blood from his tongue onto the floor.

"I am the king!"

Hmm... Crimson. Uncle was getting closer to where Cricket wanted him. Just a couple more shades of red and then he'd be angry enough to get in Cricket's face, and Cricket could utilize the knife in his boot. He felt Dashiell's grip on his shoulder lessen.

"A king understands that there is more to ruling than his own petty grievances." Cricket had heard Marwa say this enough times. "He understands that family is not blood, it is who you love. And a *king* must have enough love to not just care for an orphan who needed a home, but for all of his people. To look after them as if they were his own family. To put their needs *first*."

Uncle's hands shook against the arm rests. His muscles strained as he fought the urge to rise and storm across the room. Scarlet. Cricket was looking for Garnet. They were almost there.

"*You* are no king. *You* are a selfish, self-indulgent coward."

Uncle's hands smacked against the arm rests. Ah. There it was. Garnet.

"You insolent little brat!" Uncle flew from the throne, his hands outstretched and ready to latch onto Cricket's throat. Dashiell fumbled, a moment of hesitation, enough for Cricket to shake off his hold and reach for the blade in his boot. He got it out, and raised the point digging into Uncle's stomach hard enough to stop Uncle just as his fingers wrapped around Cricket's throat. The color drained from

Uncle's face, leaving him pale. "You wouldn't. You don't have it in you."

"A lot can change about a man in two months, Uncle." Cricket pressed the tip harder into Uncle's soft underbelly. A warning.

"Not that much. You're still soft." Uncle breathed, a hard laugh leaving him. He jerked his chin to the figures behind Cricket. Cricket turned; the blade still pressed to Uncle's stomach. Yoshi and Ignacia were on their knees, swords pressed to their throats. Blood trickled from where the sharp ends pressed into thin skin. "Did you think bringing them would help you? Did you think they could protect you? They made you weak."

"You hurt them, and I'll—"

"You'll *what*? Dig that letter opener into my ribs?" Uncle shook his head. "I don't think you will. You hurt me, and they all suffer. Not just these two, but everyone. The servants you love so much. Anstice. Your father. Your *people*. I'll make them all pay for what you did."

Cricket lowered the blade, letting it clatter to the floor, and held his hands up in surrender.

"You need to remember who you're dealing with, Cricket. Let's set an example." Uncle ordered nodding to the guard holding Yoshi. "Kill the boy."

"No!" The guard drew back his sword, readying the blow that would end Yoshi's life. Yoshi met Cricket's eyes, and the rage took over again. It gripped his insides hard enough to make them ache. The shackles that had been around Cricket's wrists clanged against the floor, ripped into pieces by the shift into the dragon. And then Cricket was flying across the room, knocking the guard aside with a taloned hand hard enough to send him reeling into a wall, and leaving behind cracked stone. The other guard, who'd been holding Ignacia, looked from his hostage to the fuming dragon, eyes wide.

"Don't just stand there! Kill it!" Uncle roared, as he backed away from a swipe of Cricket's long tail. His feet already taking him to the side door of the throne room. "Kill that monster!"

Ignacia took the moment of distraction, knocked the guard back, and leaped onto her feet. She caught the man's discarded sword and whirled into a fighting stance, her back to Cricket. Even with shackled wrists, Cricket knew so long as she held a blade, she'd be fine. "Get Sunil. We'll hold them off."

The guards had moved to circle them, their swords surprisingly steady for men and women faced with a dragon. Cricket looked at Yoshi, a thin stream of blood was dribbling down his neck, but he looked otherwise unharmed.

One of the guards decided to get brave and flung herself at Cricket in his distraction. Her sword made a wild swipe at his back legs, but Yoshi moved faster. Blade on blade stopped her with a clang.

"Sunil's headed for your father's rooms!" Ignacia shouted.

"Be safe, My Prince," Yoshi said, and tilted his head for Cricket to go.

Cricket nodded and leaped over the circle of guards. Talons scrabbled against the stone floors. The halls were empty, left barren by the need for guards to protect Uncle and whatever Uncle had done to the servants.

The door to Father's rooms was wide open, and by the time Cricket reached them his boots were skidding across the floor instead of talons. He could still feel the rough scales on his neck when his hair brushed them, but at least he looked mostly human again. He was grateful for how much quieter his boots were than the talons. But being quiet didn't seem to matter, for Uncle was waiting for him.

Uncle stood beside Father's bed; a dagger pressed under Father's chin. Father met his eyes, looking unafraid.

"Cricket," Father said softly, as if trying not to move his throat too much. "You are home."

"I am." Cricket nodded, ignoring Uncle who looked between them with wide eyes.

"You have a choice to make," Uncle said, voice sounding manic. "You can have the blood of your father on your hands, or your own. And seeing as you're a monster..."

Cricket didn't look at Uncle. He kept his eyes on Father. Father who was staring back at him steadily. Who didn't seem to care about the scales on his neck, or the sharpened nails on his fingers that pressed into his palms. Father who had loved him. Father who had been the first to teach him to hold a sword. Father who with one look said that he still loved him.

"Make a choice." Uncle pressed the tip of the blade further into Father's neck. Drawing blood. "Or I will make it for you."

There was a movement, a shadow out of the corner of Cricket's eye. He wasn't sure what it was, but a second later a whoosh of air preceded a dart burying itself into Uncle's neck. Uncle swung out, the dagger moving in a wide, dangerous arc for Father's neck. Cricket didn't think, he reacted. His taloned hand reached out and swiped at the hand holding the blade. There was a wet sound, talons cutting into the tendons in Uncle's arm, squelching and nauseating. Then a thud, the blade Uncle had held flinging away onto the bed somewhere. And then blood. So much blood. Dripping. Dripping. Dripping. From the wounds on Uncle's arm. From the sharpness of Cricket's talons.

Uncle fell to his knees, screaming as he tried to hold the deep cuts on his forearm closed. Blood spilling from between his fingers. He was shouting words, but they didn't make sense, and Cricket's ears were ringing. Cricket looked down at his hand, the talons had disappeared but in their wake were nails caked in skin, and fingers soaked in blood.

The ringing got louder. So loud. And his vision was starting to darken around the corners. Uncle slumped over finally, and Youta moved from where she'd been hiding in the shadows of the room. She eased Cricket to sit on the bed next to Father, who reached for his hand to try to ground him, and then crouched to check on Uncle.

Yoshi and Ignacia burst into the room a moment later. Ignacia moved to Youta to help her treat Uncle's wounds and stop the bleeding. Yoshi's hands pressed into Cricket's shoulders.

"You are safe, My Prince." Yoshi's words filtered in above the ringing, and a moment later the room went totally dark. Cricket slumping forward into the white knight.

CHAPTER 51

"Treason is an offense punishable by death." Yoshi had said that at least five times since they had gathered in the throne room to discuss what to do with Uncle.

He was right, of course. And the others who had participated in the attack, Dashiell, and his men, they would face life in prison. That had been an easy decision for Cricket to make. Uncle was a different story. Uncle had planned the whole thing. Uncle had swayed them all to his side. In the question of who had actually committed treason, it had been Uncle more so than the guards he'd won or frightened to his side. Uncle more so than Anstice who had helped in any way she could, at least on the surface.

"He's my uncle, Yoshi." Cricket's shoulders slumped forward, bracing his elbows on his knees, and burying his face in his hands. He was tired. So tired. It had been days of clean up to weed out the worst of the culprits, even with Anstice's confession and intel. And then there was the clean-up from the battle. The assignment of a new palace healer. And worst of all, he'd had to lock up his best friend, and sister, until he knew what to do with Anstice for her hand in all of this. Cricket just wanted to rest. But every night was plagued with nightmares of Uncle's white face, blood rushing from his arm. Of Cricket being too late to save Father. Of bodies, so many bodies, littering the palace and no way for Cricket to help them.

"He is a traitor to the crown." Yoshi's voice was hard. He was furious that they were still having this discussion, Cricket could tell.

"He's also the brother of the king," Ignacia interjected, her hand tightening on her sword. Her armor gleamed in the bright sunlight streaming in through the windows. Captain of the guard suited her, Cricket thought. Far better than the prince's babysitter anyhow.

"More reason for him to face public execution. You must make a statement, My Prince. You must tell your people that you will not stand for this. If you do not, you will be perceived as weak. Exile is not enough." It was the most words Cricket had ever heard Yoshi say in one breath, and Cricket wished they had been different words, kinder words, spoken at another time, in a softer tone. Cricket hated Yoshi for that. Hated him for how they hadn't spoken in days as Cricket was too busy trying to clean up the mess left by Uncle, and Yoshi had been off scouring the library for a solution as to why Cricket was suddenly turning into a dragon. An answer for the lingering scales.

"This," Cricket said, lifting his head and narrowing his eyes on Yoshi. "Is a Lunette matter, Prince Takayoshi. You are an emissary from Helio. A guest. Do not forget your place."

Yoshi's lips pressed into a hard line, but he fell into a deep bow. "Yes, Your Highness."

"Perhaps it is time you returned home to your own kingdom." Cricket grit through a clenched jaw.

Yoshi's shoulders tightened. He didn't rise from his bow,

but Cricket could see that there was tension there. Cricket's words had hurt him. "I am here to serve, Your Highness, and to find a solution to your unique affliction."

Cricket's scowl deepened. He lifted a hand to rub at the scales on his neck which hadn't gone away since his last shift. He wondered if he kept turning into a dragon if one day, he'd just stay that way. Professor Qiren had found no answers so far, neither had Yoshi. Still, Cricket didn't like the terms they used to speak of the dragon. Monster. Curse. *Affliction.* It was none of those things, but he couldn't explain what it actually was, so he remained silent on the matter.

"My affliction is no longer of your concern. You should return home."

"I will leave in the morning." Yoshi's words were soft, and Cricket couldn't be imagining the pain laced through them. Cricket shook his head. He was doing the right thing. Yoshi needed to go home. He needed to leave matters of Lunette to the people of Lunette.

"May you have a safe journey, Prince Takayoshi." Cricket nodded and rose from the throne. He reached into his pocket to pull the earring he'd yet to return from it. He held the earring in front of Yoshi's face, waiting for him to take it.

Yoshi looked up from where his head had been bowed, eyes focusing on the glittering amber.

"I meant to return this to you earlier." Cricket held it out further, the amber swaying softly as it caught the light. "Thank you very much for allowing me to borrow it while we searched for the perpetrator."

Yoshi took a breath and pulled his gaze from the earring to meet Cricket's eyes. The hurt was still there, but there was something else too. A quiet determination that Cricket had begun to appreciate in the knight. Yoshi had made up his mind about something, and like the stubborn mule he was, there would be no arguing with him.

"It was a gift."

"Don't be silly. This is Helio amber, it's basically a crown jewel. You can't gift that to someone." Cricket frowned, shaking his head.

"It was a gift, My Prince." Yoshi repeated, rising from his bow, and taking Cricket's free hand in his. He closed Cricket's fingers around the earring gently and bowed his head to press it to their joined hands before meeting Cricket's gaze again. "Please, keep it."

"I... Oh... Okay." Cricket swallowed around a dry throat.

"Good." Yoshi nodded in return, and that strange softening around his eyes appeared again. Like he was smiling, but it had not broken through the cloud of everything else he felt yet. "I will prepare my things to leave."

And then he turned on his heel and left the room without another word. Leaving Cricket standing there, holding the earring, with wide eyes.

"Okay, what in the name of Styx just happened?" Cricket asked, blinking rapidly after the knight.

"I think he just proposed to you." Ignacia snorted.

"Iggy! That's not funny!"

Ignacia shrugged.

UNCLE KNELT in the middle of the throne room; his arm bandaged from wrist to elbow. The healer had been by to speak to Cricket. She'd said that Uncle would never fully regain the ability to use his right hand, the tendons had been cut too deeply. The news had made Cricket sick to his stomach, but he didn't let himself dwell on it too long, not when there was so much else to think about.

"Yue Sunil. For the crime of treason, you will be banished from the kingdom of Lunette for eternity. Neither you nor any of your descendants will ever hold any claim to the throne of Lunette. If you should return to Lunette during the time of your banishment, your punishment will be execution." The scribe read from the scroll, his voice steady. "Do you have anything you wish to say to His Majesty before you are escorted to the border?"

"You really are soft, Cricket. What a kind, benevolent king you'll make." Uncle laughed, voice raspy, and broken.

"How dare you speak to the prince that way!" The guards holding Uncle's shoulders jerked him violently. His head lolling forward and back, but the cold hard smile stayed on his face.

"May you live a thousand years, Your Highness." Uncle cackled.

"Take him away!" The scribe shouted, and the guards yanked Uncle to his feet, and out of the room.

"I'll see him to the border," Ignacia said, her lips pressed into a scowl.

"No. Send one of the more trusted generals. I've got another job I need for you to do." Cricket sighed, slouching back into his seat.

"WAIT OUT HERE," Cricket nodded to the door. He knew Ignacia would like to be privy to this conversation, and maybe he should allow that, but he didn't think he had it in him to do what he had to with her eyes on him. He already felt guilty enough. Ignacia gave him an unsure look but moved to lean against the outside wall with her back toward him.

Anstice was pacing up and down her rooms, her hands twisting and wringing in her wrinkled dress. She'd been in the dungeons for a week, but Cricket had her released that morning with specific instructions that there be guards posted outside of her rooms at all times.

"Cricky!" She looked up, eyes bright, and a smile plastered onto her face as the door shut slowly behind him.

"Pack your things." The words were choked and brittle, but they had to be said. "You have been stripped of your title and are no longer welcome inside the palace."

"But Cricky, what I did—"

"I know you meant well, Anstice. I know you did what you thought you had to, but people died. Father nearly died thanks to you not warning me. My citizens died because you didn't tell me who was behind everything. People were hurt, and they died because you decided to gamble with their lives against my uncle instead of telling myself or father what he was up to."

"Sunil deserved what he got, he killed my mother."

"That isn't for you to decide! You don't get to play judge, jury, and executioner! That's not how things work!" Cricket sucked in a breath, ignoring how it shook on the exhale. "You know that better than anyone."

"I won't apologize for what happened to Sunil."

"I'm not asking you to."

"Then..." Anstice trailed off her brows creasing in confusion and oh how Cricket wished to wipe that look away. To pull Anstice close and make everything all better again just as he'd done so many times growing up. But he couldn't. Not this time.

"You can't stay here," he said instead. "It's not because I don't love you. You'll always be family to me. But you have to know, you can't stay here. If any of those guards talked, I'd have to charge you with treason just like them and Uncle. I know you weren't working with him, but that's what it *looked* like. And if you aren't here..."

"If I'm not here they won't bother." Anstice's shoulders sagged.

"You have a week to pack everything you need. I have gotten you a position in Helio. It's just a desk post in the palace library. I wish I could do more." He did. He did wish he could do more. But he couldn't in good conscience put Anstice back in politics, and even this was going to draw too much attention to him probably. People would want to know why she'd been let off when she'd clearly had a hand in things. He'd have to say it was because she was young, and foolish, but he hoped she'd learned her lesson. He hoped that would be enough.

"No. That's more than I could have asked for. Cricky..." Anstice rushed forward and hugged him tightly. Pressing her face into his chest just like she'd always done. "Thank you."

"No need. Just... Just keep in touch. And stay out of trouble, all right?"

Anstice nodded firmly.

THE DOOR SHUT BEHIND HIM, and Father was waiting for him on the other side. He smiled softly. He was still weak from his illness, but with a week of recovery, and a proper healer looking after him, Father had made surprising progress. He still needed rest, but he could take a couple hours to walk the grounds at least.

"Father?" Cricket frowned, tilting his head.

"You did the right thing, Cricket. Lunette will be in good hands with you as her king." His voice was soft. He lifted one hand to pull Cricket into a tight hug, letting Cricket bury himself in Father's shoulder just as he had when he was a child. And before Cricket knew it, the tears were flowing. He sniffled wetly into the fabric of Father's tunic, no doubt staining it. "I'm proud of you, son."

A choked sob, and Cricket hugged him back, perhaps a little too tightly, but Father didn't complain. Father never complained. "I'm going to miss her."

"I know, son. But you have done what's best for her." Father pressed a kiss to Cricket's head, his hands stroking over his back. "What a man you're growing up to be."

Cricket laughed wetly into Father's shoulder. Father was right. He'd done what was best for Anstice, and for the kingdom. Now it was time to move on, and to heal. To grow up and be the king Lunette needed. If he'd learned anything through his adventures, it was that there was still much to learn.

"Why don't you come out to the bunny enclosure and tell me all about your adventure?"

"Yes, Father." Cricket nodded, scrubbing at his wet face with his sleeve. "I'd like that."

Sneak Peek!

continue reading for a sneak peek of Lou's

The Prince of Daybreak

PROLOGUE

T here was once a young man, a young prince rather, who lost everything he ever thought he could hold dear in the span of a fortnight...

Long ago, in a kingdom not unlike this one, the lady Venus grew more jealous of the Sun by the day. Helios shone too brightly, drew too much attention, and was too well loved by the other gods. How could she compete? And so, out of jealousy and spite, she cursed him and his descendants. Their love would only ever end in pain, and Helios' line would only know heartbreak, until the sun and moon became one.

The first king of the kingdom of Helio knew of the curse, but thought himself above it, and was taken quite by surprise when his wife died in childbirth. The loneliness consumed him, and he died not a month later.

So it was that every man or woman who thought them-selves above the curse suffered, losing first their love and then themselves to the heartbreak.

After centuries of this trend the elders of Helio made a decision, there would be no more marriages for love, only arranged marriages. It was best, they concluded, to protect their people and their line.

Centuries more passed in this way, and while the arranged marriages continued, the curse became first legend, then lore, and then it was all but forgotten. Just a story tucked into a dusty book that hadn't been opened in several years . And so it should have been no surprise to anyone, not even Venus herself who had long since grown bored of this game, when the prince Shinjiro fell in love with and married a young peasant girl named Cayleen.

It seemed, for a time, that they had overcome the curse, outrun it as it were.

Cayleen gave birth first to a son whom they named Takayoshi. A beautiful white haired boy, with a serious countenance, and all-seeing eyes. And then two years later to a daughter named Atsuko with long flowing dark hair like her mother's, and the kindest smile they had ever seen.

But curses, while they may be delayed a while, they do not simply go away, they must be broken. And the only way to break this one was for the sun and the moon to become one, which they were not, and likely would never be. For how could the sun and the moon become a single being? It was not possible.

Takayoshi was four years, six months, and three weeks, exactly, when his mother first fell ill. She struggled with her sickness for months. King Shinjiro brought all manner of healer, and doctor, and witch to their door to help her, but nothing worked. And on the day after Takayoshi's fifth name day, Cayleen finally succumbed to her illness.

Shinjiro was distraught. He fell into a deep depression. His brother, and children did everything in their power to cheer him up. Despite their efforts, not a fortnight later, the king took his own life.

It was then that Takayoshi decided he would never suffer

nor subject another to suffer the fate which had befallen his mother and father. He would never fall in love.

The young prince turned to books for his answer, and after some guiding from the librarian he found a spell, a curse rather in his mind, which would draw his lines of fate to another, someone of his choosing. He would choose an impossible love then, one that would never exist. This was better than heartbreak, he reasoned.

"I don't think this is a good idea," Atsuko whispered, her face drawn in the candlelight as she shifted in her seat, making the chair beneath her creak. "Uncle will be upset."

"Uncle need never know," Takayoshi's bare feet padded softly on the stone floor as he pulled the dagger from its place amongst Father's things. The array was drawn in chalk, purple, from Atsuko's art kit.

"This is dark magic, Shishi. There'll be a price."

Takayoshi merely nodded. He understood this. He was willing to pay the price, whatever it was, for surely it would be less than the pain that would come later should he know the soaring sweep of love as Father and Mother had known it. He pressed the blade to the delicate skin of his inner arm, drawing in a breath to steady himself.

"What will you ask for?" Atsuko's fingers tapped at her toes where she'd crossed her feet up over her knees in a position that surely would make them lose circulation. "You'll want them to be pretty."

Takayoshi rolled his eyes. *That is not the point of this*, he didn't say.

He hissed as the blade drew the first line of crimson. Blood magic was forbidden in Helio. Considered dark, and twisted, even for all the times when the people of Lunette had proven it otherwise. Still, that would not stop Takayoshi.

The drips echoed in the silence of Father's room where Takayoshi had rolled the rug back so it would be easier to hide the evidence later. The chalk glowed faintly, pale moon-light chasing away the shadows left over by the single lit candle.

Atsuko gasped, her little legs falling to dangle over the edge of her chair as her eyes grew wide.

"What do you desire?" A voice echoed from the array, soft enough that had the room not been quiet he may have missed it.

"An impossible love," Takayoshi said, his mouth suddenly dry as he licked his lips. "He will have hair long enough to trail stardust in his wake, the color of the midnight sky. Eyes the shade of the first rays of the moon over the horizon. Freckles will dance across his nose, which will wrinkle when he laughs. And what a laugh it will be, high and bright and full of life. He will be clever beyond reason, much smarter than one so silly should ever be. His smile will rival the sun." Takayoshi took a breath, squeezed his eyes closed, and then he sealed the deal. The most impossible thing that a person, even one of magic, could be. "And his fury will be that of a dragon. It will come in a rush like the river, on talons, and scales, and the flight of the wind."

"A dragon." Takayoshi heard his sister squeak in horror.

"Is that all?" The voice questioned, and if Takayoshi did not know any better he would say it sounded amused.

"It is."

"What do you give in trade?"

"Color," Takayoshi said. He had thought long and hard about this, and he knew that color was something he could sacrifice. He had no love of art as Atsuko had, his love was in music, and he could do that without knowing color. "I would give my ability to see color for this impossible love."

All there was for a suffocating moment was the sound of Atsuko trying to stifle her worried mumbling behind her hands, and the soft *drip drip drip* of the blood still trailing down Takayoshi's wrist.

Then, "the deal is struck. You will not know color until you find your impossible love ." The array began to dim. "I wish you the best of luck, young prince," it added almost as an afterthought.

"Thank you." Takayoshi bowed his head, his eyes closed tight. He did not open them again until the white light of the array had stopped burning through the lids of his eyes, and when he did, the room was a wash of blacks, and whites, and greys.

"Did it work?" Atsuko hissed, whether she hoped the answer would be yes or no, he was not sure.

"It did." Takayoshi nodded. "Help me clean this up before Uncle sees."

THE PRINCE OF DAYBREAK
THE HEIR TO MOONDUST: BOOK TWO

Continue Yoshi and Cricket's adventure with The Prince of Daybreak web-serial on Wattpad, Tapas, Ao3, my website.

ACKNOWLEDGMENTS

First off, thank you—the reader—for joining Cricket on his journey through Lunette. The Prince of Starlight was something I started during the pandemic, and one of the projects that made being stuck inside a little easier. I hope it has brought you the same wry amusement, and smiles it brought me to write.

Although this book is over, Cricket and Yoshi's story is far from finished. Their world has so many more stories to tell, and already I've begun work on the third book. So rest assured, this is not the last you've seen of Cricket, his fiery handmaiden, and his stoic white knight.

Next, I'd like the thank my small hoard of beta-readers. You guys gave some excellent insight, and I really appreciate all of your hard work!

And last but certainly not least, thank you to my small writing support group. Tiss, Elle, and Jasmine—without you there would be no Lou.

ABOUT THE AUTHOR

Born and raised in a small town near the Chesapeake Bay, Lou Wilham grew up on a steady diet of fiction, arts and crafts, and Old Bay. After years of absorbing everything, there was to absorb of fiction, fantasy, and sci-fi she's left with a serious writ-ing/drawing habit that just won't quit. These days, she spends much of her time writing, draw-ing, and chasing a very short Basset Hound named Sherlock.

When not, daydreaming up new characters to write and draw she can be found crocheting, making cute bookmarks, and binge-watching whatever happens to catch her eye.

Learn more about Lou and her future projects on her website: http://louinprogress.com/ or join her mailing list at: http://subscribepage.com/mailermailer

facebook.com/LouWilham

instagram.com/lou.wilham

Also By Lou Wilham

The Curse Collection
    The Curse of The Black Cat
    The Curse of Ash and Blood
    The Curse of Flour and Feeling

The Clockwork Chronicles
    The Girl in the Clockwork Tower
    The Unicorn and the Clockwork Quest
    The Rose in the Clockwork Library

The Heir To Moondust
    The Prince of Starlight
    The Prince of Daybreak

The Witches of Moondale
    The Hex Next Door

Sanctuary of the Lost
    Of Loyalties and Wreckage

Completed Series
The Tales of the Sea Trilogy
Villainous Heroics

MORE BOOKS YOU'LL LOVE

If you enjoyed this story, please consider leaving a review.

Then check out more books from Midnight Tide Publishing!

The Castle of Thorns by Elle Beaumont

To end the murders, she must live with the beast of the forest.

After surviving years with a debilitating illness that leaves her weak, Princess Gisela must prove that she is more than her ailment. She discovers her father, King Werner, has been growing desperate for the herbs that have been her survival. So much so, that he's willing to cross paths with a deadly legend of Todesfall Forest to retrieve her remedy.

Knorren is the demon of the forest, one who slaughters anyone who trespasses into his land. When King Werner steps into his territory, desperately pleading for the herbs that control his beloved daughter's illness, Knorren toys with the idea. However, not without a cost. King Werner must deliver his beloved Gisela to Knorren or suffer dire consequences.

With unrest spreading through the kingdom, and its people growing tired of a king who won't put an end to the demon of Todesfall Forest, Gisela must make a choice. To become Knorren's prisoner forever, or risk the lives of her beloved people.

For fans of Sarah J. Maas, Jennifer Armentrout, A.G. Howard, Casey L. Bond, and Naomi Novik.

Add to your TBR
Available Nov. 3 2021

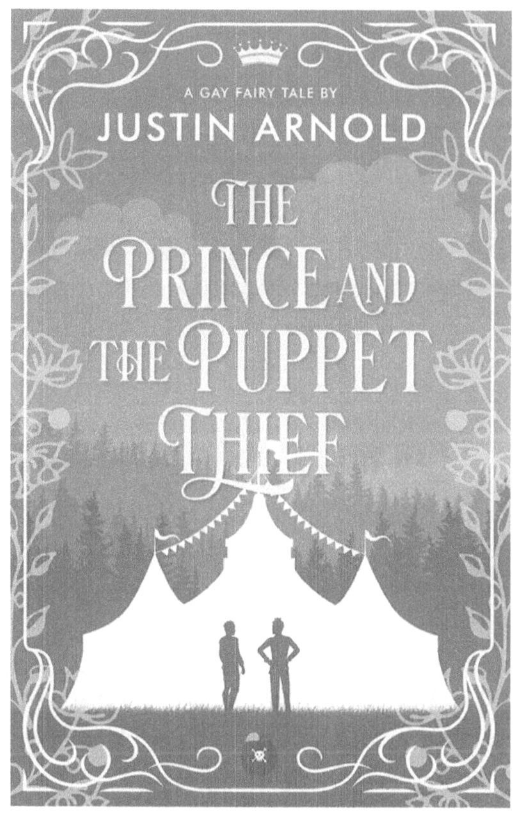

The Prince and the Puppet Thief by: Justin Arnold

Welcome to the kingdom where princes kiss thieves, princesses dance with their handmaids at midnight, and non-binary magicians see to it that everyone gets their happily-ever after.

17-year-old Simon The Squirm has spent his life on the run—and he hates it. Breaking the law gives him anxiety, and he always forgets to carry a weapon. Being the son of the 2nd most feared villain in the kingdom has never been easy, but when an ill-conceived plan to steal the Lost Princess's slippers lands him in the dungeon, he makes up his mind to take the first opportunity at freedom.

Prince Marco isn't convinced he's the one to rescue the lost Princess Isobel. Sure, he's a handsome and brave royal straight out of a fairy tale- but that doesn't mean he's ready to fall for the first damsel in distress who sends out an S.O.S. When he finds himself smitten with the sarcastic (if bumbling) Simon, a scheme is hatched to save both of them from a not-so-happily-ever-after.

The mission is simple: Simon must go in Marco's place to rescue the princess and defeat the wicked magician who stole her. But when it becomes clear that the feisty Princess Isobel would secretly rather be saved by her handmaid, Prince Marco and Simon might just end up rescuing each other instead.

Perfect for fans of The Princess Bride and The School For Good And Evil, The Prince And The Puppet Thief is a hilarious and heartwarming fairy tale rom-com by and for the LGBT community.

Available Now

The Rose and the Claw by Nancy O'Toole

A woman on a mission...

Rose Gardner never thought she'd leave the small town of West Ridge. But when her husband dies at war, she must return his arms to his place of birth to set his spirit to rest. After traveling into enemy territory, Rose falls into a trap. Held captive in an enchanted manor, she finds herself face to face with a beast who is equally horrifying and kind. Will she manage to complete her quest or be pulled in by the secrets of the manor?

A man haunted by his past...

Trapped within his own home and in the body of a hideous beast, Kris never wanted to share his prison with another. As much as Rose may draw him in with her beauty and stubborn strength, he knows she must escape before the next full moon. After all, he remembers all too well what happened to the previous caretaker.

The dead won't let him forget the blood on his hands.

Available Now

The Prince's Wing by Amber R. Duell

A royal guard. A forced rebel.

Lord Saer Tufaro was raised to be the prince's Wing—the truest and most loyal personal guard a royal could ask for. He would gladly sacrifice his life to save his best friend—the future king of Eradrist—but that may be exactly what the rebels have planned.

The Red Asters were the ones to place Saer in the palace after the old king was usurped. Close to the throne and above suspicion, he was to be an invaluable tool for the cause. But a spy is only useful if his loyalties aren't torn.

When the prince is manipulated into an arranged marriage to the former king's bastard daughter, tension in the palace grows. The Lady is as innocent as she is beautiful and would make the prince a wonderful wife. If only she didn't make Saer's heart race...

Available Now